THE
DROWNED
WOMAN

BOOKS BY CJ LYONS

THE DROWNED WOMAN

CJ LYONS

Bookouture

Published by Bookouture in 2020

An imprint of Storyfire Ltd.
Carmelite House
50 Victoria Embankment
London EC4Y 0DZ

www.bookouture.com

ISBN: 978-1-80019-195-2
eBook ISBN: 978-1-80019-194-5

This book is a work of fiction. Names, characters, businesses,
organizations, places and events other than those clearly in the
public domain, are either the product of the author's imagination
or are used fictitiously. Any resemblance to actual persons, living or
dead, events or locales is entirely coincidental.

"The best way to keep a prisoner from escaping is to make sure he never knows he's in prison."

Fyodor Dostoevsky

PROLOGUE

17 years ago...

Flying. She was flying.

Wind sliced against her face. Time was fluid, slippery. Was it centuries, or seconds? She knew she was falling from the lurch in her stomach. She took a ragged breath, in and out, then a slam jolted through her, and her entire body propelled forward until the airbag blew and the seatbelt grabbed her, holding her in place with a bruising grasp.

Her eyes fluttered open as the first splash of frigid water crashed through the open window beside her. She shook her head, startled to be awake—to be alive. Her throat was raw, every breath an effort. Her head throbbed, ears shrieked, body bruised. Hands flailing, fighting...

More water, seeping up from below, streaming through the windows—the car, she was in her car. In the river—how? She blinked, tried to focus past the pain and the rushing noise that consumed her mind. Why?

He'd tried to kill her... *Why?*

She fumbled at her seatbelt. Jammed. She had a safety tool—where, where... She tried to open the center console, but her fingers were numb from the icy water, unable to obey the commands her brain screamed out as she fought to survive. The black water was already at her neck, the car sinking, the river consuming it with primal greed. Wind howled, water flooded in, the car groaning in protest, the wail of a dying beast.

Still, she fought, tilting her face to swallow a last lungful of air, pulling at the seatbelt that kept her prisoner, straining, tugging, trying, fighting… until finally, there was nothing to fight against. Nothing left to fight with.

Silence. A sweet release of darkness beckoned as the car settled into the cradle of the river's muddy bottom. The only light a soft glow illuminating a man's face.

Luka. She strained to call out to him, bubbles escaping her as her lungs emptied for the final time. Luka. Her arms stretched, bobbing in the current now that the car had surrendered to the river. She reached out, felt his hand grab hers, so strong, so warm, his touch bringing a rush of calm.

Luka. She sighed, her body collapsing. She had nothing left except one last thought. *Why?*

CHAPTER 1

It was perfect weather for a funeral. But despite the gusting wind, chill rain, and the other-worldly fog rolling off the Susquehanna River, Luka Jericho was here to celebrate a life.

For seventeen years, every March 18th, no matter the weather, no matter his workload, in sickness or in health, Luka had made the pilgrimage back here, to the place where he'd lost everything.

After almost two decades, there was little left to mark where Cherise had driven off the road and plunged into the river. The scraggly bushes and saplings that had done nothing to slow her car on that chilly night so long ago were all now fully grown. If he'd driven here in summer, he'd be barely able to glimpse the river through their foliage. But Luka never came here in summer. He came only one day—this day—every year. To mark Cherise's life and to try to understand her death.

That mystery had changed his life and driven him to forsake his college dreams, propelling him into a career in law enforcement. Now, as the detective sergeant in charge of Cambria City's Violent Crimes Unit, Luka understood the logic behind his choices, the aftermath of trauma. After Cherise, after the gut-wrenching realization that he'd missed the signs, been oblivious to her pain, clueless… of course he'd been driven into a profession where he could help others find the answers they desperately searched for.

He sat in his pickup, watching the way the wind sliced through the early morning fog. Wet, thick spirals dancing across the river emerged on land as wisps that almost—but not quite—appeared human. They beckoned to him, inviting him into the river's intoxicating, chill embrace. To join Cherise and follow her path into the dark and lonely depths.

On the seat beside him sat his usual offering: a large bouquet of irises, blindingly blue blossoms that, despite being dead and dying, appeared almost too alive and vibrant against the shades of March gray that saturated the landscape. Or maybe it was merely his colorless mood that made it so difficult to place his faith in the promise of spring and the new life it brought. March had started hopeful, with blue skies and sixty-degree weather, but after that false promise winter had returned with a vengeance, suffocating the Appalachian Mountains of central Pennsylvania not with the crisp gleam of snow but rather with the damp chill of relentless freezing rain.

Rain that had gone on for twelve days straight and showed no signs of slowing now. Luka blew his breath out. Maybe he should stop coming, he told himself as he did every year. Maybe he should forgive, forget, and forge on with his life.

Maybe someday he could. But not today.

He picked up the flowers, tugged his hood over his head, and climbed out of the truck. As he tramped through the mud and winter grass, he imagined tire tracks gouged into the earth, sparks flying as she'd gunned the engine to bump over the railroad tracks, the crack and scratch of branches as she hurtled off the side of the hill and flew through the night.

What had gone through her mind in those last few seconds? He imagined her terror as the car pancaked against the river, cold water rushing in through the windows she'd opened, greedily stealing the oxygen, leaving her alone in the dark. That was the image that kept him awake at night. Cherise facing death, probably terrified, maybe even regretting her choice, sometimes shrieking, sometimes whimpering, sometimes silent—but always alone.

He stepped over the rusted train tracks, made his way through the brush to where the hill gave way to a steep drop off, eroded by centuries of flood waters. There he crouched, laying the flowers on top of a flat outcropping of limestone, surrounded by dead grass. Warily, he eyed the river. The clouds obscured any hope of seeing the sun rising behind the mountains to the east. No birds sang to announce the dawn, nothing stirred except the water rushing below him, the wind and rain whipping whitecaps over the river's surface. The air smelled of damp, dead earth.

He reached for a stone to anchor the irises, although he knew it was futile. They'd be scattered to the wind before he made it back over the mountains to Cambria City. What did it matter? After all, they were already dead.

Standing, he recited the poem she'd left behind to mark her decision. Langston Hughes. The book of poetry had been one of Luka's, heavily annotated and dog-eared. She'd chosen well, tearing out the well-worn page, a cairn of rocks marking it for the people who followed in her wake. Her final message to Luka, to the world.

The poem was a scant twelve words contained in three lines and was titled: "Suicide's Note."

Luka turned his back on the river and its ghosts. After seventeen years of this pilgrimage, he still had no answers, no sense of closure. Only a single question that had burrowed into his psyche and refused to let go: *why?*

CHAPTER 2

Leah Wright's Subaru rattled over the metal grating of the bridge leading into Cambria City's downtown.

"But dogs are smart," Emily argued, practically bouncing out of her car seat behind Leah. "They can tell us if an earthquake is coming."

"I don't think we're sitting on any major fault lines, no need to worry about earthquakes," Leah told her daughter. Sometime last week Emily had decided that their little family was in desperate need of a dog, taking every opportunity to introduce the idea into conversation in the hopes of wearing Leah down.

Leah blamed Emily's trauma counselor, who'd introduced a comfort dog, an agreeable and infinitely huggable chocolate lab, into their sessions. Leah had never had a dog—or any pets—while growing up. To her dogs were the creatures who bit kids and then sent them to Leah's ER at Good Samaritan Medical Center for her to patch up.

"Fall line?" Emily asked.

"Fault line." Leah glanced in the rearview mirror. Beside Emily sat Luka Jericho's nephew, Nate. She and Luka were sharing carpool duties until they both felt comfortable with the kids riding the school bus. Which might be never, given that Emily's father, Leah's husband, had been murdered in front of her last month and Nate had recently lost his mother to a drug overdose.

Nate pulled out a small notepad. He and Emily were such contrasts. She was tiny for six years old, but precocious and outgoing with an IQ the school said put her in the highest percentile. No surprise given that her father, Ian, was a genius. Nate was skinny—although tall for an eight-year-old—and had to leave everyone he knew behind last month when he moved up to Pennsylvania to join Luka and Luka's grandfather here in Cambria City. After having only sporadic opportunities to attend school while in Baltimore, he'd been placed back in first grade to finish out the year.

"Fault line," Emily repeated, and Leah knew that by the time she got home from work Emily would have drawn a detailed map of Cambria City and the surrounding mountains with every fault line precisely mapped out. And who knew, given all the coal mines and the shale formations in this part of central Pennsylvania, maybe Leah was wrong. Maybe they were at risk of earthquakes. Still, it didn't mean they needed a dog.

Leah spelled out the word, which Nate laboriously copied onto his notepad. He was a quiet kid, obviously dealing with a lot of pain along with resentment at the adults who'd continuously uprooted his life, but he was sweet with Emily. Every time Luka tried to help him with his schoolwork, Nate would glare and stomp away. Despite the difference in their ages, he was content to allow Emily to tutor him. Leah figured by the end of summer, they would both be ready to skip a grade—although she wasn't sure if that was a good thing, setting up both kids to feel like outsiders. It was why she and Ian had originally decided to keep Emily with her own age group in school. But where Nate went, Emily would insist on following and vice-versa.

"Nate, your uncle—"

"Luka," he corrected. "Just cuz I live in his house, don't make him blood."

"No, him being your mother's brother does." Leah felt compelled to defend Luka. Nate blamed Luka for his mother's death and Luka figured the kid needed someone to lash out at, so he'd allowed himself to become the target of Nate's wrath. Leah didn't agree—there was no way Luka or anyone could have saved Nate's mother. "Anyway, your uncle Luka said to make sure you remember to bring home your great-great-grandfather's army medal. The one you brought for sharing time yesterday."

Nate nodded, his eyes tightening, adding Leah to the list of adults trying to run his life for him. She had to stifle her laughter—it was the exact same look Emily had given her when Leah first told her they couldn't get a dog.

"Yeah, okay," he said.

Something about his tone made her wary. "You still have it, right?"

"Yeah, yeah. I know where it is." A little on the vague side, but she let it pass.

"And both of you remember, Ruby's coming to pick you up today."

"Because you started your new job and can't," Emily said in a bored singsong voice. "So, we wait for Ruby and if she doesn't come, we call you or Luka." She tugged her new cell phone from her backpack and waved it so Leah could see it in the rearview. As if anyone could miss it after the bedazzling Emily and Ruby had subjected the phone to.

Leah hated the idea of giving a six-year-old a phone—hated even more that she might need it. But Leah's mother, Ruby, did not have the best track record when it came to being anywhere when needed. Although after Ian was killed, Ruby had stepped up, helping both Leah and Emily, and for some strange, unfathomable reason, Emily had forged a bond with Ruby—one that Leah was loath to break. Emily had lost too much already.

It was a terrible way to live, always hoping that she was wrong, that her mother had changed, while also fearful that she was right, and that Emily would pay the price. Instead of being grateful for having Ruby's help, all Leah could feel was a watchful wariness, constantly on guard for any hint that Ruby was reverting to the woman Leah knew from her childhood.

"I still don't understand, Dr. Wright," Nate said, his tone more respectful than earlier when she'd mentioned Luka. Although he liked using Leah's title, he never referred to Luka's job as a police detective, she'd noticed. Maybe in the Baltimore foster homes he'd bounced around, having an uncle who was a cop wasn't something to boast about. "You're a doctor and your job is in the ER, but it's not really the ER? Like you don't get to see shootings or stabbings? Don't you want to be a real doctor anymore?"

Leah sighed. Street-savvy Nate had nailed it. Even her former ER colleagues had been teasing her about agreeing to take the position of medical director of Good Sam's Crisis Intervention Center. The CIC handled abuse cases, sexual assaults and other domestic traumas, performing physical examinations, social service evaluations, and forensic interviews. Her new job meant giving up everything she loved about working on the frontlines of the emergency department—but also meant no more overnight or evening shifts, although she would be on call for emergencies.

It was worth it, for Emily, to give her a sense of normality, a routine. Before he was killed, Ian had handled most of the child-rearing responsibilities because of Leah's work schedule, and she'd been fine with that. But now she was playing catch up, forced to learn "how Daddy does it" at every turn from braiding Emily's hair to how much cereal she liked in her milk.

It'd been hard enough while Leah was home during her four weeks of bereavement leave. Now she had to juggle caring for Emily, watching Ruby to make sure Ruby didn't break trust with Emily, taking care of all the paperwork and financial details that came with losing a spouse, along with the responsibilities of her new job.

She felt barely able to take care of herself, much less Emily. It might help if she could sleep. Ever since finding Ian's body and learning that he'd been targeted because Leah had saved the wrong patient, sleep had eluded her. But Emily was healing, and that was all Leah cared about. It would be a long, long time before Leah slept through the night or trusted anyone—or herself—again.

Hypervigilance, the trauma counselor called it during their last session. A symptom of PTSD. Meaning, an abnormal state of being.

Who cared, Leah thought. Who was he to decide what was "normal" after what she and Emily had been through? As long as it kept her daughter safe, gave Emily room to grow and be happy, live the life she deserved, then any strain on Leah's psyche was worth it.

"She's still a real doctor." Emily surprised Leah by coming to her defense. "But now she gets to help people with toys." She was referring to the child-friendly interview room where she'd given her own statement after Ian's murder. "So now your job is fun, right, Mommy?"

Leah didn't answer right away, distracted by her daily dilemma of navigating a labyrinthine route to school to avoid their old house—the house Emily still thought of as home, and Leah as a nightmarish crime scene. It was difficult because the school was only two blocks up the street from their old place, but the last thing she needed was Emily to break down, screaming about wanting to go home again.

"My job is always fun, pumpkin," she answered as she diverted down a one-way street heading past the park. "But you know the most fun part?"

"Bullet wounds? Getting an arm cut off?" Nate asked, leaning forward with excitement. Leah made a note to ask Luka what the kid was watching on TV. He made a karate chopping motion accompanied by sound effects. "Pow-ee! My arm, my arm! Where'd it go?"

Now Emily was getting into the roleplay. "I cut it off with my space-pirate knife! And now I'll cut off your head, too!"

"Not before I blast you with my alien ray gun!" Both kids were turned in their seats, filling the air with sound effects as they ducked and wove, avoiding imaginary weaponry.

"Enough," Leah called out as she pulled into the school drive, behind the other parents' cars in the drop-off lane. "No one's shooting or blasting or stabbing anyone. Not here and not in school. You hear?"

"Oh boy, not in school," Nate said. "You play space pirates and aliens in school and they send you to the dungeon for sure."

"I think you mean in-school suspension. But I want you guys to think of another game, use your imaginations—"

"But, Mommy—" Emily started, a hint of a whine in her voice.

"Think of a game like Daddy used to play with you. Only instead of the computer, make believe in real life, okay?"

Ian said Emily was a computer prodigy and had taught her programming skills that were far beyond anything Leah could offer—or understand. But with their electronics all taken by the police as evidence, Emily had gone a whole month computer-free. Leah rather liked it.

She edged the Subaru forward to the drop-off point. A volunteer opened the door, helping Emily out of her car seat, while Nate jumped out on his own.

"Have a great day!" She injected a note of false brightness into her voice, trying to mask the undercurrent of anxiety that threatened to devour her every time she let Emily out of her sight. She remembered the words of Emily's trauma counselor, stressing the need for Emily to return to a normal life. Structure, routine, independence. All vital to the healing process. "I love you!"

Too late—they were already running hand in hand, splashing through puddles, laughing as they raced away from Leah.

She stared after them until the car behind her honked. Jerking with a guilty start, she waved at the other driver and pulled away, steering down Jefferson. Her street. Their street. Would she find the courage to actually stop today? Go inside the house that once upon a time was her dream home?

The crime scene cleaners—trauma remediation, the company called it—had finished their work last week, rescuing as many personal possessions as possible, removing the rest—labeled as biohazards—and repairing the damage left in the wake of the attack on Ian. At least that's what their bill itemized in excruciating detail. Leah still hadn't stepped inside, despite Emily's nightly recitation of things she'd left behind that she really, really, wished and hoped she could have back. Clever girl had even figured out the best way to make sure Leah knew exactly how important each toy or book or stuffed animal or hair clip was by invoking her father.

"Please, Mommy. I need it to help me remember Daddy," she'd say, hugging Leah tight and whispering it into her ear like a prayer. "Please, Mommy."

Today Leah slowed the Subaru and pulled to the curb, despite her clammy palms and heart racing so hard she felt her pulse throb in her throat. Nothing to worry about, just a little panic attack. Look, no hyperventilation, no crushing chest pain. Gripping the steering wheel, she forced herself to breathe. *I'm fine, just fine.*

It was a lie, but one she was willing to live with.

What other choice did she have?

CHAPTER 3

Luka was driving down the mountains west of Cambria City, heading into work, when his phone rang. Naomi Harper, the patrol officer assigned to his team. She was awaiting a potential promotion to detective, which made her the most likely to be given the job of calling the boss with bad news.

"What's the problem, Harper?" he answered.

"No problem. Just a—a situation. Krichek said not to worry, he just wanted you to know."

Scott Krichek was almost as green as Harper—the detective had only joined Luka's Violent Crimes Unit last year. Ray Acevedo, Luka's second-in-command, was still out on medical leave after getting shot last month, which meant Luka hadn't only temporarily lost a trusted member of the team, he'd also lost two decades of experience at his disposal.

"What situation?" he snapped, his mood still raw from his pre-dawn pilgrimage.

"It was called in as accidental. Old lady fell down the stairs at her apartment building. DOA."

"What's Maggie say?" Despite being younger than either Harper or Krichek, Luka trusted Maggie Chen's instincts. The coroner's death investigator had an uncanny ability to see beyond the obvious.

"She's not here yet. Fog caused a multi-vehicle crash on the other side of the river. She'll get here soon as she can."

"Give me the address."

Harper told him. Luka knew the apartment building, the Falconer. It was in a quiet neighborhood that catered mainly to seniors. Last year, after his gran's death, he'd tried to convince his grandfather to move there, where Luka could keep an eye on him, but Pops had refused. Said he'd lived on his farm all his life and he'd damn well die there. Luka had eventually compromised by giving up his own place to move across the river to Jericho Fields. Good thing he had, because he now had a nephew to raise, his grandfather to watch, and a live-in caretaker to pay. It stretched every penny of Luka's paycheck, but so far, he was making it work, and living at the farm kept them all under one roof.

"Even if it looks accidental, treat it as suspicious until we learn otherwise," Luka told Harper.

"Right. We are. Even found a possible suspect. The husband…" Her voice trailed off as if she were searching for words. "But… he has some kind of mental health issue. Went nuts after he saw his wife's body. Barricaded himself inside his apartment along with a neighbor who was trying to help calm him down. Before we arrived," she added hastily. "Patrol called in ERT. We're still trying to sort out exactly what happened. Krichek wanted you to know."

"Are you serious? Why the hell—" He took a breath.

Harper side-stepped his question. "Krichek wanted to know if you want to give ERT the green light to go in."

"The neighbor is barricaded inside with the EDP?" Incidents involving emotionally disturbed persons were unpredictable, but calling in the Emergency Response Team was usually a last resort. For McKinley, the ERT leader, every option began with lethal force. Having a mental health issue shouldn't condemn someone to die, and it didn't sound like the uniforms had even tried to calm the situation down before making the call. If anything, it seemed as if they had exacerbated things.

"No. I talked the husband into opening the door and she's out. The neighbor and I are now standing just outside it, close enough so she can talk to him, but he's beyond reasoning with at this moment. Neighbor said before we got here, when she was still inside, she almost had him calmed down but then a uniform barged in, ready to Taser him. That's when things escalated."

"Escalated how? Weapons involved?"

"None that I've seen. Uniforms said the guy became violent and they had no choice but to call ERT. But the neighbor is saying the husband didn't become violent until after the uniforms grabbed her and threatened to Taser him."

The truth probably lay somewhere in the middle. But either way, there was bound to be hell to pay. Either patrol had been too aggressive, or the husband truly did pose a threat that the neighbor was blind to—although she seemed ready to tell anyone who listened that the uniforms had mishandled the situation. "Tell McKinley to hold until I get there. Make sure everyone knows the husband has medical issues—which means no Tasers. We need to de-escalate." Then he had another thought. "What's the husband's diagnosis? Anyone know?"

"Not sure. Manager says some kind of dementia. We found prescriptions with the husband's name on them scattered near the wife's body, but we haven't been able to get ahold of the doctor yet."

A physician's input would be valuable—and subduing the man might require medication beyond what paramedics could offer. Exactly what the new crisis intervention program was designed for. "Call Leah Wright."

"Boss?" Harper's voice upticked not only with a question but also with disapproval. She and Leah had clashed during Leah's husband's murder investigation. It didn't help that Harper had been convinced Leah was behind her husband's death.

"Call her, Harper. Tell the neighbor to keep talking to the guy—as long as you both are safe. And keep the ERT cowboys from killing anyone before I get there. I'll be there in ten." He hung up.

He'd driven his private vehicle over the mountain to Lewisburg this morning, anticipating exchanging it for an unmarked one after he arrived at police headquarters. But since Luka was basically on call 24/7, his truck had wig-wags installed behind the grill. He flicked the emergency lights on and sped up as he rounded the final curve leading down the mountain.

Usually he loved this view of his city carved into the side of the mountain and stretching out to the river and beyond. Even today with the glooming clouds, the morning sun still managed to filter through, turning the soot-stained peaked roofs, wet brick and stone masonry into something out of a painting. A fantasy, to be sure, because in reality, Cambria City was a down-and-out rustbelt town hanging on purely through audacity and stubborn pride.

As Luka drove, he called the ERT leader, McKinley, and got a situation report from his more tactical perspective. Definitely more gloom and doom and portents of bloodshed than what Harper had given him. Luka drove over the final hill leading into the heart of the city and turned down Second Avenue. A few minutes later he was being waved through a police barricade, parking in front of the Falconer, a brick pre-war building, five stories high. At least McKinley hadn't brought the armored vehicle—that damn thing always attracted attention.

As Luka sprinted past puddles on the street, hood up against the rain, he assessed the crowd gathered beyond the barricade. Mostly men, working age, a few college students, almost everyone with cell phones at the ready, sharing the buzz of anticipation, hoping for a show. Anything to kill the dreary monotony of the endless days of rain.

Luka grimaced. He hoped he could resolve the situation upstairs calmly, leave the crowd feeling like they'd wasted their time. Krichek spotted him and opened the first set of two ornate-leaded glass doors leading into the building's lobby, waving Luka inside.

"Detective Sergeant Luka Jericho, Violent Crime Unit," Luka told the recording officer stationed at the inside door. He unzipped his parka and glanced around.

There was a security camera inside the small entrance formed by the two sets of glass doors and a keypad below it, requiring visitors to be buzzed in if they didn't have a key. The foyer had a marble floor and columns enhanced with art deco-style embellishments. There was an elevator bank directly across from the front doors, a walnut reception desk on the left, and to the right, a wide staircase with intricate wrought-iron railings circled the lobby's perimeter to create a spacious atrium.

And near the foot of the stairs sprawled a woman's bloody corpse.

CHAPTER 4

Other than discovering her husband's body, Leah had never been to a crime scene before. As she drove up to the Falconer Apartments, she wasn't certain if the tightness in her belly was from excitement, anticipation, or anxiety. It felt different than the usual rush she had when heading into a fresh trauma in the ER. Maybe because here, she was trespassing on someone else's territory, subject to their rules.

She gave her name to the officer at the barricade and showed him her ID, then parked the Subaru where he pointed. Her new job at the Crisis Intervention Center included what her boss termed "call-outs," aiding the police in interviewing upset or fragile witnesses and using her medical expertise to help with volatile subjects, like drug users or people with psychiatric diagnoses. The program was part of a federal grant her boss had received that allowed the CIC to keep its doors open, but it was uncharted territory, this forced collaboration, for both the medical center and the police.

As she ran through the rain, trying to look like she knew what she was doing, Leah hugged a knapsack containing her trauma kit. Last month she'd been forced to treat a gunshot wound with nothing more than a kitchen towel and a belt for a tourniquet. Even though she'd saved the detective's life, she vowed never to be caught off guard like that again.

Another officer stopped her inside the doors to the apartment building and she gave him her name, even as her attention was riveted by the sight of the woman sprawled face down on the marble floor. Blood had pooled beneath her broken body and, even if Leah hadn't spotted Maggie Chen attending to her, it was obvious she was dead.

"I'm hoping that's not my patient." The joke was born of nervous anxiety and she regretted it as soon as it left her lips, felt her cheeks warm with a blush.

The officer didn't answer, merely jerked his chin to the reception desk along the other wall of the lobby. Not wanting to contaminate the crime scene, Leah edged along the perimeter. Luka Jericho and one of his team members, a young detective named Krichek, stood at the desk, along with an older uniformed officer wearing body armor and carrying an assault rifle. Luka wasn't dressed in his usual suit and tie; instead he had on muddy hiking boots, jeans, a button-down shirt, and a parka. Was something about this case so important that they'd called him in from home? A thrill of anticipation shot through her, not unlike the feeling she had in the ER when greeting a fresh trauma. But then she quickly sobered. Unlike her old life in the ER, where each new case brought with it the chance to save a life, Luka's team calling her in meant a fragile or vulnerable witness, either the victim of a crime or a family member left bereft by violence. Just like she'd been when she first met Luka herself.

The older man spotted her. "And now he goes and brings in the welfare lady," he said in a tone of disdain. "Gonna try to tell me that talking and listening works better than a bullet to the brain stem." The man had a severe case of rosacea that left his face florid red. Probably why he worked on the SWAT team instead of undercover or investigations, Leah thought. Every emotion flashed like neon across his features.

"Dr. Leah Wright," she introduced herself and held out a hand, which the other man ignored.

"This is Sergeant McKinley. Leader of the Emergency Response Team," Luka told her. "Don't mind him. He's never happy unless he gets a chance to bust in a door or use his toys to ruin someone's day. Which I'm hoping won't be necessary."

"He had a hostage—" McKinley protested.

"His neighbor is at the door, trying to help calm him down," Luka corrected. "Harper's on scene, says there's no immediate threat."

"Not what my boys are telling me. Says Orly is tearing the place up, totally unhinged."

"Orly?" Leah asked.

"Walt Orly." Luka nodded to the dead woman. "Husband to Trudy. Sixty-one years old. The building manager says they've been married almost forty years." He gestured to a man Leah hadn't noticed before, he'd been standing so quietly at the far corner of the reception desk, partially hidden by a large potted palm. He wore jeans and a khaki shirt with the name "Cliff" embroidered over his left chest pocket. "Mr. Vogel, can you tell Dr. Wright what you told me? About Mr. Orly's health?"

The man shuffled forward, head down, a sheaf of lanky dark hair falling into his face. He smelled of floor wax and machine oil stained his fingernails. When he finally looked up, not meeting anyone's gaze, Leah realized he was in his late forties even though his posture was more like a shy teenager's.

"Not sure, of the exact—" He picked at his cuticles. "I mean, I know it's not Alzheimer's. Walt isn't that old, that's for sure. And he wasn't sick, not that I could see, not until sometime last year, at least." He cleared his throat, looked to McKinley first and then to Luka, avoiding Leah entirely. "When Walt saw Trudy's body, he just lost it. Screaming for her to come back. Me and Miss Risa tried to calm him down, but he won't come out of his apartment, won't talk to no one but her—"

"Making him a risk to himself and others," McKinley put in, gesturing with his rifle for emphasis.

"*Possible* risk," Luka corrected him, then turned to Leah. "Harper reports no obvious weapons and the neighbor, a Risa

Saliba, seems to be making progress in calming him down. Which is why I've asked McKinley's men to switch to nonlethal options."

Leah's head buzzed as she considered all the parameters—this was nothing like subduing a patient in the ER. "If he's only wrecking his own apartment, why intervene at all?"

"He could harm himself and we have a duty of care to him and his neighbors. Plus, we need him out of the apartment and able to talk to us," Luka answered even as McKinley made a noise of disdain. "As soon as possible." His tone gave her the subtext she'd been missing—Luka was afraid the SWAT team might rush in and kill Walt if Leah couldn't help quiet him down and get him to cooperate with Luka's team.

"The victim could've been pushed or thrown," McKinley said. "The husband's a suspect in a potential homicide."

"Or a witness," Luka corrected. "Either way, we need to talk to him."

"Let me at least evaluate the man before you take action." Leah aimed this at McKinley. Situations like this were the whole reason they'd gotten the Department of Justice grant to bring her on board with the Crisis Intervention Center; she just hadn't expected to be coming into such a complicated encounter on her first day in the field. No one had even had a chance yet to define her role other than acting as "an advocate" for victims, witnesses, and people taken into police custody. She'd expected she'd be interviewing distraught family members—but not one who had a sniper's scope focused on him.

Leah had to take two deep breaths to quiet her nerves, glancing up past the steps that circled the atrium, her gaze climbing all the way to the top where a skylight was shadowed by rain clouds. Luka was here; he wouldn't let anything happen to her. In the month since Ian's death and the violent aftermath that followed, she'd grown to trust the detective. Since their homes were only a few miles apart, they helped each other out with childcare duties, and, although most of their discussions centered on Emily and Nate, Leah considered Luka a friend. After Ian's death she'd been surprised to realize how few friends she really had. Before, her life had centered on work and family. "What floor?"

"The top." Luka turned to the other detective. "Krichek, you stay here. Mr. Vogel, could you give Detective Krichek any footage from your security cameras?"

"Don't have any. That camera's been busted for over a year."

"Okay, then. Please stay close in case we need more information from you."

"I'd like to go up, see if Miss Risa is all right."

Luka's tone turned firm. "Please stay here. Krichek, you coordinate with McKinley." Given the scowl he threw the younger detective, Leah translated this as: stop the SWAT team from rushing in and killing anyone. Then Luka turned back to Leah. "Let's go."

He led the way around the edge of the foyer to an elevator with embossed brass doors. The Falconer was a bit frayed around the edges, but Leah could imagine that once upon a time it'd been a gleaming masterpiece of pre-war architecture. She couldn't help but think of Ian, who would have loved to explore it. But thinking of Ian always carried with it a constant echo of memories. Of her loss. Of his death. Of his blood...

"Now remember," Luka said as Leah struggled to focus on his words. "Your job is to simply talk to him, try to assess his volatility and what next steps we need to take to get him safely out of the apartment. He might seem like an old man dealing with the shock of his wife's death, but he's a suspect too. I can't guarantee he's not a threat." The elevator stopped at the top floor and the doors slid open. Leah swallowed, forcing away thoughts of Ian.

Luka paused on the landing, facing her. Two SWAT guys waited a few feet away—their escorts. "Leah. We'll be watching the whole time—we won't let anything happen to you." He drew in a breath.

"But if you're uncomfortable, we can go another route. Pilot program and grant money be damned. You don't have to do this."

But she did. She couldn't risk Walt Orly being harmed unnecessarily. She'd had the training, she handled volatile patients in the ER all the time. This was no different—except for the men with guns surrounding them. Leah glanced around the landing. Two shopping bags had been abandoned between the atrium's railing and an open apartment door that was guarded by two more SWAT officers. A set of keys hung from the outside lock, a bright pink smiley face dangling alongside them. You could never lose your keys with that keychain, she thought.

In the open doorway stood Naomi Harper, another member of Luka's team, along with a woman in her early thirties, barefoot and dressed in leggings and a baggy Hard Rock Café sweatshirt, leaning heavily on a wheeled walker angled so she could speak to whoever was inside the apartment. Risa, the neighbor Luka had mentioned. Leah was surprised to see someone so young using a walker. She didn't see any signs of an injury. Then she noticed the trembling in Risa's hands. Maybe a neurologic condition? Beyond Risa, inside the apartment, a man's form moved in and out of sight.

Risa spoke to Walt in a soft, soothing voice, keeping it low. It was a good approach, but as soon as Walt paused in his rampage to listen, he'd quickly shake his head, dismissing her words, more agitated than before.

Leah craned her head over the landing railing, looked down to where Maggie's bright blue hair marked the bottom. Trudy's body had been covered with a sterile shroud and Maggie and her team were gently bundling her into a body bag for transport.

Leah closed her eyes for a moment. She could hear Walt sobbing; the primal noises echoed deep inside her, reminding her of how she felt when she'd found Ian's lifeless body and crawled through his blood, desperate to reach Emily. She remembered thinking this wasn't real, this wasn't her life, this wasn't happening.

"Where's Trudy? What have you done with my Trudy?" Walt Orly raged. He was tall with a barrel-chest and wide shoulders, shoving furniture out of his way as he stalked through the living room—the only part of the apartment Leah could see past the narrow hallway that formed the foyer. He wore a baggy sweater that hung on him and striped pajamas.

As Walt continued his rampage, Risa turned and Luka beckoned her over to join them. "Risa Saliba? I'm Detective Sergeant Luka Jericho and this is Dr. Leah Wright."

"A doctor?" Risa scrutinized Leah.

"What can you tell me about Walt?" Leah asked. She was certain she'd never met Risa before, but something about her was familiar. Maybe she'd seen her in the ER?

"He has Huntington's." Risa leaned heavily on her walker. "Do you even know what that is?" she asked, her tone sharp. "Because the other cops didn't, made things worse."

"I know about Huntington's." Leah eyed Walt's body movements as he came into sight once again. "His voice is still strong, but the choreiform movements, agitation—he's already passing the early stages, isn't he?"

"Doctors told Trudy he was moving into the next stage. Trouble swallowing, periods of catatonia."

"What's Huntington's?" Luka asked. Leah liked that he didn't pretend to know what they were talking about just to salve his pride.

"It's a genetic disease," Leah answered. "It causes severe dementia, muscle weakness, memory loss, among other things. Including emotional lability and violent outbursts. Which explains his extreme reaction and inability to calm down."

"Walt would never hurt Trudy," Risa added. "The other cops, they kept asking if he threw her over the railing. But he'd never…"

Leah made up her mind. She didn't know how Trudy ended up five flights down at the bottom of the atrium but it didn't matter. Walt was her patient now and it was her job to protect him—which meant doing whatever it took to get him safely out of the apartment and into proper medical care. She had a plan, but she doubted the police would agree to it.

She stepped past the SWAT guys at the apartment's front door, moving so fast that she was inside the apartment before they could question her actions. Luka would be angry, but she didn't have time to explain her every decision—after all, wasn't that why they wanted her here? To use her medical expertise and judgment.

"Trudy?" she called out in a worried tone, matching Walt's. "Trudy, where are you?"

Walt whirled to her, the crystal vase in his hand, held high, ready to strike.

CHAPTER 5

If there was one thing Leah's chaotic childhood had trained her to do, it was how to pretend. In school, Nellie, the great-aunt she lived with, convinced her to try out for the school play, and Leah had found a home on the stage. She knew why she did it: as a little girl she'd thought that if she changed, if she acted different, her mother might return for her.

Even today, most of her time in the ER was spent playing the role of whoever the patient before her needed her to be: a confidante, a stern maternal figure, a team leader. Whatever helped her to learn their every secret, unravel every lie, every truth behind an injury. For Leah, it was the most satisfying part of working in the ER, more so than the adrenaline rush of a trauma. Being able to offer help without breaking down whatever lie that person had carefully constructed to keep them safe. The lies of an alcoholic vowing never again; the cries of a victim of domestic violence unwilling to forsake their abusive relationship; the blind denial of patients suffering chronic diseases they refused to acknowledge.

In the ER, everyone lied. And Leah did not judge them. That wasn't her job. Her job was to help them live, with or without their lies. The truth was a luxury some people couldn't afford.

When Walt cried out for his dead wife, refusing to believe she was gone, Leah knew it was more than his dementia driving his fury. It was heart-shattering grief.

"Walt, have you seen Trudy?" Leah drew on her own experience of loss to fill her voice with empathy that she hoped Walt would respond to. If Walt was going to make it out of here unharmed, he needed to believe her, trust her.

"Trudy?" His wife's name was a plaintive wail. The vase slipped free of his grasp, hitting the wood floor, crashing into pieces. He was barefoot, she saw. He ignored the shattered vase, his gaze fixed on Leah, pleading. "Where's my Trudy?"

She felt his denial. It echoed her own grief, a gut-twist of despair. So, she gave Walt what he needed right now, in this moment. Later, medication might help him accept the truth, but right now, her job was to give him peace—or the illusion of it. At least long enough so that they could get him help, keep him safe and allow the police to do their job without anyone else getting hurt.

Leah reached a hand toward him. "Let's go, Walt. Let's go find Trudy together."

He stared, his lips moving but no sound emerged. She tried to keep his focus on her and away from the men with guns standing behind her in the doorway. She took a step forward, sweeping her feet to clear a safe path through the broken glass. "Will you help me find Trudy?"

He nodded but didn't move. His expression was a kaleidoscope of emotion: fear, anger, sorrow, confusion, relief, and finally, hope. He grasped her hand, his grip trembling. "I'll help you."

"Good. Let's go find Trudy." For the benefit of the officers at the doorway, she added, "I'll bet she's outside. She went shopping, right?"

"We need eggs. And my medicine. Spilled it last night." He jerked a finger up to point to a stain on his pajama top.

Together they shuffled forward, another step toward the door. It was slow progress, but Leah was in no rush. The whole point of this was to help Walt to calm down so they could safely remove him from the apartment.

Walt stopped, glanced back at the destruction he'd left during his rampage, but it didn't seem to register. Instead he called out,

"It's time for my medicine. Trudy?" His voice quavered. "Trudy, where's my medicine?"

"She went to get more, remember, Walt? And she sent me to help you—I'm a doctor."

"Doctor? No. Trudy takes me to the doctor. They don't come here."

"I'm a special kind of doctor. And we're going to meet Trudy. She's waiting for you, Walt."

"But how?" He stuttered to a stop. They were only halfway to the door. "We sold our car. Trudy said it cost too much."

More likely Walt didn't want to give up driving, Leah thought. Dementia patients lived in a world of denial and immediate gratification; if they wanted something, they wanted it *now*, and refused to accept the limitations of their condition. "I brought an ambulance." Leah patted his arm. "Just for you. To take you to Trudy." She hoped he wouldn't remember her lies, but it was the best way to protect him. "Are you ready?"

Two more steps and he stopped again, this time frowning down at his feet. Leah had navigated him past the broken glass—danger he seemed oblivious to—but now there was a new problem. He tugged against her arm, reluctant to move forward. Somewhere deep inside the confusion that roiled his brain, he knew he shouldn't go outside in bare feet. "Walt, do you know where your slippers are?"

He glanced around, then spotted Risa at the door. Somehow, he didn't seem to notice Harper or the men with guns. "Risa, what have you done with my shoes?" he snapped. Then he told Leah, "Risa is our cleaning lady. She likes to play games. Hides everything."

Leah knew this was what he believed even if it obviously wasn't true. The police kept Risa from moving closer, so she called out from the door, "Sorry, Walt! Try the closet by the door, I think there's a pair of slip-ons."

"Perfect," Leah said as she continued to coax Walt down the short hallway leading to the door. Harper pulled Risa back onto the landing, to make room for the paramedics, who wheeled a stretcher within sight. The closet door and the outside door both had childproof latches to guard against Walt's wandering, Leah noticed. She opened the closet door—just a few inches, far enough to reach in and pull out a pair of loafers, but not enough to block the police officers' view of Walt. She knelt, helped Walt into the shoes. Beneath his pajamas she could see the evidence of wasting and muscle loss that came with his disease. Now that his anger and agitation had passed, he really did pose no threat.

"We're going to pick up Trudy," he declared as they finally emerged from the apartment. Luka and Harper watched from a spot near the elevators, out of the way of the medics and SWAT guys who still held their guns at attention, aiming at Walt.

Leah ignored them, focusing on Walt. "That's right, Walt. These nice men are going to take you in the ambulance. That way you won't be tired when you see Trudy."

He sank onto the stretcher, his shoulders sagging as the medics raised his feet and helped him lie back. "I'm so tired." His eyes fluttered shut, but he still held Leah's hand in a surprisingly strong grip. The medics made quick work strapping him to the gurney, including wrist restraints. Then Walt opened his eyes and stared at Leah with a gaze clouded with sorrow. "Trudy. She's gone. Put me to sleep, please. I don't want to... I can't—she can't..." Tears choked him, and his entire body shook. His gaze landed on Risa, who leaned on her walker behind Leah. "Risa. Please. It's over. It all needs to end. Please."

Leah leaned against the gurney. She stroked his arm, squeezed his hand in hers. "It'll be okay, Walt. Just lie back, close your eyes. It'll all be okay." She hated how convincing her lies were. Walt closed his eyes once more and dropped her hand.

She stepped back, suddenly feeling drained herself. "You guys might need Haldol," she told the medic in a low voice.

"Got it, doc," he said. "Med control said his doctor is waiting at Good Sam, has a room on neuro-psych ready for him."

"Good. Thanks." She sagged against the railing—not far from the spot where Trudy had gone over, she realized when she glimpsed yellow police tape from the corner of her eye. But she didn't care, she was so tired, more exhausted than after a trauma in the ER. She watched the medics, accompanied by Harper and the SWAT guys, leave in the elevator.

"Good job," Luka said as the doors closed behind them. "When can I talk to him?"

Leah shook her head. "Probably not for a while—later today, maybe not until tomorrow if he requires sedation. He's going to get agitated again, may never be able to tell you much."

He considered that. "But you'll help, right? Get him talking to us?"

"As soon as his physician allows, we can do a forensic interview at Good Sam."

Risa Saliba approached, her weight sagging against her walker. She seemed wary of Luka but caught Leah's eye. "Can we talk? When you're done?"

The elevator doors opened and Krichek appeared along with the building manager, Cliff. "Got the warrant to secure the premises, boss."

Cliff turned to Risa. "Can I help you home?" he asked, one hand on her elbow.

She shook it off and straightened, pushing her walker toward the corner apartment. "I'm fine."

"Mr. Vogel," Luka said before the manager could follow Risa. "We'll need a list of residents along with contact information, plus any information you can share about suspicious activity, and details about building maintenance and security."

Cliff stared after Risa like a lost puppy. Then he jerked and refocused on Luka. "Yeah, sure, whatever you need."

"You called 911," Luka continued as Krichek took notes. "Can you tell me what you saw?"

"Already told him and the first cops." Cliff nodded to Krichek.

"I'd rather hear it straight from you if that's okay."

"Yeah, okay. I was a little late today, usually I'm here by eight, but my car wouldn't start at first, so I got here around eight-ten, eight-fifteen."

"You came in through the front door?"

"Me? No, that's for residents and guests. I come in the back. Maintenance entrance. There's a hall, comes out beside the mail room behind the desk. So I'm coming down the hall and even before I open the door behind the desk, I hear screaming. Like something out of a horror movie. I ran the rest of the way and came through and—" He stopped, swallowed, his Adam's apple jerking. "And then I saw. It was Miss Trudy. Lying there. Blood everywhere. And up top was Mr. Walt, crying and wailing like a baby. Miss Risa must've heard him, too, because she came and got him to go back to his apartment. And I—I called the cops and they came and that was it."

"Any history of trouble in the building?" Luka asked.

Cliff appeared surprised by the question. "Here? Nope. I've been here eleven years and only time cops ever came before was one Halloween a drunk pushed past Mr. and Mrs. Robeson, got through into the lobby. But no one was hurt or nothing."

"Thanks, Cliff. Wait downstairs, please. Detective Krichek will need you to show him all the exits. You know, all the ins and outs of the building that only a manager like you knows."

"Sure, sure. Happy to." Cliff turned to leave.

"Do you know if Walt and Trudy have any relatives I could call, let them know where he's at?" Leah asked him.

Slowly, Cliff answered, his gaze directed at her feet. "Nope. Far as I know, there's no one. They never had kin come visit and there's no emergency contact listed on their lease agreement."

"We'll need a copy of that as well," Luka told him.

"Yeah, yeah. I'll go get it ready for you right now." He fled toward the stairs, realized his error, and spun around, striding back past them at a fast pace, muttering as he punched the elevator button.

"Strange bird," Krichek observed as the elevator doors closed behind Cliff. "I'll have Harper run him, see if he has a record."

Luka nodded. "What did Maggie say? Any signs it wasn't accidental?"

"Said it was too early to be certain, but there were no obvious signs of inflicted trauma or a struggle."

Luka nodded and sighed. He wasn't his usual self today, Leah noticed. As if something was weighing him down. Or maybe that was her projecting her own feelings. He and Krichek turned to head toward the Orlys' apartment, leaving Leah uncertain of what she was meant to do next.

"If you find any medical records, can I review them before our interview with Walt?" She made a note to herself to also speak with Walt's physician once they got him stabilized at Good Sam. As a police consultant, she wasn't sure if he could speak with her without Walt's consent. And Walt was in no state of mind to give informed consent. "I'd like to be prepared."

"I'll see if I can get a judge to sign off on a court order for them," Luka replied.

"Maybe the neighbor knows more about his condition," Krichek suggested.

"Good idea. I'll go talk to her." Risa had asked to speak with Leah anyway and it gave Leah something productive to do. She started toward Risa's apartment when Luka called her back.

"Leah." He was frowning. "Remember. You're not here to play detective."

"I know that." Why was he being so snippy with her?

"Didn't seem like it the way you waltzed into that apartment."
He took a breath, obviously trying to calm down. "Krichek, go
ahead, I'll meet you inside."

Krichek glanced at both of them, then went into Walt's apartment.

"I knew he wasn't a danger," Leah said before Luka could
continue. "I've dealt with patients like him before and I knew how
to reach him. I trusted you guys to have my back."

"And we did. But you're not in the ER where you call the shots.
Out here, you're part of a team. My team."

"I just didn't want him to get hurt—"

"Neither did I." He blew his breath out. "I'm not saying you
did the wrong thing. I'm just saying, next time, talk to me. We'll
come up with a plan. Together. No more rushing in on your own."

Leah bristled. "Maybe we need to come up with a plan for this
entire partnership. If you don't want me here, I can head back to
Good Sam—"

"No." His tone softened—slightly. "No. You were very helpful.
Thank you. But you're right, we need to draw up some parameters."

Leah had to restrain herself from rolling her eyes. The Department of Justice grant had come with six four-inch binders filled
with parameters and protocols and procedures. She'd spent hours
wading through their administrative jargon and had emerged with
no clear idea of what her new job actually entailed other than filling
out a myriad of budget reports, staffing reports, and reports on
the reports she'd already filled out.

"Yeah," she told him. "That's probably a good idea. Because if
you and I can't work together, there's no way we'll be getting the
rest of the department, much less the SWAT team, on board."

He glanced at his watch. "Probably not today, but soon, I
promise. In the meantime, you seemed to have a rapport with
Saliba. Want to start with her, get your medical questions answered,
while I finish here? I'll join you shortly." He pulled on a pair of

nitrile gloves. "Oh, and we don't call them SWAT. It's Emergency Response or ERT."

Then he entered the Orlys' apartment and closed the door behind him, leaving Leah alone outside.

Her cheeks burned with humiliation. This job was meant to be easier than working in the ER, but she felt lost. Leah sighed, pulled out her phone. Not to call anyone, but simply to look at the photo that filled the screen: Ian and Emily, playing on the lawn of their house—their old house—both caught laughing as they tumbled in the grass.

She felt a hand settle on her shoulder, calming her. It wasn't real, she knew that, but she couldn't help but place her own hand there, straining, yearning to feel his. *You can do this*, Ian's voice whispered through her mind. *For Emily.*

Leah closed her eyes and took one breath, then another before opening them again. She touched her fingers to her lips then to the phone, a silent promise to Ian. She put the phone away and walked over to Risa Saliba's apartment.

CHAPTER 6

Luka closed the door to Walt and Trudy Orly's apartment behind him and took a moment to rein in his emotions. He hadn't meant to take out his frustration on Leah. After all, the whole point of the pilot program was to determine the most effective role of civilian crisis intervention workers to assist law enforcement. Leah was basically inventing her new job as she did it and it was going to take some trial and error.

Krichek said something from the other room and Luka pushed thoughts of Leah aside to face more immediate concerns: how had Trudy Orly died and who had allowed his crime scene to mutate into a full-blown tactical call-out? He needed answers before Commander Ahearn or the Chief himself demanded them.

He found Krichek standing by the fireplace in the living room, photographing the damage done by Walt's rampage: overturned end tables, a smashed lamp, scattered knick-knacks, the shattered vase. The kitchen was on his left, an island bar separating it from the living room. The living room had spacious floor to ceiling windows, a large fireplace, and soft, comfortable furniture. The walls were filled with photos of Walt and Trudy at various exotic locales.

Luka scrutinized the photos nearest him—the dates inscribed on the mats were only two to three years ago, yet both Walt and Trudy appeared a decade younger than what he'd seen of them today. Walt's illness must have progressed rapidly. "Walk me through it."

"What?" Krichek replied. "You were here, saw—"

"Before I arrived. How the hell did ERT get involved?" Thank God there'd been no press to document McKinley's men aiming assault rifles at a sick old man. Or to film the presence of civilians on scene. If it turned out Luka's team was responsible for the screw-up, Ahearn was going to eat him alive.

Krichek was a solid worker, good with tedious details like financials and cell records, but he was also green, prone to wild theories. "Honestly, boss, it went to hell before Harper and I even got here. We arrived to find the body unattended, a screaming match up here. Two uniforms trying to corral the husband, one of them with his Taser out, ready to deploy. That Saliba woman, the neighbor, was trying to help but the uniforms kept shouting at Orly to comply. The old man was like an animal—I don't think he understood a word they were saying. The uniforms had already called for backup—no idea how that turned into ERT, but next thing I know, just as Harper and the neighbor are working to calm Orly down, McKinley and his guys arrive. I left to deal with them and asked Harper to call you." He turned one palm up, as if uncertain if he should be asking forgiveness. "Not sure what else I could do. It all happened so fast."

"Both you and Harper need to document everything that happened—a complete timeline of your actions, down to the second." Not for the first time, Luka wished Cambria City had the budget for bodycams. "And pray that the neighbor backs you up, that it was the uniforms who escalated things."

"Yes, sir." Krichek's expression turned grave, the seriousness of the situation finally sinking in.

Luka turned his attention to the task at hand. "We don't know yet if Trudy's death was suspicious, so what should we be looking for?"

"If she was arriving home when she fell, there wouldn't be any physical evidence inside the apartment. We could look for indications of pre-meditation like a life insurance policy or other motive…" He trailed off, turning in a circle, suddenly uncertain. Given the violence the living room had suffered it was easy to lose focus.

"How about we see if we can document Walt's mental impairment," Luka suggested. "Rule out any possibility that he's faking that. And help assess how bad off he really is, for when we interview him."

"Our warrant doesn't cover medical records, but we could document his prescriptions, especially if they're in plain sight." Krichek moved past Luka to the kitchen where, above the sink, an array of prescription bottles could be seen through the cupboard's glass doors. It, like all the cupboards and the pantry door, was held shut with a child-proof lock. Soft foam had been placed over the sharp corners of the countertop as well, while knob protectors covered the stove's controls.

"We need to find a next of kin for the Orlys." Luka tugged at one of the stove protectors. Given his grandfather's forgetfulness, they might not be a bad investment. "Did Maggie find Trudy's phone?" The coroner's investigator would have control of any personal items found on the body.

"Said there wasn't one," Krichek said in a distracted tone as he photographed the prescriptions and then looked up each drug. "Wow, this is some powerful stuff. If Orly needs all this, he must be nuts—er, I mean, extremely mentally impaired."

Luka was more concerned with Trudy's missing phone. "Keep an eye out for a cell phone."

"She was old, probably forgot it."

"Not while leaving her sick husband home alone." Which reminded him of the other thing bothering him. "Walt was in pajamas; maybe he was in bed when Trudy went to the store?" Perhaps she'd left early, in time to be first in line when the pharmacy opened, hoping Walt would still be asleep when she returned. Luka drifted down the hall to the bedroom. Two twin-sized beds, one neatly made, the other with covers tossed back. On the nightstand beside the second bed was a baby monitor with a video camera. Which meant Trudy definitely took her cell phone with her so she'd be alerted as soon as Walt got out of bed.

He returned to the kitchen where Krichek was still documenting the various medications. "Do you have the victim's cell number?" Krichek nodded. "Call it for me."

Krichek dialed and they waited. Nothing sounded in the apartment. "Straight to voicemail."

"I'm going to check her shopping bags, maybe she slipped it inside." Luka stepped out of the apartment to the landing between the front door and the elevator. A crime scene tech was dusting the railing over the atrium for prints near where Trudy's shopping bags had been abandoned. "Wilson, did you hear a phone ring just now?"

"No, sorry." He didn't look up from where he was gently swirling his brush, barely touching the walnut surface. Wilson had been with the department for decades, but despite his seniority, he preferred evidence collection on scene to examining it in the lab.

Luka moved to the crime scene tape, but didn't cross it, respecting Wilson's space. "Anything?"

"Nothing to point to suicide." He gestured to the palm prints the powder had uncovered. "See how they're facing in the same direction? If she'd climbed over to jump—"

"They would be going in different directions as she changed her grip."

"Right. And so far, these are the only ones I'm picking up. They must do a good job of cleaning. Plus, top floor, not much traffic up here."

"But if she was gripping the railing—how did she fall?" Luka craned his neck to see more closely. "She was facing forward, holding the railing like she was looking down into the atrium, right? Not backwards, like she was struggling with someone?" He reversed his own position, demonstrating.

"Nope. Definitely forward. See the fingerprints lined up on the far side of the railing?" Wilson pointed to an area he hadn't dusted yet. "Trust me, they're there. I'll get to them in a minute."

"No rush, I believe you." Luka leaned his weight over the railing. It was just low enough that he could see someone—maybe—leaning forward too far and losing their balance. It would be more difficult for someone short like Trudy, but not impossible. "Did you collect her purse?"

"Yep. Bagged and tagged. It was with the shopping bags."

"Was her phone in it?"

Wilson shook his head. "Wallet, cash, credit cards, lipstick and stuff like that, but no phone."

"Okay if I go through the shopping bags?"

"Already finished with them. No usable prints. No phone, either."

"Thanks, Wilson. Let me know if you find anything interesting." Luka moved a few steps away and called Maggie Chen. If the phone had been in the victim's pocket, it would have been transported to the medical examiner's office with the body. "Hey, it's Luka. Did you find a phone with Trudy Orly?"

"No, sorry."

"It's missing and I'm certain she had it with her." He explained about the video monitor and Walt's condition.

"The husband has Huntington's? That's like my greatest fear come true," she said. "It's a nightmare diagnosis, not just for the patient but their entire family."

"Did you find a next of kin besides the husband to notify?"

"No. If Walt can't direct us to other family, we might need to get a court order to see if there's someone listed in their wills or on their bank accounts. I hate doing that, it takes so much time and paperwork, but—"

"We can help cut through the red tape for you," he offered. "Anything on your preliminary exam?"

"So far, everything is consistent with trauma from a fall of that height. No defensive wounds." Which meant Trudy hadn't fought off an attacker. "We'll know more after the postmortem."

"Any idea when?" In non-urgent cases like accidental deaths, a PM could take days to schedule. Luka mentally crossed his fingers. Something felt off here; his gut was telling him there was more to Trudy's death than mere accident.

"You caught a break. Ford Tierney has a conference tomorrow, so he's fitting Trudy in this afternoon. Start time is two o'clock, so don't be late."

"I'll be there. Thanks, Maggie." Luka hung up, his gaze following the path from the elevator to the Orlys' apartment. Trudy's keys were in the lock, but her grocery bags were positioned between the railing and the apartment. Why had Trudy detoured over to the railing?

At least the fingerprints ruled out suicide, he thought. Thank goodness. Because he didn't think he could deal with that, not on today of all days.

The image that was his constant companion clouded his vision: Cherise in the water, changing her mind but unable to escape, her face filled with terror. How long had it taken her to die?

Now, haunted by Cherise's ghost, he looked down over the railing, down to the lobby floor far below. How long had it taken for Trudy to hit the floor? No one had reported hearing her scream. Why didn't she shout for help? A shudder shook him as he glanced back to Trudy's apartment. Maybe she knew who killed her and couldn't bear to see him go to prison. Maybe she thought her husband, given his devastating illness, had suffered enough.

CHAPTER 7

Leah knocked on Risa Saliba's door. "Coming!" she heard through the solid oak. But it took over a minute, after the click and clank of several heavy-duty locks, before the door finally swung open.

Risa stood swaying, one hand pressed against the foyer wall keeping her upright. She appeared ashen, her entire body covered in a cold sweat. "Sorry," she mumbled, then spun away, using the wall to guide her into a small powder room across from the hall closet. Retching noises sounded along with moans of pain.

Leah rushed in to help her, her instincts taking over. She understood the aftermath of adrenaline, but this seemed more than that. She grabbed a washcloth, wet it, and knelt beside Risa on the old-fashioned octagonal black-and-white tiles. "Here."

Risa nodded her thanks as she took the cloth and ran it over her neck and forehead. She flushed the toilet, cleaned her face, but didn't try to get up, simply cradled the toilet, her breath coming in panting gasps.

"Do you need me to call someone?" Leah asked. She remembered Risa's leaning on the walker, the way her hand shook. A list of possible diagnoses ran through her mind, but she'd just met Risa. It would be rude to pry. So instead, she focused on making Risa comfortable, rinsing out the washcloth and replacing it with a clean, wet one over the back of her neck. "How can I help?"

Risa sighed, took in a deeper breath. "It's the nausea." Another breath. "I'll be fine once the medicine kicks in."

The tiny bathroom had pink tiled walls, a black porcelain sink with sweeping curves as if it aspired to be an ornamental fountain, and an oval mirror with etching along its rim. Risa took a few more slow, deep breaths and finally, pushed away from the toilet. Leah stood and offered a hand to help Risa up. Like her neighbor, Walt Orly, she was much too thin.

Together they shuffled into the living room where Risa collapsed into an overstuffed chair that sat in the corner formed by the long wall of windows and the fireplace. There was a rolling computer stand beside it with a laptop and a stack of papers waiting. An assortment of medicine bottles was arrayed on the coffee table along with a cup of tea that appeared abandoned.

"Sorry," Risa said. "I didn't get a chance to take my morning meds on time, what with Walt and all." She was only in her mid-thirties, but right now seemed decades older as she huddled in the chair, pulling a well-worn quilt around her shoulders.

Leah's concern overcame her sense of politeness. All those medications—clearly whatever they were meant to treat, it had to be quite serious. "Can I ask, what's your diagnosis?"

"They don't know what I have," Risa scoffed. "Two years and the doctors have pretty much given up on me. I think they think I'm faking, that it's all in my head. Functional disorder, they call it."

Functional disorder? Leah hadn't been expecting that. She'd thought Risa would tell her she had end stage cancer or a neuro-degenerative disease. Functional disorder was often the diagnosis of last resort, when physicians threw up their hands in frustration but had to give a patient a label, if only for insurance purposes. She'd always hated that about modern-day medicine. It forced doctors to never admit that sometimes they just didn't know all the answers. "I'm sorry to hear that."

Risa turned tear-filled eyes toward Leah. "Days like this, I worry they might be right. That my own mind is doing this to me." She glanced away, raising a shaky hand to wipe her eyes. "Sorry."

"Let me reheat your tea." Leah took the mug, allowing Risa to compose herself. The layout was a mirror image of the Orlys' apartment. An assortment of herbal teas was arranged on the kitchen counter, some in tea bags, some loose in colorful glass jars. Leah took a mug from the shelf above and selected a peppermint tea for herself and put both mugs in the microwave. As she waited for the tea to heat, she looked around. A pharmacy's worth of medication and supplements were lined up on a shelf above the sink. She couldn't help but glance at a few—medications usually used to treat chronic pain, Crohn's, inflammation, arthritis, anxiety, seizures, migraines, asthma, and even Parkinson's. If Risa had half the symptoms these drugs were meant to treat, then she was one very sick woman.

The microwave dinged. Leah returned to the living room, this time taking in the decor. A tufted couch faced the chair that Risa obviously called home along with a second, matching chair beside it. A thick, handwoven Persian rug filled the space between them with bright colors. But what really caught her eye was a wall of photos. Africa, the Middle East, Asia, Alaska, and locales Leah wasn't certain of. But it wasn't the exotic locations that were so striking. It was the people in them. Normal people. Young, old, very old. Happy, sad, terrified, angry. The spectrum of human experience captured in a wall's worth of photos.

"These are amazing." Leah handed Risa her tea.

Risa sipped it gratefully. Her color was better, her breathing back to normal. "Thank you. And thank you for coming. I wanted to talk with you."

"Right." Leah sat down on the chair beside Risa and dug out one of her new business cards to hand to Risa. This was where she had to be careful. Make sure that the people she spoke to understood she wasn't acting as their physician. "I'm a doctor at Good Samaritan's ER. But I'm here this morning helping the police."

"I'm glad. They might have shot Walt. And you were so good with him. Have you done that before? Talked someone away from a violent confrontation with the police?" Risa leaned forward, eyes fixed on Leah as if her new job was the most fascinating thing in the world. Again, Leah had that strange sense of familiarity even though she was certain she'd never met Risa before.

"It's a new program. Good Sam's Crisis Intervention Center is working with Cambria City police when they have—" She searched for the right word to use with a civilian. Emotionally disturbed sounded far too clinical. "Fragile witnesses."

Risa considered that as she took another sip of tea, her trembling easing. "I've never seen Walt like that. He frightened me. It was very brave of you to go in to talk with him."

"Was it? You went in as well."

"But that was before he got so violent."

"I didn't feel brave. I just knew what he needed and concentrated on that. I mean, I've been more afraid in the ER. Usually right before a trauma arrives, when I'm imagining the worst. But then, during a trauma? It's like standing in the eye of a hurricane, everything moving around me at lightning speed, but I'm calm and focused." Leah felt like she was rambling; maybe she was more nervous than she'd thought.

"In the zone. That's what I used to call it when I was in the field. I'd focus on my subject, on getting the story, bombs would be going off—I mean literally going off around me, and I barely noticed. Like being in my own world, just me and the story I needed to tell." She sighed, her gaze passing Leah to look out the rain-streaked window. "Out there, everything seemed so clear…"

"Story—" Leah glanced over at the wall of photos, took in the small items she hadn't noticed before aligned on the mantle: a large bullet encased in a Lucite box sitting on a charred scrap of bright blue fabric. An ornamental knife displayed on a stand beside the desiccated cervical vertebrae of what had to be a giraffe, it was so elongated. "Risa Saliba. I knew I'd heard your name.

My husband is a huge fan. We've watched you on Nat Geo and PBS and the BBC and—you've been everywhere." Leah realized she was gushing. Ian would love— The thought brought her up short and she blinked, refocused, before tears could ambush her.

Risa glanced toward her walker. "My traveling days are over." She sat up straighter. "Temporarily."

"What are you doing here in Cambria City?" Leah grew up here, which was why she'd returned when her great-aunt got sick, but she'd also fought like hell to escape when she was young. What did a downtrodden rustbelt city have to offer a sophisticated journalist like Risa Saliba?

It was the first time Risa had smiled since Leah met her. "My boyfriend. We tried the long-distance thing, but after I got sick, he insisted I move in with him so he could take care of me." Her smile widened at the memory. "I refused. Refused to move in, refused to get engaged, refused to get married immediately."

"Because you were sick?"

"Because I refuse to be a burden to anyone I love. I admit, I sometimes pushed the line, was more reckless than I needed to be when I was chasing a story. But it was only myself I was hurting. I live my life on my terms…" Her gaze settled on a small framed photo beside her computer: Risa and a handsome man, arms around each other on a beach, the sunset silhouetting them as if they shared one body. "But then Jack came along and—"

"Suddenly there's a huge complicated emotional calculus to solve."

"Yes, exactly."

Leah chuckled. "Wait until you have kids. That equation turns into quantum physics, a search for a unified field theory."

"I just want to get healthy enough to be with Jack. He's been so patient through all this." She gestured down the length of her body. "Since I can't work in the field and he's based here, last year I moved here to be closer to him."

Leah glanced at the wide variety of photos and mementos. "What are you doing? Writing a book? I mean, since you aren't traveling anymore…"

Risa's expression fell as Leah's words trailed off. *Way to say the wrong thing*, Leah thought. "I am trying to write a book, but it's hard going between doctor visits and my bad days. And it doesn't pay the bills, so I actually work as a fact checker for several media outlets."

"Fact checker?"

"For features and opinion pieces, to make sure no one's twisting the facts. Obituaries, as well."

"Obituaries? I thought families wrote those."

"For most people. Anyone considered a celebrity or historical figure, famous, the news outlets keep their obituaries on file, pre-written, but they have to be updated frequently. Those are pretty easy. The tough ones are the victims of newsworthy crimes or events. When things are breaking fast and there's little time. Then, you need to be sensitive but at the same time, you can't get anything wrong and you don't have the safety net of the pre-written obituary to work from. Usually the reporter on the ground gathers the facts, sends it to the main desk who will assign a writer, then it comes to me to read and proof."

"I never knew."

"Sounds more interesting than it is. I mean, compared to boots-on-the-ground reporting." Her gaze settled on her computer and she frowned. "But there is one story I've stumbled on. I think it's a story. All the meds the doctors have me on, some days I think I'm just imagining."

"What is it?"

A knock at the front door sounded. "Want me to get that?" Leah asked.

"Yes, please."

Leah set her tea down and walked to the door, peering through the eyehole. It was Luka. Great. She hadn't even begun to ask

Risa about Walt. She opened the door and ushered him into the living room.

"Hello again, Ms. Saliba. Luka Jericho—"

"I remember, Detective Sergeant." Risa sighed as if resigned to more disruption in her day. But Leah noticed the painful wince and the way she held her belly. She could tell the other woman was trying hard not to be sick again.

"Luka, maybe we could do this later?" Leah suggested.

"I need to hear what Ms. Saliba saw—"

Before Luka could finish, the door behind them banged open and a tall, athletic man wearing a suit and tie rushed inside.

"Risa!" He ignored Leah and Luka to cross to Risa's side, dropping down to his knees, taking both her hands in his. "I saw the police and the ambulance and they wouldn't let me in until now. You weren't answering your phone and I thought—" He stopped, out of breath, and simply stared at her, as if reassuring himself that she was actually there.

"I'm fine, Jack. It's just been a rough morning."

"You're sure you're okay?" He buried his head in her hands for a moment, kissing both her palms, then looked up again. "I was so scared—I've never been that terrified in my life. I don't know what I'd do without you. What happened?"

CHAPTER 8

Luka couldn't believe his poor timing. If he'd arrived here just two minutes earlier, he could have gotten Risa's statement. Now he had an overwrought significant other to slow things down. He stepped forward, extending his card to Risa, but the man stood, turned to face Luka and took it himself.

"Detective? What happened? Did someone break in or something?" The man's concern morphed into a defensive posture as he squared off as if Luka was the enemy.

"No," Risa said. "It was Walt and Trudy. Jack, it was horrible."

"Walt and Trudy?" The man's expression softened, no longer on alert. "Are they okay? What happened?"

"Mrs. Orly died this morning," Luka told him. "I need to ask Ms. Saliba a few questions about what she saw." He tried to edge around the boyfriend, but instead the man thrust his hand out.

"Jack. Jack O'Brien." He shook Luka's hand with an assertive grip. Then turned to Leah. "And you are?"

"Dr. Leah Wright. I'm assisting the police."

He took her hand as well. "A doctor? Interesting. I'm one as well. PhD in environmental chemistry."

"Jack's the environmental compliance officer for Keystone Shale," Risa put in, her tone filled with pride. She reached for Jack's hand and guided him to the chair beside her, nodding to Luka and Leah to also take a seat. Up close, Luka realized her color was off and despite appearing a few years younger than him, her skin was stretched thin, cheeks hollow and gaunt like a much older woman.

"Environmental compliance officer. What's that?" Given the exuberant energy the man exuded, Luka was surprised Jack wasn't a used car salesman.

"Jack travels to all their sites," Risa answered. "Makes sure there's no chemicals polluting the groundwater, things like that."

"Things like that?" Jack said in a gentle, chiding tone. As if this was an ongoing private joke between them. "Things like that are what keep everyone safe." The two were holding hands and couldn't stop looking at each other. Luka smothered a wince—he remembered all too well feeling like that. The way Cherise had beamed when he proposed, despite his being barely able to get any words out.

"We met when I was doing a piece on the environmental impact of fracking." Risa's words interrupted Luka's memories. "Jack helped me understand the reports the companies released and how they were hiding contamination."

"Not Keystone," Jack piped up. "We run a clean ship—I make sure of it. No sense having all the energy you need if your kids and grandkids won't be able to drink the water or have a clean environment to play in, right?"

"Do you live here, Mr. O'Brien?" Luka asked, desperate to steer things back on track.

"I wish." Jack glanced meaningfully at Risa, who blushed. "I'm out in the field most of the time, but I have a place a few blocks away. I stop by here every morning when I'm in town. To check on Risa—sometimes she has a rough night."

"Not always," she said, her posture defensive. "Besides, I'm pretty much a night owl anyway. Get most of my work done then."

"Were you still awake this morning when Mrs. Orly left?" Luka continued. "Did you see or hear her leave?"

"No, I must have finally fallen asleep." Risa frowned. "I was up all night—"

"Why didn't you call me if you were having a bad night?" Jack asked.

"I'm fine now." Risa's tone made it clear she didn't like being taken care of, but it was obvious that Jack thrived on being a protector. "Trudy and Walt lost their home health aide. I try to help out when I can, and I told Trudy to call me anytime if she needed me to keep an eye on Walt." She stretched a hand to the computer desk and grabbed her phone. Her expression fell. "I missed her call. Seven thirty-four. I should have been awake—usually I would have been. I should have had the phone closer so it woke me. Then maybe—"

"Even if you had taken her call, she still would have gone to the store," Leah said. "There was nothing you could do."

"May I see that?" Luka gestured to the phone. Risa handed it to him. He took a picture of the missed call on her screen. "Trudy left you a voicemail. Okay to play it?"

"Of course."

He pressed the icon and a woman's voice sounded. "Risa, are you there? Oh, you're probably in the shower. Walt spilled his medicine last night but Mr. McMahon at the pharmacy keeps extra ready. I'm going to pick it up now, shouldn't be long, maybe a half hour. Walt's sound asleep—was up most of the night, so probably will sleep all morning, but just in case, could you keep an eye on him? Thanks! And if they have those tea cookies you like, I'll grab you some. You deserve a treat!"

They sat in silence for a moment. Luka had the sudden urge to call home to check on Pops, even though he knew his grandfather was being well cared for by Janine, the live-in aide who'd joined their household after his nephew's unexpected arrival. But all Trudy had to help her was the kindness of her neighbors. Silent tears streamed down Risa's cheeks.

"It's not your fault." Jack moved to sit on the arm of Risa's chair, pulling her close to him. "There's nothing you could have done." He glanced up at Luka, searching for affirmation. "Right, Detective?

Luka ignored the question. "Did you hear Trudy return?"

Risa shook her head and swiped a hand at her eyes. "No. I didn't know anything was wrong until I heard Walt shouting."

"What time was that?"

"I'm not sure. Cliff would know—it was when he called 911. I came out of the apartment and saw Walt looking over the railing. Then I saw—I saw Trudy. At the bottom."

Jack's eyes widened. "Trudy fell? From up here?" He wrapped his arms around Risa's shoulders, burying her face in his chest. "What a terrible accident."

"We're not certain what happened," Luka replied.

Jack said, "Surely you don't suspect—I mean, Walt's sick. His mind, he gets angry, confused. But he'd never hurt Trudy. Never." Despite his words, he seemed uncertain. He turned to Risa. "I think you should come home with me. I'll call off work—"

Risa was shaking her head. "I'm fine. Really. They took Walt to the hospital." Her tone turned sorrowful. "I'm not even sure he understands that Trudy's gone. He won't be able to take care of himself. I don't know what will happen to him." She glanced at Leah.

"They'll find a place for him," she said in a soothing tone. "Most patients at his stage of his illness need long-term care facilities."

"What if their insurance doesn't cover that? They won't just put him out on the street, will they?" Risa yanked on Jack's sleeve. "We need to help him. It's the least we can do." The color had drained from her face and she put one hand to her mouth.

"Did you take your medicine this morning?" Jack asked.

Risa nodded. She swallowed, took a breath.

"I think you need another dose. Let me get you into bed and I'll get it." Jack helped Risa to her feet, her weight sagging against him. "That's enough for today."

"Just a few more questions," Luka tried. Even if Risa hadn't seen Trudy's fall, he still needed to know what happened in the Orlys' apartment before his team arrived.

"They'll have to wait. Come back later, Detective." Jack's tone was firm as he pivoted Risa away from Luka toward the bedroom.

Luka glanced to Leah, a silent plea for help. Strongarm tactics would only antagonize the overprotective boyfriend. Maybe Leah could get Risa alone, away from Jack, so they could take her statement.

Leah gave him a small nod and stood. "Let me help."

Risa nodded. "Thank you, yes. Jack, Leah is a medical doctor. This way you can get to the office. If you're okay to stay a few minutes, Leah?"

Jack frowned. "No. I can—"

Risa patted his arm. "I'll be fine. Imagine. A doctor who still makes house calls." Her tone sounded strong, despite the fact that her entire body was shaking with chills. Jack frowned and half-carried her into the bedroom, Leah following.

Luka stood alone in the suddenly empty living room. How had such a simple case become so complicated, so quickly? He only hoped Leah remembered that Risa was a witness, not a patient.

He made his way to the door, but stopped to glance back. It wasn't Leah's fault that she was a healer first. Although it was damned inconvenient. Because he had a niggling feeling that there was more going on here than a simple accidental death.

CHAPTER 9

After Luka left, Leah watched as Jack helped Risa into her bed. Despite his handsome looks and engaging manner, there definitely was a mother-hen side to him, she noted with bemused appreciation. Ian was like that on the rare occasions when she or Emily were sick, donning a metaphorical apron, taking pleasure in cooking their favorite comfort foods, tucking them into bed, wrapping them in quilts and robes and his love.

She smiled as Jack used a remote to adjust the bed just so, elevating both Risa's head and feet, arranging her pillows, bringing her a glass of an electrolyte solution, and then making certain her walker, phone and medications were close to hand. All the while hovering between Risa and Leah protectively, as if uncertain if he trusted Leah.

"Jack, you're being silly," Risa protested. She pulled him down for a quick kiss. "Seriously, I'll be fine. Go to work."

He sat on the edge of her bed, caressing her hand—especially her empty ring finger. Leah turned away, edging toward the door, but Risa called her back. "No. Please, stay. I'd like your help if you have the time."

Leah nodded and pretended to study the framed photos lining the top of the bureau: Risa and Jack covered in mud at an oil field as rain poured around them; rafting the New River, both raising their oars triumphantly; a portrait of Jack stoking a campfire, the flames casting his face in relief, his expression contemplative. Caught in a moment of stillness, he looked a little older.

"We're in this together," she heard him whisper to Risa. "I'm not giving up. Not on you, not on us."

"Neither am I. Which is why you need to go, so I can talk with Dr. Wright."

Leah turned at the sound of her name. Jack's shoulders slumped but he nodded, gave Risa one last kiss, then rose. He gestured for Leah to follow him out to the living room, now empty since Luka had left. "I hadn't realized Risa found another doctor. I'm not sure who you are or how long you'll be around, but her medication schedule and medical records are on here." He handed her a thumb drive. "Please don't interfere with anything until you've read them all. Risa likes to be involved in her medical decision-making—"

"Of course, but—" Leah protested, trying to insert a quick explanation as to why she was actually there, but Jack didn't give her a chance.

"We usually discuss any new treatments together. But," his voice lowered as his gaze targeted the bedroom door, "if you really think you can help her—I mean, just please, don't give her any false hope. She's been through so much." He nodded to the thumb drive in Leah's hands. "Read it. You'll see."

One last longing glance toward the bedroom and he left. At the sound of the door closing, Risa called out, "Lock it, please."

Leah went through the living room and down the short hallway to the front door. Risa had an assortment of locks, from old-fashioned deadbolts to a large, heavy gauge steel brace that swung down from the doorknob and inserted into a cradle bolted into the wood floor. It was very different from her neighbors the Orlys. Leah had noticed that they only had a single, ancient deadbolt. What was Risa so afraid of? Leah secured all the locks, then returned to the living room to find Risa slowly making her way out of the bedroom with the help of her walker.

"I thought you needed to lie down—"

"I'm fine." Risa collapsed into her chair, shoving the walker aside. "Sometimes it's easier for Jack to leave if he thinks I'm resting." She frowned at her own words. "He's just… overprotective. It's hard to constantly fight both my illness and him when all I want to do is live my life. Does that make any sense?"

Leah knew all too well what Risa meant—since Ian's death, she'd faced similar attitudes. Family, friends, and strangers all seemed to want her to fit their image of a grieving widow—and yet they also simultaneously wanted her to act "normal" again, get on with her life.

"Why all the locks? Aren't they a fire hazard? Take so long to open, especially—" Leah nodded at the walker.

"It's not fire I'm worried about."

"What are you worried about?"

Risa opened her mouth, then closed it. She nodded to the thumb drive Leah still held. "Jack gave you my medical records."

"He thought I was here for a medical consultation." Leah tried to hand the thumb drive back to Risa.

Risa waved a hand in dismissal, too busy pulling her computer desk into position. "Keep it. If you're interested, you have my permission to review anything on there. Jack makes a dozen copies anytime we start a new protocol. That way we're ready for the next round of consults once it fails." She opened her laptop, her forehead creasing. "And they all fail."

Leah hesitated, searching for words to clarify her position. "I can't really give you medical advice, Risa. Not while I'm here to interview you for the police." She set the thumb drive on the computer stand and stepped away.

"So I'm one of your 'fragile' witnesses?" Risa chuckled. "You've got it backwards. I didn't ask you here for a medical opinion, although I'd respect an objective evaluation, of course. But I've been to Johns Hopkins, NYU, Columbia *and* Cornell, plus the NIH, their division of rare diseases. Seen all the biggest names.

Infectious disease guys thought it was a parasite or something I picked up while traveling. Immunology and rheumatology thought the same but that the reason there was no sign of infection was because it wasn't the bug or parasite or virus causing my symptoms, but my immune response to it. Neurology thought a toxic exposure, probably from my time doing that article on the burn pits our military used in Iraq and Afghanistan—"

"I read that. The story with the picture of them burning an entire airplane rather than leaving it behind."

"Yeah. And they're right, inhaling all those toxic fumes—I mean you wouldn't believe the stuff they burned, right next to troops' barracks. It's probably part of why we're seeing so many chronically ill returning veterans. But I wasn't there long enough for a significant exposure. And so they send me to someone else and then someone else and now..." She shook her head. Her tone turned bitter. "Now, there's no one left. Functional disease. What do you doctors call it? A diagnosis of exclusion? But they made it very clear what they really thought. That it's all in my head."

"You know functional neurologic disease isn't a psychiatric diagnosis, right?" Leah rushed to console her. "It simply means that the way your body functions is causing symptoms not in direct response to any underlying cause that current medicine can determine."

Risa gave her a resigned shrug. "Review my case. If you want to throw out any ideas, I'm all ears." She went silent for a moment, staring again toward the front door with its ponderous weight of locks. "But I wanted to talk to you *because* you're working for the police."

"Was there something you didn't feel comfortable saying in front of Detective Jericho?" Leah slid her phone out, ready to record. "Maybe you could walk me through what happened this morning?"

Risa's gaze remained distant, then she gave a little shake and turned to face Leah. "Of course. Let's get that out of the way." She tucked her feet under her, curled up in the chair. "If I'd only heard Trudy's call—I could have gone over, watched Walt."

"Trudy obviously wasn't expecting him to wake up before she left, much less…" Leah trailed off. It wasn't up to her to speculate about Walt's possible actions. They had no facts, not until the autopsy results came in. Maybe not even then.

Risa kept shaking her head, small uncertain shakes, trying to deny the obvious. "He loved her so much. I mean, every time they left the apartment, they'd hold hands. Jack would watch them and say, 'That's us in thirty years.' But over the past year Walt's symptoms grew worse. And he stopped leaving the apartment. It was so heartbreaking, seeing Trudy leave the apartment alone." She reached for her computer, scrolled through it. "Here, see for yourself."

A black and white image filled the screen. Walt, his back turned to prevent the elevator doors closing, holding Trudy's hand as she joined him. Both staring at each other, Trudy with a shy smile at Walt, and Walt's face filled with a grin that creased his eyes as if they shared a silent joke known only to each other.

Then she brought up a new photo. Trudy entering the elevator. Alone. Her shoulders hunched, her gaze directed back behind her as if longing for something no longer there. She physically occupied the exact same space as in the previous photo, only the time stamp had changed. Time lost, Leah thought, her mind filling with thoughts of Ian, of the myriad moments never recorded and now at risk of being forever forgotten. She looked away, blinking hard.

"I thought you were mainly a reporter," she said after clearing her throat and refocusing.

"When I'm on assignment, I work with professional photographers—they get much, much better shots than my amateur attempts. But I learned a lot from them over the years and I discovered a taste for shooting people. Just candid cell phone shots, but since I've grown more and more isolated—I barely ever leave the apartment anymore—it's my last connection to the real world. A reminder that it's still out there, waiting for me to explore."

"They're very good."

Risa blushed. "Thanks. I've never shown them to anyone except Jack—he sent them to my agent, Dominic Massimo. Dom wants me to use them in my book. If I can ever get the damn thing finished."

"Did you take any pictures this morning?" It felt like an awkward segue, but Leah knew the questions Luka would ask.

"No. When I heard Walt, I rushed out and forgot my phone."

"What happened?"

"I'm not even sure how he got out of the apartment, but he was at the railing, shrieking at Trudy. Telling her to get up, come back. I got him into his apartment and had him almost calmed down when the cops showed up, asking him all sorts of questions he didn't understand. I tried to explain that they were making things worse, but Walt got agitated and one of them pulled out his Taser, so I stepped between them and the other guy laid hands on me… and Walt, he just lost it. Screaming, knocking stuff over. I would have been able to calm him back down, but it was too late, the cops were already calling for backup." She hung her head. "I feel so bad for Walt. Seeing Trudy like that… They're not going to charge him, are they? For resisting arrest? He was just trying to defend me, he wasn't trying to hurt the cops."

"Did you see or hear anything else?"

"No. Like I said, I was asleep when it… happened. Only woke when Walt began shouting."

Leah turned off the recorder. If Luka needed more, he could always come back, ask for himself. During their conversation she'd noted Risa's tremors returning, her posture collapsing with fatigue. "It's not writer's block keeping you from finishing your book, is it?"

"No." Risa took a sip from her long-cold tea mug, used it to swallow a pill from a small box on the table between them. She leaned back, closed her eyes for a long moment, as if savoring the effects of the medication. Professional curiosity had Leah wondering what she'd taken that could have such a quick impact, but the pills weren't labeled.

"Is it because you're sick?"

Risa opened her eyes and sat up straight once again. "It's more than my physical condition distracting me from the book." She nudged the computer toward Leah. "It's this. This is what I wanted your help with. The first email came last spring, a few months after I moved here from New York. I thought it was a joke. But then... Well, read it for yourself."

Her curiosity piqued, Leah settled into the chair beside Risa and began scrolling through the letter displayed.

Dear Obituary Reader,

First time caller, longtime fan.

You'll ask me why. Why I've chosen my victims. Why I chose you. Why?

It's the least important question, but I understand your need to know. An attempt to feel in control, as if by understanding you regain some slim illusion of power. But why is of no consequence. Because I am Chaos.

Why do I do it? Because I can. I've the intelligence, the raw cunning, the courage and the willpower others lack. Why shouldn't I celebrate my superior gifts? The ones I take are all easily replaced, sheep oblivious to their small lives, their lack of destiny. My choosing them, elevating their lives if only in death, it's the one thing that makes them less than ordinary.

Although to be honest, I don't actually choose them at all. That's my secret to success. I embrace Chaos, allowing chance to guide my destiny. Everything I do is random. Where, when, how, and yes, even who.

I'm the important one in this equation, not my victims. If I want to play the game, I had to be smart, find a way to never be caught. Because a mind like mine, trapped in a cage, surrounded by imbeciles and thugs? Can you imagine anything more tragic? Almost as wasteful as a talent like yours trapped by your own body, relegated to meaningless busywork instead of exploring the world's secrets.

No, to play the game, I must have no connection to those I touch, including you.

There is no why. No motivation beyond my own enjoyment. No signature or modus operandi, no victim profile. I am a cipher, random and unique, able to strike anywhere at any time, driven by chance alone.

No rhyme or reason. Only my unrelenting need for more, more, more…

Leah looked up in alarm. *Victims?* Was Risa's letter writer claiming to be a serial killer? This had to be a hoax. "Risa. This reads like a confession. Have you told the police?"

"Yes. But there's no proof of any crime, nothing for the police to go on. They said there's nothing they can do." Her tone turned bitter. "Other than to laugh me off the phone."

If the other letters were as vague as this, Leah wasn't surprised that the police dismissed them. After all, a well-known journalist like Risa had to attract fans who wanted her to tell their story.

Risa continued, "I read about your husband in the paper, what happened, how he was killed. So when you showed up at my door, as if…" She paused. "Anyway, I thought if anyone might understand, might give me an objective opinion, it would be you. Keep reading, then we can talk."

Leah's heart pounded, the memory of entering her darkened house last month overwhelming her. Frantically searching for Ian and Emily, dreading what she knew she'd find; that primal instinct screaming for her to stop, to run... but like last month, Leah ignored it now as well. She couldn't have stopped if she'd wanted to.

She kept reading...

But why you?

Why choose you as my confessor, my chronicler, my cohort in Chaos... my silent partner?

Perhaps you were selected by a throw of a dart or toss of the dice. Maybe it was less than random. A glimpse of that bemused smile beaming out from the headshot beside your byline. The intelligence obvious behind your insightful interviews. A regard for the courage—almost as reckless as my own?—that drove you to explore the dark heart of humanity.

I hope I haven't scared you away with my frank admiration. No. Of course not. You're intrigued, compelled to follow the breadcrumbs I've dropped for you, determined to find the truth. No illness could conquer that relentless curiosity that once compelled you to risk life and limb for a story.

I'd read some of your work—honestly, I thought your piece on the Kurdish women snipers was much better than that series on the Thai child prostitutes that they gave you the Pulitzer for—so I was surprised when someone shared a link to a fundraiser page set up by your boyfriend.

I was certain it was a scam. I mean, he was just so damn needy. And the whole thing seemed beneath you, asking strangers to help you raise money for doctors and tests. I was angry—on your behalf—and determined to out him as a fake.

Then I found his videos of you, withered away to nothing, that tube down your nose to feed you, and the doctors with no idea what was wrong. And I kept looking, saw that you hadn't been published in almost two years, that you were freelancing, even writing obituaries, of all things.

And I couldn't help but think what a waste that was. A journalist of your caliber being forced to beg for scraps.

I can't help with the medical stuff but I can help ease the boredom, exercise your mind. So here I am, offering what might be the greatest adventure you've ever undertaken—a journey into the heart of a killer.

Or maybe everything I've said is a lie—that's what you're thinking. But what if it's not?

What if I've told you the truth? What if you have been chosen for something more, the most important story of your life?

Would you choose to join me, experience the vicarious thrills that only someone like me can offer? Or will you settle for your current mundane, homebound, monotonous existence, your talents wasted?

No need to tell me your answer. I already know it. And I'll prove it with my first offering.

You'll know it when you see it.
Your devoted fan.

CHAPTER 10

Leah felt Risa's eyes on her, watching her reactions as she finished reading the chilling letter. Finally, she turned away from the computer. Unsettled, she left Risa and went to the kitchen to reheat her now-cold mug of tea. As the microwave hummed, she took a few deeps breaths to settle herself. Her stomach churned, her shoulders tightened as if guarding against an attack. More insidious than fear. Dread.

If one letter could do that to her...

And Risa had been living with this guy in her head for a year, she'd said.

The microwave dinged, making Leah jump. She retrieved her tea and returned to the chair beside Risa. "You're sure this isn't some joke or a scam?" Wouldn't it be nice if it were that simple. "I mean, you're a celebrity, easy to target."

"You read it. Did it feel like a joke to you?"

"No," Leah admitted. "No. But I'm not sure that he's actually a killer. This devoted fan—"

"More like obsessed," Risa scoffed.

"Risa. You need to take this to the police. We need to make certain you're safe. Sometimes stalkers start online but move to real life."

Risa looked away, past Leah to the door. "I know," she said in a strangled whisper. "But every time I talk to the police, they act like I'm crazy."

"You're not crazy." Anger stirred in Leah. How could the police be so dismissive? Risa was smart, an investigative reporter used to dangerous situations. Not exactly someone who would imagine a threat. If they wouldn't listen to her, maybe they'd listen to Leah.

"Besides, this guy is untraceable," Risa continued. "I know because I hired the best cybersecurity specialist I could find to try to track him down." Risa took another sip of her tea. From the way she gripped the mug with both hands, Leah got the feeling that she did it not because she was thirsty but rather because she needed something to hold on to. She paused, her gaze meeting Leah's. "Your husband."

A shiver crawled over Leah. It was a small city; of course she'd be running into people who knew Ian. "That's why you're telling me. You didn't just read about Ian's murder, you knew him. Ian wasn't able to track him down?"

"No. He said this guy totally erased his tracks. But when I read about Ian's murder—"

"You thought—" Leah shook her head vigorously. The real facts behind who killed Ian hadn't been released to the public, so there was no way Risa could have known that the cases weren't connected. "No. Believe me. Ian was not killed by your stalker."

Risa leaned back, obviously relieved. "I was afraid to go back to the police after that," she said, her voice choked, her fear palpable. "Because if he tracked Ian here, if that was why—" She closed her eyes for a long moment, gathering her strength. "I haven't left the apartment since I heard about Ian. Was afraid who he might target next."

Leah was aghast. For a woman as strong as Risa to be made to feel so powerless, in fear for her life… No one should have that kind of control over a person. "We're going to the police. I'll talk to Luka myself, make him take you seriously."

"Ian said he'd prepare a report I could take to the police, said it might help."

It sounded like Ian.

"And he installed special software to document any new messages because the first ones were set to auto-erase as soon as they were read."

"Messages? Plural? There's more?" Leah leaned forward, toward the computer between them, but then pulled back.

"Dozens over the past year," Risa answered. "This guy, whoever he is, he sends me obituaries—he calls them gifts—that are people with the same name or birthday or who died exactly like people in the obituaries or feature stories that I've worked on. People all over the country." She hesitated. "I think he killed them. For me. To get me to notice him or something, I'm not sure."

"They were all murdered?"

"No. That's just it. They all appear to be natural or accidental. When I call to talk to the local police or coroners, I pretty much get laughed off the phone."

The stories Risa had worked on over the years were of course easy to find, but… "How could he know whose obituaries you've worked on? You said that was mainly fact-checking."

"Exactly. There's no byline or credit, my name isn't on any of those. At first, Ian thought the stalker might be accessing my files via malware on my computer. But he couldn't find any. I switched to a new computer, but still they kept coming. So then Ian thought maybe he's someone with the hacking skills to access editorial proofs or emails—but my work is for several news outlets and he had their IT departments check. Nothing."

"Is there anyone who links them all?" Leah asked, intrigued despite simultaneously wanting to believe that this was all a hoax. "Besides you, I mean."

Risa paused. "I'm on a few online professional forums—the people who do what I do, it's a pretty small group, so we help each other when we can. There's also my agent. Dom got me the fact-checking gigs. He's part of a larger agency in New York, so it's possible someone who works there could access our correspondence."

"Maybe Jack mentioned something in social media?" From the letter, it sounded as if Jack was as unguarded in his social media postings as he was in person. As an introvert who shunned revealing anything of her private life, Leah found extroverts like Jack more than a bit overwhelming.

"No. Jack has no clue about the specifics of my work. He respects that I can't really share details for ethical reasons."

Something in Risa's tone caught Leah's attention. "You haven't told him, have you? About the emails or your devoted fan."

Risa sighed. "It's pretty clear the stalker doesn't like Jack. I was worried if I told him and Jack tried to do anything—"

"You'd be putting a target on his back."

"Exactly. Besides, you've seen how Jack is. My knight in shining armor. He'd never stop trying to protect me—even if it meant me giving up my work, this place."

"He loves you."

"I know." The words emerged with a smile of contentment.

"If your stalker is serious or there's a risk of him escalating… I know it's not fair, it's not right, but the safest thing might be for you to leave, go off grid, someplace he can't track you. If he can't engage you, he'll get tired, move on." Because if Ian couldn't find the stalker, what were the odds that the police with their limited time and resources could? It was a harsh reality, but the unfortunate truth. And the psychology behind stalkers was similar to that of domestic partner abusers—an obsession that would never be broken as long as the object of that obsession, their victim, was accessible.

"I know." This time Risa bit the words out. "I've read the books, done the research. Hell, I once wrote a feature on victims who end up murdered by their stalkers. These women did nothing but walk down the wrong street at the wrong time, smile or say hello to the wrong man. They didn't deserve to have their lives stolen from them." Her voice rose, echoing through the cavernous room. Risa clamped her lips shut, turning her glare onto the rain battering the windows.

"You don't deserve it either," Leah told her. "No one does. That doesn't change—"

"I have resources those women didn't have. I can investigate—"

"Right. And what have you found? Is this guy really a killer like he says?"

"I'm not sure." Risa shifted in her chair, wincing with pain as she rearranged the pillows supporting her. "Years ago, I wrote a piece for *Rolling Stone*. My first major feature story. A tribute to forgotten musical artists who seemed destined for greatness until their lives were cut short by freak accidents. One of them, Jimmy Santiago, was killed after his car got stuck on train tracks outside of Corinth, South Carolina."

"Never heard of him. He was a musician?"

"Blues guitarist. Only twenty-four, but brilliant—some said he was Robert Johnson reborn via another deal with the devil."

Leah remembered the legend, that the famous musician had sold his soul to the devil in exchange for his remarkable talent.

Risa continued, her grip on her mug tightening. "Jimmy died at 12:07 on the night of April 21st, 1967. That first email came on April Fool's Day, last year. Another reason why I thought it was a bad joke. But then the next message came just after midnight on April 21st. It was a text with a video of a train hitting a man in a car. A man named James Santiago. His car stalled at the same railroad crossing where Jimmy was killed all those years ago."

"Was there a message with the video?"

"It said: *The beginning of a beautiful friendship.* It disappeared as soon as I watched it."

"And was it real?"

"Corinth doesn't have its own paper, but the next day the Greenville news mentioned it. A tragic accident. The reporter didn't even realize that it had happened before, almost exactly the same way, on the same day, over fifty years ago." She blew her breath out. "I couldn't prove anything, but I did call the Oconee County Sheriff's department. They said the guy was drunk—three times over the legal limit—it was clearly an accident."

"It could have been." Leah had to admit, Risa's story was compelling, but it could also just be that: a story. After all, Risa was a storyteller. Maybe that explained her inability to make the police take her case seriously—a desperate desire to solve it herself, return to the job she loved and lost. "Couldn't someone have had an online search running? Looking for strange accidents or criteria that tied to you and your work? Then when he found something you would see as proof, he used it to reel you in."

"That's what Ian thought. At first. But where did the video come from in the first place? Ian couldn't find it anywhere online after the message vanished."

"Maybe it wasn't even this specific accident?" Leah suggested. "Easy to fake, especially with footage shot at night."

Risa shrugged. "Since then he hasn't sent anything like that video again. Only emails, teasing hints. Nothing that could be used as evidence against him. It's as if he wants me to devote myself to unearthing his crimes, wants me to admire his work. But I haven't come up with anything solid."

"And it all started when you moved here?"

"Yes. I moved to Cambria City several months after I got sick, before the first email. There's nothing I can prove, but ever since I got here, I've felt as if I'm being watched."

"So it's not only your illness keeping you housebound?" Leah couldn't help but wonder if some of Risa's symptoms were psychosomatic—a way to deny her fear of going out in public where her stalker might see her. Then she had another thought. "Do you think Trudy's death might have something to do with your stalker?"

Risa pulled away, as far as the chair would allow her, but gave a guilty nod. "Maybe." She shuddered. "I just don't know. Maybe I am crazy. Maybe this is all in my head, these feelings. Hell, maybe I was all wrong about everything. I had myself convinced I was on the trail of a serial killer no one else knew about. The story of a lifetime. But I should have never forgotten the first rule of journalism."

"What's that?"

"Trust no one, assume nothing."

"It's also the first rule of emergency medicine. Because everyone—"

"Lies," Risa finished for her. "Exactly."

The gaunt, anxious woman before Leah was nothing like how she'd imagined Risa Saliba would be after reading her articles or seeing her on TV. As if her confidence and vibrant energy had been whittled away, leaving an empty husk. A rush of sympathy engulfed Leah—she'd felt the same after Ian was killed. She still felt like that most days. As if she'd been emptied out, a puppet going through the motions of living for Emily's sake, but not her own.

"When I met you this morning," Risa continued, "it felt like… finally someone who could help. An objective second opinion—and, if you think my stalker is actually killing people, maybe you could talk to the police? Help make them believe."

Leah stood, her decision made. "Send me everything you have. I'll take a look, pass it on to Luka Jericho." She nodded to the thumb drive Jack had given her. "I'd also like to help you with your diagnosis, if that's okay." Reviewing Risa's medical records would give her some idea as to any underlying delusions or mental health issues that might be at play. Because something about this whole situation felt off. Maybe it was just that Leah didn't want to admit that Risa's stalker was smart enough to outwit Ian—she wasn't sure. Either way she was going to find out who Risa spoke with at the police department and find a way to make sure they learned to take victims' complaints more seriously. Maybe have them spend a few days observing the victims that came through the CIC. Might make for a good way to get the police on board with the new pilot program as well.

Risa sank back in her chair, obviously exhausted. "Thank you. I'd love any opinions or ideas you have." She hesitated, glancing toward the wall of photos depicting her former life. "You or Detective Jericho. I just can't—I can't live like this. Not anymore."

CHAPTER 11

The little boy's shriek startled Emily. She froze; the parachute's silken hem jerked from her numb fingers. She wanted to run and hide, but there was nowhere to go in the wide-open gymnasium filled with kids. The boy's noise turned to laughter as he dashed under the colorful parachute the other children raised. Emily's section of parachute fluttered at her feet, just like her ballerina sheets had after she'd crawled under her bed that night last month. Suddenly the taste of blood filled her mouth.

Someone else yelled and Emily blinked back tears, clutching her stomach, not sure if she wanted to cry or throw up or run. Mostly, she wanted to curl up in a ball and crawl into the dark. She couldn't live like this anymore. She was scared. All the time. Even when she was sleeping. That's when the bad people like the bad man who killed Daddy came.

Be brave and strong, Daddy always said when he wanted Emily to do something Emily was scared of doing, like her first time on the teeter-totter or when he took her training wheels off her bike. She remembered Daddy's long fingers, the way they danced over the keyboard of his laptop like he was playing piano. And the way he smelled—a lot like the trees in the back of their new house where it was just Mommy and Emily and Miss Ruby—who was Mommy's mommy, but no one ever called her Mom and especially not Grandma.

Daddy wasn't here anymore. They'd locked him away in a box, dug a hole, and threw dirt on him. He was gone forever and ever, amen. The first few nights after they put his box in the ground, she had nightmares about him waking up in the dark, buried alive. Mommy told her it wasn't really Daddy in the box, that Daddy would forever live in Emily's heart, except she sometimes felt like he was slipping away, leaving her heart as cold and empty as the hole they'd buried him in.

She couldn't tell Mommy how she felt, not when Mommy was so sad all the time. And Emily wasn't sure if she could trust Miss Ruby. Mommy definitely didn't trust Ruby; it was like they were always fighting without ever saying any words out loud.

Mostly Emily whispered her fears to JoJo, the puppy in Dr. Hailey's office. JoJo was the only person she could tell her biggest secret: it was her fault Daddy was dead. She hadn't been brave and strong that night.

A girl jostled Emily out of the way to take over Emily's spot around the rim of the parachute. The rain had kept all the kids trapped inside for recess for the entire week and no one was happy about playing the same games over and over. Emily didn't really care—it was the way the gymnasium made every noise echo and bounce back at her that she hated. She couldn't tell where the noise was coming from, couldn't find a safe place to guard against any bad people, leaving her vulnerable and alone despite the crowd of kids and the teachers sitting on the bleachers.

She thought coming back to school would be different, especially now that she had Nate as a friend. He was her first real friend, not just someone who would let her sit at their table during lunch but never talk to her. Where was Nate? Her moment of panic had left her disoriented and she'd lost track of him. Right now, she needed to keep track of everyone she loved, making sure they were safe. Couldn't let anything happen to them. Not like what happened to Daddy.

Because of her. Because she hid. Because she wasn't strong and brave.

She whirled around, searching for Nate. There he was, over in the far corner with a bunch of boys playing dodgeball. The boys had Nate backed up against the wall. None of the teachers noticed; they were too busy checking their phones and talking to each other up on the bleachers. Nate didn't look upset—instead his face was blank, the way it got when he talked about his mom or what happened at the foster homes he used to live in.

Emily didn't trust that look. She headed toward the boys, flinched when they threw their balls at Nate, every bounce and thud reverberating through her. Then she heard someone whispering a very bad name.

"Hey!" she called out to the boys, all of them much taller than she was. The Homan twins were the ones whispering the very bad word, and throwing the balls hard enough to hurt Nate, their elbows arcing back, entire bodies winding up with the effort.

"Stop it!" She grabbed the closest Homan boy's elbow as he prepared to throw another ball. She twisted her own body, keeping her feet planted, and he tottered off balance, tumbling to the floor. The other boys laughed.

Ruby said the Homan brothers were stupid—which was another bad word Emily wasn't allowed to use, but Ruby was a grownup and grownups never followed their own rules. The Homans' farm was just through the woods and over the hill from Nellie's house and sometimes they came over on their four-wheelers, tore up Nellie's flower fields and gardens. Nellie was dead, but even though Emily couldn't remember her great-great-aunt, she still felt protective of Nellie's farm. Which meant she already didn't like the Homans, even before they decided to pick on Nate.

Then the boys turned and suddenly she was surrounded, on the other side of a semi-circle, her and Nate against five boys. Nate stepped between her and the two Homans, using his body as a shield.

"Get out of here, Em," he told her in a low voice. "I'm fine."

"Yeah," the standing Homan, Billy, said as his brother, Jimmy, scrambled to his feet. "He's fine. We're just playing."

"What'cha gonna do about it, anyway?" Jimmy said, grabbing a ball and taking aim, the other boys doing the same.

Be brave and strong, Daddy whispered. Emily stood tall despite the butterflies that filled her stomach trying to fly away and hide, wanting to take her with them.

Instead of retreating, Emily stepped forward, standing beside Nate, facing the boys. She'd let Daddy down and now he was gone forever. She wasn't about to let her friend down. No matter what.

CHAPTER 12

As Luka drove from the Falconer to police headquarters, he tried unsuccessfully to stifle the feelings of frustration and irritation that Trudy Orly's death had instilled in him. This wasn't like him, not at all. Usually he enjoyed the start of a case, that sense of anticipation, where everyone's story was important and anything was possible.

It was better than closing a case. Unlike in the movies or on TV, there was frequently a let-down when a case was solved. Either the solution was too easy—especially now that it was almost impossible to avoid some kind of video catching people in the act—or, all too often, they knew who the perpetrator was, but they didn't have enough evidence to take it to trial.

He loved the feeling of calmness he felt when he entered the chaos of a fresh crime scene. He'd once dated a yoga instructor who'd told him that the Sanskrit word for that feeling was *praśāntacārin* or "walking tranquility." The ability to control your emotions to better observe the world around you. Like all his relationships since Cherise, theirs hadn't lasted very long. But what she'd said had reminded him of college: when he'd be working on a poem, that feeling that the rest of the universe flowed around him, leaving him untouched as he searched for the right words, completely at peace. Of course, those days were long gone. After Cherise, he had changed career paths, leaving poetry far behind.

Why did Trudy Orly's death nag at him? Was it the thought that her husband might have killed her? Or the fact that Walt's health condition might prevent him from being convicted? No, he'd arrived at the scene already frazzled. He never should have gone to the river…

Maybe it was the echoes from Cherise's death that had created this sense of unease. He remembered that night. He'd been home, waiting for her to return from her study group. Washing dishes, staring out the kitchen window, watching the rain duel with the darkness, so lost in thought he'd let a coffee mug slip through his fingers, had cut himself. Blood swirling through the sudsy water… and then the doorbell rang. The police. Cherise, gone.

Death by misadventure, someone had told him that first night—he had no idea who, could barely hang on to any of the words hurled around. That was before they found the suicide poem she'd left, a message aimed to strike straight at Luka's heart: his book, the poem he'd been fascinated by. Before they realized that she'd taken off her engagement ring and stopped her medication. There were tire tracks, gouged into the ground as she'd accelerated. No misadventure, no accident, now they were certain—so certain, beyond all reasonable doubt, beyond any argument Luka could make with the cops, the coroner, even Cherise's parents.

Suicide.

Trudy's death wasn't suicide. And no accident, he was certain. Not with a missing cell phone but an intact wallet full of cash. Which left one possibility. Murder.

He pulled into the secure parking lot beside the anonymous yellow brick building that housed Cambria City's police department. He despised the ugly cube of a building, and yet, somehow, in this unrelenting month of rain and gray, color had blossomed uninvited in the small corner of unattended mud beside the employee entrance. Yellow and purple miniature irises, immune even to the plummeting nighttime temperatures, had appeared first, followed by a clump of crocuses. And now what he'd thought were weeds had proven themselves to be flowers—his gran had had them in her garden as well, called them Lenten roses.

His first theory had been birds carrying seeds from residential gardens, but he'd worked in this building for over fifteen years and had never seen flowers before. It definitely was not the result of any municipal beautification project. Whatever or whoever was responsible, the mystery made him smile every time he came to work.

As Luka climbed the stairs to the investigative division on the third floor, his phone rang. Pops. "Everything okay?" Luka said.

"About to ask you the same question," his grandfather answered. "You left before sunrise and I know where you went. You may treat me like a doddering fool, but I can still read a calendar. How you doing, son?"

Not even Luka's father had ever called him "son." Only Pops. As if reminding Luka that even at thirty-seven, he was still a boy to the old man. "I'm fine. Caught a case on the way back. Will you tell Janine I might not be home until late?"

"What about Nate?"

"Leah's mother is picking the kids up from school." Given Luka's new duties as a surrogate father to an eight-year-old, it was lucky for him that Leah had moved out to her great-aunt Nellie's house, only a few miles down the road from Jericho Fields. The kids also saw the same trauma counselor—someone Leah had recommended. Luka had never dreamed that when he finally became a father it would require a crash course in psychology. It helped to have someone like Leah to talk to about Nate and what he was going through—she was experiencing the same rollercoaster with Emily.

"Leah's mother? That Ruby woman." Pops' tone dripped with disdain. "Don't like her, don't trust her."

"Her record's clean—criminal and driving." Luka didn't mention that Leah didn't entirely trust Ruby either, although Luka wasn't sure why. She'd assured him that the kids were safe with Ruby, leaving him with the impression that her mother had betrayed Leah on some deep emotional level when she was a child.

All he knew was that Ruby had left Leah in her great-aunt Nellie's care when Leah was eleven—but he had no idea why.

"Yeah, but she isn't family," Pops continued. "That boy needs folks he can count on."

Translation: Luka was already failing Nate. "And he has them," Luka defended himself. "He has you and Janine, now that she's living at the farm—" Janine was hired as a home health aide for Pops, but she'd been helping to look after Nate as well.

"Who's gonna help him with his homework and such? I don't know nothing about this new-fangled math they're teaching."

Luka reached the door leading into the detective's bullpen. He blew out his breath. "Nate will be fine, Pops. And so will I. I'll get home as soon as I can."

"See that you do. Not like it does the dead any good, you running yourself ragged." Always one for the last word, Pops hung up.

Luka opened the door, the cacophony of a dozen men and women working rolling over him like a wave. The investigative division included vice and drugs, domestic and sex crimes, as well as Luka's own Violent Crimes Unit, which focused on homicides, serious assaults, and robberies.

He skirted the periphery of the collection of desks until he reached his tiny glass-fronted office that always made him feel as if he were on display like a department store mannequin. After carefully removing his parka so as not to dump water over the collection of files arranged on his desk, he grabbed the spare suit he kept hanging in the tiny closet and went to change. On his way back from the men's room he grabbed coffee, wincing as he spilled some on his hand. He'd switched out his old mug—one that Cherise had bought and that now sat on his desk beside her photo—for a new travel mug, but it still didn't feel right in his hand.

As he settled into his desk chair, he finally felt in control of the day. He was just getting ready to dig into the intricate details of

Huntington's—Luka wanted to be able to understand the disease before he spoke with Leah about the particulars of Walt's case—when he glanced at the clock on his computer and realized he had only twenty minutes before the sergeants' meeting with Commander Ahearn. A meeting that McKinley would be at, no doubt trying to shift blame for this morning's fiasco at the Falconer onto Luka's team.

Krichek would have called him with any new info on the Orly case, so Luka quickly checked for updates on his other open cases. The first was a hit and skip, car versus bicyclist. Forensic results on the paint chips and broken headlight found on the victim's body were still pending, the computerized traffic reconstruction was in his inbox, and there was nothing new from patrol after re-canvassing the area for potential witnesses. He glanced through the crime scene photos to choose which ones to print out for Ahearn, settling on one of the mangled orange bike rather than the one of its equally mangled deceased owner.

Gary Wagner was a thirty-one-year-old customer service worker training for a triathlon. He'd left behind a pregnant wife and a two-year-old. From the reconstruction, the truck or SUV that had hit him hadn't braked until a quarter a mile past the point of impact. And they'd found boot prints suggesting that someone had returned and left again, abandoning the bicyclist to his fate.

That's the part that made Luka so intent on finding the driver—Gary Wagner had still been alive when he'd been found by a farmhand on his way to work hours later. He'd died en route to Good Sam. All that time, lying alone in the dark and rain, suffering, no way to call for help, his phone shattered not by the impact, but by a man wearing boots. That act, taking the time to return to the scene of the impact but deciding not to render aid, but to rather allow the victim to die; that made it pre-meditated murder, which made the case Luka's.

Luka called the state forensic lab. "Anything on the Wagner case?"

"We're narrowing down the vehicle's make and model from the paint, but it's going to take time."

"What about the headlight fragments? Can you use them to narrow it down?"

"Nope. It's a generic replacement, could've bought it anywhere. Oh, but the bike shows evidence of transfer. Your vehicle will have a significant amount of Tangerine Daze-glow ruining its paint job. It's a proprietary color, so easy to confirm the match once you find the vehicle."

"If it's not already scrapped and scattered over the tri-state area." Luka hung up and turned to his next case, an armed robbery at a pharmacy. The suspect seen on video from security cameras in the store and on the street fleeing the scene now had a confirmed ID, patrol was searching for him, and the DA had approved an arrest warrant.

And last, a LOL mugging. Their little old lady was still in a coma but was now breathing on her own, not that that helped Luka find the actor behind her attack, but it was a nice bit of good news given that the trauma surgeons at Good Sam had been fitting her for a body bag when she first came in.

He made a note to follow up with her when he went over to Good Sam for the Orly autopsy after lunch—if he had time for lunch.

A rap came at his door as he was closing down his computer and gathering his notes for his meeting. Krichek had returned from the Orly crime scene.

"Anything?" Luka asked, although he knew the answer. Krichek would have called if he'd found anything.

"Nope. But wanted you to have our reports and timelines before your meeting with Ahearn. Harper texted hers from Good Sam." He handed a sheaf of forms to Luka. "I printed them all out. I know Ahearn likes his paper trail."

Luka glanced over the timelines. They made it clear that the uniforms had called in ERT and escalated the situation prior to his team's arrival. "Good." All he needed now was Risa Saliba's witness statement confirming everything. "Keep working neighborhood CCTV and retracing Trudy Orly's steps. Did Harper say when we can interview the husband?"

"Yeah. His doctor said maybe in an hour or two—whatever drug they gave him to calm him down also put him right to sleep."

Luka made a note to pass the info onto Leah. "You know where to find me if you need me."

Krichek flashed a "better you than me" grin, knowing how much Luka hated the twice weekly meetings—it wasn't as if he didn't also keep Ahearn briefed via daily emails and phone conversations. But Ahearn was old school, enjoyed the power trip of face-to-face confrontations.

"Don't worry, boss. Any excuse to get you out of there—"

"Don't hesitate to use it." Luka sighed, grabbed his coffee—he'd need the reinforcement—and his files and left.

He'd only made it as far as the stairwell when his phone rang. It was Nate's school. "Mr. Jericho? It's Robin Driscoll, the vice principal. I wanted to alert you to an incident."

His face went cold as the blood drained, but he managed to keep his voice steady. "Is Nate all right? What happened?"

"Nate's fine. But I'm afraid we need to address some behavioral issues. Can you come in for a discussion today?"

"Today? What did he do?"

"We're still sorting things through, but apparently Nate bullied some classmates. From what I can tell, nothing serious, but we do have a zero-tolerance policy, so he'll be spending the day in ISS."

"ISS?"

"In-school suspension. We find it's better than immediately sending a child home. This way they can keep up with their academics and we can address any counseling needs during the school day." She paused. "But I'll need to meet with you before we can allow him back into class."

Luka frowned. Nate was already being held back—something Nate viewed as a punishment, one more strike against Luka—making him older and bigger than the other kids in his class. Luka wasn't sure if he felt more angry or disappointed that Nate was taking advantage of his size. But part of him also felt sad and wanted to give Nate the benefit of the doubt. During Luka's sister's years as an addict, she'd lost custody of Nate and he'd bounced around between foster homes growing up. It'd only been during the past year and half that he and his mother had lived together, giving Nate his first taste of stability, all ripped away when Tanya overdosed last month.

"What time do you leave for the day?" he asked.

"Four o'clock."

"I'll be there by then." He had no idea how—he still had the Orly autopsy, which could take hours, plus interviewing Walt, once the doctors cleared him. Leah had texted that she was emailing him a copy of her recorded interview with Risa Saliba, but he still wanted a chance to speak with Risa himself. It would be good to compare anything she told Leah with what she told him. Not that he needed to double-check Leah's work—he appreciated her help this morning, he really did. But sometimes he didn't know the right questions to ask himself, not until face to face with a witness, watching them tell their story. The Falconer was only a few blocks from the school; maybe he could somehow squeeze it all in and still be there by four.

He climbed the steps to the administrative offices on the fifth floor, wondering how other single, working parents did it. If Nate had been his biological son, his from infancy, would he somehow have already mastered the art of being in two places at once? Was there some magic formula, a secret he should know?

Luka stared at the door, then at the useless waste of paper that were the files he held. There'd be hell to pay from Ahearn, but if Luka was ever going to be the parent Nate needed, then he had to step up. *Now*. Not when it was convenient.

He turned and headed back down the steps, hitting redial on his phone. He'd send Krichek to take his place with Ahearn—good training for the detective, learning how to sit through interminable meetings when you'd rather be working a case. "Ms. Driscoll? I'm on my way."

CHAPTER 13

Emily squirmed in her plastic chair, one of four lined up against the wall in the reception area outside Vice Principal Driscoll's office. The room was large, with a reception desk guarding the offices behind it, dividing the grownup area from the kids' area. The office ladies on the other side of the desk occasionally glanced over at her, giving her an encouraging smile or nod. Emily liked most of the office ladies, but she didn't like Vice Principal Driscoll, who always patted her on the head and called her "cute" while never listening to what Emily said. As if just because she was a first grader, nothing she said could make a difference.

Nate was on one side of Emily, sitting rigidly as if he was afraid to breathe, while the two Homans boys sat on her other side, heads together, getting their story straight before their dad came for them. Emily wished it was *her* dad coming to intercede on her behalf. Daddy always listened to her and he always made sure the other adults—even Ms. Driscoll—did as well.

Luka appeared in the doorway and Emily felt Nate stiffen even more, like he was trying to shrink into the pale green paint on the wall behind him. Nate always seemed scared around Luka. Not scared *of* him, just extra tense, like he was waiting for something bad to happen. She didn't get why—she loved Luka. He listened to her almost as carefully as Daddy and he always asked very, very good questions. Plus, he was a policeman—the same policeman who'd caught the bad people who hurt her daddy. Making him *her* policeman. And one of the few grownups who made her feel safe now that Daddy wasn't here anymore.

Heedless of her teacher's admonition to sit still and stay put, Emily hopped down from her chair and raced to greet Luka. He looked particularly smart in his suit and tie, the perfect grownup to make their case.

"Thanks for coming," Emily told him, taking his hand to lead him to the chairs where Nate waited. "We could use a good detective."

"Really?" His grin wrinkled his eyes but then vanished when he saw Nate. "What seems to be the problem?"

"These boys took Nate's great-great-grandad's medal." She stood and pointed to the Homans with her free hand, the other still gripping Luka's. "And then they called him a very bad name and threw balls at him during recess."

"Did not!" Billy retorted while Jimmy made a smirky face at her. "Emily lies. Everyone knows that."

"Yeah," Jimmy joined in. "Like how she said her dad's a hero who catches bad guys when he was really just a computer geek who got himself killed."

Emily dropped Luka's hand and launched herself at the twins. Two against one, both twice her size? She didn't care. They couldn't talk about her daddy that way. But Luka grabbed her by the waist, lifting her off her feet, even as Nate sprang out of his chair.

"Leave her alone," Nate said without raising his voice. She'd noticed before that Luka did that too—he was most serious when his voice went low and quiet. "Want to pick on someone, you pick on me."

"No one's picking on anyone," came a voice from behind them. Everyone straightened up, even Luka, who gently set Emily back on her feet before turning to face Ms. Driscoll.

Emily could never figure out how old Ms. Driscoll really was. Her hair was all one color, like it had been painted on, and her face was too smooth, maybe because she never frowned or smiled or laughed—she just stared, her two dark, beady eyes like laser beams. When Emily and Nate played Space Aliens, the evil robot overlord was always Ms. Driscoll.

"You must be Nate's uncle," Ms. Driscoll said, eying Luka.

He met her gaze without a flinch. "I am. I'm sure we can get to the bottom of this—"

"He shoved me." Jimmy pointed at Nate. "I fell down. Hurt my arm. Maybe even broke it." He dramatically rubbed his elbow.

"Right," his brother chimed in. "It was Nate. He did it."

Nate stood silently, his face down but his gaze angled up, aimed not at Ms. Driscoll, who would decide his punishment, but at Luka. Afraid. Not of being punished, Emily knew, but of disappointing Luka, of being sent back to foster care.

"They're lying." She turned her back to the Homans and focused on the grownups. "Nate didn't shove anyone. They were hitting him with balls and calling him names. Bad names."

Billy opened his mouth to interrupt but Ms. Driscoll silenced him with a glance. "My office. All of you. Now."

They marched inside, Jimmy and Billy bumping against Nate until Luka inserted himself between them, separating them effortlessly as he wrapped his arm around Nate's shoulders. Emily trailed behind, feeling suddenly very alone.

"What are you doing to my baby!" A shout echoed through the reception area. Miss Ruby ran into Ms. Driscoll's office. "Don't you touch my Emily. She hasn't done anything wrong." Ruby laid a palm on each of Emily's shoulders, ready to haul her away if need be. It felt good. Only Emily wished it was Mommy. Where was she?

Emily sighed. Where Mommy always was. At work.

Ms. Driscoll took her seat behind her desk. She smoothed her hands across the paper calendar that covered most of it. "The Homans didn't answer my calls, so we'll begin without them."

There weren't any other chairs in her office, so they all had no choice but to stand and face her. Ms. Driscoll focused on Nate. "What do you have to say for yourself, Nathaniel Jericho?"

Nate hung his head, both fists swinging at his sides. Emily felt more guilty than ever. It was her fault he was in trouble. She'd only wanted to help, but now she realized that the consequences of her actions might be worse than Billy and Jimmy's name-calling had been.

Before she could figure out what to say, Luka spoke up for Nate. "Sounds like my nephew is the victim here. I know for certain that he would never willingly part with his great-great-grandfather's medal. It's a family heirloom and Nate treasures it. You two," he turned to the Homans, "need to return it. Immediately and undamaged."

"Do you have it? William? James?" Ms. Driscoll asked.

They shuffled their feet. "It's at home," Billy finally answered. "He can come for it, he wants. We live just down the lane from him."

Ms. Driscoll jerked her chin as if the issue was settled. Before Emily could protest, Ruby squeezed her shoulders, hard, silencing her.

"Then there's the issue of Nate shoving James," Ms. Driscoll continued. "We have a zero tolerance—"

"Nate didn't do it," Emily said, summoning all her courage to squirm out of Ruby's grip and step forward to face Ms. Driscoll's lethal laser glare. "I did. I tugged Jimmy's arm. Just a little. He was getting ready to throw another ball at Nate—" She broke off when she saw Nate shake his head at her, frowning her into silence. Why? She was telling the truth, being brave and strong, like Daddy said.

"My granddaughter was obviously simply defending her friend," Ruby said. "That's not bullying."

"It is if she used physical force on another student," Ms. Driscoll replied, her tone frosty. "And we have a zero tolerance—"

"Yeah, I heard you. Well, I have zero tolerance for ignorant petty bureaucrats who like to use their position to bully little kids and who don't even know the truth when they hear it. It's obvious Nate and Emily did nothing wrong here. As far as I'm concerned, this meeting is over." Ruby extended a hand to Nate, keeping her other one on Emily's shoulder, using it to steer her toward the door. "C'mon, kids. School's out early today."

She marched both Nate and Emily out into the hallway, ignoring Ms. Driscoll's commands to return. A few minutes later Luka joined them, stretching his long legs to catch up.

"Sure that was wise?" he asked Ruby.

"Don't know, don't care. It sure felt good, putting her in her place."

Luka's phone buzzed and they paused just inside the doors, at the safety officer's desk. He glanced at his text. "Sorry, I have to get back to work."

"No problem. Kids, go get your coats and we'll head home." The safety officer glanced up at that. Ruby tapped his notebook with her purple-painted fingernail. "I'm on the list. The grandmother. So don't you even try to stop me."

Nate was already almost all the way back to their classroom where all their stuff was. Emily ran hard to catch up. "Why didn't you say anything? Why didn't you tell them the truth?"

"Either way they'll think I'm too much trouble. I told you to leave it be," he muttered out of the side of his mouth like he didn't even want to talk to her. "Besides, don't ya know? Snitches get stitches."

Emily wasn't sure what he meant—her mom gave people stitches all the time when they got cuts. Maybe it was a Baltimore thing or a foster thing. "What I know is friends don't let friends get bullied. Or get in trouble when they haven't done anything wrong."

Nate stopped outside the classroom door and went silent, staring down at his shoes.

"Besides," she continued. "You know they're never going to give your great-great-grandad's medal back."

"Yeah." Nate glanced down the hall to where Luka and Ruby waited. "But I can't ask Luka to fight my fights for me."

"Then it's up to us." Emily wrapped her arm in his. "We just have to be brave and strong."

CHAPTER 14

When Leah emerged from Risa's apartment, she was struck by how quiet the top floor of the Falconer had become. A bright orange evidence sticker had been fastened over Walt and Trudy's apartment door and the only police presence on this floor was a crime scene tech taking photos of silver-dusted fingerprints on the railing. Cliff, the building manager, stood behind him, waiting to pounce with his mop and cleaning rag.

Cliff perked up when he spotted Leah, tucked a rag in his back pocket, and abandoned his cleaning cart to join her. "Is Miss Risa okay? Does she need anything? Maybe I should check on her."

"No. She's fine. Resting." Leah wasn't sure why, but she felt the need to protect Risa's privacy.

"Good thing there was a doctor here to check her out." He followed Leah as she made her way to the elevators. "Most days she never even leaves her apartment anymore. I have to bring her mail up for her."

Leah glanced over the railing, bracing herself for the sight of Trudy's blood. But the marble floor below was immaculate, gleaming even. The only sign of this morning's trauma was the bright yellow caution signs warning of the wet floor. Cliff clearly did a good job caring for his building—and the people in it.

"You know," he said without her asking. "I don't believe Walt did it. I mean, sure, he's been acting all sorts of crazy these past few weeks. I found him riding the elevator up and down wearing only his jockey shorts just the other day. But he loved Trudy."

"When was this?" Leah asked as she waited for the elevator. It arrived and she stepped inside, Cliff followed.

"Last month. That's when Miss Trudy had me put all those childproof locks on the doors. So he couldn't wander out of the apartment no more. He was so furious. Wouldn't talk to Miss Trudy for a week after, kept begging Miss Risa to set him free." They arrived at the lobby. "But no way did he kill her. He loved her. He really loved her."

Leah started to leave but then turned back. "You said he asked Risa to help him?"

"Oh yeah. He's kinda fixated on her. Some days she's his little sister—she's dead though, his real sister, car crash a few years back. Other times, Risa is his nurse or housekeeper or, I don't know, his guardian angel?"

"Why didn't he ask you for help? Was it because he knew you installed the locks?"

He shook his head, his hair falling into his face. But he didn't bother to brush it back, content to hide behind it. "No, ma'am. Like most folks around here, Walt just stopped seeing me. Especially after he got sick. Trudy and Risa, they were his life—like it took all his energy he had left to remember who they were. Well, kinda remember, best he could." He shrugged. "Me? I'm nobody, the invisible man." Before Leah could ask anything else, he stepped back onto the elevator, pushed the button, and the doors slid shut between them.

Leah skirted the wet patch on the marble floor and left the Falconer. Outside the rain had turned to a dreary sleet, thick, wet blobs that fell half-heartedly from the sky. On the street, normal traffic had resumed now that the police barricades were gone and the few pedestrians passing by kept their heads lowered, hoods and umbrellas up, taking no notice of her or the building that had so recently become a crime scene.

Preoccupied with thoughts of her conversation with Risa, Leah arrived at Good Samaritan barely noticing her drive there. She parked the Subaru and walked in through the emergency department's entrance, waving to the security guard. As she passed the triage desk, she felt a pang of regret: only three days in on her new job at the CIC and she already missed the ER. An ambulance crew rushed a patient into the resuscitation bay down the hall, and Leah ached to join in on the excitement.

Instead, she continued past the nursing station and through the secure doors leading into the Crisis Intervention Center and her new office. As medical director, she had an assistant, Monique, who did most of the administrative work necessary to keep the CIC running. Both Leah and Monique were in their mid-thirties, but Monique had been working at Good Sam for almost fifteen years, giving her an air of authority that Leah couldn't compete with.

"Veronica is with an assault victim in Interview One," Monique announced as she handed Leah a sheaf of paperwork. "Dr. Chaudhari called, said his patient responded nicely to medication and he's willing to allow you and the police to interview him in an hour or so, but only in the interview room on the neuro-psych ward. A Detective Harper has stopped by twice—something about needing a witness report from your call-out this morning?" She arched an over-plucked eyebrow at Leah.

"Yeah, sorry, I should've called, given you an update."

"Don't worry, I covered for you with Dr. Toussaint."

Leah looked at her blankly—Andre Toussaint was the Trauma Chief, in charge of trauma surgery, the ER and CIC, but Leah couldn't remember any appointment with him.

Monique barely suppressed her eye roll. "You were supposed to send him your preliminary budget and workforce requests? I put it on your calendar."

Ah, the calendar that Leah never checked—it was a proprietary app that required she sign into the hospital system every time she accessed it, which made it more of a pain than it was worth. She'd never used it at all while she worked in the ER.

"Should I add the interview with this Mr. Orly to your sched-ule?" Monique continued. "Anything else I should be expecting?"

"No. But if Harper calls or comes by, send her through." Leah stepped past Monique's desk and opened the door to her office. So close to an escape. But then Monique pivoted her chair to face Leah once more.

"If this new partnership with the police is going to have you out of the office, we should discuss a procedure so things don't fall apart here." Monique's tone made it clear that she did not approve of her newly appointed medical director gallivanting around with the police at crime scenes.

"This is new to everyone. But I'd love your ideas. Maybe you could write up a proposal and send it to me." Leah hoped that would empower the assistant—after all, the CIC had done just fine with only Monique running things before Toussaint went after the grant money that necessitated placing an MD in charge. Probably Monique's main source of aggravation. But if the CIC was going to continue to function, serving the needs of victims, they needed the money the grant was bringing in, so the change was out of their hands.

Monique huffed, then spun back to face her computer, dismiss-ing Leah.

Leah closed the office door behind her, thankful for the solid walls that allowed her some privacy. She shed her dripping raincoat, shoved the paperwork into one of the cubbyholes behind her desk, and sank into her chair. She hadn't had time to personalize the office, except for a framed photo of Ian and Emily that held the place of honor beside her computer. She smiled at the image and blew a kiss in their direction.

You wouldn't believe what your friend Risa has gotten me into, she silently told Ian's image as she opened her work laptop and inserted the thumb drive containing Risa's medical information. She copied the files and, while the hospital system ran its automatic virus and malware scan on them, she clicked through to her email. Four from Risa, all with attachments.

Leah wished Ian was here to tell her what he'd found on Risa's hard drives. She only had Risa's word and she wasn't sure if she could trust her. Leah considered this as she clicked through Risa's emails—the journalist had helpfully named the files in the order Leah should read them. It wasn't that Leah thought Risa was intentionally lying. But given her underlying illness, maybe Risa was delusional. Except… Leah liked Risa. Wanted to believe her. Even if believing her meant that there was a serial killer out there.

She could almost feel Ian's scowl of warning. After what happened last month, she of all people should understand the danger of getting involved. Even though observing from the sidelines went against every grain—it was what drew Leah to emergency medicine in the first place, that urge to rush in and help when others were running away or standing by, frozen. She loved that sense of calm and certainty that came in the center of chaos, the moment in the middle of a complex resuscitation when the path revealed itself with stunning clarity.

She clicked on the first set of attachments—a text file containing the letters from Risa's stalker.

As Leah began reading, she wondered if Ian had read them as well. He'd never mentioned it. They'd rarely discussed his work, but if he truly believed there was someone dangerous walking around Cambria City, wouldn't he have said something? It was what made Leah question Risa's theory. She didn't trust Risa yet, but she did trust that her husband would have gone to the police if he thought people were in danger.

Still, even if there really was no killer, Risa felt threatened—Leah guessed that her reluctance to leave her apartment with its many strong locks had as much to do with her stalker as it did with her illness. Unmasking the stalker might do more for Risa's health than any diagnosis Leah could offer.

The second letter was dated April 22 of last year, the day after the video of the man killed at the railroad crossing had been sent to Risa.

Dear Obituary Reader,

Hope you enjoyed the show! As you can see, I always deliver on my promises.

Let's get back to me. Take your mind off your squalid circumstances. Who knows? Maybe there's another Pulitzer in it at the end? A chance to win your job back.

How did I start killing, you'll be wondering.

First off, there was no abuse or childhood trauma, so don't expect me to whine or cry like those babies they're always showing on the TV. They're the cretins who get caught—too stupid to live, if you ask me.

I had an excellent childhood despite my parents getting divorced when I was young. My mom remarried a guy who was a great role model. We lived in the country and he taught me how to hunt and fish, take care of myself. He gave me everything, except his last name.

My biological father insisted I keep his, which seemed only fair since he was also good to me, but in different ways. He flew me out to visit him in California and we'd do stuff my stepdad couldn't afford. I even got to meet a few Hollywood stars, men who were my heroes. Remember, I was just a kid. But I still was smart enough to see behind their masks—smart enough to know they were just faking it, acting just like they did in their movies and TV shows.

That's when I decided that whatever I did in life, it would be real. Honest. Something important that would change people's lives forever, not just for a few minutes between commercials.

It wasn't too long after my last trip out to LA for my dad's funeral—heart attack—when I killed my first human. I was sixteen and had no idea what I was doing. The whole thing started out so damn messy—a total disaster. I thought for sure I was going to prison forever.

But even if I hadn't been able to get away with it, I was still glad I'd done it. It was... glorious, the hand of God reaching down to touch me.

Eager for my next kill, thirsting for that sense of excitement, the thrill of power, I almost got caught stalking my next victim. I realized that if I wanted to keep pursuing this, my passion, my bliss, then I needed to hone my skills, learn discipline, how to think better, control my emotions. And I had to find a much wider hunting ground, one where nobody would ever suspect me.

So I joined the army where the taxpayers—aka my future prey—were so thankful for my service even as they paid to teach me better ways to kill.

I returned home with more skills, more kills—sanctioned and unsanctioned—and a thirst for more thrills. Unleashed from the military's constant surveillance, I could go where I wanted and do what I wanted, as long as I never got caught.

That became my new obsession. Not my next kill, but how to win the freedom to keep killing for years and years to come.

I studied my fellow killers—those who had gotten caught, especially. And I realized that their biggest mistake was allowing themselves to fall into a pattern. Lazy bastards deserved to get caught. But not me. I wouldn't repeat their mistakes.

I bought an assortment of dice, coins, I Ching divination rods, Tarot cards, and a random number generator app for my phone. And I began to allow them to control my life, every decision made guided by pure, unpredictable, capricious random chance.

If killing was to be my destiny, then I had to embrace Chaos in all its glory.

More—much more, I promise!—next time.

Your devoted fan.

Leah stopped there. The next file wasn't a letter from the stalker but Risa's notes: a running list of clues the stalker had revealed. Parents divorced, father moved to LA, heart attack, etc. A second list held a series of questions with possible research avenues and annotations on what Risa had found.

There were pages and pages of research, everything from obituaries of men who'd died of heart attacks in LA county during a span of years, survived by teenaged sons and ex-wives, correlations with the names of the sons and databases of army enlistment, to overseas deployments, sniper and special ops training. Leah wondered how Risa had gotten those records—obviously the reporter had her sources in the military. But every lead Risa followed turned into a dead end.

Leah scanned the files Risa sent and realized the largest one was a spreadsheet. She hated spreadsheets but with this kind of research, she could see why it would be the best way to organize the information. Leah opened the file, just to see how many leads Risa had followed over the past year.

The spreadsheet was huge. 3019 entries with 212 data fields. Each. And that was only the first tab—the tabs went from A to the end of the alphabet and then from AA to HH. All color coded and labeled with Risa's shorthand notations, like GEO, WITS, etc.

Leah stared at the dizzying display splashed across her screen. How much time had all this taken? These were only the data points, the end result of painstaking hours and hours of research. How had Risa found time to do her paying work? Clearly she was as obsessed with her stalker as he was with her.

She clicked the spreadsheet closed, her screen returning to the text of the next letter, dated only three weeks after the previous one.

Dear Obituary Reader,

I feel we've gotten close enough for me to share some intimate details. I thought you might enjoy a moment-by-moment account of how I go about my business. I warn you, I won't make it easy for you, but I'll play fair and leave enough clues that you'll eventually work things out. Who knows, maybe you'll be able to reunite my chosen one with his family… if you're not too late.

Wish I could help you with a name, but honestly, I have no idea. The dice led me to him. I will tell you he lives in Indiana. I watched him for most of a day. He worked at a landscape company and I've never seen anyone so… More than happy—content might be a better word, yes, he was content with his job. All day long, a smile on his face, he helped people pick out shrubs and trees and rocks and dirt. He loaded their cars and SUVs, loaded pickup trucks and even used a forklift to load bigger trucks headed out to some suburban development or a new golf course or wherever.

That was his life. Digging in the dirt. And it was clear that he loved it. It was as if he had some special shine to him—despite the grime that covered him. The way he leapt to greet each new customer, the way he hummed and sang as he watered and tended the plants, even the way his body moved when he shoveled fertilizer—as if he were performing intricate choreography, a ballet. Joie de vivre, the French call it.

I feel that way about my own work, so I knew when his time came, it had to honor his love for his work.

He was the last one there after closing. Bedding the plants down for the night as if tucking children into beds, complete with a lullaby sung in Spanish. Using a tractor to push fallen dirt, fertilizer, and mulch back up into their small mountains. Even sweeping around the base of this tiny mountain range, despite the fact that as soon as he turned his back, wind and gravity would cascade more down to the ground again. And he knew it—as soon as he finished sweeping and walked away, a breeze gusted, rippling across the display of ornamental ponds, and he glanced back at those mounds of soil with a grin that said, Tomorrow. Tomorrow, I'll return to fight again. You can't beat me, but have fun trying.

And that's exactly when I knew how he had to die. No need for casting the dice, not when it was so blindingly obvious what Fate had in mind for him.

He's still there to this day. Waiting for you to find him, reunite him with his family—or what's left of him.

Let the games begin, dear Obituary Reader. The clues are all there. Good luck!

Your devoted fan.

Leah leaned back. She felt dirty; the urge to go wash her hands overwhelmed her. Turning a man's death into a game? Surely the stalker hadn't actually killed anyone? No, he'd said he wanted Risa back working; this must have been a way to try to lure her into writing again.

Except… it felt real. The way the stalker's mind worked, the lovingly drawn description of his victim, the strange combination of clinical detachment and intimacy.

There was a knock on the door, and she jumped, chiding herself for allowing herself to be drawn into the stalker's macabre game—just like Risa had. Still, a shudder sent goosebumps racing across her skin as she took a breath and called out, "Come in."

It was Naomi Harper. "Walt Orly," the young detective said as she came inside and plopped herself down in Leah's sole guest chair. "His doc says he couldn't have done it. Can you talk to him, translate the medical jargon? Because the man is stronger than he looks—you saw him tear apart that living room."

"Sure. Is he ready?" Leah reached to close her computer, the words she'd been reading still glowing on the screen. She hesitated—should she ask Harper to read the files? No. Better to give them directly to Luka. After all, Harper was the youngest person on his team, a patrol officer allowed to wear plainclothes. Not yet a real detective.

"Yep. Guy's awake. Calm, lucid. It's like Jekyll and Hyde compared to the way he was this morning. I'm just waiting on Luka to get here." Harper said it as if she assumed Leah was sitting at their beck and call, nothing better to do than come when summoned. True, she didn't have anything other than paperwork, but that was only because she'd just begun this job this week—a job that was hers to define within the parameters of the funding.

For the first time, Leah realized the possibilities of her new job were endless. She could be more than a figurehead scribbling her signature on administrative forms and advising the CIC's staff—who were already experts at their jobs. The sexual assault nurse examiners underwent rigorous training as did the social workers they partnered with.

Leah had enjoyed the call-out this morning—it felt like being back in the ER. How could she do more of that? She was already certified in CISM—the crisis debriefing that first responders underwent immediately following a major trauma or disaster. How hard would it be to get training in hostage negotiation? Or more acute mental health interventions—other than dosing someone with Haldol, like she almost had to do this morning.

She'd seen courses for tactical training for physicians so they could work with SWAT. No, ERT, she reminded herself. Except… It was too dangerous. She had to think of Emily. After all, Emily was the reason why she'd left the ER. Stable hours, decent paycheck, no more night shifts. Those needed to be her goals. Not chasing the thrills she'd left behind in the ER.

Leah sighed and pushed back her desk chair to stand. Maybe she was destined to spend the rest of her career tied to a desk after all. A vision of herself buried in a mound of unfinished paperwork flashed through her vision.

"Let's go talk to Dr. Chaudhari while we wait for Luka," she told Harper.

"Thanks, doc. Knew you'd sort it out for us."

As they left the office, Leah glanced longingly at her computer, feeling the compulsion of the stalker's words. She understood why Risa couldn't let it go.

CHAPTER 15

Luka hoped he'd done the right thing, sending the kids home with Ruby. He wished he had time to take them to Jericho Fields himself, but blowing off one of Ahearn's interminable meetings was one thing; missing the interview of a vital witness—and their only viable suspect—was something else completely.

He was having second thoughts about how he'd handled things with the vice principal. They all knew the reason why Nate would be targeted by kids like the Homan twins—and it had nothing to do with the fact that he was a newcomer to the school. Was saying nothing, focusing only on finding the truth of what happened instead of why—was that the right thing? It worked for Luka in his professional life. But was it right for Nate?

Anger seethed through him and he almost turned the car around to go back and give Driscoll a tongue-flaying, like his gran would have—or Pops for that matter. But the vice principal hadn't done anything overtly racist, not that he'd seen, and Nate needed her on his side. It rankled, though, the thought of giving an eight-year-old "the Talk" and adding to the burdens Nate already carried after Tanya's death and having his life uprooted. But the kid had to be prepared—in this country, in this world, in this city, this wouldn't be the last time he would have to deal with people who only saw the color of his skin and not the person inside.

He'd calmed himself by the time he pulled into Good Sam's parking garage and followed the instructions Harper had texted him to the secure neuro-psych ward. A guard at the reception desk had a pass ready for him and buzzed him through glass doors into a short hallway decorated with soft, woven tapestries and Amish quilts. No sharp edges, he realized. Just as there was no furniture lining the walls, only thick, rounded handrails, at the right height to catch a patient who lost their balance. The ward even smelled different than the rest of the hospital. Instead of the strange scents of cleansers and fake citrus air freshener, here it smelled almost like… A memory filled his vision: Christmas or Thanksgiving, his gran and mother pulling pans and pans of cookies from the oven, waving him away when he and his sister tried to sneak one.

He followed the signs to the counseling room Orly's physician had said they could use for the interview. Like the CIC facilities down in the ER, it was a suite of rooms with an observation area in the center. That's where he found Harper, Leah, and a middle-aged man wearing khakis and a button-down shirt, with no tie. His hospital ID said DR. CHAUDHARI.

"You can't be in there asking questions," Harper was telling Dr. Chaudhari as Luka entered the tiny room. Harper, only a few inches shorter than Luka, practically towered over Chaudhari. Add in the intimidating posture she'd assumed, her face mere inches from Chaudhari's, and he was surprised the man appeared so placid, almost amused. "We can't have any information you elicit thrown out as hearsay."

Leah moved to intervene between the two—reminding Luka of the way Ms. Driscoll had separated her warring first-graders. "I understand why Dr. Chaudhari wants to be the one to conduct the interview. He's right. A familiar face will help keep Walt calm and focused." Chaudhari aimed a smile at Harper that was subdued yet triumphant. "But Officer Harper is also right. We need to make it clear for everyone involved, especially Mr. Orly, that this isn't a medical interview but a witness interview so that we avoid the hearsay exception. I can ask the questions in my capacity as a consultant for the police, while Dr. Chaudhari monitors Mr. Orly's mental and physical status."

Luka rapped his fingers against the wall since it seemed no one had noticed his arrival and Harper immediately backed off.

Luka stepped forward and offered his hand. "Dr. Chaudhari, I'm Detective Sergeant Luka Jericho. I'm in charge of the investigation into Trudy Orly's death." They shook hands and Luka continued, "I think Dr. Wright's solution is the best all around. I know your primary goal is to protect your patient, but learning the truth behind his wife's death could also have serious implications for his welfare."

"I've been treating Mr. Orly since his initial diagnosis three years ago and I have never seen any evidence that he's capable of violence." Chaudhari's composure slipped, but only for a brief moment. He gathered himself. "But I do agree with you. Dr. Wright and I were discussing this, and I am concerned about the ramifications to Walt's prognosis and treatment if he does believe he caused his wife's death."

"Now that we have the court order, I checked his chart. There was an incident several days ago, was there not?" Leah asked.

Chaudhari blew his breath out. "An isolated incident. Walt has been fixated on driving again; he stumbled across the keys Trudy had hidden from him and became irate."

"What happened?" Luka asked in a low tone, noting that Harper had pad and pen out, documenting everything. Because of Walt's cognitive decline, they had a court order for his medical records and permission to interview him, but anytime a doctor–patient relationship was involved, things could get dicey in the hands of a good defense attorney. If Walt was their actor, his case might never make it to court, given his diagnosis.

"No one was hurt," Chaudhari said. "Not seriously. Walt grabbed Trudy by the arms, shook her, shouted at her. Left a few bruises. She called me and I adjusted his medication, arranged for respite care. And that's when we both decided it was time."

"Time?" Luka asked.

"To find an alternative living arrangement. I gave Trudy a list of several facilities in the region and she visited them. I believe she decided on one in Smithfield, placed Walt on a waiting list for the next available bed."

"And that's the only time, to your knowledge, that Walt has laid hands on his wife?"

"The only time Trudy told me about."

"Patients with Huntington's—I understand they can be volatile, unpredictable. Could they snap, do something in the heat of the moment, but not realize it or remember it a short time later?" Leah asked.

"Mr. Orly definitely seemed to have no awareness of hurting his wife, or even that she was dead, when we finally calmed him down," Luka explained to Chaudhari. "Despite witnesses saying that he'd been at the railing, had seen his wife's body, probably moments after she fell. Is that normal for someone at his stage of the disease?" He didn't add the question he could tell by Harper's scowl she was itching to ask. Could Walt Orly be faking his confusion after his wife's death? Maybe he'd pushed her in the heat of an argument, then realized what he'd done.

Chaudhari considered carefully. "Unfortunately, with this particular disease, almost anything is possible, Detective."

"Does he know Trudy is dead now?" Leah asked. Last thing they needed was to agitate Walt with news of his wife's demise.

"Yes. I explained it to him and he seems to have retained the information. But I can't predict how long that clarity will last. Which is why, although he's much calmer and more coherent, I doubt this interview will yield anything helpful. But let's not keep Mr. Orly waiting any longer." He opened the door and waved

Leah through it, leaving Luka and Harper to watch and listen from the monitoring room.

"Talk about your bedside manner," Harper said to Luka as they closed the door.

"He seemed fine to me."

"No, you. The way you got him to cooperate. Guy's been stonewalling me all morning."

Luka met her gaze and raised an eyebrow.

She sighed. "Yeah, I know, honey instead of vinegar. I was just so riled up over McKinley and the patrol guys trying to blame me and Krichek for this morning's fiasco—"

"How about if you let me handle McKinley and you focus on the case. What other loose ends need following up?" Naomi Harper's test scores had proven she was capable of being promoted to detective, but her attitude often made Luka wonder if she was ready.

"I haven't had any luck tracing next of kin—"

"Maggie and the coroner's office will help with that."

"Then the biggest thing I want to tackle is finding the victim's cell phone. A woman her age, sick husband at home, no way in hell she's forgetting it or losing it. But it wasn't on her body or with her personal effects, so where is it?"

Luka nodded. The missing cell phone was top of his list as well. "Get with Sanchez in the cyber unit. There was a video baby monitor in the apartment, no doubt sending footage to Trudy's cell. Maybe he has a way to access that. Also see if the cell provider has the data on her recent activity ready. If not, follow up on it. I don't want to wait until Monday." Weekend or not, he and his team would be working, so why shouldn't the damn phone company?

"And you'll take the autopsy?" Harper seemed relieved to be spared that particular duty.

Luka didn't mind attending postmortems—he often came up with questions he didn't even know he had during the examination of the victim's body. The only thing he hated was how damned long they took—especially if assistant medical examiner Ford Tierney was on duty. The guy was brilliant but he had a tendency to make everything take twice as long while he checked and double-checked his findings. But that was also why the DA loved him in court. No defense attorney had ever been able to rattle Ford on cross-examination. "I've got it from here. Go on back to the office. Call me if you find anything."

"Will do. Later, boss."

Luka turned to the monitoring window. The counseling room reminded him of his dentist's waiting room—soft, rounded chairs, a cushioned loveseat. Walt Orly sat in one chair, the only sign of agitation the constant drumming of his left foot. His hands were palms up in his lap, his shoulders slumped, jaw slack.

Leah sat in the chair beside Walt while Chaudhari sat across from them. Leah began by asking basic questions, making sure Walt was oriented and agreed to be interviewed. Luka was impressed by how she was able to document everything they needed legally while also putting Walt at ease. Then she said, "Walt. Thank you again for meeting with us. Do you know why we wanted to talk with you?"

Walt hunched his body, his gaze centered on Chaudhari's shoes. He began rocking slowly. "Something happened. I saw—"

Leah waited much longer than Luka would have done before gently pressing the issue. "What did you see, Walt?"

Walt shook his head, still focused on the floor. Hard, small shakes of denial. "No! Trudy! No!" Despite his agitation, his voice was low, mournful, coming from somewhere deep down in his gut.

Chaudhari reached across the space to lay a hand on Walt's knee. "Are you all right? Do we need to stop, Walt?"

Luka aimed the psychiatrist a glare even though he knew the man couldn't see it through the two-way mirror. Chaudhari was only doing his job, trying to protect his patient, but Luka needed to hear what Walt had to say.

Walt kept rocking, but said nothing.

Leah waited until his movements slowed and some of the tenseness left his body. Then she asked, "Walt, do you remember Trudy coming back from the store this morning?"

"Meds, I spilled my meds. I should've never—she thought I couldn't open the door..." He held up his trembling hands, drew them into fists. "But I went outside, and, and, and, and—" His jaw clamped tight.

"It's okay, Walt. Hey, can you take a deep breath for me?" Leah asked. "Like this?" She moved her hands up and down in time with a long inhalation and even longer exhalation. After a few breaths, Walt relaxed a bit. "Good, good. Now, you went outside, was Trudy there?"

Walt shook his head vigorously.

"Did you see anyone?" Leah tried again.

The room grew silent except for Walt, heaving one breath in after another, as if gathering the strength to answer. Leah and Chaudhari sat perfectly still, while behind the glass Luka found himself holding his breath.

Then Walt launched himself out of the chair in an explosion of fury. He flew across the space, a primal shriek emerging as he flung himself headlong into the mirror. He pummeled the image of himself with both fists—to Luka on the other side, it felt as if the blows were aimed at him. Tears streaked his face as he screamed, "She's dead! Trudy's dead!"

Chaudhari came up from behind but stopped short of coming within range of Walt's fists. "Walt, listen to me—"

"No! She's dead, she's dead..." Walt's body deflated and he fell to the ground, sobbing, both arms circling his knees, head bowed, rocking his body into a tight ball. "Dead, and it's my fault..."

CHAPTER 16

After Walt Orly's disastrous interview, Leah invited Luka to lunch in the physician dining room. It was the least she could do, given how badly her first interview for the police had gone. It wasn't her fault; she had warned them that given Walt's dementia, there might be little he could tell them, but it was frustrating that it had gone downhill so fast.

"So this is the doctors' dining room," Luka said as they sat down at a table near the rain-streaked windows. He glanced around, eyebrow arched. "Feels like a teacher's lounge."

"It's not meant to be fancy," Leah said defensively. She liked it—it was small, sparsely furnished since most physicians grabbed and ran, but most importantly, it was almost always empty, making it so much quieter than the bustling main cafeteria next door. "The idea is to be able to get something without waiting in line." She nodded past him to the three open doors on the other side. "The conference rooms are nicer. Good places to have classes and meetings without missing lunch."

"Because a hospital runs on its stomach." He scooped up a forkful of pasta Bolognese. "Tastes good. I feel like I'm carb-loading for a marathon."

"Exactly." She took a bite of her sesame chicken and green beans.

"Could you send me a summary of Walt's medical records? And anything you know about the medications he's taking. I want to make sure we cover all our bases."

"Of course." After another bite she asked the question that was bothering her. "You're not going to use what Walt said as a confession, are you?"

"That wasn't a legitimate confession," he answered, to her relief. "That was a portrait of a guy in pain, barely hanging on, much less understanding what happened…"

She glanced up, not liking the way he left the statement hanging as if it was a question. "A portrait? You think maybe he was faking?"

Luka shrugged. "We'll see what the autopsy shows, but right now I'm exactly where I started. Unable to rule Walt Orly out as a suspect and with no one else to look at."

"I just don't see how a man with his state of cognitive decline could—"

"Cognitive decline," he echoed back at her. "As measured by what? His and his wife's self-reporting? That's why I want you to double-check what Chaudhari has documented in the medical records. Because who's to say Walt didn't decide to kill Trudy when she began looking to move him out of the house? Maybe he's faking getting worse, setting up an affirmative defense."

"What's that?" Leah asked.

"The defendant admits their guilt but also that they were mentally incapacitated, unable to judge right from wrong."

"Not guilty by reason of insanity." She thought about it. "I still don't see it. Walt seemed genuinely distraught."

"Yeah, so did Nate." He set his fork down and met her gaze. "Why weren't you there to back me up with Driscoll this morning?"

"Nate? What are you talking about? Did something happen at school?" She slid her phone out: no missed calls.

"Yeah. They accused Nate of bullying some other kids. Emily stuck up for him, but they didn't believe her. That Ms. Driscoll is a piece of work. Acts like she can see into the souls of kids—and she definitely doesn't like what she sees when it comes to Nate."

"You went to the school? Why didn't they call me?"

He wiped his plate with a piece of garlic bread. "Ruby was there. I sent the kids home with her since it was either that or in-school suspension for the rest of the day. Figured it was Friday, so why not." He broke off. "Ruby didn't tell you? I assumed you were busy and you sent her in your place—"

"Too busy to take care of my daughter?" she snapped as she dialed Ruby. She turned away to shield Luka from her anger and frustration. "Why am I just now hearing that Emily was sent home from school?" she demanded as soon as Ruby picked up.

"Excuse me for taking care of things so you wouldn't be interrupted at your very important work," Ruby answered. "You're so very welcome. For that and for having two kids stuck inside running around while I fix them lunch."

"What happened? Why did they call you?" Last thing Leah wanted was for Emily to feel as if she didn't have time for her—or to learn to rely on Ruby. Because someday, one day, Ruby would let Emily down, would not be there for her—just like she had Leah when Leah was a little girl. More times than she could count.

"Said you'd called to remove Ian as primary and gave them my name instead."

"Not instead of Ian. Just to add you to the list so you could pick her up. They were meant to move my name to primary contact."

She could practically hear Ruby's shrug. "Guess they messed up. Worked out, though—would you have left the hospital to drop everything and go listen to that stuck-up principal get all high and mighty about their zero tolerance rules? Believe me, you were better off without it. Total waste of time."

"Is Emily all right? What happened? Did someone bully her?"

"As if," Luka sputtered, earning a glare from Leah.

"She's fine. I'll tell you everything when you get home from work." Ruby was loving this, a chance to prove her superiority as a parent. She hung up on Leah.

Leah turned back to Luka, not certain if she was more embarrassed that he'd seen her blow up at Ruby or that she hadn't been there when Emily needed her. "I hate her passive-aggressive power plays."

"Power plays? Tell me about it. I went from living alone, no one to answer to, to moving in with an eighty-three-year-old man who wants to act like he's still nineteen and an eight-year-old kid who I barely know but am now responsible for. And, oh yeah, don't forget Janine—old enough to be my mother, raised four kids on her own, so not afraid to tell me exactly how I'm doing everything wrong."

His tone of mock aggrievement coaxed a smile from her and she added, "Maybe Ruby's not so bad after all."

"It takes time," he assured her. "You guys are practically strangers—all she sees is the girl she left behind and all you remember is who she was back then. But you're both adults now, both changed."

"At least I've grown up," she scoffed. "Not so sure about Ruby. But she loves Emily. That much I do know." She glanced up at him. "What really happened this morning? At the school?"

"Seriously, it was nothing. A few boys tried to gang up on Nate, then claimed he bullied them. But Em saw what was happening and she stepped in."

"Wait. Are you saying she hit someone?" What would Ian think? It went against everything they'd ever taught Emily. "That's not Emily; she knows better than to resort to violence."

"Not sure I'd call it actual violence. It sounded more like she tugged a kid's arm who was trying to get to Nate. They definitely aren't telling us everything though. Yet. But I'll get it out of Nate, I promise."

She fussed at her now-cold chicken.

"Don't worry. Emily's fine," he reassured her.

"I should've been there. Not Ruby." She hated the bitterness that colored her tone, but now wasn't the time to get into all the reasons why she couldn't bring herself to fully trust Ruby. She knew Ruby would never intentionally do anything to hurt Emily. In fact, Ruby had risked her own life to save Emily last month. But a few weeks of living with her mother wasn't enough to erase over twenty years of mistrust and resentment. Not to mention a deep-seated fear of abandonment that Leah was trying hard not to let Emily see.

"Believe me, that Ms. Driscoll would agree. The way Ruby stormed in—" He chuckled. "Reminded me of my gran. Seriously, though, she did okay, Leah."

Leah nodded, forced herself to take another bite of her food. "How's Nate?"

"Nate's Nate. Shut down. Kid's like a turtle—any sign of the slightest disturbance in his environment and he withdraws into his shell. I have no idea what to say or do to help him. And those Homan kids today weren't any help."

"It was the Homans?" Her jaws clicked shut, biting off what she was about to say about the sprawling clan. "I've treated a few in the ER."

"Back when I was in uniform I once got called out to their place for a D&D—drunk and disorderly," he translated, "that involved skeet shooting, only instead of throwing skeet targets into the air, they'd rigged a slingshot and were shooting at live chickens—any small living thing they could get their hands on."

"Hope you called the SPCA on them."

"Luckily none of the animals were hurt—they were so drunk they couldn't figure out the concept of trajectory. Have they bothered you since you've moved into Nellie's?"

"No. Guess with the bad weather, they've been staying home. But I hate that they're our neighbors." The Homan farm was over the hill, between Nellie's place and Jericho Fields.

"Let me know if they do anything. And we should make sure the kids stay away. Believe me, Billy and Jimmy are the least dangerous of the bunch." He took a drink of his milk, ready to change the subject. "How'd it go with Risa Saliba?"

"I've emailed you a copy of the interview. She backs up Harper and Krichek's accounts of what happened with Walt."

"Good. Should get the brass off my back. Did she say anything helpful?"

"Not about Trudy—well, maybe." She explained about Risa's stalker, his letters and vanishing videos and texts. "He's obsessed with Risa. And I tell you, his letters freaked me out. I don't understand why the police wouldn't take her seriously."

"She came to us?"

"Said she did."

He slid his phone free. "When?"

"Sorry, I'm not sure. But the letters began last April."

He dialed. "Krichek, pull any complaints filed by Risa Saliba. Forward them to me. They should all be from the last year. Thanks."

"What if he was there, at the Falconer?" Leah asked. "Maybe he's a suspect."

"You think this stalker could have killed Trudy?" His tone was skeptical. "This has been going on a year, but despite being a reporter with a ton of media connections, she suddenly decides to confide in you, an absolute stranger? Why would she do that if she really believes this guy is a serial killer?"

"Because she thought it might be tied to Trudy's death," Leah argued.

"But you don't know her, Leah. How do you even know the letters are legit? That she's not sending them to herself? She's used to being in the spotlight. Maybe with this illness, she's using this stalker to plan a big, dramatic comeback? Would be a damn sight more likely than a serial killer deciding to share all his innermost secrets with a reporter. Hell, maybe she's not even sick, is faking everything?"

His vehemence surprised her—not at all like the Luka she'd come to know over the past month. That Luka loved brainstorming every possible angle of an argument. Although, in a way, that was what he was doing, playing devil's advocate. He didn't have to be so damn good at it, though.

"She's not faking her stalker."

"How can you be certain?"

"Because she hired Ian to try to trace him."

They both went silent at that. Finally, Luka glanced up. "I'm sorry. If Risa Saliba made an official report, I'll follow up, open an investigation, get our cyber squad on it." He made it sound as if Risa's willingness to involve the police was a test of her veracity. "Could you get me Ian's records of what he did? They'd be helpful."

"I guess they're at the house." The house—as in, her and Ian's home. The one Leah hadn't stepped foot inside since that night. She swallowed. "I can look for them."

"And I'll have another chat with Ms. Saliba."

Registering his tone, she glanced up. "You think she made up meeting Ian, don't you? You think she heard my name, and is using Ian's murder to suck me in."

"You're a sympathetic audience, a respected physician, you've been in the news lately. If you believe her, that gives her story credence."

"You didn't read his letters. I believe her, Luka. She hides it well, but she's genuinely terrified."

"All the more reason to make this official, open a real investigation."

"So you'll read the files she shared with me—I promised her you would at least take a look."

"Send them my way. I'll try to skim them during the autopsy. It's Tierney, so—"

"You'll have plenty of downtime."

"Unfortunately, yes." He paused, his gaze focusing on the rainy window beyond her. "About this morning."

Leah knew what Luka was going to say. "I had it handled—"

"No. Leah. I know this is all new to you, but you can't be rushing in like that. Every scene poses potential danger. And all this talk about serial killers—"

"I'm not saying Risa's stalker is an actual serial killer. Just that we should look into him as possibly killing Trudy. Maybe start with Cliff, the building manager." She'd already forgotten Cliff's last name; he really was the invisible man. "He was hanging around Risa's apartment, asking about her. I definitely got a stalkerish vibe from him."

"He's on my list. But that's not the point and you know it. You can't treat everyone as if they're a patient under your protection."

As usual, he'd nailed her dilemma. She fussed with stacking her dirty dishes on her tray, avoiding eye contact. "I know, I know. Honestly, I feel like such a fraud, taking this job. If I'd known Toussaint only hired me because the grant funding required a physician as medical director—the money they're paying me would be better used to help hire more psychiatric social workers. They'd be able to save a lot more lives out on the street than I ever could, preventing more deaths and injuries by intervening right away."

"If the pilot program is successful, we can get more money and do that."

"They're already doing it out in Oregon. It has saved the city millions of dollars. Not to mention civilian lives—"

"And the police officers saved as well," he added. "I know, I've read about it. But first—"

"We need to make this program work." She crumpled up her napkin and threw it onto her tray. "Which, I guess means that I take orders from you." The words tasted bitter. One of the great things about being in the ER was that while she listened to the opinions of everyone on her team, in the end, she was in charge.

"And my first order is no more armchair sleuthing. I appreciate how people open up to you, but don't go looking for trouble. Understand?"

"So you don't want me to go back and talk to Risa again? I'm not sure she's comfortable talking to you and, besides, she also asked me to look into her medical case."

He arched an eyebrow.

"I know, I know," she hastened to add. "You think I'm getting too involved. But besides her stalker and medical problems, Risa is also a key witness. No one knew Walt and Trudy better than she did. It would be good for her to trust me."

"Okay," he relented. "I'll review the information Risa gave you. In the meantime, you can speak to her about the Orlys and her medical issues. But," his tone underscored the word, "only as a prelude to her coming in for a more thorough formal interview first thing tomorrow and also opening a case on her stalker." He glanced at the clock on the wall then pushed back his chair to stand. It was almost two o'clock, the time Trudy's autopsy was scheduled to begin, and they both knew how punctual Ford Tierney was.

Leah mirrored his movements. "Hey, is something else going on? Other than Nate getting into trouble? You just don't seem yourself today."

He gave a small shake of his head and grabbed his raincoat, fisting the material in his clenched hand. "This day—" His gaze returned to the rain-darkened window. "I'm fine. Just a bad day is all."

CHAPTER 17

It was a little past two by the time Luka made it to the medical examiner's offices in Good Sam's basement. He'd stopped by the ICU on his way. Their little old lady, the victim of a vicious mugging, was still unconscious. But the good news was that her daughter had finally arrived from New Mexico. It was painful to confess to her that they had no firm leads yet, but Luka was glad that at least she wasn't alone.

As he signed in at the morgue's security desk, he braced himself for Ford Tierney's lecture. It would begin with a dissertation on punctuality, segue into how lucky Cambria City PD and Craven County were to have a medical examiner, much less an assistant ME who was also board-certified in forensic pathology, and conclude with a final tirade on the idiocy of the two centuries-old system that left the vast majority of the state with undertakers or politicians elected to the position of coroner.

Didn't matter how often he'd heard it before, Tierney would repeat his speech, exactly the same every time, and wouldn't allow Luka a word in edgewise until he'd finished. Luka had learned to simply swallow his medicine with grace and goodwill. But today when he arrived at the autopsy suite's observation room, there was a body wrapped in a sterile shroud on the stainless-steel table, but no sign of Tierney.

Luka glanced at the clock in surprise. Was the hyper-punctual medical examiner actually late? He smiled and began composing his own lecture on timeliness when Maggie Chen entered the suite and waved at him to join her. She tapped the intercom. "Ford got called away. But I've got something to show you."

Luka made his way into the autopsy room and cloaked himself in a surgical gown and booties, then pulled on a face mask and gloves.

"Found a few things on my preliminary examination," Maggie told him. "I'm thinking maybe you don't need to wait for Ford to finish."

That sounded promising, Luka thought as Maggie gently removed the shroud on the body. Trudy Orly had been positioned face down on the table, her forehead cradled on a curved stand. Her clothing had been removed and her hair cleaned of the blood and bone fragments left by her head injury. Maggie didn't have to say anything—there was obvious bruising along the woman's shoulder blades and the outer parts of both arms.

Bruising in the shape of a man's hands as he shoved Trudy into a wall? "How old are these?" Luka asked, thinking of what Chaudhari had said about Walt shaking Trudy.

"Old. Maybe a week or so. But that's not what I wanted to show you."

"No bruises from today?" Luka didn't bother to hide his disappointment.

"Nothing obvious. And I think I know why—also why no one heard her scream or shout as she fell." Maggie turned the overhead lights off, grabbed a handheld alternative light source wand and handed Luka a pair of special filtered goggles. Then, with a flourish, she raised Trudy's hair to reveal two small oval discolorations at the base of her scalp, on the opposite side from where her skull had been dented by its impact with the lobby floor.

"Are those what I think they are?"

"Stun gun. Not police issue—the prongs are too narrowly placed. I'll try to get a manufacturer, but it might take a while." She clicked the lights back on. "They're fresh. Within minutes before death—Ford can confirm that she was still alive when she was stunned once he takes tissue samples."

He handed her back the tinted goggles. "Maggie, you're amazing. Anyone else would have missed those." Luka ran his fingers along the back of his own neck. "Someone must have been very close to her. Very close."

"Maybe someone she knew?" Maggie suggested. "My guess is, given the way they're slightly off center, the killer stood right beside Trudy as they both faced the atrium. If she'd been afraid of this person, I can't see her standing so close to them. Maybe they dropped something as a distraction, to get her to look down."

"Then they stunned her." Luka brought two fingers to the back of Maggie's neck. "And as her body went limp—"

"He or she simply rolled her forward over the railing, let gravity do the work."

"Which means there would be no bruising other than from impact."

"And with the railing acting as a fulcrum, it wouldn't take someone very strong at all. Man or woman. They're easy to buy for personal defense. It could even have belonged to Trudy."

Luka made a note of that. If the stun gun was Trudy's maybe they could track the purchase. Then he had another thought. "If strength and muscle coordination weren't important, then even a man with Huntington's could do it."

"You're thinking the husband?"

"He had motive—she wanted him out of the home, was looking into long-term care facilities."

"Anyone could have done this," she replied. "If Trudy let them get close enough."

Which meant his list of suspects had narrowed considerably, limited to people with access to the Falconer and who Trudy would allow to enter her personal space. Putting Walt firmly at the top of his list. "Thanks, Maggie," Luka told her as he shed his protective gear and headed through the doors. "I owe you one."

"I'm keeping a tab," she shouted back before the doors slid shut behind him.

Luka called Krichek as he walked back to his car and told him about Maggie's findings.

"Gives us enough for a search warrant—including all of the Orlys' electronics," Krichek replied before Luka could give the order. "But if Walt is faking his symptoms, he wouldn't be stupid enough to leave the stun gun in his apartment."

"See if the judge will also cover the common areas inside the Falconer and get the uniforms on it. Make sure they don't forget things like flowerpots, the elevator shaft." He remembered what Leah had said about Cliff Vogel. The man would open up more to a woman than a man. "What's Harper doing? She can join them, get that manager to show her every nook and cranny."

"Harper's downstairs working with the cyber guys now trying to track Trudy's cell. And I just finished with the Orlys' financials."

"Anything?"

"Sorry, no."

"What about those complaints from Risa Saliba?"

"Next on my to-do list. Oh, but the staties called, their lab says our hit and skip vehicle in the Gary Wagner case was a Dodge Ram. 2006 to 2010. They emailed you the full report."

"Thanks. Ask Harper to—"

"Start compiling a list of registered owners. Already on it."

Luka reached his car. "I'm heading back, be ready for a debrief in twenty. Hopefully by the time we're done, we'll have the warrant." He got into the car but didn't turn it on right away.

That niggling feeling that he'd missed something had intensified. He replayed the few coherent parts of Walt's interview while glancing at the crime scene photos and finally it clicked. Trudy's keys were still hanging from the door to her apartment. He remembered the childproof guard on the inside doorknob. Maybe Walt wasn't faking everything, and he really couldn't open the door without assistance. Had he been waiting for her to unlock it? That would explain why her keys were left in the lock and why she'd abandoned her shopping and went to the railing, trying to corral her wayward husband. But it also meant Walt had to be prepared, waiting and ready to use the stun gun.

He imagined Trudy talking softly, trying to calm her husband, putting a hand on his arm, gently pulling him into a hug, telling him it was okay, everything was okay, and to come with her back into their apartment, back home. And as they embraced, Walt nuzzling her neck, lifting her hair off her collar, and hitting her with the stun gun. Trudy's body stiffening, electricity sparking down her nerves. The effects would have only lasted a few seconds at most, but during that time she'd have been powerless.

Yet still conscious, still able to watch as her husband pushed her over the railing. Her last image, his face, watching her fall.

CHAPTER 18

When Leah got back to her office, Monique had all the paperwork she'd missed from the morning ready and waiting for her. Monique practically herded Leah into her office, arranging the files in front of her in order of importance.

"Shouldn't we be doing all this via computer?" Leah protested. "Instead of killing trees?"

"It's a federal grant. Not sure they even know about computers."

Ah, so Monique did have a sense of humor. "Sorry it's so much work for you. But the money—"

"I'm the one who found the grant, told Dr. Toussaint about it. Otherwise he was going to shut us down." Monique finished rearranging Leah's desk and stood up straight. "Guess you could say it's my fault you're here." She looked down at Leah with a stern frown. "We need to do this right, or we'll lose the CIC."

"I understand. I'll make these my top priority," Leah promised. "And I want to see if there's a way we can chisel out the money to get a psychiatric social worker on the team—someone to do outreach in the field."

"Build a real crisis response program. Not just someone riding with the cops, but training them and training the 911 dispatchers to triage crisis intervention calls direct to us. Then it would be the cops backing us up, not beckoning for us to come when they're in too deep," Monique replied.

"You've been thinking about this."

"I've got a plan," Monique answered. "Grew up in the Kingston Towers, saw how many times the cops made things worse when all people needed was someone to listen, to get them the help they needed." She shrugged. "Not the fault of the police. They're trained to use the tools at hand, meet violence with violence. But—"

"It's not working. Not anymore. You're right, Monique. We need to start with a fresh idea, focusing on what the people in the community need, then build a system that will really serve and protect them." How many times had Leah had the same debate with her fellow ER physicians? Violence, drug use, mental health issues, economic inequality—they were all public health problems, not just laws broken.

Monique had her hand on the doorknob, eyes narrowed at Leah as if judging whether Leah would stand by her words. Finally, she nodded. "Once you're finished with this first round of paperwork, I can take over. And I'll get as much of it on the computer as possible."

"Thanks, Monique." Leah wasn't sure, but she might be more intimidated by Monique now. Because now she didn't dare to let her down. "Maybe we could do lunch sometime? Go over your ideas, then create an official proposal, see what everyone else thinks?"

"Sure thing." Monique stepped over the threshold, then turned back. "Of all the docs they could have stuck us with, guess you're not so bad." She closed the door before Leah could reply.

Basking in the glow of Monique's approval, Leah quickly went through the paperwork. Most of it was authorizations for database collection and other file sharing of grant documents, so Monique was right: in the future they could avoid paperwork. Shaking her head at the irony—paperwork so they wouldn't need paperwork—Leah signed all the areas Monique had highlighted for her, and began to read the areas where Monique had filled in the grant's mission statement, purpose, financial plan, workplace safeguards, harassment policy, and quickly felt her eyes glaze over out of sheer boredom. All this tedious minutia had accompanied the original grant application so why were they now making them repeat everything?

She gave the finished stack back to Monique. "Good work."

Monique simply nodded, busy typing a report from one of the sexual assault nurses. Leah retreated back to her office, but made a note to find a way to give Monique a raise. She opened her laptop, tempted by Risa's research on her stalker, but instead began sorting through Risa's medical records. Once she had them in chronological order, she settled in and began reading.

At first, Risa's physicians seemed confident that they could find a diagnosis. But as test after test came back, each contradicting the last one, their tone grew almost angry, as if Risa were somehow to blame for their inability to find an answer.

Risa's symptoms were consistent: muscle weakness, diffuse pain, tremors, nausea, vomiting, severe fatigue, headaches, weight loss, a rash that came and went. All symptoms of a myriad of possible diagnoses. But when her physicians tested her, trying to pinpoint the exact cause, the test results were conflicting. First, she'd have an abnormally low sodium along with a metabolic acidosis, then, a few weeks later her sodium would be normal and the acidosis resolved but her liver functions would be elevated.

By the time she'd reached the end of the files, Leah understood the frustration that bled through the physicians' clinical notes. Risa's story never changed, but somehow her lab results were all over the place, totally inconsistent one visit to the next. Two of the specialists even suggested Munchausen syndrome—a psychological disorder when patients either lied about symptoms or produced them by ingesting various substances or via artificial means.

The more Leah read, the more she heard Luka's voice in the back of her mind, telling her to look at all possibilities, even the ones she did not like. Like the possibility of Risa faking both her illness and her stalker.

Leah closed her laptop with a sigh. She needed Ian's files on Risa, needed to see what he'd written, needed to read between the lines. Risa might be able to fool doctors—if she was faking her symptoms—but no way in hell would she be able to fool Ian.

It was time. Time to go home.

CHAPTER 19

When Luka arrived back at the police department, Krichek was at his desk on the phone and Harper was nowhere to be seen, so he parked himself in his office and caught up with his emails and reports.

The first was Ahearn blasting him for not making the sergeants' meeting and implying that he was inclined to favor McKinley's take on what had happened this morning. Thankfully, Leah's email with the recording of her interview with Risa Saliba along with a summary report was also in his inbox, allowing him to dispatch the problem quickly, cc'ing both Ahearn and McKinley as well as the commander in charge of patrol. *Let them sort it out upstairs,* he thought.

Leah had also forwarded Risa's emails and attachments with her files on her stalker. Luka should have been writing his own reports on the Orly death as well as his other open cases, but couldn't help but take a peek. That one quick look soon turned into a journey down a rabbit hole as he skimmed the dozens of emails, Risa's notes, and then her database.

He read the stalker's emails first, fascinated by the psychology of the writer. More than simple narcissism, they revealed a depraved egotism typical of psychopaths. Yet, somehow, the stalker also seemed to genuinely care about Risa.

Then he turned to Risa's notes and research. She'd collected an overwhelming amount of data. After almost an hour, he closed all the files and sat back, wondering if he'd gotten everything wrong. This level of obsession was dangerous, even in someone healthy.

Not Risa's stalker's obsession with her, rather Risa's obsession with her stalker. It was statistically unlikely that an actual serial killer was behind the letters. Certainly, the letters contained no real evidence. How could a seasoned investigative journalist not see that? Maybe she was desperate to regain the spotlight, win another Pulitzer and return to her former glory?

As he clicked through the myriad of tabs in Risa's database he wondered if maybe it wasn't Walt faking his symptoms, but Risa. After all, who better to get close to Trudy outside her apartment than her neighbor, the one who helped her with Walt? And the stun gun changed everything about the mechanics of the crime—their killer didn't have to be stronger than Trudy Orly, only quicker. He made a note to ask Leah more about Risa's medical condition, see if her symptoms could be fabricated.

Before he could take his musings farther, Krichek and Harper waved at him through the glass wall of his office. Luka nodded to the conference room where they'd have space to work, grabbed his laptop and a notepad and joined them there.

Krichek sprawled in his chair, a smirk on his face, but it was Harper who was doing the victory dance.

"Warrants come through?" Luka asked as he slid into his seat.

"Got patrol searching for the phone and the stun gun," Krichek answered. "Also have the financials and—"

"But that's not—" Harper cut in.

"And the phone records," Krichek drawled, clearly enjoying tormenting the junior member of the squad. "But I think maybe Harper has news from the cyber squad."

"Yes," she exclaimed. "Sanchez figured out that the baby monitor you found was loading to the Orlys' cloud account and we have the password, so he was able to remotely access the monitor videos." She paused to take a breath as she clicked her tablet. "Watch this."

A grainy night vision video revealed Walt sleeping. The time stamp was from 8:19 this morning. Walt was tossing and turning, his hands flapping about, despite him seeming sound asleep. The chime of the doorbell made him jerk upright, eyes open. "Trudy?" he shouted. After waiting a few moments with no answer, he threw back the covers and got out of bed, his gait slow and shuffling, moving past the camera's range. With no motion to activate it, after a minute the camera went blank.

"Did you see the time? When the doorbell rang?" Harper asked. "It was only two minutes before the first 911 call."

Krichek was not impressed. "So? She locked herself out, he's pissed, opens the door, argues with her, she drops her bags, he shoves her over the railing. Bing-bang-boom, two minutes is plenty of time."

"Her keys were in the lock," Luka reminded him.

"There's a safety latch on the inside to prevent Walt from leaving," Harper added. "Either Trudy or someone using her keys had to open it for him. Walt couldn't have opened that door himself."

Luka wasn't sure that Walt couldn't have opened that door, but he let Harper's comment slide. "Maggie found marks from a stun gun on Trudy's scalp, hidden by her hair. So whoever did this—"

"Planned it." Krichek blew his breath out, conceding the point to Harper. "Unless they just happened to be carrying a stun gun and just happened to see Trudy right after she unlocked her door and just happened to know Walt was asleep inside so they needed to ring the bell to wake him and open the door from the outside for him…"

"We need to test those childproof latches, see how difficult they really are," Luka said, reluctant to give up on Walt as a suspect totally. After all, the vast majority of the time, the domestic partner was involved in cases like this one.

"Dr. Wright could maybe help us know if Walt's symptoms are as bad as everyone thinks," Krichek said. "He could still be our actor." He frowned. "Except for the damn monitor. It shows he was asleep before the doorbell—so who rang the doorbell? No reason for the wife to use it when she had her keys."

"Wait." Harper was still up, practically bouncing on her toes. "That's not the only thing Sanchez found." She clicked through to the Orlys' cloud account. There were two folders labeled with numbers correlating to each of the Orlys' phones. Harper clicked on one and the screen filled with dozens of photos.

"Look at the dates," she told them.

Most of the photos were of nursing facilities. The final ones were a stately colonial-style mansion on a well-manicured lawn. "Trudy's been searching for a long-term placement for Walt," Luka said. "His physician said she'd decided on a place in Smithfield."

Krichek tapped his own device, scrolling down to squint at a report. "Cell records show she was there last week and again yesterday."

"There were photos taken yesterday that were deleted from her phone. These six," Harper said. She highlighted the photos and enlarged them to fill the screen. They showed the grounds around the nursing home, its street, and the neighboring houses. Somehow Trudy had found a window of opportunity to take the photos when the rain had stopped, leaving behind puddles that reflected the parked cars and trees along with a row of smaller, but still elegant homes that lined the avenue.

"Why would she delete them?" Krichek asked. "To save room on her phone?"

Harper shook her head, her grin wide. "Trudy didn't delete them. The metadata says they were erased from the phone *after* she died."

That earned a raised eyebrow from Krichek. "The killer didn't want anyone to see them."

"But he didn't know they were still in the cloud's trashcan where Sanchez found them," Harper finished.

"Where's the phone now?"

"Sorry, boss, that's all I have. Sanchez said as soon as the photos were deleted, the phone was turned off and its GPS disabled. Said the actor probably removed the battery and SIM card. Last tower it pinged to was the one nearest the Falconer at 8:24 this morning, only a few minutes after the murder."

"It might still be there. Along with the stun gun." Luka narrowed his eyes at the photos. They were perfectly ordinary pictures of a perfectly ordinary street. The only human visible other than Trudy's reflection in a car side mirror was a faint silhouette of a man at the far edge of one shot. "Sanchez is enhancing these images?"

"Yes, sir. Running them through every program he can think of."

"Where are we on motive?" Luka asked Krichek. Even if the photos were the reason why Trudy was targeted, they still needed to rule out any other motives. And they didn't rule out Walt entirely; he could have been working with an accomplice.

"Financials look fairly benign. No excessive debt, but their retirement accounts have taken a hit because of Walt's medical bills. Last year they established a family trust so that if anything happened to Trudy, the money would be earmarked for Walt's care. That's where her insurance payoff is going. Half a mill, should buy Walt a nice room at that nursing home."

"No other beneficiaries? Next of kin?"

"Nope. Just the two of them. No one other than Walt stood to profit financially from Trudy's death."

"If Walt isn't our actor—and we also need Sanchez to analyze the monitor footage, see if it's been tampered with—then the killer knew to ring the doorbell to wake Walt. And to open the door for him," Luka said.

"Setting Walt up to take the fall." Krichek grinned at his own joke, ignoring Harper's groan and eye roll.

"Bad puns aside," she said, "if our actor intended to implicate Walt, they knew about Walt's medical condition and the safety latches Trudy had installed on the door."

"So someone who's been inside their apartment. And someone with access to the Falconer," Krichek added.

"Maybe they were disguised as someone in a position of authority?" Harper suggested. "That would also explain how they got out without anyone noticing them. Dressed as a cop or a medic."

"Or they just moved fast, knowing that Walt seeing Trudy's body would provide a distraction when he called for help."

As Luka listened to Krichek and Harper's ping-pong of theories, he couldn't help but think that there was one person who fit every aspect of the profile they were building.

"Krichek," he interrupted their debate. "Did you find that report I asked you about? The one from the neighbor about a possible cyberstalker."

"No report ever filed by or about Risa Saliba. Not with us, at least. Maybe since it's cyberstalking she went straight to the feds? It's their jurisdiction."

Luka sat back, absorbing the implications. Had Risa lied about filing the police report? Or had Leah misunderstood which agency Risa had spoken with? Krichek was right; a journalist with Risa Saliba's experience would definitely know that the FBI investigated cybercrime. Hell, she'd written a story on it.

He needed to talk to Risa Saliba. But not until he had a chance to do a thorough background check on her and go over her so-called stalker files again. And look at what stories she'd covered before she got sick. If she was hiding anything, he was determined to find it.

CHAPTER 20

Despite the fact that Good Sam was only a mile away from her home, Leah lost her nerve halfway there. Luka was counting on her to get Ian's files, but she couldn't even make the turn onto Jefferson, her old street. Anger simmered through her. Not just anger, shame at her weakness. More than a hint of despair and dread—she couldn't even perform this simple errand, and it was only one of an overwhelming myriad of tasks Ian's death had left her with. She had an inbox filled with forms and phone calls waiting to be returned to insurance adjustors, attorneys, bankers, his former employers, retirement advisors, credit card companies, the DMV—the list was daunting and endless.

Instead of wallowing in grief and self-pity, she allowed herself the luxury of anger. And, as she drove past the school, she realized she had a target other than her own wounded psyche to direct it at. Classes were out, the kids all gone, but the lights were on in the administrative wing, she noted as she took the spot closest to the main door. She ran through the rain to the door, glad to find that it hadn't been locked yet.

The guard post was empty and the only person in sight was a custodian waxing the floors at the far end of the corridor. She strode into the administrative offices, past the vacant secretary's desk, and into the vice principal's office.

Ms. Driscoll glanced up from her computer, its screen bathing her face in an orange-yellow light. No wonder the kids called this place the dragon's den, Leah thought as she almost turned to flee. But her anger squashed the impulse and she held her ground.

"Mrs. Wright," Ms. Driscoll began before Leah could say anything. "I was not expecting you. Did you make an appointment?" Her tone implied that if Leah had, then Leah must have gotten the time or date wrong, otherwise she would have been expected.

"You made a mistake. You called my mother in today, instead of me. If there's a problem concerning my daughter, I expect to be called."

Ms. Driscoll said nothing, merely arching an eyebrow of disbelief as she clicked on her computer. She read down a screen, taking her time—and leaving Leah standing, rain dripping from her coat, feeling more and more like a child waiting to be disciplined rather than an adult. Power games meant to manipulate. Everything in the office was arranged to intimidate, from the lack of chairs to the wall filled with framed diplomas to the bookcases filled to the brim with officious-looking volumes. What kid wouldn't immediately be cowed into obedience?

Leah smiled. Any kid, except her Emily.

Finally, Ms. Driscoll looked up from the screen. "It appears you made the mistake, Mrs. Wright. Usually your husband, Dr. Wright, was our primary contact for events concerning Emily." She gave an arch smile, as if Emily was so out of control that she caused such events on a daily basis. "Dr. Wright was always readily available when we needed his presence to… intervene and modify Emily's behavior."

"I—" Leah was about to protest. Ian was a regular fixture at the school, volunteering with Emily's class, and he'd also sometimes taken Emily out of class early to work on their father–daughter computer projects, but he'd never mentioned any occasion when Emily had required discipline.

But the vice principal cut her off before she could even start. "I see here that you called to change the primary contact from

Dr. Wright to your mother, a Miss Ruby Quinn. So, no mistake. At least not on our behalf."

"No," Leah fought to keep her voice calm, "I called to add my mother to the pickup list and emergency contacts. I should have remained primary contact."

"But, Mrs. Wright." Ms. Driscoll's smile widened, showing even more teeth. "You were never a primary contact. Only Dr. Wright."

Leah forced herself to count to ten, but made it only to four. "Please correct the error immediately. And explain to me how your school allowed my daughter and her friend to be both physically and psychologically abused by two of their classmates?"

There was click as the lights in the outer office shut off. Leah glanced at the clock: four o'clock. Ms. Driscoll closed down her computer, stood and brushed past Leah to retrieve a trench coat and old-fashioned umbrella from a coat stand beside the door.

"I'd love to, but I'm afraid we've run out of time for the day." She stood in the doorway, one hand on the light switch, her body angled in an invitation for Leah to either leave or remain in darkness. "However, feel free to call and schedule an appointment to discuss Emily's behavior and potential consequences. At your convenience, of course, Mrs. Wright."

"It's *Dr.* Wright," Leah said as she stalked past, already wondering how difficult home-schooling might be.

Satisfied that at least she'd gotten the last word, she fled to her car and started driving. Rage simmered through her, but there was little she could do about it. On the surface, any objective evaluation of their conversation would reveal only that the vice principal was acting in a professional manner. But Leah understood the truth of the matter: Ms. Driscoll was as much of a bully as the Homan brothers.

Seething, the encounter replaying in her mind, she was startled when she realized she'd turned onto Jefferson and was only a few houses away from her old home. As she pulled into an open space across the street, a queasy feeling swamped her. She couldn't do it.

But Luka needed Ian's copy of his work for Risa. Leah had to go inside sooner or later, if only to grab her and Emily's personal belongings and retrieve the boxes of evidence the police had returned to the house a few weeks ago. If she kept giving in to her fear and anxiety, they would only fester and build. Best to face them now.

Still, she sat, her gaze fixed on the brick Victorian divided into two townhouses, all thoughts of Ms. Driscoll forgotten. The azaleas beside the front stoop had gone from naked branches to budding, the rain making their green appear otherworldly. Had they been so green and alive this morning when she'd stopped after dropping the kids at school? Honestly, she had no idea, she'd been so trapped in a haze of grief. She thought of the day when Ian had planted them. She'd been working on the hydrangeas on the other side of the walkway, Emily plopping small containers of annuals in between, more dirt covering her than made it into the ground.

A good day. One of many that this house had gifted her.

Hanging onto the happy memory, she left the car before her courage could desert her and crossed the street. Her fingers were numb—from the cold, not from fear, she lied to herself—as she fumbled her key into the lock. The door swung open and Leah stepped into the house, feeling like a stranger in her own home. It was cold, so physically cold that she shivered. And the smell... nothing horrible, no scent of blood, but stale with the faint underlying tinge of chemicals.

She shut the door, the thud echoing through the house before dying into silence. It was the quiet that made Leah falter. Her house was never quiet, not like this, not this soundless vacuum devoid of life.

She hugged her arms around her chest. She couldn't focus beyond what was right in front of her: her good wool coat, the one she saved for church and special outings, hanging from the coatrack. She brushed her fingers against its sleeve, trying not to remember the last time she wore it—coming home from church, her and Ian arguing about something the priest said. Well, she'd been arguing, and Ian, as always, treated their difference of opinions as an opportunity for debate. It was the one thing that drove her mad about him, the way he became excited when they argued, as if it was some kind of intellectual exercise, stimulating, fun. So much so that he'd often end up arguing her side for her, which, of course, only infuriated her more.

And now, she couldn't even remember what they'd been arguing about. All she remembered was at one point yanking her hand away from his, her need to gesticulate, hammer home a point, more important than her need to keep hold of his hand.

Hanging onto her coat with one hand, she reached for Ian's herringbone coat beside it, raising the sleeve, inhaling his scent. She tucked the cuffs of both coats into the pockets of Emily's pink jacket hanging between them, creating a family.

Only then did she turn to face the rest of her home. Evidence boxes were stacked on the coffee table. She'd asked the police to deliver them here instead of to Nellie's house, because she hadn't wanted Emily asking questions. And because she hadn't had the strength to deal with what was inside them. She still didn't.

Several were small and flat, sized for computers, the other two were larger, and on top was a small plastic envelope that held Ian's wedding ring. All were marked with a case number scrawled in a thick marker. As if Ian's entire life—and death—could be contained by an anonymous seven-digit number.

Leah wove her way around the armchair and coffee table, past the sofa and basket of Emily's toys, until she ended up at the fireplace with its mantle full of photos. She stretched a hand out, yearning, but immediately pulled it back, afraid to contaminate memories so precious and pure with the despair of her current reality. Her breath came quick and gasping. Her lips were numb, her face tingling with pins and needles, and the pressure on her chest had a stranglehold on her breathing.

She knew it was a panic attack, but no amount of logic could ease the overpowering sense of impending doom. She whirled, ready to bolt, but some last strand of rational thought had her grabbing the laptop boxes and envelope as she fled to the door. Arms full, she almost dropped everything as she struggled to turn the knob.

And then she was outside, stumbling down the steps. She made it to her car, and threw the boxes into the back, closing the hatch and collapsing against it, rain streaming down her face and hair, rivulets of cold seeping between her parka and her skin.

Had she locked the door? She dug into her pocket and found her keys. No. Her hands had been full.

Reasoning through that one simple question somehow helped to calm her, the pressure in her chest giving way, although her pulse still throbbed in her temples. A few more deep, slow breaths and she was able to clear her vision and focus on the next task: going back.

Not inside, she promised herself. Just to the door. Lock it and leave. She could do that. Lock it and leave.

She focused on her feet as she retraced her steps until she faced the solid oak door once again. Despite her panic, part of her was desperate to escape inside, never leave the world where she could imagine Ian still alive. But she denied herself the luxury of escape. She couldn't afford it—she had Emily to think of.

Ian would understand, she thought as her trembling fingers locked the door. She pressed her palm against the wood, making a silent promise: *I will be back. You aren't forgotten. Never forgotten.*

As she walked back to her car, breathing still ragged, her phone rang. Risa.

"Leah?" Risa's voice trembled. "There's a new message."

"What's it say?"

Then Risa said, "It's addressed to Detective Jericho."

CHAPTER 21

Risa Saliba's background check came up clean, and as Luka combed through her files, he couldn't find any evidence to prove the existence of her stalker. Much less whether he'd killed anyone.

All of the people the stalker suggested that he'd killed shared some similarity to people Risa had interviewed, written feature stories about during her career as a journalist, or, more recently, had worked on their obituaries as a fact-checker. But the similarities were small: a shared name, shared date of death or manner of death—a clever internet researcher could easily have found these "doppelgängers," as Luka thought of them, using them as examples of his killing prowess by claiming responsibility for their deaths.

Or an equally clever investigative reporter determined to reclaim her fame and fortune could be using them to create a fictious stalker.

Frustrated by his lack of progress, Luka decided to head over to the Falconer. Time to interview Risa himself, without interruptions from distraught boyfriends or distractions from her medical issues.

He parked in the lot beside the building, recognizing Leah's Subaru as he jogged through the rain to the front door. Leah said she'd be talking to Risa about her medical issues. He wondered if Leah should stay during his interview—he could use her medical expertise to dissect Risa's symptoms, see if they were genuine. If he caught Risa lying about those, it would be a short journey to discrediting her stalker "evidence" as well.

He pulled open the Falconer's heavy glass front door, shutting the furious elements behind him. After texting Harper to come let him in—he didn't want to alert Risa to his arrival, give her time to prepare by asking her to buzz him in from her apartment—he relished the silence of the space between the two sets of glass doors. Fingerprint dust still stained the keypad, although the brass door handles had been polished bright. The lobby was empty, the decorative sconces casting a ring of light around the space where Trudy's body had lain.

What role did Trudy's death play in all this? After all, she was his real case. Not this unlikely serial killer–stalker drama that Risa Saliba had engulfed him and Leah in. He remembered Leah's naïve first instinct to believe Risa, that the killer stalking Risa may have killed Trudy. Far-fetched, for sure. But at this stage, with no concrete suspects, he had to keep an open mind.

Movement behind the reception desk caught his eye—Harper emerging from a door hidden by the tall potted palms, the same one the building manager had used this morning. She waved at him and crossed the lobby to open the door, her expression one of wide-eyed enthusiasm. "Perfect timing, boss. Wait until you see what I found."

"Trudy's cell or the stun gun?" he asked as he followed her back through the same door.

"No. Maybe better, though." The door led to a short hallway. A doorway leading to the mailroom was on one side, a janitor's closet on the other. And at the end was a door labeled: MANAGER. Here Harper hesitated. "Not sure how it ties into Trudy's murder, but—look for yourself."

With a flourish she flung the door open. The lights were on in what appeared to be a simple office: cheap desk with an outdated computer, file cabinets, whiteboard filled with maintenance items to be addressed. Beside it was an open door leading to a walk-in closet. Luka stepped inside.

And found himself surrounded by images of Risa Saliba. On one wall, a collage of candid photos caught from a variety of angles. The back wall held a collection of printed headshots from her various publications.

"Where's Vogel?" he asked Harper.

"No idea. Left before I got here. His shift officially ends at four, so no one thought too much about it. But there's a sleeping bag tucked under the desk and the address we have says he hasn't lived there in months—"

"Put out a BOLO. Local and state."

"Already done."

Luka scrutinized the images on the first collage. A few showed Risa working in her living room and were taken from above. Hidden camera? Probably in the fire detectors—easy enough for the building manager to place under the guise of replacing the batteries. "Did you check the computer?"

"Nothing on this one, but I'll bet his phone or home computer has a lot more than these. Who knows how many cameras he's had on Saliba." She backed out of the small space. "Big question is, what does this have to do with Trudy Orly? Did she catch him spying on Saliba and he killed her to silence her?"

"Someone has been sending Risa anonymous letters. Claiming to be a serial killer who wants her to tell his story."

Harper's eyes went wide at the implications. "Boss. Did we just let a serial killer escape?"

Luka's phone rang, saving him from answering. Risa's boyfriend, Jack O'Brien.

"Detective Jericho?" he said, his tone rushed. "I think you need to come here. The killer sent Risa another message. I can't explain, just get here as fast as you can."

CHAPTER 22

To Leah's surprise, after Risa buzzed her into the Falconer, her door wasn't opened by Risa or even Jack O'Brien, but instead a reedy man with a shaved head and a pair of very small, round glasses perched on his nose.

"You must be Dr. Wright," he exclaimed as if he'd been waiting all day to meet her. He thrust out a hand. "Dominic Massimo. Risa's agent. Call me Dom."

Leah followed him inside where Risa waited in her customary chair. Jack stalked the narrow space behind the island that separated the kitchen from the living area, talking on the phone in a low voice. He hung up and turned to Risa. "He's on his way. But as soon as he gets here, we should leave. Let me get you out of here."

"Why? It's not like he doesn't already know where I live." Leah frowned at Risa, who shrugged. "Jack was here when Dom called, so I told Jack about the stalker, showed him the letters. Thanks for coming. I just don't know what to do—and these two aren't being much help." Her almost flippant attitude surprised Leah until she realized it was all an act of bravado. When Leah looked closely she saw the fear hiding behind Risa's calm façade.

"Excuse me?" Dom said, hands on his hips. "The letter was sent to me, not you. Who dropped everything to drive here from Manhattan?"

Jack glared at the other man. "Only to protect your own interests. You want Risa to turn this into some kind of media spectacle."

"We all want Risa to return to her former level of success. If this serial killer story is our ticket, then I say we take it and run with it."

"Except it's her life on the line." Jack walked over to Risa's chair, settling on its arm.

"Mine as well—the killer obviously has my address."

"Wait," Leah put in, drawing both men's attention. "How did the killer send you a letter addressed to the detective investigating Trudy's death when she only died this morning?" It sounded terribly complicated and meant the killer—or stalker—had been close enough to know Luka was on the case and where to reach Dom.

"Exactly why I want Risa out of here. The guy is toying with us," Jack said, one hand laid protectively over Risa's arm.

"Anyone care to know what I think?" Risa asked. "I don't think Trudy's murder was planned—or at least not like his other killings, which despite his victims being determined by a throw of the dice, otherwise were so meticulous no one has ever labeled them as murders. And he had plenty of time after he killed Trudy to email a letter to a courier service, ask them to print it out and deliver it to Dom."

"Even required my signature. I thought I was being sued or something."

"You called Luka, right? He's coming?" Leah asked.

"I just spoke with him. He's on his way," Jack assured her. He seemed the only one taking the potential threat seriously.

"In the meantime, we might have had a breakthrough on one of the other cases the killer mentioned. The guy from Indiana?" Dom sounded excited by the prospect of helping to unmask a serial killer. More than excited, rapacious. Making Leah wonder exactly how far he'd go to resurrect Risa's career.

"Jack thinks I was looking in the wrong place for the dead landscaper," Risa explained.

"Problem was, Risa grew up in Kansas and then lived in New York City," Jack said. "She doesn't know this area. Not Indiana the state, but Indiana, Pennsylvania. It's a town not far from Pittsburgh. Making it much too close to here," he finished with a worried expression, edging his hip closer to Risa.

"Any missing landscape guys from there?" Leah's tone matched Dom's and she realized how easy it was to get caught up in the exhilaration of hunting a serial killer—never mind that ten minutes ago she'd been convinced that Risa might be making the whole thing up. And who was to say she wasn't? She could have arranged for the letter to be delivered to her agent. It was a great way to divert suspicion.

Before Risa could answer Leah, there was a knock on the door. Dom rushed out and returned with Luka and Harper, neither of whom appeared happy with the circumstances.

"I understand you have a letter addressed to me," Luka began after introducing himself and Harper to Dom.

"Actually, it's a letter to me," Dom corrected him. "Containing instructions to deliver a message to you. In person." He raised his phone to video the encounter. "I saved everything for fingerprints and DNA and such." He turned to Harper, who was donning a pair of nitrile gloves. "I assume that's your department?" With a flourish he reached to the coffee table and handed her a clear plastic folder containing an envelope, sheet of paper, and receipt.

"Please stop filming, sir," Luka told him. "What was the message?"

"I have my rights," Dom argued.

Risa intervened. "Dom. Stop. It's distracting. And this is important. Give Detective Jericho the message."

Dom shrugged and pocketed his phone. "It's all there, in the letter. You didn't expect me to memorize it, did you? It's just a bunch of numbers. Said to bring them to Detective Sergeant Jericho. So I did."

Harper held up the plastic-encased sheet of paper. "Looks like maybe an IP address?" She snapped a photo. "I'll ask Sanchez." She moved to the foyer to make her call.

Luka took a breath and Leah knew he was sorting through priorities—she'd seen that expression on him before, when he was questioning her after Ian's murder. "Ms. Saliba. I'd like to know more about your stalker. Take me through everything. When exactly did the emails and texts begin?"

Leah remained at the bar separating the kitchen from the living room, but when Luka began questioning Risa, Jack quietly moved from the kitchen to Risa's chair. He said nothing, simply sat on the arm of the chair, one hand on Risa's shoulder, offering his silent support.

"Last April 1st. You can see the timestamp on the first email. The video about the man hit by the train came a few weeks later but I don't have any proof of that; it was sent by a text that deleted itself."

"And who else have you told about his correspondence?"

"Me," Dom said, chest thrust out as if it was a point of pride, his gaze not on Luka but rather on Jack. Leah had the feeling it wasn't the first time the two men had competed for Risa's attention. "I'm her agent, Risa tells me everything."

"It wasn't until a few months later—May or June, last year— after I'd hired a private cybersecurity consultant, that I told Dom," Risa corrected him.

"That consultant was Ian Wright?"

"Yes. I contacted him through the college, thought that way I'd be sure to get someone reputable. After he couldn't track the stalker via my computer, we asked my most frequent contacts to allow Ian to check their computers for malware and tracking software."

"Contacts? Including Mr. Massimo?"

"Right. And my editors at the news bureau along with a few research contacts. Since I became ill and began working from home, I haven't been in touch with as many people as I used to be." She grimaced and shrugged one shoulder.

"The stalker seems well aware of your illness. How many people know about it?"

"That's my fault," Dom interjected before Risa could answer. "When it became clear that Risa's condition precluded any travel, I put out feelers, called in some favors to get her work she could do from home." Then he aimed a glance at Jack. "Not that it was any secret. Jack started a fundraising campaign to help Risa with medical expenses."

Luka nodded his understanding and returned his attention to Risa. "Ms. Saliba, have you noticed anyone taking an unusual interest in your activities?"

Risa seemed surprised by the question. "No. But I don't actually have many usual activities—lately I haven't even left the apartment."

"Because of your medical condition?"

She hesitated, raising a hand to cover Jack's. "No. Because of Ian Wright's murder. I thought, maybe, his death could be tied to my stalker."

Leah noticed that Jack's jaw tightened at Risa's admission, but he said nothing, only squeezed her hand.

"And yet you never reported your stalker to the police," Luka said, his tone calm—too calm, like a cat waiting to pounce.

Leah turned to Risa. "But you did. You said—"

"I said I'd spoken to the police. And I have. I've chased down every lead the stalker left, trying to confirm his victims. Without evidence, no one would believe me. Several threatened me with charges of making a false report." She kept her expression and tone business-like despite her obvious frustration. "So, no, Detective Sergeant. When an expert like Ian Wright couldn't track my stalker, I realized there was no way your department would be able to. I did submit a cybercrime complaint to the FBI but never heard back from them."

"Do you have documentation of any of that? A copy of your report to the FBI?"

Jack jumped up, taking a stance between Risa and Luka. "Are you calling her a liar?"

Before Luka could answer, Harper returned, her phone held up in front of her. "Boss, you're going to want to see this." She handed the phone to Luka. "The message led to a webpage."

He peered at the screen. Leah had the urge to step closer, to try to see what he saw, but it was Dom who actually sidled up to Luka, shamelessly reading over his shoulder.

"It's addressed to Risa," Dom said.

"What's it say?" Jack asked.

Luka said nothing, simply cleared his throat and handed the phone back to Harper. "Go ahead, read it," he told her, stepping back, his posture rigid as he observed the others' reactions to the message.

Harper began, "My dearest Obituary Reader, You're the one person I can trust with these insights because even if you went to the police, there's nothing to lead back to me. I know you're hungry for details, facts you can check and validate and use to springboard your investigation. I've whetted your appetite, perhaps given you a new reason to live given the pathetic prison your health has sentenced you to? I hope so. In fact, my guess is that Detective Sergeant Jericho is there with you now, reading this. You have my permission to share everything with him. He, of all people, will take an interest in my very first kill. After all, he was engaged to her. Her name was Cherise."

The phone shook in Harper's hand and she turned to glance at Luka. He blinked rapidly and jerked his chin, nodding at her to continue. Leah was certain no one except her noticed his reaction; everyone else was focused on Harper. But then she saw that Risa was staring at Luka as well.

Harper continued, "Luka will think I'm lying, taking advantage of the fact that it's public knowledge that he'd be lead investigator on any violent crime committed in your city. But I'd never not tell you the truth, my dear Obituary Reader. You're the one person I trust to chronicle my achievements; I'd never tarnish our relationship with tawdry lies. Tell Luka to open the encrypted image below. Welcome to the game, Detective Sergeant Jericho. Just call me Chaos."

Everyone was silent as Harper finished. "Sanchez told me not to click on the image, but he's going to decrypt it, run it through software to make sure it's not infected, and text it to you."

"Is it true?" Jack asked. "Your fiancée was murdered?" He sank back onto the chair arm and wrapped an arm around Risa's shoulders, pulling her close to him.

Luka's face remained blank. "My fiancée killed herself. Seventeen years ago today. Facts anyone could easily discover after two minutes with Google."

"Maybe it wasn't suicide?" Dominic said. "How can you be sure?"

Before Luka could answer, his phone chimed. The mystery image. Everyone, even Leah, leaned forward in anticipation as he slid his phone out and glanced at it, turning his body to shield the image from everyone else.

After a moment, he hauled in a breath, his shoulders rigid, and slid the phone back into his pocket. "Ms. Saliba, I'd like permission to search your apartment and take your electronics in for our cyber squad to analyze."

That got both Dom's and Jack's attention. Jack spoke first. "Search her home? Why? You can't suspect Risa had anything—"

Dom's protests overrode Jack's in volume. "Absolutely not. Risa's livelihood depends on those electronics. Maybe, if you sign a waiver and NDA, we'll let you monitor incoming communications, share any new information the killer sends us—"

"Wait," Risa said in a quiet but commanding tone. "Detective Jericho, I can't afford to be disconnected from the world, especially not right now. In fact, if the killer is watching me so closely, won't he be upset if he can't communicate with me? Maybe lash out at an innocent victim? Is there a compromise we could reach?"

"Exactly," Dom put in, as if it was his idea.

"How often is your building manager in your apartment, Ms. Saliba?"

Risa gave a shake of her head as if confused by the abrupt change of topic. "Cliff? He brings me my mail and packages if I can't get downstairs. But he doesn't do more than place them on the table for me. Why are you asking?"

"We have evidence that Mr. Vogel may have planted cameras inside your apartment."

Jack sprang off the chair at that. "He's spying on her? Where is he now?" Not waiting for an answer, he turned to Risa. "That's it. You're out of here. Tonight."

"We're searching for Vogel," Luka told Risa. "But you understand why we want access to your electronics and your apartment."

Risa pulled the quilt from the back of the chair around her shoulders, huddling under it.

Jack said, "Leave the damn computers; you can live without them. And if this Vogel creep is the killer, then he knows the game is up, he's on the run, so he'll be way past thinking about reaching you."

"She needs her files for the story," Dom put in. "But we'll agree to some kind of remote monitoring." He made it sound as if it was his decision.

"We have a warrant to search the common areas of the Falconer. I'd like to—with your consent—widen our search area to include your apartment." Luka took a step closer to Risa, blocking Dom. "Perhaps Mr. O'Brien has a point about you leaving. At least until we've finished."

Jack's head bobbed along with Luka's words, obviously agreeing. Risa frowned, took a breath, and threw off the quilt she'd been sheltering under. "No."

"Risa—" Jack started.

"No. This is my home, the only place I feel safe. Now that the police know about Cliff, he won't come back here, so it's the one place

I *am* safe. I'm staying." She turned to face Luka. "I would appreciate it if your men could remove any cameras, and I'm happy to allow you to monitor my communications, but what exactly would you be searching for if I gave you further access to my apartment? I have sensitive files—physical and digital—which are confidential, relating to my work. As a journalist, I need to protect those."

Luka's lips tightened, but he nodded. "We can limit our search to any hidden surveillance devices along with Trudy's cell phone and a stun gun that we believe was used during her murder. Would that satisfy your criteria?"

Leah could tell by the expression on his face that he would never leave it to that, was simply buying time until he could persuade a judge to grant him full access to Risa's home and life. She wondered how difficult that might be given a reporter's right to protect their sources.

Risa nodded. "I would consent to that limited search, yes."

"I'm leaving Officer Harper here to monitor the situation." He gave Harper a curt nod. "Perhaps you could get more complete statements from everyone involved," he told her, holding his hand for the plastic bag containing Dom's note. "I'll get this to forensics, have them put a rush on it."

He was out the door before anyone could move. Leah hurried after him—whatever had been in that image, it had shaken him. By the look on Harper's face, she'd seen it as well.

"Luka, wait," she called to him as she left Risa's apartment. He took another two steps but then stopped halfway to the elevator lobby. Almost exactly where Trudy had fallen to her death. The crime scene tape was gone, everything sparkling clean as if it had never happened.

She caught up to him. "Was the killer telling the truth about your fiancée?"

He said nothing but his gait slowed as he led her to the elevators. "Her name was Cherise Sumner. We met sophomore year at Bucknell. I asked her to marry me start of our senior year." He shook his head, his gaze arching skyward as if addressing the heavens more than Leah. "We had so many plans…"

The elevator doors slid open and they both stepped inside. Luka took advantage of the privacy to slump against the far wall while Leah pushed the button for the lobby.

"How did she die?" she asked when he remained silent.

"She was at a friend's house—they had a LSAT study group. Cherise was brilliant but struggled with tests. She was always a bit up and down, had been on anti-depressants since high school, but thought they messed with her focus, so, unknown to me or her doctors, she'd stopped them. Her friend said she hadn't done well on the practice tests for law school, was upset—and resentful of me for already being guaranteed a full ride for grad school. At least, that's what everyone believed—" He stopped, a small choking sound emerging. "I shouldn't have, though. I should have never believed, should have fought, should have—"

"Luka, you were just a kid."

"Still… She never came home that night. A passing motorist saw her car partially submerged in the river. All the windows were down and she left a poem behind, weighted down on the river bank. A message to me, to the world."

"A poem?"

"One of my favorites, I'd just done a paper on it. So elegant, so poignant, I'd thought at the time. Three lines, twelve words total. But the title says it all."

"What was it?"

"Langston Hughes. 'Suicide's Note.'" He shrugged, less an expression of uncertainty than of frustration. "I should have known—"

"The killer's just playing mind games," Leah protested as the doors opened on the empty lobby. "Don't believe anything he says."

"No. He's telling the truth." Luka slid his phone free and thumbed the screen, then held it to her. It was a photo of an engagement ring, taken at an angle to reveal the inscription: *Cherise, my beloved. Forever, Luka.*

"It's hers," Luka said, his voice gravelly with emotion. "They never found it on her body, thought maybe she'd thrown it in the river. But now I know. He took it. There's no other explanation. He killed Cherise."

CHAPTER 23

Luka stalked through the empty lobby, ignoring the fact that he was crossing the space where Trudy Orly's body had lain a mere eight hours ago. Leah kept pace with him and while he was glad for her company, he also wished she wasn't here to witness the tsunami of emotion swamping him.

Guilt, grief, fury, confusion all collided, screaming that he do something, anything, shrieking that the past seventeen years of his life had been a lie. Energy shuddered through every nerve—he couldn't have stopped and stood still if he'd wanted to. He paced, first crossing then circling the lobby, his footsteps ringing through the vast expanse of the atrium, moving faster and faster until finally Leah simply stood and watched, letting him go.

Then it hit him. This was what the killer wanted. Chaos.

Luka halted so abruptly one foot skidded along the newly cleaned marble. The clarity that had eluded him since the case started was now stunning. Above him he heard the two patrol officers working, but they sounded very far away.

Leah joined him. "Are you okay?"

Luka swallowed, searching for his voice, and settled for nodding. "If you need to talk—"

"No." The word sounded clear, like the old Luka, as if nothing had changed. But everything had changed. Everything. *Focus*, he told himself. *Prioritize. Family first.* "Leah, can Nate stay at your place tonight?"

"Of course."

"Thanks." And Pops? Any way this played out it would devastate the old man—not only the implicit threat to Luka, but also the truth of Cherise's murder. Pops had adored her. Best to let him stick with his routines, remain in his home. Far easier for Luka to be the one to leave. He'd ask Ahearn to arrange for patrols to swing by the farm. Then he faced Leah. How could he be so stupid, letting her get involved in this? "You need to go back to Good Sam. This wasn't the right case for a civilian to be involved with."

"You're kicking me off the case? Why? Did I do something wrong? I mean, you wouldn't even know about the killer if I hadn't gone the extra mile to spend time with Risa."

He started for the doors and she followed. "It's nothing you did. But think. If this guy is responsible for Cherise's death, then he's been killing and getting away with it for seventeen years. He's had that ring in his back pocket to use for all that time."

"Right. He's a serial killer—" She sounded almost flippant, and a rush of disappointment flooded over him. After what Leah went through last month, he thought she, of all people, would understand how serious this was.

"You've been watching too many movies. Real-life serial killers, the ones who make a career of it, who don't get caught early on—it's because they're smart and careful. They don't go around leaving clues and letters and taunting the police—especially not after BTK was caught—not unless it's part of their plan, a way to force an error from the police or…" He trailed off, still fighting to follow the tangled threads of the tapestry unfolding in his mind. The picture was sprawling, so much larger than he'd ever imagined. How much of it was truth and how much misdirection? Could all three cases—Cherise, Trudy, and Risa's stalker—really be the work of one man, undetected for seventeen years?

"If Cliff is Risa's stalker, then did he kill Trudy and Cherise?" Leah's question echoed Luka's thoughts. "He didn't strike me as very cunning."

"We're getting a full background," Luka said absently. He agreed with her—his initial instincts when he'd met the building manager were of a socially awkward man with a limited skill set. But maybe they'd seen only what the killer wanted them to see. "But Cliff had the opportunity and the means to kill Trudy." It didn't feel right, but the facts in hand trumped Luka's instincts. Until he discovered new facts that gave him a reason to doubt Cliff's guilt. Either way, they had to find the man and question him. Soon.

"Why involve Risa? Why give her clues to follow? Why the letters? And why kill Trudy?"

"He has a plan." No, that wasn't quite right. "He *had* a plan. Involving Risa. But something changed. Trudy did something, saw something, said something that threatened him. He didn't kill her because he wanted to or because his damn dice told him to, he did it because he had to kill her, to silence her, immediately. Somehow, she posed a threat to him. Maybe something in the photos deleted from her phone." Except that they'd found nothing unusual in any of the deleted photos. What might have made them worth killing for?

"Why not just lie low, then? Or make a run for it? Why keep engaging Risa, why tell you about Cherise? Have you met Cliff before? Did he know Cherise?"

As much as he appreciated Leah voicing all the questions roiling through his mind, giving them some semblance of order, he wished she'd be quiet, give him a minute to think. "I never met Vogel before. Cherise never mentioned him. I have no idea why he's doing this or how he got Cherise's ring."

"Maybe when he learned you were in charge of Trudy's case, he saw an opportunity to create some chaos?" she mused. "Live up to the name he's chosen for himself?"

He didn't answer. Suddenly his case was in shambles, despite now having a viable suspect. Chaos. The killer worshiped it; Luka's face grew cold as realization hit him. Chaos. That had been his life after Cherise. An abyss of confusion, rage, despair, and endless questioning, scrutinizing his every decision, blaming himself for missing vital clues.

Despite being in the cavernous empty lobby facing Leah, suddenly Luka felt claustrophobic, trapped in the tightest vice imaginable: of feeling alone. Then Leah touched his arm, breaking his reverie.

"He sees a way out—and it's through me," Luka said in a low tone. "They'll remove me from the case—personal involvement. Like how you doctors can't treat family members. Which means, I'm out of the game. Exactly what he wants."

"If they take you off the case, who will replace you?"

"It doesn't matter, you're off it as well." Her glare forced an answer from him. "It'd have to be a sergeant or higher, but not someone too close to me, so they won't be tainted, just in case—"

"In case what?" she scoffed. Then she sobered, took a moment to consider. "In case they think you're a killer? That you were involved in your fiancée's death? No. Who would believe that?"

He wished he could joke about it. This was his life—past, present and future—on the line. "Leah. This guy is smart enough to go undetected for seventeen years. I don't have an alibi for Cherise's death. Maybe he'll claim I gave him the ring or he stole it from me or who knows what. Point is, this could easily spiral out of control. Whatever happens, the department will need to investigate any role I may or may not have played in her death. They can't afford even a whiff of impropriety. Otherwise this guy could walk, even if we do catch him."

She frowned at that. "They'd really suspect you?"

"There's no innocent until proven guilty, not when you're a cop—not in the eyes of the public, at least."

"So who will take over? Will they take over Trudy's case or just Risa's? How does it work?"

He could tell by her earnest expression that she wasn't asking out of curiosity, but rather because she wanted to know how best to intercede on his behalf. "My guess? Ahearn will personally supervise, and he'll put McKinley in charge of the day to day of the search for Vogel and the investigation into Risa's stalker and any deaths he might have been involved in. Maybe they'll let me stay on Trudy's case, I'm not sure."

"McKinley? The SWAT guy?"

"ERT," he corrected automatically. "Listen. I have to go, try to get ahead of this. And you are no longer involved with this case, with Risa Saliba, or with me. Other than taking care of Nate. Understand?"

Defiance flashed across her face.

"Leah. I'm trusting you with Nate. With my family. If I'm in this guy's sights, I need to make sure no one else is targeted along with me. Especially not Nate."

"Right." She blew her breath out. "Okay. But you need to keep me in the loop—if I don't know what's happening, I can't protect him. Especially once this hits the news—"

"And you know the killer will make sure it lands with a splash, gets everyone's attention. Only a question of when."

"We'll need to tell Nate as much as we can. He needs to understand—"

"I don't even understand," he snapped. Then he softened his tone. "No, you're right. I'll come by tonight, tomorrow at the latest—as soon as I know something."

They walked toward the large glass doors at the front of the building. Despite their weight, the rain and wind lashed at them hard enough to make them shake.

"What will happen? To you?" she asked as Luka opened the first set of doors. "I mean with your boss?" But her tone made it clear it was more than his career that she was concerned about.

He looked out at the rain, not at her, not back at the scene of the crime he'd been lead investigator on up until a few minutes ago. "Same thing that happens with every suspect, guilty or not. They'll tear my life apart."

CHAPTER 24

As she fixed Emily and Nate their dinner, Ruby kept talking about how proud she was of them both. But that didn't make sense to Emily. Shouldn't she be in trouble? She didn't hit anyone, but she had made Jimmy fall.

"When's Mommy coming home?" she asked Ruby. Miss Ruby was good when you needed loud voices or to run away, but Emily had quickly realized that she wasn't the best at actually thinking through a problem. Not like Mommy or Daddy.

"Late. She's busy at work."

Emily sighed. Mommy was always busy at work. Helping other people. Guess it was up to her to figure this out on her own. Nate was in worse trouble now because of her—trouble with the Homans, trouble with Luka for losing Nate's great's war medal, and trouble with Ms. Driscoll. She couldn't help with Ms. Driscoll, but maybe she could help with the Homans and the lost medal.

"Why'd you stand there?" she asked Nate in a low tone as Ruby stirred the flavor packet into the chili. Emily liked how Daddy cooked better—he let her decide which spices to try so every time it was like a new experiment. Daddy always said to start with "why" when approaching a problem. "Why'd you let them throw those balls at you and call you those names?"

Nate shrugged. "Got called worse back home. Your mom gonna let us sleep in our fort? We don't have to tear it down?"

"Why not? It's not hurting anyone."

His eyes grew wide. "Never got to do anything like that back in foster. Everything had to be cleaned up before bedtime."

"How're we going to get your great-great's medal back?" Emily said it only to be polite—she already had a plan. And now that she understood Nate's why—he was afraid of speaking up and being sent back to Baltimore or foster where people treated him even worse than the Homans did. She couldn't ask the grownups for help; it was just her and Nate. When Nate shrugged, she continued, "You know Billy and Jimmy's house is just through the woods? There's a path down the mountain they come four-wheeling on. Ruby was swearing at them for tearing up the far lavender field, said she'd get a shotgun and shoot them next time."

"No, sir." He shook his head. "We're not gonna shoot anyone. I can't afford any trouble. They want the medal so bad, they can have it."

"Won't Pops and Luka be mad that you lost it? That could get you in trouble, too." Besides, it was just wrong, the Homans taking Nate's medal. Emily couldn't stand by and let that happen.

He considered that, gulping down his own glass of Quik, leaving a milky brown mustache in its wake. Emily took another drink, so now they matched. It was one of the good things about having a friend; you didn't have to be different all alone.

"What's your plan?" Nate asked, dropping his voice to a whisper. He gave Ruby a sidelong look, but she was humming to herself and dancing in front of the stove as she stirred the chili.

"The rain is supposed to stop tonight—my phone told me. It has maps on it, too, so we don't get lost."

He paused as he thought, then gave a slow nod. "We need a compass. Pops has one."

"So did Nellie—I found an old one in one of the trunks in the attic. Do you know how to use it?"

"Yeah, kind of. Pops showed me." From his tone, she could tell he was starting to get excited by the idea.

"So tomorrow we go over there and we get your great-great's medal back. Then we bring it home and we'll be heroes. Maybe my mom will even let us have ice cream. Or we can walk from the Homans' farm over to Jericho Fields—the map says it's not far. We could surprise your Pops, show him how you used the compass."

Then everyone would know how brave they'd been, facing the Homans. It didn't make up for what happened last month, when she'd been too scared to help Daddy, but maybe it was a start. She needed to do something to get rid of this constant, awful feeling inside.

Nate considered. "Sure we won't get into trouble?"

Emily shook her head vigorously. "No. Just you see. We're going to be heroes."

Just like her daddy was a hero. Brave and strong.

CHAPTER 25

Leah was tempted to head home. It had been an exhausting day—and she still needed to deal with Emily and what had happened at school. But she'd also promised to talk to Risa about Risa's medical problems, so she took the elevator back up to Risa's apartment.

As the elevator made its slow ascent, Leah wondered again about Risa's illness. Her test results didn't fit any one diagnosis, but if Cliff was her stalker, could he also be causing Risa's symptoms? If he had access to Risa's apartment, maybe he had tampered with her food, was poisoning her? A thrill ran through her at the idea that she could maybe solve the mystery and help both Risa with her symptoms and Luka with proving that Cliff was the killer. That would keep his bosses from coming down hard on him, right?

When she reached Risa's apartment the door was ajar and Harper was standing outside it, where she could still hear everything happening inside as she spoke on her phone. It sounded as if she were arranging for the search of Risa's apartment for surveillance devices. She jerked her head at the door indicating it was okay for Leah to enter.

Inside, Leah found Jack in the kitchen chopping herbs with an agitated pounding motion while Dom and Risa huddled over Risa's computer. The smoke detector in the living room was down, its parts strewn over the coffee table.

"We think we found him," Risa announced when Leah approached. "The landscaper. His name was Miguel Rivera and he went missing last year, body never found."

"How do you know it's him?" Leah asked, startled by their excitement. They'd all just discovered that Risa's stalker had at the very least killed Cherise—and that he'd been watching Risa's every move—yet Dom and Risa were so calm, focused on their own investigation.

"The clues in the letter Chaos sent," Dom answered. He stopped himself. "Or is 'Chaos Killer' better, do you think? Maybe The Chaos Killer for the title and simply call him Chaos. Oh, yes, I rather like that." He sat back, his obvious pleasure at successfully branding a serial killer taking Leah aback.

"Ignore him," Risa said with a smile. "I gave all the details we've found to Detective Harper; she's checking with the Indiana police department. If I'm right—"

"We're right," Dom corrected.

"Leah, you staying for dinner?" Jack called from the kitchen.

"No, no thank you."

"Anyway," Risa continued. "We think he's buried in one of the hills of mulch or topsoil at his own landscaping place. His brother-in-law took it over after Miguel vanished, so they're all still there. According to my research, the temperature inside one of those mounds can go as high as four hundred degrees. Sometimes they'll even have a fire smoldering beneath the surface. So after all this time, there might be nothing left; even bones could be dissolved."

"But his missing person's report said he wore a white gold wedding band and had dental work, so they could find those if they sift through everything," Dominic put in.

"If some unsuspecting gardener didn't haul them home in a load of mulch."

They sounded excited as they discussed the grisly demise of the landscaper, debating the possible condition of Miguel's remains, arguing about the size of the mulch pile and how often it was turned. Leah could somewhat understand. A false front, denying the reality that a killer had been so close? But still, the casual, almost cheerful mood felt… off.

If Cliff was really the killer—even if he wasn't, he absolutely was obsessed with Risa, so maybe her half-baked theory about his causing Risa's symptoms still held? It was a long shot but wouldn't hurt to ask. "Would Cliff have had access to any food you ate?"

Risa seemed startled. "No, I don't think so. I mean, like I told the police, he's been in the apartment, but I was always here and I never saw him go into the kitchen."

"Maybe delivering groceries or takeout you ordered?"

"Jack does the shopping and the takeout guys come up—so they can get their tip."

"Okay, it was just a thought."

"We thought about it as well." Dom spread his hands wide as if evoking a cinema marquee and lowering his voice as if he were a movie announcer. "Imagine a man so obsessed he'd poison a woman to keep her near. A man obsessed enough to kill, simply to entertain her with a story to investigate." His eyes brightened. "A modern-day reverse Scheherazade. How's that for an angle?"

"Dom, stop," Risa snapped. "We don't know that that's what happened. Even if Chaos is Cliff, we can't be sure he actually killed any of the people he wrote to me about."

"We're pretty sure about the landscaper," Dom argued, not apologizing at all. "And definitely the cop's girlfriend. Plus, how else do you explain your neighbor? It's him, it's got to be. And we've got the inside track on the story of a lifetime."

"A reporter isn't supposed to be part of the story," Risa said. "I didn't ask for this, I didn't want any of what he wrote to actually be true. I mean—poor Trudy. And now Walt's in the hospital. I still can't believe it was Cliff."

"You saw the camera they found," Dom argued. "Believe it, get over it, and let's nail this story before someone else does."

Risa glared at Dom, who simply smiled in return.

Leah retreated to the kitchen, rethinking her theory. She realized that she'd gotten the timing all wrong: Risa's symptoms had begun before the stalker began to write her. And before she'd moved to Cambria City, so Cliff couldn't have caused them. Risa's illness may have triggered the stalker but otherwise was unrelated.

As Leah helped herself to a glass of water, Jack gave her a bemused smile. "Don't mind those two." He put a large pot of water onto the stove. Jack's movements around the tiny space were almost a dance; obviously he was familiar with the location of every utensil and ingredient. "When they get on the trail of a story, they're incorrigible. Get lost in their own world."

Risa had said something like that earlier, Leah remembered. "And you?"

His knuckles grew white as he wrenched a salt mill over the water with more force than the action required. "Me? I know better than to interfere. Risa, she's been in the middle of battles—actual battles with bombs and bullets. To her, this is just another story. And Dom? He's in full-on hustle mode. Knows that the first to break the story is the one who will cash in. But I won't lie. I'm frightened—" He broke off, banging the salt mill on the counter.

"You're angry she didn't tell you about the stalker sooner," Leah interpreted.

"Damn right I'm angry. It's my job to protect her." He glanced over his shoulder at Risa. Took a breath and blew it out. "Except I guess now it's the police who will be doing that. So I—" He waved his hands at the assembled ingredients. "I cook. Maybe I don't know anything about armies or wars or being shot at, but I know people need to eat."

"It's more important, in many ways, that you're here for her. She'll need that. Someone she can trust, talk to when it all hits her. It's not easy, having your life dissected by the police."

"You talk like you know—"

She grimaced. She still wasn't sure exactly how to talk about Ian to strangers. "My husband—he was murdered."

"Oh. I'm sorry." He turned away, busying himself with the food prep. "Can I ask? Did the police catch his killer? I know I won't sleep, not until they get this guy."

She didn't want to tell him that even after Ian's killer was caught the night terrors didn't get any better. Instead, she stuck to the simplest truth. "They did. Ian's killer was caught the day after Ian died."

"Good."

As he lifted three pasta bowls down from the cupboard, she asked, "Is Dom staying, then?"

"Are you kidding? With all this drama? Of course." Jack sounded bitter. "He's here all the time anyway, practically rents a suite in the hotel across the park." His knife kept up a rhythmic smack against the cutting board, mincing parsley with such vigor that tiny bits of it flew into the air. "I want her to leave, but she'll never go—not with Dom here. Too much pride. He's the one person who has always believed in her—she'll never risk letting him down or appearing weak to him. As soon as we finish eating, I'll grab my stuff from my place."

"I think Harper is arranging for the police to watch the apartment tonight," she told him. "That should help her feel safer."

"Think I'm going to trust the police to keep Risa safe? The lead detective's own fiancée was a victim and he had no clue. There's no way am I trusting her to anyone."

Leah wanted to defend Luka, but there was no arguing the truth. Chaos knew exactly what he was doing when he sent the photo of Cherise's ring to discredit Luka.

Laughter rang out from the living room where Dom was acting something out for Risa.

"He does make her laugh," Jack said with a sigh. "Better than I can. She says I'm a worrywart, but you watch. After he leaves, she'll stop pretending everything's fine. She never lets him see her symptoms, her pain."

"Does she have the same symptoms every time? I was reading her records before I got here, but they were much more complex than I imagined."

"No. There's definitely a pattern in the timing, but the symptoms are different almost every episode. Sometimes it's like a bad stomach flu, lasting a few days, sometimes migraines with muscle shakes and cold sweats, where her face turns beet red, and her breathing speeds up. Then there's all the medication—how do you know where the symptoms begin and the side effects take over?"

He was right. Especially given the variety of prescriptions Risa was juggling. "I'll cross-check their side effects, see if maybe the doctors or pharmacists missed a possible interaction."

"Thanks." He frowned and was silent as he concentrated on stirring his red sauce. The delicious aroma reminded Leah that she needed to get home to her own dinner.

"There's one other thing," Jack said in a low voice that wouldn't carry out to the others. "A few weeks ago, I found something."

"What?"

"A bottle of ipecac hidden in Risa's closet—tucked inside a pair of boots she hasn't worn in years. I looked it up, it causes—"

"Severe vomiting," Leah finished for him. Could Risa be harming herself? "Why would Risa hide the ipecac from you?"

"I don't think she's doing it to herself," he replied; his expression was both earnest and concerned as he glanced over his shoulder at Risa. "I really don't. I read about women who do that—her personality just doesn't fit. She'd never…" His words trailed away. "I mean, why? She has everything—she's smart and talented. Honestly, most days I'm not sure I deserve her. I have no idea why she's stuck around a boring guy like me. So why would someone do that to themselves? Destroy their chance at happiness?"

Leah couldn't help but glance at the wall of photos that Risa had taken. "Maybe she doesn't think she deserves it? Happiness."

"No way. If anyone deserves to be happy, it's Risa." He nodded to himself as if sealing a deal. The pasta water came to a boil. "Sure you're not staying?"

"No, but thanks. I have family waiting at home."

"See—that's all I want. Me and Risa, a home. Together. Knowing that when you open that door, there's someone waiting. Give me that and the rest of the world can go to hell, all I care. Know what I mean?"

Leah turned away, blinking hard. She'd had all that and more with Ian. But now she was alone—and worst of all, she couldn't let anyone know how she felt, the anger and fear, the guilt, the sadness that threatened to smother her some days and most nights. She couldn't even bring herself to tell her counselor everything—if she dropped the façade for a single instant, even with someone like him trying to help her, she'd never be able to pick it back up again.

"I'd better go." She crossed back to the living area. "Risa, is it okay for me to share your medical records with a colleague? She might have some helpful insights." Leah thought she'd call Maggie—the death investigator was better at puzzles like Risa's than most physicians Leah knew. Maggie had a gift for seeing details but processing them in a way that allowed her to think outside the realms of conventional wisdom. A lot like Ian that way—and Emily.

"Is she going to bill me for a consult?" Risa answered with that falsely bright tone that Leah found so jarring.

"No."

"In that case, you have my permission to share them with anyone you want. Dom keeps trying to get me to post them online, set loose the entire internet on solving my medical mystery."

Leah cleared her throat. "I'd better be going."

"Of course." Risa pushed herself up out of the chair with some effort, Dom watching from where he sat, not moving, simply watching.

"Don't get up," Leah hastened to say, but it was too late. Risa waved her off when she tried to help.

"I'm fine," Risa said through gritted teeth. "I just want to thank you, Leah. I know I've taken a lot of your time today—and things have turned out a bit crazy—but I'm really glad to have met you."

Leah couldn't help but smile. "Me, too. I'll let you know if I find anything about your symptoms. Take care."

"Thanks," Risa said, leaning against her walker as she watched Leah walk away.

Leah closed the apartment door behind her. Somehow it felt a relief to leave the tiny space that was so overcrowded with emotions. She half-expected her ears to pop with the change in pressure.

Harper said goodbye to whoever she was talking to and hung up. "They're a bunch, right? I mean, a serial killer stalking her and she's throwing a dinner party for boyfriend and whatever-the-hell that Massimo guy is. Did you notice how he never stops looking at her? Gives me the creeps just to be in the same room."

"Was that Luka?" Leah nodded to the phone.

"No. That was Sanchez—he's all set with the remote monitoring of Saliba's electronics."

"So you're sure it was Cliff? That he killed Trudy?" The stronger the case was against Cliff—or better yet, the faster they found him—the less damage done to Luka's career, Leah hoped.

"He was on scene, actually called 911. He knew about Walt, how easy it would be to trigger his emotions. Hell, he even installed the damn childproof locks, knew to open the door to get Walt out onto the landing. Who else could it have been?"

"But why send the note to Dom? And let Luka know that he also killed Cherise?"

"He wanted to buy time, forcing us to waste time chasing leads in another state. I mean the whole thing with the courier and signed note and telling Dom to bring it here in person. That kind of thing never happens in real life, is straight out of Hollywood. Vogel obviously never dreamed that we'd catch on to him so quickly—I'll bet he shit his pants when we came back with the warrant to search the whole building."

"I don't know. It all seems so—"

"Like I said, this isn't the movies. Ninety-nine point nine percent of the time, the killer is right there, in plain sight. But for Vogel to be an actual serial killer?" She bounced on her heels. "Now, that's wild."

"Not if the killer has you in his sights."

"*Luka.*" Harper sobered. "You're right. We need to watch out for the boss. Can you imagine? Losing someone you loved—" She stopped, but didn't appear chagrined, even though Leah of all people knew exactly what that kind of loss entailed. "Luka still uses a coffee mug she gave him, you know. All these years later. Bad enough the love of your life kills herself, but then to learn she was murdered?"

"They can't punish him or hold it against him, can they? I mean, I know they have to look into his life back then, but he had nothing to do with her death."

"People talk, they'll always look at him different." She glanced over the railing down to where Trudy's body had landed. "You know, when we got here this morning, Krichek was letting me act as lead, thought it was a simple accidental death. I was so excited. But now, with the boss involved, with someone he loved a victim…" She raised her hands and shrugged. "I'm not sure what to think or how to feel."

"Yeah, I know…" Leah was familiar with the unique mixture of adrenaline and dread that accompanied every major case into the ER. It was a strange tightrope to walk: balancing the thrill of saving a life with the overwhelming knowledge that these were real people—people with families, with loved ones, with hopes and dreams and prayers—and their lives rested in her hands.

They reached the elevator and hit the call button. "Will you let me know—" Leah started but wasn't certain how to finish. She didn't have the right to pry into Luka's career problems, but she also wanted to be there for him if he needed anything.

Harper shifted her feet. "Any internal investigation will be confidential."

"So there's nothing we can do to help Luka?" Leah hated the idea of standing by, doing nothing. It went against every fiber of her being.

"Didn't say that, doc." Harper's posture straightened as if she'd decided to take a chance on Leah, despite Leah being a civilian. Or more likely, she simply wasn't about to turn down anyone who could help Luka. "I'll call you if I think of anything."

"Thanks, Harper."

CHAPTER 26

Luka reached Ahearn's office just as the commander was leaving for the night. At first, Ahearn was irate—he'd been heading out to a black tie charity event, was already in his tux—but as soon as Luka painted the broad strokes of the turn of events, he'd grown quiet, sat back down in his desk chair and gestured for Luka to take a seat. "Tell me everything, from the beginning."

Ahearn listened attentively, asking a few questions—often the same questions Luka also wanted answers to—and jotting the occasional note. It reminded Luka that the commander was also a detective once.

Luka finished his recitation of the facts. He hadn't included his theories or suspicions—the situation was complicated enough already. It didn't matter that Luka had nothing to do with Cherise's death. Until they were able to prove that, the mere suspicion would allow defense attorneys to question Luka's integrity—which could be twisted to create reasonable doubt in a jury's mind. Chaos involving Luka in his web of deceit could lead to every case Luka had been a part of being reexamined and picked apart by rapacious attorneys. All the good he'd done since Cherise's death could be unraveled, guilty men walking free again.

"The press will have a field day with this," was Ahearn's first conclusion, defaulting to his role of administrator. "You can be damn sure Chaos will alert them, chum the waters to create a feeding frenzy. We have no choice but to investigate every avenue—including re-opening your fiancée's case. I'll put in a call to the Lewisburg PD as soon as we're done here."

"Yes, sir. I understand."

Ahearn's forehead creased, his gaze sharp as he scrutinized Luka. "I'm not sure you do. In this scenario you're the chum and the press and public are going to eat you alive. There's nothing the press loves more than a crooked cop to crucify. You prepared for that, Detective Sergeant? Because we can't be seen as favoring one of our own—at least not to the public. But please know, off the record, you have the department's full support."

"Thank you, sir." Luka couldn't help but wonder if learning doublespeak was mandatory once you reached his rank.

"There's nothing to thank me for. There's no way in hell I'm letting some pissant coward who throws little old ladies off balconies use a tragedy from one of my people's past to derail an investigation. This guy is not getting away with it, I promise you that."

It was a promise they both knew Ahearn couldn't keep, but still, Luka appreciated the sentiment.

The commander took a breath, tapped his pen against the notes he'd taken. "You said Saliba refused to hand over her electronics."

"Best I could do was get her to allow our cyber squad to monitor her computer remotely. We need a warrant to do more."

"Damn right we need a warrant. Not just for her computer. For all her electronics."

"I have Krichek working on it. I left Harper at the Falconer to monitor the situation." Luka had also texted Krichek a list of other high priority items, since he was now in charge of the Saliba investigation until Ahearn appointed someone to fill in for Luka.

"Good. This is going to be a multi-jurisdictional nightmare. Have we heard anything from the NYPD on the courier or the agent?"

"Dominic Massimo. No."

"Massimo. Right. Does he have an alibi or not? Is he coming in for an interview?"

"I came to you straight away, didn't want to possibly taint any aspect of the case by conducting a formal interview with Massimo."

Ahearn nodded. "Right. We'll get him in tomorrow. In the meantime, you're off this case, but not suspended or under investigation. As of now, you are a cooperating witness. I want a firewall between you and anything to do with this case—one so thick and impenetrable that no fast-talking defense attorney can tear it down in court, suggest that you were given special treatment or imply that you might be responsible for any of this. Understand, Detective Sergeant?"

His tone made it clear that the discussion was over. Luka stood at attention and nodded. "Yes, sir, Commander. You have my full cooperation."

"Good. Go home, get your affairs in order before the vultures descend. Then first thing tomorrow, I want you here for an official interview with the assistant DA, myself, and Sergeant McKinley. If you want your union rep or an attorney present, that is certainly your right. But as a witness, not a suspect, I expect you to cooperate fully and answer every question put to you." His tone made it clear that Luka had no choice. "Will that be a problem, Detective Sergeant?"

"No, sir." Luka was agreeing to have the most painful time of his life flayed open and dissected, but if he wanted to both save his career and help catch Cherise's killer, it was his only option.

"Good. Go. You have a long day ahead of you tomorrow." Ahearn waved a hand in dismissal.

Luka hesitated. This case—no, these cases, were spiraling out of control. Exactly what Chaos wanted. Someone had to fight back, look beyond the path the killer was leading them down. "Sir." He stopped. Better to ask for forgiveness than permission. He cleared his throat. "I'll see you tomorrow."

Luka left Ahearn's office and headed down the steps to the investigative floor. He needed to start fresh, be objective, follow the facts not his feelings. It was what he'd struggled to do after Cherise's death, until his overwhelming grief forced him to abandon his poet's instincts and embrace a cop's cold, hard logic.

At his office, he packed his personal possessions into a box so that McKinley could use his desk since the ERT leader didn't have an office on this floor. Luka could run his other open cases from anywhere. Then he dictated his reports for the day, including his final meeting at Risa Saliba's apartment. It felt surreal, objectively reporting on an event that he'd become personally involved in. It was as if he was talking about someone else's life, not his own.

He remembered the very first time he'd met Leah Wright. It was a few hours after she'd found her husband murdered; he'd interviewed her in her daughter's hospital room. At the time he'd marveled at her calm and control, the way she clearly and concisely answered his questions. He'd attributed it to her training as an ER physician, being able to compartmentalize her emotions, but now he truly understood the depth of that dissociation.

More than shock. More than mental control. It was denial. A refusal to accept that life had irrevocably changed. Forever.

He closed the door to his darkened office, carrying with him the only thing of importance: Cherise's mug.

This feeling, this distance, this numbness, it wasn't a mere coping mechanism, he realized. It was a matter of survival.

CHAPTER 27

By the time Leah arrived home, the rain was starting to let up, clouds thinning enough for a faint halo of moonlight to shine through. Ruby waited for her at the kitchen table, the aroma of chili scenting the air, a pile of dishes in the sink.

"Where are the kids?" Leah asked as she hung up her coat. She'd left the evidence boxes she'd picked up earlier in the car, not wanting to risk questions from Emily. "It's too early for bed."

"Not by my clock." Ruby took a sip from a rather large glass of wine. "Thank God it's supposed to stop raining tomorrow. Those two need to get outside and run off some energy."

Leah debated whether to hear the story of what happened in school from Ruby or go up to question Emily and Nate. Despite Ruby being the adult, she decided the kids' version would probably be closer to the truth. She crossed behind Ruby, noting from the dirty glasses in the sink that she'd given the kids chocolate milk. Again. While Leah didn't mind it as an occasional treat, she hated it when Ruby turned choices like that into a good guy–bad guy situation—with Leah, being the responsible adult charged with setting reasonable limits, always coming out the bad guy. "I'm going to check on them."

"Emily insisted on building a fort in her room, says they're going to sleep there. Don't be surprised if it's a mess and you might not have sheets left on your bed."

"Right." Leah walked through the rarely used formal dining room to the foyer inside the front door where the stairs were.

Through an arch opposite was the living room with its large fireplace. She glanced in, assessing the damage. Books and art materials, playing cards scattered about. A path created out of pillow and couch cushion stepping stones wove between stuffed animals posed as if they were ready to pounce on unsuspecting travelers.

She smiled at the mess. How could she not find joy in the fact that Emily and Nate could find the energy to harness their imagination, despite the trauma they'd both been through? Messes were easy to clean—two kids' broken hearts were more difficult to mend. But it was a hopeful start.

She remembered Luka's worry, urging her to protect Nate. In the moment, she'd assumed he meant physically, was worried that Chaos might target his family. But now she realized he meant more than that. He'd meant protecting Nate from the worry that Luka might be in trouble, avoiding any hint of instability. Last thing Nate needed was to lose someone else he cared about or to have his world come crashing down again.

Leah climbed the stairs, avoiding the creaky third one, and went down the hall to Emily's room. She'd recently moved out of Leah's bed, and so far had made it one whole night without waking from the night terrors that had forced Leah to crawl in with her on the narrow lower bunk of Emily's new bed.

Slowly, Leah opened the door, expecting to surprise Nate and Emily mid-giggle. But the room was silent.

The mattress from the top bunk had been moved to the floor beside the lower bunk and a sheet was tied to the top railing, creating a lean-to. It emitted a soft glow—a combination of Emily's nightlight and the fairy lights she'd had Leah string around the bunkbed frame.

Leah crouched down to peer under the sheet. A rush of pride made her put her hand to her chest—Emily, who often had trouble remembering to be kind and polite, she was so busy trying to be grown-up, had given Nate her bunk and had taken the mattress on the floor. She'd even shared a few of her new favorite stuffed animals, which were arranged along the railing and the nightstand to stand guard over them.

Blinking back tears, Leah fought the urge to crawl in beside the children. Emily's snores were deep and steady, while Nate slept on his belly, arms and legs thrown out as if they were growing too fast for him to keep them tucked under the covers. Leah leaned forward, head brushing the sheet overhead, and gave them each a kiss on the forehead before backing out and quietly closing the door.

Ruby stood in the hallway, holding her glass of wine, watching. "I was gonna go out, meet some friends, but with the rain and all, guess I'll stay in. I'll be in my room if you need anything."

"Thanks for picking them up from school. I told them to call me next time so you won't be bothered."

"No bother." Ruby took a step down the hall but turned back. "They're good kids." Then she walked away, leaving Leah to decipher her tone. Did she mean, good kids unlike Leah, who Ruby had abandoned time and again when she was a child? Or that Leah was failing at making certain Emily knew she was a good kid, now that she had to juggle twice the parenting duties and all the disciplining?

It was hard to know with Ruby. With her nothing was ever the simple truth—most of the time, it was nothing even close to the truth. Ruby's life had always revolved around Ruby—and her constant need to be the center of attention—which was why Leah was so puzzled by her comment. Maybe she was wrong, maybe Ruby was finally growing up. Or at least trying.

Puzzling over her mother's intentions and realizing she might never understand Ruby, Leah went back downstairs and retrieved the evidence boxes from the Subaru, carrying them inside to the kitchen table.

Luka needed Ian's files, but there was something else more important to Leah. Before tackling the computers, she tore open the small plastic envelope and retrieved Ian's wedding ring. It was too wide for her to wear on her finger, but she retrieved a spool of braided silk thread from the mudroom where her great-aunt Nellie used to tie bouquets of flowers. Leah hung the ring around her neck, the gold metal chill against her skin.

Then she found the box with Ian's computer, unpacked it and plugged it in, but couldn't bring herself to turn it on. Instead, she sat at the kitchen table listlessly eating a lukewarm bowl of leftover chili, not really tasting it as she stared at the dark screen.

She yearned to see what was in the computer—it was as much a part of Ian as his fingers or toes—but was also afraid that it wouldn't feel real, that seeing his words glowing on the screen would be a letdown, a reminder that he was never coming back. Finally, she dared tap the power button. The machine whirred to life with the soft exhalation of someone startled from a dream.

Tears ambushed her as the home screen filled with a photo of her and Emily. She was reading Emily a bedtime story, snuggled on Emily's old bed in their old house, surrounded by all her favorite old stuffed animals and dolls. The same bed Ian had died on.

Guilt bowed her shoulders and she had to close her eyes to stave off the dark tsunami of grief that ambushed her. She choked back bile, the chili turning rancid, churning through her gut. How long would she feel this way? The rest of her life?

A gentle rapping at the kitchen door had her jerking her head up. Luka stood there, waiting on the back porch—only company used the front door. She pushed her chair back, stood, and opened the door. The rain had finally stopped—his coat was dry and the pitter-patter that had been a constant these past few weeks as it drummed against the metal roof was silent.

"Nate up?" he asked as she stood aside to let him into the kitchen. He held a Batman knapsack in one hand—Nate's clothing, no doubt.

"No, they're both asleep."

"Already?" He seemed disappointed as he set the knapsack on a chair.

"He was asleep by the time I got home so I didn't have a chance to talk to him. How much are you going to tell him? About why you want him to stay here?"

"Not sure. I'd love it if I never have to tell him anything. It's overwhelming to me—what's a kid going to think or feel? I mean, how do I even start to explain?"

She motioned for him to sit as she brewed them both cups of tea. Luka was a fan of Nellie's cinnamon and rosehip blend and it was Leah's favorite as well. "I think," she answered as she waited for the water to heat, "a kid like Nate needs the truth more than anything."

"Right. Which truth? The one where a killer reached out after seventeen years to tell me he murdered my fiancée? Or the truth that as a cop there might always be people—past, present, and future—willing to target my family to get to me?" He leaned back, his gaze vacant as he stared at the embossed tin ceiling tiles overhead. "Honestly, I never dreamed I'd ever have a family to worry about…"

The kettle whistled and she poured the water through the strainer into their mugs, releasing a soothing aroma. "Luka Jericho, lone wolf cop prowling the streets."

He grimaced at her words. She returned to the table and took her seat, setting a mug before each of them.

"But now I've got Pops and Nate to worry about." He sat up, raising his mug to inhale deeply and then take a sip. "Maybe I'll wait before talking to Nate. Make sure I have not only the truth but also more than that—a plan, a way to move forward so he feels safe. Kid's just so damned vulnerable right now. Those Homan kids and that Ms. Driscoll aren't making things any easier."

"I have a confession to make," she said. "I went to the school. Was ready to give Ms. Driscoll a piece of my mind."

"And?"

"I'm not sure how, but she put me in my place so fast, I felt like I was the kid."

He nodded. "Right. I know the feeling. I barely got a word in edgewise."

They sipped their tea in silence. Then Luka said, "You know, when the school first called, there was this jolt through my gut. I heard 'bully' and 'Nate' in the same sentence and my first instinct wasn't to argue or disbelieve—it was disappointment."

"Because you thought he might have done it?"

"Yes. No… Because I was afraid I'd already let him down. That if he had bullied someone it was because I hadn't taught him better. And then I was angry. How could I have already given up on a kid—my sister's own flesh and blood—as quickly as the rest of the world had. As if he were disposable, not worthy. So I rushed to the school determined to stand up for Nate—"

"To fix things. I know the feeling."

"But that Ms. Driscoll, she acted as if Nate was already convicted. Then Ruby showed up and there was no more talking or discussion or negotiation. She believed—no, she *knew*—Nate and Emily hadn't done anything wrong and she just… she was like a tornado. Whisked them away, like it was in her nature to do whatever it took to protect them. No thinking, no debate, just doing."

Leah bowed her head for a long moment. "That's not the Ruby I knew as a child." She glanced up once more. "But it sounds like the mother I always dreamed of having."

"It was humbling to watch," he admitted. "Made me realize how much I need to learn. She reminded me of your great-aunt Nellie. I felt that same weird combination of awe, terror, and respect that I did whenever Nellie came by the farm."

"Talk about your forces of nature." The memory of Nellie brought a smile.

"I'm just saying—maybe Ruby has changed, is changing. After everything, with Ian, with you and Emily moving in here, maybe it's good for her, for all of you."

"You're telling me to trust her. I am, I'm trying. The way Emily loves her… It's torture, watching her open her heart to Ruby and all I can do is hold my breath, thinking of all the ways Ruby could break it."

"Maybe it's not about trust at all. Maybe it's about having a little faith. I know she's disappointed you before, broke your heart when you were a kid, but I think she's trying. And after this morning, I'm realizing that that whole 'takes a village' stuff about raising a kid—there's something to it. You can't do it alone, and neither can I."

She glanced at her face reflected in Ian's computer. It bore little resemblance to the face of the smiling mother cuddling her daughter from his desktop photo. "Honestly? I'm terrified. Maybe it's not Ruby I can't trust, but myself."

"Why?" He leaned forward, abandoning his tea, his expression earnest.

"Ruby blamed how she acted when I was a kid on depression triggered by my father's death. Depression that took her decades to get over, to the point where she abandoned me time and again when I was too much to handle. And now, after Ian, I finally understand what she felt." She sagged in her seat, didn't have the energy to sit up straight. "I'm exhausted, it's like the world is surrounded by a fog so thick I can't find a path through it. I'm lost without Ian." She glanced away, blinking hard. "What if this feeling never goes away? What if I'm just like Ruby? I don't want that for Emily, can't let her lose me as well as Ian."

"She won't." His tone was firm, not allowing for any argument. "Because you're not Ruby. First, you're already dealing with Ian's death—you're seeing a therapist, you're focusing on what's best for your daughter, you're trying to heal, not clinging to the pain. And second, you're not alone. You've got Ruby and me and Pops and Maggie and your friends at the ER. We're all here for you. All of us."

As reassuring as his words were, they couldn't ease the constant knot of fear that held her heart in a vice. She took a sip of tea but its soothing magic was gone. "I need to know: when will it get better?"

His gaze focused on the depths of his tea mug, as if he could read the future. "Know where I was this morning? Before we got called to the Falconer? I drove over the mountain to Lewisburg. Sun wasn't even up yet, rain was pouring down, fog so thick you could walk across the river on it. But I do it every year. For seventeen years now. I go to where she died, and I bring her favorite flowers." He looked up, met her gaze. "Guess I'm not the right person to ask how long before the pain goes away."

They sat in silence for a long moment. "How are you doing?" she asked. "I mean after that letter, knowing Cherise was killed—does that make it better or worse?"

"Both, I guess. Worse because I fought and argued with the police when it happened, even tried to get her folks to pay for a second autopsy—which didn't help their pain. Eventually I gave in, I let them convince me. Only that meant if she did kill herself, then it was my fault. That I missed the signs or I somehow drove her to it. God, how I beat myself up. But now, knowing the truth—"

"It means it wasn't your fault."

He nodded. "More than that. It means I can actually do something. All these years, wondering where I'd gone wrong, asking myself what I missed. Now I have something—someone—to fight. I can bring her justice."

"All we have to do is find him." She pulled Ian's laptop close. "Let's get to work."

CHAPTER 28

While they waited for more information on Cliff Vogel—which Luka hoped Krichek would be supplying soon—he and Leah spent the next several hours dissecting everything they knew about Risa's stalker and the people he claimed to have killed. Hoping to organize the wealth of information Risa had collected and translate it into actionable lines of investigation, they moved to the dining table which they covered with craft paper taken from the kids' art supplies, making lists in neon-colored markers. Despite the informal office supplies, it wasn't much different from how he led his team when approaching a new case. The main difference was that officially Luka wasn't involved—he'd need to feed any ideas they generated to his team via Krichek. Frustrating, but necessary.

"Somehow I thought police work would be more action, less talking," Leah joked as she stood back to appraise their work. "Where are the car chases and shootouts?"

They shared a grimace at that—they both knew Luka had never had to use his duty weapon until last month when he shot and killed Ian's killer.

"It's not like TV," he assured her. "Real detective work is all about the walk and talk."

"But everyone lies."

"Exactly why we talk to them more than once," Luka said, rifling through their notes. "Sooner or later they trip up. Or we keep talking to other people, widen our focus. Sooner or later someone sees something that leads us back to our actor."

"Why do you call them actors? I thought they were suspects or perps or persons of interest?"

He chuckled. "Never perp. Suspect has a negative connotation that defense attorneys can use against us, say we have tunnel vision or targeted someone, built a case to fit. Persons of interest, or subject, sometimes, but usually in reports. Actor, I guess because it's a legal term. Someone who took action."

"Another thing TV gets wrong."

"I'm sure all the medical stuff is just as bad."

"Oh yeah. Don't get me started." But she sounded distracted. "Everyone lies," she repeated. Then she snapped to attention. "Everybody lies. Especially Risa's stalker. We've been looking at this backwards."

Luka nodded for her to continue. Leah tore off a fresh sheet of paper and began making a list. "He says he only kills victims that he finds by random chance, but he killed James Santiago because he wanted to prove himself to Risa, duplicated his death to look like the Jimmy Santiago she wrote about in a story. James wasn't merely chosen by the toss of a coin; his death was staged, manipulated."

"It's on the to-do list I left for Krichek and Harper—to follow up with the South Carolina authorities. But I see where you're going. He's claiming to work at random. But these so-called gifts of his…" He gestured to the names from the list of possible victims Risa had included in her database. "They were all people with similarities to people in stories or obituaries Risa worked on. They weren't random. He targeted them because of Risa."

Leah tapped the marker against her teeth, the neon purple cap bobbing in the air. "Except, I think he lied. I mean, look at them. They're scattered all over the country and the only ones that the police were involved in was the drunk driver who died in the car crash and the old lady in the house fire. The rest died of natural causes."

"But the stalker still claimed them as his, said he made their deaths appear as if they weren't murders." Luka turned to her. "You think he lied about that as well. That he didn't actually murder them, and make their deaths appear accidental?"

"Not all of them. I mean, if it's Cliff, he's worked at the Falconer for over a decade. But somehow over the past year since he met Risa, he found time to travel all over the country, to find victims who correlated with Risa's work, and committed not one or two but a dozen perfect murders?"

"You think the killer found random people who correlated with Risa's work and used their deaths to what, pad his résumé?"

"If Cliff is Chaos, I don't see any other way. I'll bet if you check his work records, he'll have alibis for all the deaths over the past year."

"But if it is all lies and no one mentioned in Risa's letters was actually killed, are we even sure that Risa's not involved?" he asked. "Either Cliff Vogel is Chaos and is as brilliant at deception and misdirection as he said in his letters, or he's actually who he appears to be: a guy obsessed with a woman he can never have, not in his wildest dreams. Guys like that, they're easily manipulated. She could be building him up as a fictional Chaos to resurrect her career and then when she's ready, he takes the fall." One of the items on the to-do list he'd left Krichek was to verify that Risa had actually reported her stalker to the FBI's cybercrimes unit. Although simply filing a report wasn't enough to prove her stalker was real.

But Cherise's ring… Now, that was proof. How could anyone not involved with Cherise's death have gotten it?

"But if we're not trusting what anyone has told us—certainly not what Chaos put in his letters—than where do we start?" Leah asked. They stood side-by-side, taking in the maelstrom of data Risa's hunt for her stalker had created.

"First we eliminate the 'doppelgänger' victims, the ones whose names or details have been used by Chaos, but who we have no proof of having been murdered. Then we narrow in on the ones who he probably did kill." Luka began crossing names off the list.

"Santiago, for sure he killed," Leah said. "And landscape guy—he's a definite."

"We don't have confirmation," Luka reminded her, but still starred both names. "Indiana PD is going to search the manure and mulch hills tomorrow."

"You keep letting facts get in the way of my theory." She gave him a mock grimace and rolled her eyes, reminding Luka of Harper. Not that he'd ever tell Leah that. "Let's focus on what we know for sure, then. We know he's obsessed with Risa."

"And we know whoever killed Trudy didn't want anyone to see those photos from her phone." Luka made a mental note to follow up with Sanchez, the cyber squad tech. Then he remembered—he was meant to be off the case, so he couldn't ask directly. He'd have Harper get him the info; she and Sanchez were buddies. Though it was already bad enough he had Krichek and Harper feeding him information, risking censure from the brass. Damn, this was becoming a nuisance already.

"Which brings us to the one person we know he killed. He had her ring after all. You said there's no way he could have gotten hold of it unless he killed her," Leah said. "Cherise."

Luka looked away. He wasn't sure if he was ready for this, but he'd already come to the same conclusion. All roads led to Cherise.

"Why do you think he killed her?" Leah asked. "If it really was his first killing, she had to have meant something to him."

"You think he knew her?"

"Were there any signs of her being stalked at the time? Maybe she was involved with someone before you came along?"

A kaleidoscope of ancient memories swirled through Luka's vision—Cherise at the heart of each of them. Throwing one of her campus-famous "soirees" where they'd open their house to everyone; Cherise sitting at a table surrounded by their friends, beaming at each in turn. He remembered them cheering him on the first time he ever dared to get up and perform one of his poems in public. So many times and places, where she was not only the sun Luka's world revolved around, but she burned so bright, the rest of the world couldn't help stare and admire her brilliance.

He sank into one of the dining chairs, rested his head in his palms, elbows on the table. He was so tired. This case... Every time it spun in one direction, it ricocheted back to blindside him from another.

After a moment, he looked back up, the colorful notes in front of him swimming in his vision. "I can't remember anyone in particular. Cherise went out with a lot of guys before me, but she'd said none of them were ever serious. She stayed friends with a few of them, but I never suspected they could have wanted her dead. I'll forward the ones I know about to Krichek, just to cover all bases."

"If it was Cliff, he'd have been older than you guys. By—"

"Eight years," he supplied. "I definitely would have remembered someone that much older hanging around Cherise. But I'll see if he was enrolled or working on campus or nearby." He shook his head, irritated. "I mean, I'll ask Krichek. Damn it."

"The killer said he was just a kid when he killed Cherise—but if it was Cliff, then that's another lie. Which makes sense, since he manipulated everyone into believing Cherise killed herself. That's a fairly sophisticated level of thinking. Hard to imagine a kid doing that." Leah took the seat beside him, her gaze on their handiwork. "Did the autopsy find any evidence that she wasn't alone in the car that night?"

"No. The river took care of that, erased everything." He didn't bother to hide his bitterness. "Forensics came up empty."

"Why were you so certain it wasn't a suicide? You said she'd had problems, was off her meds?"

He considered that. He could've given her all the arguments he'd offered to the police back then: that Cherise was too proud to give up, not with her dreams in sight; that if she had, she'd never have been so mean, focusing the blame on him by leaving his book with the Langston Hughes poem; that she'd been acting fine, was excited, making wedding plans, plans for her future—for their future…

Except none of those were the real reason. "Honestly, I just couldn't accept that I'd been living with her, had seen her every day and I had no idea. I couldn't handle the idea that I'd missed every sign. For months after, I'd lie in bed every night dissecting those past few days and I couldn't for the life of me see what I'd missed. It tormented me, the not knowing why." His breath was ragged as he sucked it in. "I imagine her in the water, in the dark, alone, the water tugging at her, holding her down. I imagine her changing her mind. But it's too late."

"But now you know that it wasn't her fault. And not yours, either. The killer wanted you to feel guilty, to shoulder his blame." She took the seat across from him. "Because despite what he says about allowing chance to control his actions, he loves manipulating other people. For him, it's all about power and control. I mean, he's practically run Risa's life for her for a year now. He's manipulated you right off the case."

"But that means he *was* there back then, watching us, stalking Cherise. And I missed him. I never saw him, never noticed him." Luka cursed, caught in the bitter shadows of memory. "If so, then it was my fault that he got to her. And I never even knew that he was right there."

CHAPTER 29

Luka ended up sleeping on Leah's couch—by the time they had finished dissecting the case, it was late, and they were both exhausted.

They'd gone over everyone from college that Luka could remember, and even a few he didn't whom they'd found via an alumni message board. Cherise's friend who'd hosted their study group that last night had created a memorial website for her. It pained Luka to see all the hearts and prayer hand emojis filling the screen. He didn't know most of these people—and was certain Cherise hadn't either. But he diligently checked all their names, finding no one who seemed suspicious, and forwarded them all to Krichek for full background checks.

He woke early as sunlight was beginning to crawl through the windows, showered and dressed in the mudroom. Leah's great-aunt Nellie had installed a washer, dryer, toilet, laundry sink, and a small shower in a location convenient to both the back porch and the kitchen since her work had meant she was always out in the flower fields or making chocolate and candles.

Luka had visited Nellie's home a few times as a kid when he spent summers with his grandparents, but he remembered her more from her trips out to Jericho Fields. She'd come during the harvest, the orchard dripping with apples, and she and his gran would create the most marvelous concoctions using Jericho apples, Nellie's lavender and roses, and, of course, chocolate. They sold them at all the nearby fall carnivals, Amish auctions, and county fairs.

When he was a kid, he'd be on the lookout for Nellie's rickety old green truck and would run to greet her, knowing his efforts would be rewarded with a piece of chocolate. No matter the weather, she always looked the same—red hair escaping her sun hat, flannel shirt, jeans, work boots. He hadn't seen her in over a decade before her death, but somehow in his mind she lived on, kept alive by his childhood memories.

Now, he wished he'd spent more time at his grandparents' farm when he was a kid. Since he was several years older than Leah, he had never met her during the time Leah lived with Nellie after Ruby left for good. Leah was eleven then and Luka would have been fourteen, much too old to leave Pittsburgh and his friends to come hang out with his grandparents. He'd been such an arrogant brat back then—like most teenaged boys.

As he tied his tie, he couldn't help but think of Nate sleeping upstairs. How would he remember this time after being torn from everything and everyone he knew? It was already clear he saw Luka more as a cop than a surrogate father. No matter. Luka was determined to give Nate a childhood that one day he could look back on and smile at. Just like what Luka had.

Luka finished dressing, folded the quilt and sheets Leah had given him, then grabbed his bag and keys. He hesitated at the bottom of the stairs, his gaze climbing to where Nate slept. Should he talk to him, warn him about what he might hear about the case?

With a sigh, Luka turned away. Better to let the boy sleep while he could. There were no TVs in Nellie's house—neither Ruby nor Leah had brought any in after they moved here, honoring the dead woman's wishes—so maybe Nate wouldn't even hear about it. Why not protect the kid for as long as possible?

Luka left, the kitchen door latching behind him with a quiet click.

Nellie's farm was only a quarter mile beyond the city limits, but because of the winding topography of the river and the hills, it took over twelve minutes for him to drive the four miles to the police department downtown. Even with no traffic on a Saturday morning, it was almost eight by the time Luka arrived for his meeting with Ahearn. He parked and walked to the staff entrance, pausing to regard the latest efforts of the mystery gardener. The rain had stopped and the clouds were clearing, leaving blue sky in their wake, so he'd expected the small corner of color to be even more brilliant this morning.

Instead, he was greeted with a pile of sodden trash and dead leaves that perfectly matched his mood. The downspout that fed into the corner and the gutters it was connected to had finally surrendered and overflowed. Someone had cleared the sidewalk of the debris by sweeping it all into the corner, over the tiny flowers. The irony of the blue skies above and the dead mud smothering spring's hope below was not lost on Luka. He could only hope it wasn't a harbinger of his own fate.

By the time he reached Ahearn's office on the fifth floor, he was three minutes early for their meeting. But when he opened the door to the conference room, he was the last one to arrive. Ahearn sat at the head of the table, a videographer was setting up her camera in one corner, the ADA was to Ahearn's right, while McKinley sat on his left, both using the seat beside them as coatracks, leaving Luka a seat at the far end of the table, as if in quarantine.

"Are we waiting for anyone?" Ahearn asked. "Your union rep or attorney?"

"No, sir." Luka took his time removing his coat, folding it over the chair back, and retrieved his notes and laptop. Finally, after enough time had passed to make it clear that he was here because he wanted to be here, not because of any summons from on high, he sat down.

"Now then," McKinley took the lead, "why don't you start at the beginning and tell us about your involvement with Cherise Sumner."

Luka took a deep breath, held Cherise's image firmly fixed in his mind, and began. "She was my fiancée. She died our senior year of college. We were both undergrads at Bucknell in Lewisburg."

He kept to the facts, reciting everything he had told the police seventeen years ago, only this time he maintained an emotional distance, as if he were an objective observer rather than the man whose life had been shattered and put back together, with missing pieces never to be found again. He hated knowing that the killer wanted him here, wasting his time, wasting everyone's time, distracting them all from the real work at hand. All he could hope was that his team was having more success.

"Sir, we should be focused on finding her killer—the man who sent the photo of her ring," Luka said.

"We as a department are absolutely focused on finding your fiancée's killer," Ahearn answered. "As are the Lewisburg police and the state police. But, in this room right now, our focus is on damage control. Finding any weakness or flaws that could be used against us once this becomes public."

Meaning weakness or flaws in Luka's story and his actions handling Trudy's case.

"It's our job to plug those holes before they can hurt the case we'll be eventually building against the killer," the ADA added in a slightly kinder, gentler tone.

"Continue," Ahearn ordered.

Luka finished giving them the background on his and Cherise's relationship. McKinley turned things over to the ADA. She grilled him relentlessly, comparing his answers to the statement he'd given the Lewisburg police seventeen years ago. When she was satisfied that he hadn't changed his story and couldn't catch him in any contradictions, Ahearn waded in, meticulously combing through the police report as well as the coroner's findings.

"You knew she had a history of depression, but not that she'd stopped taking her medication?"

"Correct."

"But you were living together. How could you not know?"

Luka stifled his flinch. Ahearn couldn't know it, but he echoed the exact words Cherise's father had flung at him when the officials closed the case as suicide. At the time Luka had still been fighting for them to keep it open, investigate it as a possible homicide. But there'd been absolutely no evidence to suggest foul play or anyone else's involvement, leaving the blame for Cherise's death to fall on Luka.

Before Luka could respond, there was a knock on the door and Krichek poked his head in. "Just to let you know, sir," he said, not specifying which superior he was addressing, "Dominic Massimo failed to show up for his interview. He's not at his hotel, his car is gone, and his cell phone has been turned off. He's in the wind."

CHAPTER 30

It had been years since Leah had stayed up most of the night talking to anyone other than Ian. When she had finally crawled into bed, her brain was spinning with all the various ideas she and Luka had generated for the case. It had felt good to be useful—and hopefully it had helped Luka not feel as frustrated about being sidelined. He'd sent his team a list of possible avenues of investigation. It seemed that police work wasn't all that different from medicine. Create a list of possible diagnoses, eliminate what you could, start testing for the rest. But then came the most difficult part: waiting for answers.

Which made her think of their other mystery, the one she could maybe solve: Risa's medical symptoms. She finally closed her eyes, diagnoses dancing in her mind, and created a list to check Risa's records against. All those abnormal but contradictory lab tests. What had been missed? Could Risa be self-harming? The ipecac Jack had found would cause some of her symptoms but not all of them. Was she fabricating the rest?

Leah had tossed and turned all night. Her arm kept searching out the cold, empty half of the bed—Ian's side, that until a few nights ago had been filled by Emily's warmth. Finally, she curled up in the center of the bed, hugging a pillow, and drifted off.

Only to be awakened when a girl-sized planet spun off its axis and hurled itself onto Leah. "Daddy's back! Daddy's back!" Emily shouted gleefully into Leah's ear, first one then the other. Her palms squished Leah's cheeks between them as she bounced on Leah's chest. "Mommy, he's back, he's here! He found us!"

Leah slit one eye open and grunted in response. Emily's face was pressed against hers, nose to nose. She blinked and rolled Emily off her so she could breathe. "What?"

"Daddy. He's here." Emily was kneeling beside Leah but still managed to bounce the bed hard enough to rock the headboard into the wall. Then she peered at Leah. "Wait. You already knew." She tugged at Ian's ring hanging from Leah's neck. "Why didn't you wake me?"

Her mind still blurry, Leah clasped Emily's hand holding the ring. Oh hell. She should have seen this coming. "Honey—"

"Mommy, he's here. I saw his computer on the table and then he brought my computer and my iPad and my Xbox back, too. It's like Christmas all over again." More bouncing. Leah caught Emily by the waist and drew her into a tight hug. Emily traced Leah's cheek and lips with her finger. "Mommy, what's wrong? Why aren't you happy? Daddy's back. Now we can all go home," she continued in a singsong voice. "Now everything can go back to the way it was." Leah remained silent, hugging Emily even tighter. Emily's face softened and Leah felt her fantasy slip away in the way her body went slack.

Still Emily tried one last time. "Daddy's home and we don't need to cry anymore..." Finally her tears choked her, and she flung her arms around Leah's neck, sobbing into her shoulder.

"I'm sorry, baby. We talked about this, you know Daddy's not coming back. Not like it was."

"But I saw—"

"I stopped by the old house. The police returned your computers, so I brought them here. I was going to tell you, but you were already asleep when I got home."

"We built a fort. I dreamed Daddy came and helped. He likes Nate. Says I'm lucky to have a friend like him." She rubbed her nose in Leah's hair. "I miss him," she whispered. "I want him back. Why'd he have to go away and die?"

"I miss him, too, pumpkin. But he's always here. You know that." Leah shifted Emily's weight until they were face to face once again. "Daddy is here." She placed a palm on Emily's heart. "And here." Her other hand went to her own heart. "Forever."

Emily raised her own hands to cover Leah's and nodded solemnly. "Even if I can't remember sometimes? Even if I can only see him in my dreams?"

"No matter what. He's never leaving you." But Emily was right, it wasn't fair to her not to have more reminders of her father in plain sight, even if every time Leah saw a picture of Ian, it shattered her heart all over again. *Be strong. For Em.* That had to be her mantra. She could break down and deal with her own emotions later. Like after Emily went to college or something. But right now, Leah was all Emily had. She couldn't let her down. "Tell you what. I'll try to go over to the house today and bring back pictures of Daddy. Then you can decide where they should go."

Emily nodded at that. "Can I come? I miss our old house. I want Huggybear and all my other animals and my PJs—the softy, soft ones with the pretty ballerinas. And I need—"

"Honey, I don't think you can come. Besides, you're grounded—Luka told me what you did to those boys and what you said to Ms. Driscoll."

"But they were picking on Nate. They stole his great-great's army medal. They're bad guys and bad guys need to go to jail!" Her indignation had her bouncing again. Leah decided this wasn't the time for a lesson on the nuances of dispensing justice—not with her daughter's tears still wet on her face.

"We'll talk about it later. Right now, I need to shower and wash your boogers out of my hair, and you need to go be a good hostess to your guest. You remember what that means?"

"Let Nate play any game he wants, don't fight over toys, and he gets to choose what he wants for breakfast first, even if there's almost no Sugar Loops left and only one piece of cinny bread."

Leah sighed. She'd meant to stop at the store on her way home last night. One week on the job and she was already failing as a working single mom. "Make me a list. Two of them. One for what you want from the house and one for shopping. I'll be down to help you with the spelling in a few minutes. Okay?"

Emily bobbed her head and jumped off the bed. "I'm gonna show Nate my tablet with the games Daddy and I programmed." She was out the door, a blitz of bright color and motion.

Leah sighed. She needed to do better. It was just so hard—as if gravity was weighing her down more than the rest of the world. Most mornings she could barely make it out of bed, had to force herself to shower and brush her teeth. But she did it. And she'd keep doing it. For Emily. But if the hours she'd put in yesterday were any indication, then this new job might not be the solution she'd thought it would be. Unless she limited herself to only the administrative aspects—but then she'd be miserable and surely would bring home her frustrations to Emily as well. She needed to learn how to create a balance—one that tilted toward Emily, no matter what. After all, it wasn't as if she was a detective or would actually find a killer. Her job was simply to advise. To facilitate. That was all.

She'd just finished getting dressed, her hair still wet as she pulled on jeans and a fleece top—the sun might be finally shining, but it was still March and they'd be lucky if the thermometer made it past fifty—when her phone rang. It was Jack O'Brien.

"Leah? I'm sorry, I know it's Saturday, but I didn't know who else to call and Risa won't let me take her—" His words tumbled over each other, he was so agitated.

"Slow down, Jack. What's wrong?"

"It's Risa. She's been sick all night. I've tried everything, I don't know what else to do. Could you come over? Please?"

Leah blew out her breath. "Is she awake? Can I talk with her?"

"She hasn't slept at all. Vomiting and nausea. I've gotten sips of electrolytes into her, so I don't think she's dehydrated—not yet. But I just—" His voice broke. "It just never stops. I can't—she can't take much more. She's in so much pain, she tries to hide it, but I can tell. I just... I don't know what else to do. I've tried everything." Jack sounded close to tears himself.

"Keep up with the fluids, small sips every few minutes. If she gets worse before I get there, promise me you'll call an ambulance. I'm on my way."

CHAPTER 31

When Leah reached Risa's apartment she had to show her ID to an uniformed officer before he let her get close enough to knock. It was Jack who opened the door. "She seems better now," he said as he led her into the living room. "No more vomiting, at least."

Leah paused, observing her patient. If this was "better" then she wished Jack had called sooner. Risa was pale, shaking so badly that she had to hold her mug with both hands, and sweat stained the T-shirt she wore over a pair of leggings. She raised the mug to her lips but instead of drinking from it, she spat into it, then wiped even more drool from her mouth with a washcloth. Finally, she seemed to notice Leah standing there, holding her knapsack containing her medical gear.

"I told him not to call you." Risa's voice was flat with fatigue. She closed her eyes and curled up in the chair. "I'm fine."

Leah approached her, glancing into the mug Risa clutched, then at her patient. Despite her vomiting, Risa's lips were moist—in fact, she seemed to be swallowing frequently. "Headache?" Leah asked.

Risa simply nodded, her eyes still closed. She raised the mug and spat again.

"Does that happen often? The spitting?" Leah tapped the mug and Risa looked at Leah wearily. Her eyes were red, her pulse strong but rapid as Leah closed her fingers around Risa's wrist.

"Sorry." Risa set the mug on the table beside her. "I know it's gross, I can't help it."

"Excessive salivation, it's a pretty specific symptom."

"It's new, only happened a few times," Risa mumbled.

"Not yesterday when I saw you," Leah said. "You weren't as sweaty then either."

"Yesterday was more like usual—the medicine works better when it's like usual."

"Zofran," Jack volunteered. "The doctor gave it for her nausea and it usually helps the headaches as well."

"Not so much this time, but whatever it was, I'm feeling better."

"Any diarrhea? Or just the nausea and vomiting?"

"No diarrhea. The vomiting stopped, but I'm still nauseated."

"When did it start?" Leah asked.

"The nausea hit her a little bit after dinner," Jack answered.

"Later than that," Risa said. "Dom had already left, right? At least I think so."

"What did you have for dinner?"

"The pasta you saw me making—we all had it," Jack said. "Dom and I had wine, Risa just tea." He stopped. "Risa, I opened the wine and poured it, I remember that. But I didn't get you your tea."

"Dom got it for me." Risa frowned as she saw Jack's expression close down.

"Of course he did." He turned to Leah. "You know how I said I thought there was a pattern to Risa's episodes? She gets worse every time Dom visits."

Leah blinked. Did he seriously suspect Dom of poisoning Risa? "Risa, is that true?"

"What? No. You're both crazy. Dom would never—"

"Why?" Jack snapped. "Because he's your friend? Because he's stuck by you when you stopped taking all those high-paying dangerous assignments and the money stopped flowing in? Don't you get it? He's not your friend, you're his money-maker and that's all he cares about."

"But I said no to those jobs before I got sick," Risa protested.

"So maybe he's punishing you for it. Or is using your illness to turn you into a spectacle he can cash in on. I don't trust him." It was clear this was an argument that Jack had been building to for a long time. "I don't think he's good for you. There. I said it."

"You think—" Her eyes went wide. "No. Why would Dom want to hurt me? How does that benefit him at all?"

"It's that damn book. If you're sick that's one more publicity angle to help him sell it."

Risa shook her head. "But it's because I've been sick that I haven't been able to finish the book. You can't have it both ways."

"Hang on," Leah interjected, feeling like a referee. "Let's slow down and focus on Risa and what's happening now. The symptoms you have today fit a few toxins—"

"Toxins?" Jack's voice rose to near shouting. "You mean poison—"

"Wait, wait." Leah let her voice rise to match his but then lowered it. She took a deep breath and he followed. "Let's think this through. If Dom—or anyone—did this, then they either brought the toxin with them or they found it here. Any pesticides, bug sprays, plant sprays in the house?"

"No," Risa said. "I'm not good with plants."

"There's that mold killer stuff for the bathroom," Jack said. "Would that—no, different chemicals." As he calmed down, his expression cleared. "You're thinking organophosphates or carbamates, aren't you?" Leah remembered he was an environmental chemist. "No, nothing like that in the apartment. Besides, it would need to be a commercial product, like what professional landscapers use."

"Landscaper?" Risa sat up straight. "Like the man killed in Indiana?"

"The man missing in Indiana," Leah corrected, Luka's voice in her head. She wondered if, with him off the case, someone would still be following up on the search. She hoped so. "Another possibility is nicotine. Do either of you smoke?"

"No," Risa said. Then she let out a long exhalation, her shoulders sagging. "But Dom vapes."

"Wait." Jack crossed into the kitchen, returning with a small trash can. "I saw something—" He rummaged through the garbage, then held up a tiny cartridge. "I think this is his."

Too bad Jack had just put his own prints all over it, Leah thought, knowing Luka would be frustrated at that. "Risa, how about if we go to the ER and get you tested?"

"Wouldn't a toxin have showed up in my other tests?"

"Nicotine has a short half-life. It would have already been out of your system by the time your doctors ordered any toxicology tests. Plus, they would have had to ask the lab to look for nicotine specifically."

"C'mon, Risa. One more test, you can do it," Jack urged, taking her arm as she tried to push out of the chair. "I'll help you get dressed."

Risa's phone chimed. They all pivoted to where it sat on the table. "Unknown number," Risa read from the screen, her voice barely above a whisper. Leah handed her the phone and they all gathered around it as Risa began the screen recording app Ian had installed for her. Even with it, Leah was glad that the police were watching everything that came through Risa's phone and computer.

Then Risa tapped the message.

It was a video. Although the timestamp showed that it was being livestreamed, the location was dark; eerie shades of grey and white appeared to be reflections on rushing water. Then the image shifted, and a white blur shaped like a body slowly came into focus. It was a man, naked, gagged and bound, lying on his stomach, hogtied, his limbs contorted behind him.

At first Leah thought he was dead. But then water surged around him, the small space he was confined in filling fast. He kicked against his bonds, struggling to lift his torso higher out of the water. Already, in the few seconds the video had gone live, water seeped several inches up his thighs. He thrashed, his head colliding with some unseen obstacle, forcing him to remain bent in an unnatural position, his face hidden from the camera.

At the corner of the screen was a countdown clock. It had twenty-nine minutes and fourteen seconds remaining. Thirteen, twelve…

Then another chime as a text appeared.

Ready for the endgame? Be the hero I know you were in the beginning. Save him. Your devoted, Chaos.

CHAPTER 32

Before Krichek could begin to detail his efforts to locate Dominic Massimo, Luka's phone buzzed, as did Krichek's and McKinley's. Luka peered at his phone. A group text from Sanchez, the cyber tech.

Livestream intercepted. New victim. Still alive.

Both he and Krichek were halfway out the door before he realized Ahearn was shouting his name. Luka gestured for Krichek to go and then turned around.

"Sir, I might be of assistance—" he started, desperate to be allowed to be involved in the case in some way.

"Background only," the commander growled. "And everything goes through McKinley."

Good enough. Luka could interpret "background" to mean almost anything—exactly why Ahearn had phrased it that way. Luka didn't wait for the elevator but dashed down the steps toward the cyber squad's basement offices. He wondered why Ahearn didn't want to see for himself, and realized if things went south the commander would have plausible deniability by distancing himself. For a moment he almost pitied McKinley, who would bear the brunt of any backlash, but then he focused fully on the task at hand.

"Fill me in," Luka said once he'd caught up with Krichek. Last they spoke, Krichek had still been waiting for vital information on

Vogel's background last night. Especially his military service record: Vogel hadn't been in the army as Chaos had claimed to have been, but had served in the navy. Despite automation, databases under the control of government entities still required humans to query them and release the results, which meant waiting.

Krichek was talking on his phone as they continued their jog down the stairs but quickly hung up. "No reported sightings of Vogel. Talked to people at his old address, nothing there. Best we can tell he's been living in his office at the Falconer last few months. No wants, no warrants, never been in any trouble. Tenants at the Falconer say he's a bit slow but friendly; they talk like he's as much a part of the building as the light fixtures— essential but invisible."

"Did we get his service record yet?"

"No. I put a rush on the request." Not that that meant much to the military.

"Has Vogel ever lived or worked near Lewisburg?"

"No. He's been here in Cambria City for the past eleven years, working at the Falconer. We haven't been able to trace anything before that. I'm hoping his military records will fill in the gaps."

They arrived at the basement level that housed the cyber squad, the PD's gym and indoor firing range, along with the records department. Sanchez was anxiously awaiting their arrival. "I don't know what to do," he greeted them in a breathless tone as they dashed through the maze of empty workstations to a large video screen. "I can't find—"

Luka pulled up short at the image filling the screen. A man, naked, hog-tied in a narrow, enclosed and darkened space with water rushing in from below. His face was in shadows but his scalp appeared to be shaved. His shoulders contorted in pain as he fought against his restraints. A countdown below him read: twenty-seven minutes, three seconds.

"Any way you can trace the camera feed?" Luka asked.

"No. I've been trying everything." Sanchez sank into the chair behind a computer monitor, his gaze fixated on his keyboard. "Damn it!"

"Take a breath," Luka instructed as his phone rang. He handed it to Krichek to deal with. "Tell me what you do know."

"It's been re-routed and bounced around the globe and back. There's no GIS info either so we can't use that to pinpoint the location."

Krichek held out Luka's phone. "I've got Dr. Wright. She's with Risa Saliba and Jack O'Brien, watching on Saliba's phone."

Luka took his phone back as McKinley burst into the room. He quickly assessed the situation and nodded to Luka. The ERT commander was smart enough to let Luka do his job—McKinley had never worked investigations.

"Leah, do either of them recognize the man?" Luka was pretty sure he did, but the night vision camera in the dark trunk revealed too little detail for him to be certain.

"Risa is certain it's Dominic Massimo. We just tried to call him and he's not answering."

"Okay. Hang on in case I need you." He turned to Sanchez. "See if you can track Dominic Massimo's cell. Krichek, get Harper and some uniforms over to his hotel room."

"McKinley, that look like a car trunk to you?" Damn image was so dark, it was difficult to make out background details. "Look at how the metal curves."

"Yeah, I'd say American, large sedan. Hard to tell more from this angle."

"What's Vogel drive?" Luka asked Krichek.

"2004 Honda Civic."

McKinley squinted at the image. "Too big for a Honda. What's Massimo drive?"

"Hang on a moment." Krichek pulled up the information from the NCIC database. "Black Town Car."

"Bingo," McKinley breathed, bouncing on his toes, ready for action. He was texting on his phone, no doubt calling his team in.

Luka had a sinking feeling they wouldn't be needed. The countdown kept ticking, relentless. Twenty-two forty-one. A shudder raced down his spine.

"Pull up the VIN info on Massimo's car," he instructed Sanchez. "Contact whatever navigation service he uses and see if we can ping the car for a GPS location."

"On it." Krichek dialed his phone.

Luka paced between the workstations, thinking about the text sent to Risa. The killer's last message had been addressed to Risa but was meant for Luka—could this one be as well? If so, then Chaos had to be referencing the beginning of everything: Cherise's death.

"Krichek, who have you been coordinating with in Lewisburg PD? We need them to send everyone they have to search along River Road, but focus on the area across from the sewer plant first. That's where they found Cherise."

"I've got the State Police Troop F's commander on speed dial," McKinley volunteered, dialing his own phone. Leaving Luka with nothing to do but watch and wait, trying to send telepathic messages of hope to the struggling, terrified man. His first impression of Dominic Massimo hadn't been favorable, but that didn't mean he deserved to die.

"Why Dom?" he wondered. His phone rang. Harper.

"Boss." She sounded out of breath. "Massimo's room shows signs of a struggle and his car is missing from the hotel garage."

"Call in the crime scene techs and start reviewing any security footage they have."

"Staties are mobilizing, but they're at least fifteen out," McKinley said. "Are we sure we're sending them to the right place?"

"It's where he killed Cherise," Luka said through gritted teeth. "Why repeat his MO if not to send a message?"

"Except the message wasn't to you, it was to Saliba." Krichek nodded to the text. "Is there some place near here where she was a hero? Or maybe she should've been a hero but wasn't? Something personal to her?"

Luka grimaced—he should have thought of that himself, but he'd been too caught up in memories of Cherise's death. He raised his phone only to hear Leah repeating Krichek's question to Risa. A few moments later she came back on the line. "Risa says no. She can't think of anything that might fit. There's also nothing to tie her to any specific location in Pennsylvania. She only moved here after she got sick, barely knows anyone here other than Jack and her neighbors and doctors."

"Thanks," Luka told her, grateful at how thorough she'd been. The countdown passed nineteen minutes. "Listen, if this gets close—"

"I've taken the phone from her so she can't watch," Leah assured him. "She didn't like it—she's a reporter, said she's seen worse."

"Not the same, believe me. Stay on the line." He turned to Sanchez. "Can you tap into any traffic cameras over in Lewisburg? Especially along the river?" Luka doubted there were many. Outside of downtown and campus, the area around Lewisburg was rural, similar to Cambria City, with few homes and businesses. Plus, the riverbank was steep and forested—a car in the water could easily be missed from the road.

As he waited, the countdown continued. The water was now surging up to the man's chest and Luka feared the time on the clock might be an overestimation of how long he had left. The man was thrashing, rocking his body side to side, obviously fighting to free his hands. But still the water kept coming and the seconds kept ticking away.

"Leah," he said into his phone. "Who's there with you?"

"Just Risa and Jack."

"You were there with both of them when the video went live?"

"Yes." Giving both Risa and Jack alibis. And Walt couldn't have done it; he was still in the hospital's locked neuro-psych ward. Which left Vogel as their main suspect. The man must be a brilliant actor, was all Luka could think. "Ask them if they ever saw Cliff and Dom interacting."

Nothing about this case felt right. He was missing something. What had the message said? *Endgame... hero... beginning.* That all pointed to Cherise and how she died. Except Luka never really had a chance to be a hero for her, never had a chance to save her.

Leah eventually replied, "Jack says he saw Dom and Cliff arguing a few weeks ago. I guess Risa had given Dom a key to the Falconer so she wouldn't need to buzz him up every time he visited and Cliff didn't like the idea. Said keys were for residents and immediate family only. Jack didn't catch it all, but he heard Dom threaten to get Cliff fired." She lowered her voice. "Do you really think that's Dom in the car?"

"His hotel room showed signs of a struggle and his car is gone."

Her tone turned grim. "Luka, you need to tell the searchers, if he's in the river, the water will be cold, might buy us some time. They can't give up."

Luka relayed the message to the others.

Sanchez and Krichek called out reports as they came in, but it was all bad news. The clock passed eleven minutes. Despite his best efforts, the water was up to the man's shoulders. "Leah?"

"I'm here."

"Any thoughts why this guy thinks Risa could save Dom? Beyond her knowing him? I mean, 'be the hero I know you were,' that sounds very personal and specific."

Leah paused. "Maybe to torture her? He blames her that he has to change his plans because of the police investigation of Trudy's death. Maybe he wants her to feel guilty if Dom dies?"

"If so, then—"

"It's not just Risa he's upset with. It's you as well. He knew Risa's electronics would be monitored, knew she'd call you right away even if they weren't. I think it's all a show. Designed to demonstrate his power over Risa but more importantly—"

"His power over me," Luka said in a grim tone. "That message. It's not just to me, it's about me. Not Cherise. A hero in the beginning— Hang on…" He turned to McKinley. "Get everyone you can out to the wharf."

"What wharf? Here in Cambria City?"

"Pier three—no, no, pier four." Luka closed his eyes, straining to remember. He'd just finished his field training, was only days patrolling solo. "Sanchez can you pull that area up on the screen?"

The tech tapped his keyboard and a Google Earth image appeared. "It was fourteen years ago," Luka said, scrutinizing the image. "A college kid OD'd outside a warehouse on the wharf. His friends thought he was dead and ditched him. I found him, gave him Narcan, but while we were waiting for the medics, he freaked out, jumped into the water. Almost drowned. I had to fish him out." He pointed to the spot on the image. "Here. Right here. First time I had my picture in the paper." First time anyone called him a hero.

"Pull up any CCTV from that area," McKinley ordered as he called his team.

"Just a few traffic cams, but they're over a block away," Sanchez said. "This is the best I can do." The image shifted, revealing the street that ran along the wharf, but no clear image of the pier. "Wait. Let me scan the recent traffic."

On the screen the man still struggled, fighting to keep his head above the water. It crept up his neck, relentless.

"How could he get a car onto the pier and dump it in the river with no one seeing?" Krichek asked. "It may be Saturday, but there are still workers down there and it's broad daylight. Someone would have seen something."

"Nothing on traffic cams in the area," Sanchez put in. "No black Town Cars down there anytime this morning."

Damn. Another wild goose chase. Luka turned away. He'd failed, just like he'd failed Cherise. All he could do was act as a futile witness.

The car lurched, the water surging. There were still three minutes on the clock when the water lapped up over the camera lens and the screen went black.

CHAPTER 33

Luka couldn't remember ever feeling so useless. McKinley and his men were out searching, Sanchez had called in his fellow techs to analyze every frame of the video as well as Risa's electronics, while Krichek was coordinating the various warrants they'd need along with maintaining communication with all the jurisdictions now involved in the search for Dominic Massimo.

"Luka? Are they close? Any word?" Leah asked. He'd almost forgotten she was still on the phone line.

"Nothing, no sightings. They're widening the search. I should have known he wouldn't make it easy, use the same spot where Cherise—" As Luka glanced around the room at the men busy trying to save a stranger's life, he realized that maybe he was the one who stood at a distance. As if a sudden chasm separated the rest of the world from him. He'd had this feeling before. After Cherise died.

"Maybe when the car lurched the water rose where the camera was but lowered on his side?" Leah suggested, pulling his focus back to the here and now. "If there was an air pocket, he could still be alive. They aren't giving up, are they?"

"No. McKinley has his men searching here and the staties and guys over in Lewisburg will keep looking there as well. But there's a lot of rivers, streams, lakes to cover and it's starting to feel like he's leading us on a wild goose chase."

"Which means he's loving all this. Probably has a police scanner, is following what you're doing," Leah said, the frustration filling her voice matching his own.

"McKinley is sending Harper over with a warrant for all of Risa's electronics and a full search of her apartment. She'll need to come in for an interview. Make sure she doesn't try to play Nancy Drew and hold out on us, will you?"

"After that video, believe me, she wants to help," Leah reassured him. "What if the killer comes after her? Can you place her in protective custody or something?"

"No. Sorry. We don't have the budget for that. Not unless she wants to camp out in my office, since I'm not using it for the duration. How's she doing?"

"She was sick all night—it sounds like nicotine poisoning to me. I'd like to take her to the ER to be tested."

How the hell could someone have reached Risa last night? Luka wondered. Vogel had been long gone by then. Krichek and Harper had searched the apartment, removed the two cameras they'd found, and hadn't found any other surveillance equipment, plus there had been patrolmen inside the Falconer all night. Maybe the poison had already been inside the apartment? He made a note to have the techs test Risa's food once they got the search warrant. "Is she okay?"

"Yes, pretty much all the symptoms are gone now."

"Go ahead, get her tested and checked out. But make it quick. Stay with her, document everything. I'll talk to McKinley, see if he'll let you take the lead with her interview. She'll respond to you better than him."

Leah hung up, leaving Luka with nothing to do other than to think, to try to gain perspective and see where they'd gone wrong. Sanchez and the other techs ignored him as he continued to pace the cramped cyber squad quarters, but every time he caught a glimpse of footage of the trapped man replaying on their screens, it only frustrated him more, so he finally fled outside where he'd have room to think.

It was hard to believe that a sky this vibrant and blue could also be sheltering a wanton killer, he thought as he turned his face to the sun, allowing the warmth to sink deep into his skin. When he looked down again, he noticed the secret gardener's bedraggled attempt at inviting color into the drab surroundings. His mind racing, shifting through the various permutations of the case, he grabbed the small folding shovel he kept in the toolbox in his truck bed and carefully sifted through the debris covering the flowers. Hard work was the best way to declutter a busy mind, his gran used to tell him before setting him to work at Jericho Fields. He could almost smell the sweet-vinegary perfume of apples in the cider press even now.

The tiny flowers emerged, a few stems broken, but most of them simply bowed beneath the weight of the debris from the overflowing roof gutters. Again, that sensation of being distanced from the physical world threatened to overwhelm Luka. If Dom died... No, he couldn't think like that. He'd done everything in his power to save the man.

But had he? Chaos obviously thought either Luka or Risa should be clever enough to unravel the riddle in his text. Maybe it wasn't about something in their past, but something in the present? He crouched and finished with his fingers, lifting each bloom and leaf above the mud, then using the dead leaves to support the flowers. The whole job only took a few minutes, but by the time he finished it almost looked like a proper flower bed.

He returned the shovel to his truck and was walking back to the building when a glint of sunlight bouncing off a vehicle mirror caught his eye. A reflection, misdirection. What had Leah said last night? About control?

Chaos was controlling, manipulating them all now. Directing—no, misdirecting—them to look where he wanted them to look. *Welcome to the endgame*, his message said. As if this was a game of chess, with people's lives sacrificed like pawns. Luka opened the door back into the building, and missed the warmth of the sun instantly.

Pawns. A game. *Chess.* Energy surged through him as he jogged down the steps to the cyber squad's office. "Sanchez, pull up that image of the area around Pier Four again." Where Luka's career had really started.

"ERT checked the wharf out—all of it," Krichek argued, a phone in each hand, but apparently on hold on both. "There's no one there."

"Just do it," Luka ordered Sanchez. A moment later the image appeared. "Zoom in over here and pan slowly. Across the river, opposite from the pier." Warped reflections, truths contained in lies, and lies wrapped in the truth—these were Chaos' real weapons, Luka realized.

"Boss, there's nothing there." Krichek joined Luka at the large screen. "Just the road. The mountain cuts too close to the river for any homes or businesses. And up the mountain is forest and abandoned coal mines. No way a Town Car could make it up there."

"Stop," he told Sanchez. Luka leapt forward tapping the screen. "Call McKinley, tell him to get his men over there."

"Where exactly is there?" Sanchez asked. He blew up the image. "I don't see anything but a small picnic area."

"See that spit of gravel? It's an informal boat landing. Called Rook's Landing. Not enough room for boats on trailers. But canoes and kayaks launch there. There's a dirt road leads to Route 11." He turned to Sanchez. "Any cameras out there so we can get a live picture?"

"No, sorry."

Krichek had lowered one of his phones to grab another handset on a landline, updating McKinley. Luka was already heading out the door.

"Call river rescue. Tell them I'm on my way," he called back, hope lighting a fire in his veins. He did a quick mental calculation. The video camera had died eight minutes ago—given the cold water and the chance that an air bubble had been created when the car tipped to the side, Dominic Massimo might still have a chance.

A few minutes later as Luka drove over the bridge, he spotted the river rescue team streaming toward Rook's Landing in their boat. By the time he'd steered his truck down the mud-slicked gravel road leading to the landing, the ERT van was also there and the siren from an ambulance sounded from behind Luka.

Concerned about blocking the paramedics, he pulled the truck off to the side, driving over a patch of dead grass. He hopped out and ran down the graded landing, splashing through puddles, until he reached the water's edge. The divers had located the car, pushed by the current until it had gotten tangled in trees growing along the bank of the river about ten yards past the landing. The roof of the Town Car was barely visible above the murky water, but Luka was more concerned with the trunk.

He and the others watched and waited as the rescue divers worked below the surface to pop the trunk and release their victim. They made fast work of it, two divers supporting a man's body, guiding it through the water to the waiting medics. Together they lifted him onto the medic's transport cot.

The divers had cut the man's bonds and he lay on the cot face up as the medics assessed him. Luka heard McKinley arrive, issuing orders to his men to help the divers winch the car onto dry land so that the CSU team could examine it. The noise and movement created a haze around Luka as he imagined another stretch of river, another car, another team of first responders.

He quickly shook himself free of the memory and stepped closer to where the medics were working. The man had been beaten, his face and body swollen with bruises. Yes, his scalp had been shaved, but when the medics moved aside to insert a breathing tube down his throat, Luka saw that he wasn't Dominic Massimo.

It was Cliff Vogel.

"How long did you say he's been down?" one of the medics asked Luka. They'd placed a machine to do chest compressions over Cliff's sternum.

"We lost the video feed fourteen minutes ago. He was alive then. But he was in the water at least a half an hour before that."

"He's real cold," the medic muttered as he used a small handheld drill on Cliff's leg, hooking up a bag of fluid. "We got no vitals." His partner finished inserting the breathing tube. "You in?" His partner checked a monitor and nodded. "Let's load and go, we'll call Good Sam on the way."

One of the ERT guys drove the ambulance so that both medics could remain in the rear and work on their patient. As Luka watched them drive off, McKinley approached. "He gonna live?"

"They said no vitals." Luka shrugged.

"So we've been searching for Vogel but really Massimo's our man?"

Luka was silent, still trying to put the pieces together. Perhaps Chaos hadn't liked the idea of Cliff spying on Risa. Leaving McKinley to process the scene, which would take hours, Luka jogged back to his truck and followed the ambulance, desperately hoping Cliff—the one person who might be able to identify the killer—lived.

CHAPTER 34

Harper escorted Risa to Good Sam while Leah followed in her Subaru and Jack in his company van. Leah had shared Risa's medical records with Maggie Chen last night, so while she waited for Risa to be signed into the ER, she gave Maggie a call and updated her on Risa's most recent symptoms.

"I'm thinking nicotine poisoning," Leah finished. "But I can't remember its half-life. Think I can still get a viable sample this long after?"

"Hang on," Maggie answered, followed by the sound of computer keys clicking. "Urine is your best bet. But given her other symptoms, I'd also run blood and hair."

"Hair?"

"For heavy metals. When I plotted her symptoms on a timeline, it looks like a rollercoaster, doesn't fit any single diagnosis. But if someone is dosing her with toxins, then it might not have always been the same one, right?"

"Which would explain both the erratic timeline and the changing lab results." A nursing assistant escorted Harper, Jack, and Risa from the registration area to the nursing station where Leah stood.

"Yeah, but your timeline for last night doesn't exactly fit either," Maggie continued.

Leah waved Risa into the minor care room she'd commandeered but remained outside the door to finish her conversation with Maggie. "How so? Isn't nicotine biphasic? Minor toxicity fits with the symptoms Risa showed—if it was a major overdose, she'd be in the second phase, getting worse."

"But if she ingested the nicotine after dinner last night, she should have shown symptoms a few hours later—not this morning."

"Are you sure?" Leah frowned. Maybe she'd misunderstood the timeline Jack and Risa had given her? Maybe Risa had become asymptomatic earlier, but Jack panicked, had still called Leah. No, Leah herself had witnessed the hypersalivation when she arrived at Risa's apartment. "Could you send me a link to that information? I haven't dealt with a nicotine OD since residency."

"Let me guess, New Year's."

"Yep. Kid woke before his parents, parents went to bed after throwing a party without cleaning up, and—"

"The kid drank the pretty drinks, not seeing that a cigarette had dissolved in one. Classic. I'll send you the link. Might stop by myself, if you don't mind. I've a friend who's a tox fellow in Pittsburgh, maybe he can fast-track your tox screens, so they'll take days to weeks instead of months to come back."

"We're in the ER now, then will be in the CIC. Thanks, Maggie." Leah hung up, wondering how to approach the confusing and conflicting history she'd been given this morning. Best way might be to separate Jack and Risa, get each of their stories, then compare the two. Once she had Risa in the CIC for her witness interview, there'd be a chance to do that.

She was just about to head in to examine Risa and order the tests when her phone rang. Luka. "We found him," he exclaimed before she could say anything. "But it wasn't Massimo—it was Vogel. Medics are en route to Good Sam."

The trauma alert sounded at the nursing station and Leah straightened. "I'm at Good Sam. The medics are calling in now."

"I'll find you there." He hung up.

Leah made it to the nursing station just as the ER attending on duty, Sam Davidson, finished giving instructions via the trauma radio to the medics transporting Cliff.

"He's part of a case I'm working on with the CIC," she told him as she followed him to the trauma bay. "Mind if I assist?"

"More the merrier." They both donned masks, gloves, and Tyvek gowns. "What's the story?"

"Abducted, held in the trunk of a car that was driven into the river." She explained about the video. "We lost the live feed at 9:21."

He glanced at the clock. "That was almost half an hour ago."

"Did he have any vitals when they found him?" She didn't need to see the grim expression on his face to know it was a long shot.

"No. Asystole and hypothermia." They both backed away as the nurses wheeled in the warming equipment. Sam assessed his troops: anesthesia ready to take over the airway, a nurse on each side to work fluids and meds and monitor chest compressions, another nurse to record, an assistant to run labs, and Leah. "Medics drilled him in the field, but we'll need a central line."

"Got it," Leah told him. The intraosseous was a needle drilled directly into bone, a quick and dirty way to give fluids and medications, but only temporary, while a central line would allow them access to the larger blood vessels leading directly to the heart.

"They're here," a nurse called even as the team's radios went off.

"Sure you're up for this?" Sam asked Leah as she prepped the central line.

It felt strange and she couldn't really admit it, not with a dying—or maybe already dead—victim arriving, but Leah felt better than she had in weeks. More than adrenaline, it was the sense of belonging, that she was home again. No second-guessing or worry about office politics; here in the trauma bay she knew every step of the choreography, as did the rest of her team.

Before she could say anything, the medics burst through the door. They'd intubated Cliff in the field and were bagging oxygen into his lungs while a mechanical chest compressor performed CPR. "Two rounds of epi." The medic at the head of the gurney called out his report. "No response. Bagging with a hundred percent O2."

They quickly transferred Cliff over to the ER's bed, the nurses swarming over him, switching monitor leads, checking the lines. As they worked, Sam and the anesthesiologist listened to his lungs. "Breath sounds equal and bilateral," the anesthesiologist said as he took over bagging. "Needs pressure, though." Maintaining adequate ventilation was always a tightrope with drowning victims: force the air in too hard and they'd blow a lung, not enough pressure and their damaged lungs wouldn't absorb the oxygen.

Leah wedged herself between the CPR machine and the anesthesiologist, then she prepped a sterile area over Cliff's right clavicle to place the central line. She palpated her landmarks, and within a few seconds had the subclavian line ready. "I'm in."

She hooked up the warmed IV fluids while beside her a nurse was placing a nasogastric tube that would also have heated fluids running through it in the hopes of warming Cliff. In the ER you were never dead until you were warm and dead. "What's his core temp?"

"Up to thirty-two," Sam said. "Time for another epi then clear for X-ray to check line and tube placement. Keep that warming blanket and the lights on him."

While the X-ray tech took her shots, Leah joined Sam. "Thirty-two isn't all that cold. Should we try vasopressin?"

Sam nodded. "We'll see what the labs come back, but—"

"It might be too late," Leah finished for him.

The X-ray tech left to process her films. Sam and Leah returned to Cliff's side. "Stop compressions, check his rhythm," Sam told the nurses.

"Asystole on two leads." Asystole or flat line meant there was very little they could do to get the heart beating again.

"Resume compressions. Vasopressin, forty units."

The nurse gave the meds while Leah and Sam watched and waited. Then the assistant ran back in. "I've got the blood gas and electrolytes." She handed Sam a slip of paper. Leah peered over his shoulder.

"Potassium 8.2, severe acidosis," she read. She blew her breath out, glanced at the clock. It'd been eighteen minutes since the medics began CPR.

"Let's treat the hyperkalemia and repeat the gas and lytes in ten. We'll give him the full thirty," Sam said, but the faces of the nurses and the rest of the team had all gone blank. They all knew that Cliff was gone.

And twelve minutes later, after exhausting every option, Sam pronounced him dead. "I'll call the coroner," Sam said as he left.

Leah stripped free of her protective clothing and went back to the nursing station. Luka was there along with Harper. Across the hall, Risa and Jack watched from the doorway of the exam room.

Without Leah saying anything, Risa made a small sob and turned to Jack, who bundled her in his arms and pulled her back into the exam room. Harper merely sighed and slid out her phone. "I'll let McKinley know."

"You did everything you could," Luka told Leah.

"I know. Doesn't make it any better." She slumped against the counter, watching the nurses do their charting, documenting the resuscitation efforts.

Luka's phone rang. He listened, made a noncommittal noise, then said, "Thanks." After he hung up, he explained, "Krichek. We finally got Vogel's military records. He was deployed during Cherise's killing, couldn't have done it. Guy was a hero, won a bronze star and purple heart. Suffered a traumatic brain injury with cognitive impairment."

"He wasn't Chaos."

"Nope. My guess is that Chaos got angry when he learned of Cliff's own obsession with Risa."

"Then it has to be someone who knew Cliff was spying on Risa. But the only people who knew that were your team and the other police officers, Risa, Jack, me, and—"

"Dominic Massimo. Who's still missing."

"You think he took Cliff as a diversion, to throw you off his scent while he escaped?" Did that mean Risa was now safe with Dom gone?

"That's McKinley's working theory. I'm not sure." He leaned against the counter. "What did you learn from Risa?"

"I was just heading in to examine her when they brought Cliff in."

"Krichek's working on Massimo's background and checking his alibi for Trudy's death."

"What are you going to do?" Leah asked.

"I'm sidelined as far as Cherise, of course, but Trudy's case is still mine."

"You said something last night about Trudy's phone, the pictures she took the day before that the killer tried to erase. Did the techs find anything when they examined them?"

"Nothing helpful. Which is why I thought I'd start by re-tracing Trudy's steps in Smithfield where she took them. Figure boots on the ground, I might see something or find someone who saw something."

"What about Risa?" Leah glanced at the closed door to the exam room.

"Finish your exam. McKinley said he'd be over to do the interview with you as soon as he finishes at the crime scene on the river."

"He's letting me do the interview?"

"Thought Risa would feel more comfortable, might be more forthcoming. Besides, isn't that what this new program is all about?"

"Yeah, sure. I'm just surprised McKinley thought of it, is all."

"Well, he might have had a bit of help." He looked past Leah to where Maggie Chen had arrived from the coroner's office. "Let me give Maggie the details of what I know, and then I'm off for Smithfield."

"When will you be back?" Leah asked. "Still want Nate to stay another night? Emily would love it, I'm sure." As long as Leah remembered to stop at the store and bring home something for dinner, not to mention breakfast tomorrow.

"I won't be long and so far I've been able to avoid any reporters, but maybe another night at your place isn't a bad idea." He grimaced. "I feel bad, leaving him, though."

"Do you need me to check on Pops?"

"No, Janine's there and Ahearn sent a patrol unit to watch over them. But thanks." He headed into the trauma bay. "Good luck with McKinley. I'll see you soon."

Leah watched him huddle with Maggie, filling her in on the details behind Cliff's death. She couldn't explain why, but as she moved to rejoin Risa and the others, she felt a sense of unease, the shiver of someone walking over her grave.

She shook it off. Losing a patient was never easy. But losing someone to an arrogant creep of a serial killer who had viciously targeted an innocent man? That brought a whole new sense of frustration and fury. Leah steeled herself. Chaos might have the upper hand right now, but she'd be damned if she was going to let him win.

CHAPTER 35

Leah opened the door to the exam room to find Risa huddled in Jack's arms, sobbing. They sat on the exam table, hips and thighs touching, Jack's fingers threaded in Risa's hair. Leah cleared her throat. "I can come back in a few minutes—"

Risa jerked upright, wiping her eyes with her thumbs. "No, no. I'm not sure why it all just hit me, usually I can hold it together better."

"You don't need to hold it together," Jack murmured to her. "It's all right to let your feelings out. This isn't like when you were on assignment and had to bottle everything inside. You're with me, you're safe with me."

"I know. It's just it feels somehow selfish—to even be alive to be upset, when poor Cliff is dead for no other reason than the fact that Chaos chose me to play his sick games with."

"That's not selfish," Leah said, sinking into the chair nearest the desk. "That's human. It's also okay to feel relief that you are still alive to feel anything."

Risa met her eyes and nodded.

"Live to fight another day, right?" Jack gave her shoulders a squeeze. "Let's get this over with so we can get you out of here." He glanced at Leah. "So, you've reviewed her records, seen her symptoms; what are you suggesting, Doctor?"

Leah was glad of his use of her title—it put them all back on neutral, professional territory rather than something more personal. "I also had a colleague review your chart, Risa. She plotted the symptoms against a timeline—"

"The other doctors did that," Jack put in. "Said there was no pattern, that was part of the reason why—"

"Why they think I'm faking," Risa finished.

"Well, we found a pattern in the lack of a pattern. When you look at each individual attack, they suggest different causes. And if we suspect someone else is behind your symptoms then they might have been using different toxins at different times."

"Someone," Jack scoffed. "Say his name, Doctor Wright. We heard the cops talking. It was Dom. It makes sense. She always got worse after he was around. And remember, Risa, he brought you those teas? Said they were from a Chinese herbal specialist—there could be anything in them. We should get them all analyzed. I can take them to my lab at Keystone." He jumped down from the table. "What else do you want me to test, doc? I should've thought of this sooner—"

"I think it would be best if we used the hospital laboratory services. Just in case we need to document a chain of custody and the like for when there's a trial."

Risa glanced up at that. "First they need to catch him."

"How long will all this take?" Jack asked. "To get results?"

"Some of it will be back in a few hours—the routine tox screen for drugs of abuse and the like. Again, I'm not expecting to find anything there, it's more for documentation. The other assays will take several weeks."

"I could do it faster in my lab at Keystone," he muttered.

"Jack, let her do her job."

"First I'll examine you and then we'll get samples of your blood, urine, and hair."

"Hair?" Risa asked. "What's that for?"

"Heavy metals accumulate in the hair and can last there for months after exposure," Leah explained. She stood and pulled a gown from the cupboard and handed it to Risa. "Do you want Jack to stay?"

"No," he said, obviously uncomfortable. "I'm going to go pack us up—and get you a new phone since the cops took yours. Call me when you're done and I'll pick you up, okay?" He kissed the top of her head. "It's almost over. You know how we're always talking about getting out of this dreary rain and gray and find a deserted beach in Fiji or Togo or someplace warm and sunny? Let's do that. Just the two of us, where Dom will never find us."

She rubbed his arm and nodded, her gaze fixed on the gown clutched in her other hand. "Thanks."

Jack hugged her again and left.

Leah started for the door to give Risa time to change into the gown, but Risa called her back. "Wait. Can we talk? I need to tell you the truth. I can't keep hiding it—not with people dying. I couldn't say anything in front of Jack. He'd be so disappointed."

Leah sat back down and waited. After several moments of silence, she asked, "Disappointed in what, Risa?"

"Disappointed in me. It was right when we started dating. Dom and editors kept pressuring me to head back out, back into war zones. Lord knew there were enough to choose from. They kept at me, blaming Jack, saying I'd gone soft, wanted to settle down. And I did—I do."

"But?"

"But Jack wasn't the real reason why I quit—not the only reason. My heart was empty… no, that's not right, it was like it was too full, but with darkness. And that darkness was eating away at me. I wasn't sleeping; every time I closed my eyes all I saw were the dead babies and children and mothers and fathers who'd tried to save them but who couldn't even save themselves…"

"You were burnt out. Maybe even suffering from PTSD."

Risa shrugged one shoulder. "Maybe. Probably. But I couldn't keep turning down assignments, not without looking weak. And if a woman in my field shows any weakness they'll never get the choice assignments. I had a reputation to protect. So…" She blew her breath out, twisting the gown in her hands as if wringing someone's throat. "I told them I was sick."

"Is that why there was ipecac in your closet?" Leah asked. "Have you been creating your own symptoms?"

"Ipecac?"

"Jack told me. He found it hidden in an old pair of boots."

Risa shook her head. "I never used ipecac. I don't even own any. I lied about my symptoms, to Jack and Dom, to my doctor, but I never took anything. That's why the first doctor couldn't find anything wrong. But then, I really did become ill, with real symptoms. After that I wasn't lying. But I guess the doctors were right—it must have been my mind, making me sick, because I wanted to be sick. Don't you see?" She was close to tears. "It's all my fault. If I'd kept working, Chaos would have never targeted me, none of this would have happened."

Leah slid up onto the examination table beside Risa. "It's not your fault, Risa. Your doctors couldn't find a diagnosis, that's true. But I think I have an idea why—and it wasn't all in your mind."

Risa sniffed and looked up. "It wasn't?"

"No. Your lab results were abnormal. But not always in the same way—which is why your doctors were so frustrated. Nothing fits with any one diagnosis. However, if you look at the pattern, it could fit with several different toxins."

"Toxins? You mean Jack was right? I was poisoned?"

"I think so." Leah paused, waited for that to sink in. Risa seemed overwhelmed, but there were still so many questions that Leah needed answers to. "You're certain the ipecac isn't yours?"

"No. Someone must have put it there. But Jack's the only person who'd go into my bedroom." She raised her head to face Leah, eyes wide. "Unless Dom did during one of his visits. But why? How does that fit with him being a killer and wanting me to write his story?"

"I've no idea." Risa was right; it didn't make sense to Leah either. "Maybe the ipecac was Plan B? To discredit you if you ever got too close to the truth about him?"

"I guess." She frowned. "I guess I'm not as smart as he thought I was, because I can't put any of this together into a coherent picture."

There was another discrepancy Leah hoped to clear up: the timing of the nicotine administration—if indeed Risa's symptoms this morning were from nicotine. "Jack said you got sick last night after Dom gave you your tea?"

"That's what he said."

"You don't remember it that way?"

Risa bit her lower lip. "Again, please don't tell Jack. I don't want him to worry. But sometimes, I wake up in the morning and I can't remember the night before—huge swaths of time, just gone."

"How often does it happen?"

"A few times a month. I just lose time."

It could be PTSD, but it could also be a side effect of a toxin. Leah was glad she'd asked the lab to run the full tox panel. "What do you remember from last night?"

"I remember you leaving. I remember Dom there, making me laugh with some crazy story about another one of his clients. I remember Jack cooking. After that, it's all a blur."

"You don't remember eating dinner or drinking the tea or Dom leaving?"

"No."

"Do you remember getting sick? The nausea and vomiting and needing to spit, feeling flushed?"

"Those woke me up this morning. Vomiting first, then the others kept me awake. Around five-thirty, it was still dark out. I woke Jack with my throwing up and he got up as well. We tried to ride it out, and after a few hours I was feeling better, keeping fluids down, but he was worried, so he called you."

"That was just after eight."

"Right. Does that help?"

Leah considered her words carefully. "Risa, think hard. Did you get up during the night to eat or drink anything?"

"I don't know. Like I said, I can't remember anything until I started throwing up. Why?"

"Nicotine poisoning has a fairly quick onset as well as a short duration for minor overdoses. Which means however the nicotine got into your system, it wasn't at dinner or while Dom was there last night. It would have happened early this morning."

Risa frowned, shaking her head slowly as if bewildered. "I wish I had an answer, but the whole night is just a blank." Leah blew out her breath in frustration. Risa reached over and gripped her hand, her gaze searching Leah's face.

"You believe me, don't you?"

CHAPTER 36

Emily couldn't help but feel sad that her daddy hadn't really come back. Last night was the first night she hadn't had a nightmare about the bad man and what happened to Daddy. Instead, she'd dreamed that Daddy was there, watching over her and Nate, telling them how proud he was of them for being heroes. Only then she and Nate weren't inside their bunkbed fort, instead they were dressed like explorers in the movies and were accepting medals for bravery for their trek through the woods to retrieve Nate's great's medal—and somehow saving Nate's great-great-grandfather as well. At least that's who she thought the man in the old-fashioned army uniform was, even though he wasn't very old and looked a lot like Luka. Then the Homan twins and Ms. Driscoll were all carted off to jail.

And then she woke up. Still half-asleep, she went downstairs, where she'd found Daddy's name on boxes and his computer was back and she'd hoped and wished… but it was all like the dream. Not real.

Still, that didn't mean she and Nate couldn't make it real. Be heroes.

By the time Nate and Emily finished cleaning her room—and the living room and the breakfast dishes—the sun was shining bright, spilling tiny rainbows over the lavender plants lined up in their rows from the house to the woods. Emily had her plan finalized. The Homans scared her, not just because they were bigger than her but because they made her afraid deep down inside, like the bad man who killed Daddy had on that night she tried so hard to forget but never could. But Nate needed her help and she couldn't let him down.

She gathered what they needed. After lunch—grilled cheese and tomato soup—Ruby told them to go play and they finished their preparations, including dressing in proper exploration outfits: boots, jeans, T-shirts under a fleece top for Emily and a flannel shirt for Nate, baseball caps, then windbreakers for both.

"Ready?" she asked Nate.

"Yeah." He didn't sound as enthusiastic as he had last night. "Did you ask Ruby?"

"Hang on." She ducked her head into the living room where Ruby was listening to a book and flipping through one of Nellie's old seed catalogues. "Ruby, can Nate and I play outside? It stopped raining."

Ruby glanced out the window. "Enjoy the sunshine while you can. Be back before it gets dark—supposed to rain again tonight."

"Thanks, bye!"

It felt so good to be out in the sun that they ran through the mud between rows of lavender plants, racing each other to the tree line. Then they came to the edge of the forest leading up the mountain.

The four-wheeler path wasn't marked on the map on Emily's phone, but it was pretty obvious where it began given the large patch of rutted and churned up dirt. Nate ran right up it, vanishing into the thick shadows of the trees, but Emily stopped. The trees were tall, with thick branches like long, knobby fingers that quivered in the wind, ready to wait until her back was turned and then they'd grab her. And the noises—they came from everywhere, above and below and around all sides. She hugged herself tight, trying to squeeze the panic away as her heart thudded and all she could see was blood…

Then Nate raced back down the path, smiling as he took her hand. "Hey, c'mon."

She took a deep breath, her fear washed away by the clean scent of pine and wet leaves, then followed him into the trees.

They quickly came to their first obstacle: the path converged with four others, all leading in different directions. Emily scrutinized the map. She'd studied it so much that she thought she had it memorized, but it was difficult to translate it into the real world. She'd googled the Homans' address and it was marked; they just had to cross the patch of green on the map to get there. The measurements said it was between half a mile and a mile. That was easy.

She held the phone flat on her palm beside Nate's hand with the compass. Nate rotated until both were pointing the same way.

"Pops said the arrows always go north," he explained. "So we need to go this way." He stretched his left arm pointing into the trees. "Not quite west."

She studied her map then the compass and nodded. "Right." She chose the trail closest to their desired direction. "This way." Emily led the way into the woods, following the ruts from the four-wheelers. The rain had left the tracks filled with puddles and the dirt around them was sticky mud, so they walked in the brush and leaves alongside the trail. The pine trees swayed in the wind and the naked trees that had lost their leaves in the winter had tiny red and brown buds breaking out. The air smelled fresh and wonderful, a promise of spring, and Emily forgot her fear. The woods weren't dark and scary like she'd thought. Just different.

Nate stopped as a large bird spiraled above them. "Is that an eagle?"

"Or a hawk. Next time we need to see if we can use my daddy's binoculars. Then we could tell for sure." The thought of Daddy and her walking through the woods, on their own adventure, made her sad. She'd never get another adventure with him again.

"We could go back for them."

"No. They're at my old house. With all my other stuff." They were both silent for a long time. But it wasn't a bad or sad quiet, more like Nate understood how she felt—probably because all those fosters left him with not much stuff, either. Luka had gone to Baltimore and brought back what was at Nate's old house, but it was mostly clothes for school and a few pictures of him and his mom.

"I miss her," he whispered into the wind.

"I miss him," Emily echoed.

They kept walking until the path forked, this time giving them only two options. "Which way?" Nate asked.

"You're the navigator." They huddled over the compass and map once more. "We wanted to go towards the ten o'clock when we had the arrows lined up." They rotated around and ended up standing in a mud puddle.

"Neither path goes the right way," Nate said.

"Yeah, but that one is more the right way." She pointed to the path that was seven o'clock away from the north arrow. "Plus the other path goes up the mountain and it looks steep."

Nate squinted at the compass and her map again. "Can you make it show where we are?"

Emily tried to refresh the map but all she got was a whirling circle. "No cell bars."

"Okay. We just need to remember we went left, so that will be going right when we're trying to get back." He broke a branch from a pine tree and stuck it in the intersection. "And we'll look for the branch." As they ran down the path, birds flew away, flapping their wings in annoyance.

But then a loud crack echoed through the forest. Both she and Nate stopped, looking around, their backs to each other as they scanned the shadows surrounding them.

The wind swirled past them, carrying a man's laughter—or was that a bird squawking? They pivoted to face the direction it seemed to be coming from, Nate stepping in front of Emily. She moved aside—he blocked her view and she wanted to see—but then came the crunch of footsteps and more laughter, this time from the other side of the trail.

"Who's there?" Emily called, trying to ignore the way her stomach churned—just like that night when Daddy's shouts had woken her, when… She squeezed her eyes shut tight, shoving the memories away, taking deep breaths like Dr. Hailey had taught her. She wished JoJo, the therapy puppy, was here with her. Mommy should have let her have a dog.

"Are you okay?" Nate whispered, taking hold of her hand. She opened her eyes and nodded. "I think we should head back."

She nodded again, her mouth too dry and throat too tight to try to talk as her eyes met Nate's. They turned, eying the path behind them. The sun was hidden behind clouds, making Emily shiver as the shadows stretched across the trail, trying to swallow her and Nate.

They took one step, then two… and then they saw him. A big man, dressed in black, with a helmet covering his face.

Just like the man who'd killed Daddy.

CHAPTER 37

Luka had already examined every detail of Trudy's photos, running every address and license plate through NCIC. After getting the okay from the Smithfield PD and Ahearn, he grabbed a pool car and headed over the mountain.

Smithfield was a smaller version of Cambria City, mirroring Cambria City's topography. Surrounded by the Allegheny Mountains on three sides and the Juniata River on the fourth, its history was built on the railroad and coal industries. Large Victorian and Queen Anne mansions anchored the nicer neighborhoods, shoulder to shoulder with white-framed colonials, brick Federal styles, and gabled Cape Cods. Go a few blocks in any direction and the architecture changed dramatically to narrow shotgun-style homes, post-war split-levels, and squat bungalows sporting roofing shingles as siding. Abandoned lots surrounded the railroad tracks alongside the river, while further away from the historic town center was a combination of forest and farmland.

Luka checked in at the police department—no sense treading on toes—made certain his map and list of names was up to date, then headed over to the nursing home situated in a stately brick Queen Anne Victorian, complete with turret and gables.

He started retracing Trudy's movements by speaking with the nursing home staff. Luckily, given the higher volume of visitors on a weekend, the administrative assistant who'd worked with Trudy was there.

"Mrs. Orly is dead?" he repeated, eyes wide, face aghast. "I just saw her."

"I know. That's why I'm here. Did anything unusual happen during Mrs. Orly's visit? Did you meet anyone who seemed to know her? See anything out of the ordinary?"

He shook his head. "Nothing like that. It was mainly paperwork—she'd already toured the facilities. We got her husband on the waiting list, took care of the insurance and financial forms. I don't think she even spoke to anyone other than me while she was here. She took some pictures to share with her husband—maybe those would help?"

"Right. Thanks." Luka headed back out to the street, taking a moment to enjoy the sunshine. He felt as if he were emerging from hibernation, it'd been so long since he'd felt the warmth of the sun on his face. It was still chilly, especially here where the wind was constrained by the mountains, giving it extra bite, but he didn't mind. He glanced at Trudy's photos and began to follow her footsteps, knocking on every door he came to.

He'd made it to the end of the block and halfway up the other side of the street without success. No one remembered seeing Trudy, Dominic Massimo, or any stranger two days ago.

He reached a nicely kept Cape Cod, white frame, blue shutters and trim, and no one was home. Not surprising given the beautiful day, but… As he was sliding his card and a note into the mailbox beside the front door, he realized that it was almost full. And there were newspapers lying on the porch. Could be nothing, but something felt off.

Luka checked the homeowner's name, Patrick Rademacher, against the list he and Leah had compiled last night. People Risa had written about, fact-checked, or proofed their obituary. Rademacher wasn't on it. Yet, the name felt familiar—a niggly, jangly, electricity under the skin kind of familiar.

He peered through the front window. No signs of anyone home or any disturbance. Which meant he had no probable cause to enter the house. He went back down the porch steps but stopped before reaching the sidewalk. There was another walkway alongside the driveway that led to the backyard. A white-washed privacy fence surrounded it, but the gate was open. Luka debated the consequences of trespassing, decided they were minor, and went through.

"Mr. Rademacher?" he called out as he followed the narrow walkway down the side of the house. He looked inside the windows as he went—nothing of note except what appeared to be remnants of a half-eaten sandwich on the kitchen table.

Approaching the backyard, he could see the framing of a deck and steps down to a flagstone patio. He stopped. Death came with a particular sensation, one that started with a metallic taste high up in the back of the throat, long before any scent alerted a person.

Luka moved forward slowly, watching where he stepped. Each inhalation heightened his awareness, his instinct that death was near. The crows pecking at the corpse floating face down in the hot tub confirmed it.

CHAPTER 38

Leah finished her exam and stepped outside to allow Risa some privacy as she changed back into her clothes. Nothing on Risa's physical had helped to either confirm or deny her suspicions. Across the hall, Harper and Maggie Chen huddled together at the nursing station.

"What's up?" Leah asked. "Did something happen?"

"McKinley's on his way for Saliba's interview," Harper answered. "I'm just waiting for him and helping Maggie with her math."

"I'm telling you, it doesn't add up." Maggie turned to Leah. "The water in the car trunk where Cliff was found was forty-nine degrees Fahrenheit."

"Not very cold. Probably part of the reason why we couldn't get him back."

"Forty-nine degrees sounds pretty damn cold to me," Harper said. "I thought cold water was supposed to buy him more time."

"Very cold water as in near freezing. Especially when associated with sudden immersion," Maggie explained.

"Like a kid falling through the ice on a frozen pond," Leah added. "In that situation, even with a prolonged down time, sometimes you have a chance. But not with a slow submersion in not-so cold water."

"Okay, so the odds were against Cliff from the start. You guys did everything you could. So what's the problem, Maggie?" Harper tapped the notepad where the death investigator had been scribbling calculations. "You keep saying the math is off. Your algebra—"

"*Algor mortis*," Maggie corrected. "The cooling of the body postmortem." She tapped her phone where an app was displayed. "I've input every variable into the Henssge equation. Water temp, resuscitation efforts at rewarming, his BMI. Nothing adds up."

"Those formulas might not be accurate since he died so recently," Leah said, wondering at Maggie's level of concern.

"Right," Harper said. "In fact, sometimes there's no obvious cooling of the body for a few hours after death." Both Leah and Maggie turned to stare at her. "Hey, I've read Sutherland's textbook, too. Besides, we already know the time of death—we were all watching it happen, live. Vogel died at 9:21 a.m."

Maggie shook her head, her robin's egg blue hair sparking in the overhead lights. "No. That's the problem. Everything in my calculations says that Cliff died in the middle of the night. Hours before that video went live."

Now it was Harper and Leah's turn to frown in confusion.

"Lies," Leah muttered. "Somehow the killer must have faked the time stamp, made it appear to be live-streamed."

"Sonofabitch set us up—had us on a wild goose chase while he was escaping." Harper grabbed her phone. "Sanchez? Could the time stamp on the video have been altered? Well, get the camera CSU found inside the trunk and find out. Please. It's important." She hung up. "He said he can't tell until he examines the camera, but it is theoretically possible." She pushed her chair back and stood up. "Got to go. McKinley's here and he doesn't look happy."

Leah stood as well and followed Harper's glance to the ER entrance. McKinley's rosacea was flaring, and his expression was just as angry. Leah got the distinct impression that the ERT commander was not enjoying his time taking over Luka's detective squad.

"Saliba ready for her interview?" he asked when he spotted Harper and Leah.

"Yes. I've got everything set up in the CIC interview room," Leah told him.

"Good. Harper, you monitor and record. Dr. Wright, you take lead. I want an exact accounting of everything Risa Saliba knows or suspects about Chaos—every detail, no matter how small. We need to get ahead of this guy."

"Sir." Harper suddenly sounded tentative. Then she took a breath and straightened her shoulders. "Maggie Chen, the death investigator—" She nodded toward the trauma bay where Maggie had gone to prepare Cliff's body for transport to the morgue. "She thinks maybe Vogel was killed much earlier than we'd assumed. Like hours earlier."

"What's Tierney or the ME say?" McKinley demanded.

"Nothing yet," Harper admitted. "But—"

McKinley silenced her with a scowl. Then he turned back to Leah. "I'll be waiting in the CIC. Bring Saliba and let's get this over with."

Leah watched him march away. "I'm guessing there's a reason why McKinley isn't a big fan of Maggie?" Or vice-versa, given the way Maggie had escaped as soon as she caught sight of McKinley.

"She once tossed him off a crime scene. He wanted to search the body before she finished documenting the scene." Harper glanced toward the trauma bay, a gleam of appreciation in her gaze. "Got into a huge shouting match, right there in front of everyone. And Maggie won."

"Good for her. Now if we can just make sure this damn interview doesn't turn into another shouting match." Not for the first time, Leah wished Luka was here.

"Good luck with that." Harper went to get Risa to escort her to the CIC interview room.

Leah lingered, her gaze caught by the scribbled calculations Maggie left behind. If Cliff really did die hours earlier, then why go through the elaborate video countdown? Like the message to Luka about his fiancée's engagement ring, it all felt so… contrived.

A magician's patter, designed to distract you with a story while the real sleight of hand was happening right under your nose.

Chaos lied. But he also did everything for a reason. What was he trying to distract them from? Was something bigger happening elsewhere? If they could find out, maybe they could catch him. Before he killed again.

CHAPTER 39

Emily froze. Her breath caught in her throat at the sight of the masked man. The mask had plastic over the eyes, reflecting the storm clouds racing through the sky above him, as if he was part of the sky. Was she dreaming? Then she saw the rifle he carried. A strangled noise slipped past her clenched lips and she clapped her hand to her mouth. Quiet… Daddy said to be quiet so the bad man didn't find her.

Nate grabbed her arm and yanked her so hard she spun all the way around, away from the man with the gun.

"Run!" Nate ordered. They hurled themselves down the trail. Emily barely saw where they were going, everything was a blur, her mind filled with flashes of memory, of the night Daddy was killed.

The trail ended in a field of broken corn stalks and mud and weeds that brushed against Emily's knees.

"Where are we? Where do we go?" Nate asked her, panic filling his voice.

Emily stood, her breath heaving in through her mouth all the way down to her toes, past her toes even, as if she was a mouse and could burrow her way into the earth, hide.

But there was no place to hide.

Be brave, be strong, Daddy whispered. Emily didn't feel brave and she wasn't strong. She was scared. But just like Daddy had saved her, she had to save Nate. After all, it was her fault he was there.

"This way," she told him, taking his arm and crouching low to hide below the highest weeds along the edge of the field.

The field ended in a rickety barbed wire fence with some cows behind it. Past the cows was a collection of buildings: a big red barn, a shorter metal building like an airplane hangar open on two ends, a farmhouse, a few smaller buildings behind it, and two double-wide trailers. The Homan farm.

"We can hide in one of the barns," Nate whispered. The sound of four-wheelers slipping in the mud, their engines whining, came from behind them.

They skirted the cow pasture and entered the main compound. Two men came out of one of the trailers and seemed to be arguing about something. They headed toward the metal hanger building where there were several cars and trucks squeezed in. It had no doors, so they crept around the back of the larger barn until they were on the other side of the building where the men were, so at least they were hopefully out of sight. There was a chicken coop with a small yard and beside it was another area behind a short chain link fence with a plastic doghouse that had a broken roof.

A sad-looking dog circled a pair of empty bowls. From the ruts it had left in the muddy grass, it must have been pacing for hours.

"Poor thing," Nate said. "He must be so thirsty. Look at how his tongue is hanging out."

Before she could stop him, Nate swung himself up over the fence and emptied his water bottle into the dog's bowl. The dog didn't make a sound, didn't even bare its teeth, as if it was used to people trespassing in its space. In fact, when Nate first raised his hand to open the bottle, the dog had cringed and slunk backwards, head ducked as if it expected to be punished.

"Nate," Emily whispered. "Get back here. We need to find a way out." She'd given up on their mission of retrieving Nate's great's medal—getting back home to Nellie's without being shot was the new mission. Behind her, two men on four-wheelers came roaring into the compound, pulling up in front of the building with all the cars and trucks. They were laughing as they dismounted, slinging their guns off their shoulders.

"No, we can't leave him." Nate picked his way through mud and grass, the dog backing up until it was against the fence near Emily. Up close she could see its eyes were crusty, its hair matted, and there were red stripes crisscrossed across its back. Nate crouched down, keeping some distance. The dog finally met his eyes but bared its teeth and gave a small growl. "It's okay, boy. I'm not gonna hurt you. Go on, get your drink. I know you're thirsty."

Nate stood to one side and the dog slunk past, edging around to keep Nate in sight. Then it got close to the water bowl and its thirst overcame any fear as it dipped its entire head in and lapped it up.

"The coast is clear," Emily whispered to him after the men went inside the main house. The clouds had almost blocked the sun and the first drops of rain were falling. Ruby was going to be so angry. "C'mon, let's go."

Nate was halfway to the kennel's fence when a noise came from the farmhouse. He froze and glanced over his shoulder.

Emily followed his gaze. Billy and Jimmy were coming down the porch, headed straight for the dog's yard. And they both held rifles.

"Nate, get out of there. Now!"

CHAPTER 40

While Luka waited for the Smithfield PD to respond, he paced the sidewalk in front of the house with the corpse in the hot tub and called Leah, hoping for an unofficial update on both the case and how Nate was doing. Her phone went straight to voicemail, telling him that she must still be in Risa's interview. He considered calling Ruby but decided he didn't want Nate to think he was being too intrusive. Then by the return leg of his third lap between the houses on either side of the crime scene, he'd decided that Leah had the right idea and that he needed to get Nate his own phone. Maybe not a smartphone, but at least an old-fashioned "dumb" one.

Finally, a cruiser appeared, pulling up to Luka, and a uniformed officer emerged. Luka gave an account of how he came to find the body to the Smithfield officer, Jon Mann. Mann called his corporal to the scene, Luka repeated everything, and then the corporal in turn called the coroner and the on-call detective. And then they waited—no one could touch the body until the coroner or one of his deputies examined it.

"Good thing the hot tub wasn't actually on," Mann joked. "Can you imagine the stink?"

"Would've found him faster," the corporal replied. He was a man in his mid-forties to early fifties with a build that could only be politely described as "stout."

"Can't believe we've got a serial killer." Mann stood straighter and rubbed his thumb over his badge, as if prepping to be featured on the evening news.

Luka answered their questions, but it felt strange, playing the role of reporting witness rather than detective in charge of the scene and investigation. As polite as Mann and his fellow officers were, they didn't look at Luka like an equal, a brother in blue. Did he act the same way around witnesses and victims? Luka wondered. Simply because they stood on the wrong side of the thin blue line?

He took the first opportunity to step away and call McKinley to update him.

"I'm at the hospital with Dr. Wright; we're starting Saliba's interview," McKinley told him. "What was your victim's name again?"

"Patrick Rademacher. I think he's connected to Saliba, but I can't place him—"

"Wait, here she is." There was a clatter as McKinley handed the phone over and put it on speaker.

"Risa, does the name Patrick Rademacher mean anything to you?" Luka asked.

"Patrick? Of course. He's a photographer, we worked together for years."

That's why the name felt so familiar to Luka. He must have seen it on the bylines of the photos accompanying Risa's articles. "And where is he now?"

There was a long pause. "He's dead. A few years now. Was working on a piece about Syrian refugees. Why?"

"Did you work on his obituary?"

"No, this was before I got sick and started taking those assignments. What happened? Why are you asking about Patrick?"

"How did he die?" Luka asked, edging off the sidewalk to allow the coroner with his gurney to pass.

"He drowned. His boat was scuttled while he was filming refugees. His boat and two more, filled with families. They were able to retrieve his final shots—won him a Capa and a Pulitzer. Wait." She paused and hauled in a breath, slow and heavy as if dragging a weight. "Wait. I didn't write about him, but I did speak about him. At a memorial event for journalists killed while covering conflicts. It was a fundraiser for their families."

"And no doubt advertised," Luka said mostly to himself.

"He's killed again, hasn't he—is it Dom, is it really Dom doing this?" Her words came machine-gun fast, leaving her breathless again. "I just—I can't believe it. I've known him for over a decade. I wouldn't have a career if it weren't for him. Who has he killed now?"

"A man by the name of Patrick Rademacher appears to have drowned. In Smithfield, on the same street as the nursing home that Trudy visited. And from the state of the body, I'm guessing he was killed the same day she was here."

"The link. That's why he killed Trudy. She must have seen him near the scene of the crime."

More than a link, Luka thought. It meant that they needed to take Chaos' list of possible victims much more seriously. If he killed Rademacher, then there had to be other true victims out there as well. He shook his head. Leah was right. Chaos lied. But how to tease the truth from the lies? Because only by finding real victims did they have any hope of obtaining the evidence they needed to locate and convict Chaos.

McKinley came back on the line. "I'll coordinate with the locals, but Smithfield has such a small department, I'm sure they'll punt it to the staties right away. Finish up there and come on home—Ahearn wants to form a taskforce with us and the state police and other local jurisdictions. He's calling in the FBI to do a profile and the marshals to help us track Massimo. I need you back here to coordinate and give them your full cooperation in regards to your fiancée's case."

He hung up before Luka could ask any questions. Pretty obvious that Ahearn was doing some punting of his own—by forming a multi-jurisdictional taskforce, he'd get extra resources and avoid the bill, all the while keeping the fame and glory for himself.

Luka trudged back to the hot tub, just in time to watch them fish the bloated, crow-pecked body out from the stew of decomposition fluids. "Would a time frame of two days fit for time of death?"

The coroner wore a medical respirator, hiding most of his face, but he bore a remarkable resemblance to the corporal, making Luka wonder if they were related. "Got to do some calculations. Check ambient temps over the past two nights, larval development, what have you." His gaze went distant as if he were doing the math in his head. "Could be. Definitely not too much longer or he'd be a lot more gone than what he is." Then he shrugged. "Whatever I say, the state police's forensic pathologist will have his own ideas. If were you, I'd wait for the report to be sure."

Luka was halfway back to Cambria City when his phone chimed. Harper. "Jericho here."

She answered in a near-whisper. "Wanted to update you." In the background he could hear a woman's voice, although he couldn't make out the words. "On Cliff Vogel."

"Aren't you with McKinley interviewing Risa Saliba?"

"He has me monitoring from the observation room. I don't think he likes the idea of a uniform working plainclothes."

"It's not that. His guys work plainclothes all the time."

"Then tell me how to make him listen. Maggie discovered something that might be important."

"Something they need to ask Risa about?"

"No." He sensed her frustration even over the static-filled connection. "Maggie doesn't think the video was livestreamed. She says Vogel might have been killed hours before it was sent to Risa."

"What does Sanchez say? And has Ford Tierney given us an official window for time of death?"

"I have Sanchez working on it and we haven't heard anything from the ME yet."

"It might be days before we do." Luka thought about it. Other than giving the killer a head start, the time of death didn't have an immediate impact on which leads to follow next. Better for McKinley to finish learning everything he could from Risa and then add that knowledge to Harper's new theory about the timestamp being misleading. "I'd wait until the interview is finished before you share all this with McKinley. He's never worked the investigative side before now. Maybe feed things to him in bite-sized chunks."

"Like you did for me on my first case. Yeah, I can do that."

"Did he let Leah take the lead on the interview?"

"Yeah. He's actually playing it smart, sitting in the back corner, listening, not interrupting, letting her and Risa find their own pace. Slow going, but we're almost done."

"Krichek will call you if anything happens. Ahearn is calling in the staties and feds for help, forming a taskforce."

"Which means I'll be off the case? They won't need two of us and Krichek is a detective, has seniority." Her yearning for a chance to prove herself worthy of promotion to detective wasn't subtle.

"We'll see. Either way, good work. Call me if you need anything."

"Thanks, boss."

Luka had just reached Route 11 when another call came through, this time from an unknown number. "Detective Sergeant Jericho."

"Luka, it's Emily. Miss Emily Wright," she repeated as if multiple young girls with chirpy-birdlike voices had his number. But he realized that she was whispering, her words coming sharp and fast. "You need to come quick, before they hurt Nate."

"Slow down, Emily. Where are you?"

"Billy and Jimmy Homan's farm."

The Homan place was only a few miles away. Luka gunned the engine. "What happened?"

"Hurry. They're going to shoot him. Luka, I'm scared."

He sped past the entrance to Jericho Fields. The Homans were just another two miles down the road. "I'm almost there. Get somewhere safe."

"I can't leave Nate—"

The fury rose in his voice. "Hide, Emily!"

Then came the sound of a gunshot and Emily screaming.

CHAPTER 41

Luka put Emily on hold only long enough to call in for backup, then returned to her call. From her rapid breathing, it sounded like she was running, and he hoped she found a place to hide. He spun onto the Homans' dirt road, now slick with mud and puddles. Past the barns there was a crowd lined up around a small fenced-in dog run. At the house across from the kennel three women stood on the porch along with an assortment of young children. No weapons visible, allowing him to turn his attention to the two boys holding paintball rifles while next to them one of the adult women held a shotgun and two of the adult males had semi-automatic pistols.

All aimed at Nate, sitting in the mud, shielding a dog with his body. Nate glared at the men, fearlessly.

Luka blasted his siren to draw their attention away from Nate. In addition to the visible weapons, Luka was sure that there would be more in the house and other buildings. He was outnumbered at least eight to one, not counting the unarmed children. Regulations said he should wait for backup.

To hell with the rules. That was his boy. Even if Nate hadn't been family, the sight of grown men and women terrorizing a young child who was trying to help a poor animal—Luka had never truly felt his blood boil before, he was usually the one remaining calm, uninvolved, but now he finally knew what that level of rage and fury felt like.

He left his car, hand resting on his weapon, and slowly approached the crowd. The woman and one of the men swung their weapons to cover him while the other man kept his gun on Nate—as if an eight-year-old unarmed boy was a threat.

"Detective Sergeant Luka Jericho, Cambria City PD," he called, making sure his coat was pulled back to reveal his badge at his belt. He'd arrested a few of the Homans when he was in uniform, but wasn't stopping to put names with faces. Right now he was more interested in what their hands were doing. "I got a 911 call of a disturbance. If everyone could please put their weapons on the ground and step away, I'm sure we can sort this all out."

The crowd was still for a long moment. Luka kept his breathing steady, forcing himself not to glance at Nate but to focus on the immediate threat. Someone in the back of the crowd sniggered, then came the sound of a child giggling. The adults relaxed.

"Sure thing, officer." Luka recognized the man in front, Dale Homan, as he spoke. Dale fanned his fingers away from his pistol's trigger and with an overdramatic, exaggerated motion set the pistol on the ground. "Sorry if our second amendment rights intimidate you. Wouldn't want you to feel scared for yourself."

That drew another round of snickers from the crowd behind him.

"We're in our rights," the woman said, still holding her shotgun but pointing it down at the ground. "Caught him trying to steal our dog."

"Trespassing and theft," Dale said. "You going to arrest him? Do your duty and lock him up?"

"Clear a path, step away from the kennel and the boy," Luka replied. The crowd shifted slightly—enough so that Nate could go through the kennel gate. Except he didn't.

"Nate, get over here. Now." Luka inserted every level of command into his tone. Not that it did any good.

"No, sir," Nate shouted, his arms wrapped around the cowering dog. Both the dog and Nate were splattered with paint ball impacts. But no blood that Luka could see in the dim light of the gathering dusk and misty rain. "Not leaving him. He's hurt."

Luka heard a car pull up behind him. No lights or sirens, which was probably for the best—no need to infuse more drama into an already tense situation. A car door slammed and the Homans all turned to look at the newcomer. Luka glanced over his shoulder just as Ruby Quinn, Leah's mother, stalked past him, going straight for Dale Homan.

"This how you people get your kicks?" she shouted. "Terrorizing little kids and poor defenseless animals? You all get into the house right now, or I'll do more than call the cops, I'll call someone who can really ruin your life and you know exactly who I'm talking about, don't you, Dale Homan?"

To Luka's surprise Dale looked down, scuffed his feet. He masked the motion by bending forward to retrieve his gun, making Luka tense his fingers around his own weapon, but simply shoved it into the back of his jeans. "We was just fooling, Miss Ruby," he said sheepishly. "Can't no one take a joke?"

"Joke's over." Ruby raised her hands and waved them. "Go on now, back inside." The crowd slowly dispersed to their respective domiciles leaving Luka, Ruby, Dale, and Nate. "Emily Wright, get your skinny butt out here before I spank it raw!"

From the shadows of a metal barn, Emily stepped forward. "Sorry, Miss Ruby. Don't blame Nate. It's all my fault. I'm the captain, he was just the navigator."

Luka had no idea what she was talking about, but at this point all that mattered was getting them out. Keeping his gaze on Dale and the house behind him, he edged over to the kennel and opened the gate. "C'mon, Nate. We're leaving. Now."

"He needs help." Nate drew back far enough for Luka to see the animal's wounds. The poor thing had been whipped and beaten, starved to the point where its shoulder blades were like two knife edges beneath its matted fur. "Can we take him with us?"

"That dog's going nowhere. Belongs to my kids," Homan said. "And that boy is the one who hurt him. You can't prove otherwise."

"The dog's been shot with a paintball gun," Luka pointed out the obvious. "And the boy is unarmed."

"Just my boys defending themselves best they could. Besides, maybe he got rid of the evidence. No matter. It's our dog and he's staying here."

"I got evidence, Mr. Luka," Emily said, running over to Luka. She handed him her phone. "Here, I videoed everything."

A patrol car pulled in and two officers emerged. Luka waved them over as he watched the video. It showed the Homan boys shooting paintballs at the dog and Nate, then their father and uncle pointing handguns at Nate, one of them laughing as he fired into the mud a few feet in front of Nate. The sight had Luka clenching his jaw so hard his ears popped. And yet Nate had stood his ground, refusing to be cowed. A flush of pride overwhelmed Luka. He couldn't wait to tell Pops. "What were you two doing here anyway?"

Emily answered. Hands on hips, she glared at Dale. "Billy and Jimmy stole Nate's medal, the one from World War Two that his great-great-grandfather won for bravery. And they wouldn't give it back, so we came to get it."

Ruby joined Emily, adding her glare to the little girl's. "Well?"

"My boys ain't no thieves. Must've been a misunderstanding." Dale swiveled his gaze to the house. "Boys! Get out here and bring whatever you too—borrowed from this kid."

Emily had done a good job of documenting several crimes: cruelty to animals, child endangerment, he could maybe even squeeze a felony assault for the weapons fire. But there was something even better caught by Emily's video.

A black Dodge Ram parked in the metal garage. Its front bumper and hood were dented and smeared with bright orange paint. Tangerine Daze-glow, to be exact.

Thanks to Nate and Emily, he'd just found his hit and run bicyclist victim Gary Wagner's killers.

CHAPTER 42

Given its traumatized clientele, the CIC's adult interview room had been designed to convey a sense of intimacy, security, and comfort. After their more than two hours of conversation, Leah was more exhausted than after a shift in the ER.

It didn't help that the only break they'd taken had come when Luka called to ask Risa about the dead man he'd found in Smithfield. Risa had refused every offer of a break, saying that she just wanted to get it over with. Finally, McKinley was satisfied that he'd learned everything he could from her and they finished for the day.

McKinley and Harper left first while Leah remained to do a bit of crisis intervention with Risa; even though the journalist denied any need of counseling—said it was no different than reporting from a war zone, and she was merely an objective observer—Leah knew firsthand the cost of walling off emotions. Together they ran through a series of breathing and relaxation techniques.

"It's been a long few days," Leah said as she escorted Risa from the CIC back into the main ER where Jack was waiting. "First, Trudy, then learning about Dom—are you sure there's nothing else I can do for you?"

"Help the cops find the bastard and we'll be happy," Jack answered, taking Risa's arm in his.

"Thanks, Leah. This has been a real help," Risa said, giving Jack a "behave yourself" look as they left.

Leah returned to her office to finish her charting and saw that the preliminary results of Risa's tox screen were back. Because of

Risa's amnesia and lost time, Leah had ordered a complete tox panel on Risa's blood, urine, and hair.

This initial rapid assay focused mainly on drugs of abuse. Leah was surprised to see that there was a positive finding: gamma hydroxybutyrate or GHB. Known for its use as a club drug, in addition to its other effects, it caused sedation and short-term amnesia.

Given GHB's short half-life, the fact that it was still in Risa's system meant she'd been dosed within the last twenty-four hours. Dom had supposedly left Risa's after dinner—unless he hadn't? Maybe Jack's confusion about when Risa's symptoms from the nicotine ingestion began was because he'd also been sedated? Maybe Dom had returned—or had never left—and then to cover his tracks gave Risa the nicotine this morning before he made his escape?

Then she thought of something else. GHB was known as a date rape drug. Could Dom have sexually assaulted Risa last night and no one, not even Risa, knew? Dom was obsessed with Risa, that much was clear by simple observation.

She called Risa. No answer. Right, the police had taken Risa's phone. Next, she tried Jack. "What do you need, Leah?"

"Are you guys still in the hospital?"

"We just finished all the paperwork and are halfway to our car."

"Which floor of the garage are you parked at?"

"The roof. Why?"

"Wait for me. I'm on my way." Leah grabbed her bag and coat and headed out to the parking garage.

Jack was waiting for her at the elevator bank on the roof. The sun had been obscured by thick clouds and it looked like the rain would soon be returning. Risa was nowhere in sight. There were only a handful of cars up here, including Jack's paneled van with the Keystone logo.

"Look, Risa's exhausted," Jack started before Leah could say anything. "I know she puts on a brave face for you and the cops, but as soon as we left the ER, she pretty much collapsed." His tone turned pleading. "Please, I beg you. You can't keep asking her to go through this."

"I have her preliminary results," Leah told him.

"Give them to me, then."

"You know I can't do that—confidentiality."

"Then it will have to wait until tomorrow. I'll have her call you." He turned to leave, when Leah stopped him.

"Jack, I can't tell you what Risa's results are, but it would be a huge help if I could test you as well."

He spun back, surprised. "Me? What for? What kind of test? I'm fine, there's nothing wrong with me."

"It's a simple tox screen."

"Tox screen. You mean a drug screen." His gaze narrowed and he positioned himself with his back to the van, also blocking anyone in the van from seeing Leah. "If you want to test me, there must be a specific drug you're looking for. What is it, Leah? What do you want to test me for? I have a right to know."

"Gamma hydroxybutyrate." He might draw his own conclusions about Risa, but he was right, he needed to know what she was testing him for.

"Gamma—that's GHB, a date rape drug." He glanced over his shoulder toward the van. "Risa—" He shook his head vigorously, then his shoulders slumped as the full implications hit him. "That bastard—" He seemed close to tears, a low moaning coming from deep in his throat. He turned away, his arms wrapped around his chest beneath his jacket. "It's all my fault. I couldn't protect her."

Leah placed a hand on his shoulder from behind. He turned and leaned into her as if unable to support his own weight. "I'm sorry," she murmured. "I hope I'm wrong."

"So do I." He straightened, sniffed. "Guess we'd better go talk to Risa, decide what to do next."

Together they walked around the other cars, heading toward the van. Suddenly Jack stopped, twisting as if he'd heard or seen something. "Leah, look out!"

Before she could turn to face the threat, pain exploded throughout her body.

CHAPTER 43

Luka had patrol officers corral the Homans and their weapons, secure the evidence, and call animal control while he waited for Krichek to bring a search warrant. Thanks to Nate and Emily, and Emily's video, they had more than enough probable cause.

Nate and Emily were now both inside the kennel, comforting the dog. "You're gonna keep him, right?" Luka overheard Emily ask Nate as he approached the fence where Ruby watched them. Nate hugged the dog tight, burying his face in the mangy creature's fur. Luka hoped he wasn't getting too attached—he wasn't even sure that the poor thing would survive.

"Who were you talking about?" he asked Ruby. "When Dale backed down."

She made a harrumphing noise. "His grandfather and I play poker together. Occasionally we entertain each other in other ways." An arch smile slid over her features. "He owns all this, runs the family. Those boys do not want to get on his wrong side, believe you me."

He filed that tidbit away for a future discussion, wondering if Leah knew who her mother was associating with. Although Wallace Homan, the patriarch of the family, kept his hands clean and had never been arrested—he left the dirty work to the younger generations. "How did you know the kids were here?"

"Couldn't find them for dinner, so I used the find-me function on Emily's phone. But the real question is where's Leah? She insists I have to call her if Emily gets a hangnail, but she's not picking up."

"That's my fault. Her phone will be off—she's doing a sensitive witness interview for us."

"And she acts like I'm the lousy mother. Wasn't that the whole reason why she took this new job, so she'd be here for Em? I don't see her picking her up from school, I don't see her dealing with that Miss Fancy-pants vice-principal, I don't see her spending her own damn money buying new toys when there's a house chock full of toys just across the river—"

Luka took her arm and steered Ruby into the barn, out of earshot of the kids. "I hope you don't talk like that around Emily. Because Leah is working damn hard at being a good mother, providing for Emily and you, while dealing with her own grief." His voice was low but filled with unexpected anger. Who was he defending? Leah or his own bad choices? Nate's mom, his own sister, was dead of a drug overdose and he could have—should have—seen how bad off she was. Cherise was murdered but he let himself be convinced that she'd killed herself.

"Don't talk to me about grief," Ruby snapped. "I know about grief. About losing someone so dear it rips out a chunk of your soul."

"Then you should take it easy on Leah. Anyone can see she misses the ER. Every time a siren goes off, she's like a thoroughbred ready to race. But she gave it all up for Emily."

"I know, I know…" She paused. "At least she has a job. And a roof over her head. Life wasn't as easy for me, you know." She narrowed her eyes at Luka. "I heard you talking about your fiancée last night, about how it changed your life, how you still visit where she died every year. I've spent my whole life struggling since I lost Leah's father and I didn't have anyone to help me. I had to go it alone."

"That's not true. Leah told me she was raised by her great-aunt Nellie, that Nellie tried to help you, too."

"Nellie's help always came with too many strings. Get a job, stop moving around, take my meds, stop drinking. I had a life to live, too, you know. But Leah never gives me credit for that, for all the good things I did for her. Like leaving her with Nellie. Or helping her now. Letting her into my house."

Nellie had left Leah the house when she died, not Ruby, but Luka didn't waste breath on arguing. Ruby was damaged, but it was clear that she was also striving to do better for her daughter and granddaughter. "I think Leah appreciates your help," he said slowly. "But you also need to appreciate what she's going through. Especially if you've gone through it yourself."

"I know," Ruby said, as if suddenly Luka was her biggest fan. "I keep telling her, don't make the same mistakes I made, that I know what I'm talking about, but she never listens to me. She treats me like she's still that sullen eleven-year-old I left at Nellie's. Never seems to realize that I gave her the greatest gift of all by leaving her behind—"

The animal control van arrived, interrupting them. Jessie Trevasian hopped out, her usual dour expression pulling her face down. She was in her mid-fifties and had been doing her job for Craven County for a quarter of a century with no intention of leaving anytime soon. People she barely tolerated, but animals she loved.

Luka left Ruby in the barn and joined Jessie, who was assessing the situation, photographing the dog's living conditions.

"The kids said he had no food or water when they arrived, seemed dehydrated." He showed her the video Emily had shot. "They saw welts on his back and the Homan boys shoot him with a paintball gun."

Jessie shot the house a glare that could have been a lethal projectile in its own right. "Lost track of how many animals we've had to remove from this family."

Luka nodded. At least this trip he didn't have to call Children and Youth.

"That boy, who's he?" Jessie asked, studying Nate and his interaction with the dog as she and Luka approached the kennel.

"My nephew. Nate."

"He's a good one, kind-hearted. Putting himself in harm's way to protect an animal—there's grown men wouldn't do that to save a human's life."

Luka found himself beaming with pride. Then he quickly felt guilty. He'd played no role in building Nate's character. So far. "Kid's been through a lot. I imagine if you repeated that to him, it would mean a great deal."

"Happy to." She left Luka at the gate and entered the kennel, crouching down to Nate and the dog's level, talking to him softly. "This guy have a name?"

"Rex," Emily supplied, obviously wanting to be part of the action. "Short for T-Rex."

But Nate only shook his head. "Dunno. Not sure."

"Then Rex it is," Jessie declared as if it were written in stone.

Nate finally met Jessie's eyes. "He gonna die?"

"Not if I have anything to do with it." She pulled back the dog's gums, glanced at its eyes and ears. "He's pretty sick and neglected, but he's young, has some fight left in him, I reckon. Don't you, Rex?"

The dog lifted its snout and gave a single wag of its tail. "Good boy," Nate told it. "This lady's gonna take care of you."

"Sure am," Jessie assured him. "Want to give him a hug before I take him?" Nate wrapped his arms around the dog, then let them fall away. Jessie carefully lifted the animal into her arms. "Honor to meet you, Nate. You should be proud, you saved a life today."

Nate said nothing, just kept staring at the empty patch of grass and mud where Rex had lain. Luka escorted Jessie to her van, then returned to the kennel. Nate still sat in the mud, Emily standing over him, both hands on her hips, their backs to Luka.

"Nate, you gotta ask. If you want to keep Rex, you need to say something to Luka."

"Can't." Nate sounded heartbroken. "Can't ask for anything that will make him send me back to foster. Can't risk it."

"But you love Rex, I can tell," Emily responded.

Nate stood, brushing grass and dirt from his jeans with swift, angry motions. "I don't love anything. Never will. You love something, someone just comes along and steals it from you. You love someone and they just go and leave. I'm never gonna love anyone, not ever."

He sounded so damn certain, as if he'd deciphered the mystery of the universe. Luka's chest tightened because Nate's words echoed in his own heart—a seventeen-year-old echo of a decision he'd made after Cherise was taken from him. Better to live alone than risk the pain of letting anyone get too close.

Emily wrapped her arm in Nate's, leaning her head against his arm. Their backs were to Luka and the silhouette they formed made him blink—yet another echo of Cherise.

"Nate, Nate," Emily said in a tone that implied worldly wisdom. "I know it hurts. But you can't go your whole life trying not to love."

"Sure I can," Nate snapped. But he didn't move away, allowed her to lean her weight on him.

"No. You can't. Because who wants to live a whole life full of nothing?"

Nate shrugged one shoulder. Luka sniffed and the kids both turned to him, surprised a grownup was paying attention. "You know, Nate," Luka said. "I'm very proud of what you did today. Once they get Rex better, he's going to need a good home."

Nate stared at Luka as if searching out some hidden trick Luka was trying to play on him.

"Taking care of an animal is a lot of responsibility and hard work. You up for that?"

Emily tugged at Nate's arm as she jumped up and down, splashing mud over them all. "He is, we are, yes, sir, please, please!"

"What do you say, Nate?"

The joy filling Nate's face was answer enough for Luka. "Yes, sir. I'd like that."

"Okay, then. You two go find Ruby. She's going to take you home."

"You're not coming?" Nate asked.

"I've got to get back to work. But tomorrow, a special breakfast, just the two of us, okay?"

Nate scuffed the dirt with his heel but nodded. Luka returned to his car and steered around the other official vehicles, heading back down the lane. He decided that he didn't care if he had to work overtime tonight, he wasn't going to miss his promised breakfast with Nate.

He stopped at the end of the lane, ready to turn right towards Cambria City, when a white van with the familiar Keystone Shale logo drove past him and turned down Old River Road. Luka wondered at that—there was nothing down there except for an old pumping station. The small station had never been able to keep the area drained enough to protect the train tracks, so the railroad had finally built a bridge over the marshlands that were periodically flooded. Keystone probably used the station to monitor water quality—otherwise why else would Jack O'Brien be headed down a road no one ever used anymore?

The van's passenger seat had been empty. Risa was probably still tied up with Leah, finishing her interview. Luka tried to call Leah but it went straight to voicemail, confirming his theory. Next he called Krichek.

"Congrats, boss," Krichek said. "Heard you nailed the Homans for our hit and skip."

"Still figuring out which Homan exactly, but it's a start."

"And you found us one of Chaos' victims in Smithfield. Ahearn's going to let me act as liaison with the feds, work with their profiler." Excitement filled his voice. "Oh, and I heard back from the Indiana PD—not much left of our landscaper, but they found enough to do DNA testing. So that's another kill confirmed."

The thought didn't make Luka feel better—he would have preferred Chaos to have lied about his other victims. Although, the more bodies the more potential evidence. Chaos might be smart, but he wasn't perfect. Sooner or later he'd screw up and leave something of himself at a crime scene.

"Any sightings of Massimo?" Luka asked.

"No. I've got NYPD watching his apartment and office, and the staties are monitoring all the LPRs, but so far no joy." The automated license plate readers covered most of the interstates and the turnpike, but Chaos was too smart for that. Luka was certain he'd stick to back roads. Plus, the man no doubt had an escape plan ready to go. Given his diversion this morning with Vogel, he was already hours ahead of them.

"Did you ever get a chance to get Jack O'Brien's statement? He seemed suspicious of Massimo before anyone else."

"No, sorry." Krichek sounded abashed. "I got too busy with—"

"No apologies necessary. I just saw him head down Old River Road toward the old pumping station."

"I think Keystone uses that place for water monitoring. O'Brien's probably trying to get some work in before he and Risa take off. Ahearn gave him permission to take her to a hotel in DC until we catch this actor. That way they'll be close enough to come back if we need them for anything and in the meantime, the feds can protect them better than we can."

More likely Ahearn was using the feds to avoid paying for the overtime it would take for their people to watch over Risa. Luka switched his indicator to left. "I'll get O'Brien on record before I head back in."

"Great, I'll cross it off my to-do list." Krichek was clearly enjoying the new responsibility he had been given. It was the best of all worlds for a detective: gaining valuable experience without the administrative hassles that came with Luka's job, the job McKinley was temporarily tasked with.

But only temporarily, Luka promised himself as he turned down Old River Road. Somehow Luka was going to find a way to be there when they nailed Chaos. Cherise deserved that much.

CHAPTER 44

Leah woke in darkness. Memories flooded over her. A visceral image of finding Ian's body, her feelings of terror and anguish. The same terror that threatened to overwhelm her now. She was panting, breathing too fast, and forced herself to close her eyes and take slow deep breaths.

Her skull throbbed, her mouth was parched, and every muscle in her body felt twisted with cramps. What happened? The question slogged through the mire of her mind. She'd seen something—no, *someone*.

She blinked, the slight movement reverberating through her head, releasing more pain. She licked her lips, swallowed, and took another breath. A cloth hood covered her head. The air inside it tasted strange, sickly sweet. Yet, strangely familiar. Her lips and the skin around her mouth burned. Slowly, painfully, she took inventory of the rest of her body.

There was a distinct area of throbbing pain between her shoulder blades. Her hands were bound behind her, numb as her weight rested against them. Thin plastic bit into her wrists—zip ties? Her legs were free, and she could stretch them out without hitting anything. Relief flooded over her as the image of Cliff's hogtied body filled her vision. She wasn't in a car trunk, thank God. The floor felt like rough concrete, cold and damp, but not wet.

Her muscles protested when she tried to sit up, so she compromised, rolling first onto her side, releasing the weight against her hands, waiting for the pins and needles to subside and feeling to return as she rubbed the cloth covering her head against the floor, finally sliding her face free.

The room—a cellar?—felt expansive but the darkness was almost complete. No matter how much she blinked, her vision remained blurred, but as her eyes adjusted to the dark, she realized there was a faint shadow of light coming from above. A partially covered window? Or maybe it was night? How much time had she lost?

She made out silhouettes of what appeared to be large pieces of equipment—a boiler, maybe? The building smelled old; more than that, it smelled wet, like algae and mildew. As her eyes adjusted to the dim light, she saw a row of several large pipes coming out of the floor to connect to the larger piece of equipment. Then she shifted her gaze to the wall behind her and realized that the patch of darkness against the floor was a human body.

"Hello?" she called softly as she scraped her aching body over the concrete floor. No response. Who was it? She strained to remember what had happened before she blacked out. Risa, she'd been with Risa… Risa and Jack.

She scanned the room, her vision slowly clearing, but didn't see anyone else. Only one person. What had happened to the other?

Finally, she reached the other person. Like her, their head was covered with a hood. As soon as Leah stretched her arms behind her back to pull the covering loose, she realized it was a woman.

"Risa?" She rocked her body to shake Risa, was rewarded with a low moaning. "Risa, wake up!"

Risa sputtered and groaned. Leah twisted her body around to face her. Risa's eyes blinked open. "Wha—" Her voice was gravelly. She licked her lips, tried again. "Where?" Then she arched up, eyes wide with panic, arms flailing behind her. "No, no! Jack, where's Jack?"

"Did you see who took us?"

"No." She shook her head as if trying to clear cobwebs. "I didn't see. Did you?"

"No, but Jack did." Leah measured her words, the memory slowly coming together. "He tried to warn me, but it was too late."

"Where is he? Is he okay?"

"I don't know." Leah fought through the fog clouding her brain. "Think, though. Chaos won't hurt him. Because if he killed Jack, you'd have no reason to cooperate."

"Maybe he's holding him hostage like us?" Risa slumped against the wall behind her. "Dom never liked Jack. Even if he doesn't kill him, he might still hurt him." She was silent for a moment then stared at Leah. "What are you doing here? Why did he take you?"

"I think it's because I found out he was drugging you."

"We already knew that."

"No. This is a different kind of drug. We found GHB in your tox screen."

"The date rape drug?"

Leah nodded. "I was asking Jack if I could test him as well since he was with you last night. It would explain why the timing of the nicotine dosing was off and why neither of you remember much of last night."

"I can't remember anything. None of it makes sense." A soft sob escaped Risa but she quickly cut it off. "I don't understand any of this. Why involve me in the first place? What does Dom want from me?"

"I think, maybe, he was trying to give you a reason to live. He knew you weren't happy not working at the job you loved, so he gave you a story to investigate, a puzzle to solve."

Risa shook her head. "No. No, that's insane."

Leah agreed. But as warped as it was, it fit with Chaos' twisted logic. "We need to get out of here."

"If it's me he wants, maybe I can make a bargain for you and Jack." Risa sounded resigned to her fate—a fate Leah refused to accept.

"No. If he comes for you, you need to engage him. We're not powerless here, Risa. You need to believe that. Believe in yourself."

Risa was silent, her chin dropping to her chest. "Listen to me." Leah used her best trauma-command-doc voice—not loud, but also not easily ignored. "You are our best weapon, Risa."

That got her attention. "Me? How?"

"You have a hold over him no one else has. If we know anything about this guy it's that he's obsessed with *you*. Use that, manipulate him like he has you. All we need to do is buy enough time to escape and get help."

"Leah, we could be anywhere." Risa's voice hardened. "I'm not sure escape is our best option. He'll just run after us, or worse, he'll hurt you or Jack. Like you said, that's probably the only reason why you're still alive."

"Then what?"

"We have no choice. If we get the chance, we fight back. Even if we need to kill him."

CHAPTER 45

As Luka drove down Old River Road, the ancient, potholed macadam tested the Impala's suspension. The heavens opened with pelting rain, howling wind, and a stroke of lightning pierced the night.

Jack O'Brien had made it clear that he was no fan of Dominic Massimo, giving Luka hope that the chemist might be able to shed some light on the psychology behind Dom's actions. At this point, any insights to help them find Dom would be helpful.

A sudden sheet of lightning illuminated train tracks crossing along the narrow bridge the railroad had finally built over the marshland once it realized that the depression-era pumphouse couldn't keep up with the river's stubborn, periodic flooding. Luka couldn't help but think of Cherise—these same tracks, this same river marked her place of death, although forty-odd miles to the west.

Not her death, he corrected himself. Her murder.

Past the marsh, the road crossed over the tracks and drifted closer to the riverbank, close enough that he could see wind-whipped froth churning only a few yards away. He rounded a bend and turned onto a dirt drive, leading to the small two-story pumphouse ahead, a flickering light beckoning from a front window. Despite its utilitarian function, the building had been embellished with Victorian-style arched windows along the ground floor and a tiled peaked roof. Even the lower level that housed the pumping equipment and that sat partially submerged by the river had leaded-glass transom windows, high enough to avoid the water. Where a residential building would have a porch, the pumphouse sported a gingerbread-trimmed portico that functioned as a carport. Two vehicles were parked beneath it: the white-paneled Keystone van, sitting behind an old Honda Civic, its hood exposed to the rain, mere yards from the river's edge.

Luka stopped the car at the edge of the trees and doused the lights. It was standard procedure, even for a benign witness interview: you never announced your arrival or parked directly in front of a building. As he trudged through the rain toward the other vehicles, another stray slap of memory came to mind—Cherise had driven a Civic almost the same color. Luka had the sudden feeling that if he edged his gaze as far as possible, he'd see her standing there, just out of reach, watching over him.

Luka approached the building cautiously, wondering to whom the Civic belonged. Then he remembered: Vogel had a Honda registered to him. If his car was here, was Dom here as well? He had only seen Jack driving the van, but Dom could have lured him out here.

Other than the dim light flickering from the front room, the building was completely dark, with no signs of life. Luka used the cover of the storm to sidle beneath the window, raising himself up just far enough to peer inside. He saw a battered couch, its back to the window, and a coffee table with an open laptop in front of it. A motionless man sat on the couch, his shaved skull bathed in the colors of the news video playing on the laptop.

It was Dominic Massimo, appearing remarkably relaxed for a killer on the run. Luka had found his killer, but the timing couldn't be worse. He needed backup. As he slid his phone free, he saw that beyond the coffee table, the laptop's glow illuminated an open door leading into a dark room. Another man slumped against the wall, in view of Massimo. Jack O'Brien, gagged, hands and ankles bound, motionless. The shadows were too thick to see what injuries he might have, or even if he was still alive.

Luka backed away silently. He had no cell service, but a text might still get through, so he alerted McKinley of the situation, hoping for a quick response that would assure him backup was on the way. Regulations dictated that he should watch and wait—in fact, that's exactly what he would tell anyone else to do. No intervention unless the hostage was threatened.

But Luka had questions. Questions he'd waited seventeen years for the answers. Questions that would decide if Dominic Massimo lived or died.

Luka sidled beneath the portico and tested the front door. It was unlocked and made a tiny sigh as he pushed it open. He stepped into the dark foyer, closing the door quickly.

He stood in a narrow, darkened hallway. The only light came from the open doorway of the front room to his left. He took a deep breath, held his weapon steady, and glanced quickly inside. The door opened slightly behind the couch into the room where Massimo still sat, intent on the video coverage of his own crimes. There were no weapons in sight, but one could easily be hidden.

Once again, Luka had a chance to back out and let McKinley's team handle the situation. Massimo hadn't noticed him yet. He took a step away from the door, allowing the adrenaline to clear slightly. He had Chaos trapped; this wasn't the time for unnecessary risks.

For years he'd had visions of confronting Cherise's killer, of beating out the answers to the questions that had driven Luka all his adult life, even killing him... but they all faded like the adolescent fantasies they were.

No. Luka was a cop now. He would do this the right way.

It's what Cherise would want, he thought as he backed away. McKinley and his men would have more chance of taking Massimo alive. Luka's responsibility right now was seeing to the hostage's safety. If O'Brien was even alive. He hadn't been moving when Luka saw him through the window.

He took one last step backwards, hoping to find a way to get to O'Brien without alerting Massimo, when he sensed a warmth behind him. Not even an impression, definitely not a thought. A whisper of instinct. Before he could turn around, a man's arm wrapped around his neck. In the man's other hand was a semi-automatic, its muzzle jammed into Luka's spine.

"Damn," the unseen man said in a jovial tone. "You cost me five bucks, Luka. Bet myself you were gonna put a bullet in that corpse there on the couch. Finish it once and for all. Avenge your lovely Cherise."

Luka still held his weapon. His attacker tightened his grip, using his gun hand to wrap under Luka's armpit, adding leverage to the arm choking the blood to Luka's brain. Luka tried to angle his pistol back to shoot the man in his leg. Anything to incapacitate him, give Luka a chance to escape. His vision was blurring, red fraying the edges, his head thundering, his brain screaming for oxygen.

His mind gave the command for his finger to pull the trigger, but he couldn't feel his hands, much less command them. The last thing he heard was the thud of his gun hitting the ground.

The last thing he saw was Cherise's face smiling, her hand reaching out, inviting him to join her. Then blackness consumed him.

CHAPTER 46

Horror flooded over Leah at Risa's words. Logically, she knew Risa was right—they might need to kill in order to survive this night. But all Leah could see was Ian's bloody body. Could she actually do it? Intentionally harm someone? She glanced at Risa's face, twisted with terror. It wasn't just about saving herself, it was about protecting Risa as well. And more than that, it was Emily. Whatever it took to get home to her, Leah would do. Could do. Decision made, she used the wall to push herself to standing. "First, we need to find a way out of these zip ties."

Risa mirrored Leah's movements. "Got you covered. Trick I learned working protests." She sobered. "In fact, it was Patrick who taught it to me."

"I know you can loosen them with a hair pin or paper clip, but I don't see anything like that down here."

"Yeah, those are the best options—less painful. This will work, but it's gonna hurt." She raised her hands behind her back. "Get your hands up as high as they'll go. Push your butt out like you're doing a squat. Now, I'm not going to do it because if I'm meant to distract him, he'll need to see that I'm still tied up. But what you're going to do is bring your arms down hard and fast, hit your butt while you're pulling your arms out." She demonstrated in slow motion. "Do it hard and fast."

Leah assumed the position, stretching her arms as high as she could, despite the pain. The zip ties were so tight that any movement caused them to bite into her flesh. The first time nothing happened except she felt a trickle of blood from one wrist.

"Again. Faster, harder," Risa instructed. "Think snapping motion."

Leah took a deep breath, strained to raise her arms even higher, then brought them down hard and fast as she blew her breath out forcefully. To her surprise, the zip tie snapped in two and she was free.

"Nice trick. Now let me see if I can find a way out." Leah retrieved the broken zip tie to use as camouflage for when their captor returned.

"And find a weapon." Risa leaned against the wall, watching Leah. "Do you think he could have drugged me before last night?"

"No way to know. GHB clears the system so fast we were lucky to find it this time." Cautiously, Leah felt her way around the periphery of the room. It was empty except for the large pipes feeding into an even larger round container. Not a boiler like she'd originally thought, not with those pipes that were a foot or more in diameter. More importantly, she found no tools, not even any loose pieces of pipe or fittings. Nothing that could be used as a weapon.

"Did the GHB cause my symptoms?" Risa asked as Leah explored their prison.

"The amnesia and lost time, yes. But probably not the other symptoms."

"So he was poisoning me with something else." Risa's indignation was undercut by fear. Leah wished she had answers for her, but right now she was focused on getting them out of here.

The room was definitely subterranean, the only light a dim glow entering through narrow windows near the ceiling. There was a set of open-backed metal stairs leading to a closed door above.

"Can you see me?" She waved to Risa. "I found the stairs. If he comes, he'll be coming from this direction."

"I can make you out, barely."

Leah climbed the steps, taking care to hug the railing closely and test each step for telltale creaks and rusty groans. Despite the obvious age of the building and the sense of long neglect, the steps felt solid. She tried the door at the top—bolted from the other side.

She returned down the stairs, then searched the area beneath them, cobwebs sticky against her face and hands. Thunder sounded from outside and rain pelted the tiny windows. Leah returned to Risa empty handed. "Nothing." She wiped her grimy hands against the back of her parka and stopped. "Wait. Maybe something. Hold on." The parka's hood, waistband and hem were threaded with lengths of adjustable paracord. She tugged at the one around her waist.

"If Dom drugged me last night, why didn't he just take me then? Or both me and Jack?" Risa asked as Leah worked on removing the paracord. Leah got the cord loose. It was thin but strong, with small adjustment caps at both ends. She pulled it taut. A garrote? She'd need something to use as leverage, otherwise even with the element of surprise, he could overpower her, break free.

Leah searched her pockets. Their abductor had taken her bag and with it her keys and cell phone, but deep within the inside pocket she found an old ballpoint pen. Some random gift from a pharma company, ubiquitous around the hospital, but it might just save their lives.

She wound one end of her makeshift garotte around the pen and secured it—it really was a lot like a thin tourniquet, Leah realized. She'd need to get close, very close to use it, but it was better than nothing. Except, even with Risa distracting Chaos, he was trained military. He'd never let her get close enough to reach over his head, loop the garrote, and twist it tight.

She held the length of paracord out for Risa's inspection. "Maybe tie it to the base of the stair railing? Trip him when he comes down?"

Risa nodded. "But promise, when he falls, you don't wait for me. If we can't kill him, then you need to run and get help. You hear me? You run. Leave me. Okay?"

Leah ignored her by pretending to be too busy selecting a railing low enough that she could hide beneath the stairs and reach the cord to pull it, yet high enough that the fall would have some hope of at least stunning Chaos.

"What was he doing while we were watching Cliff die?" Risa mused as Leah tied the cord and leaned her weight against it to test it.

Something fell into place for Leah at Risa's words. Suddenly she understood. Everything. There was one person who benefited from Risa being drugged, from her being unable to remember large swaths of time. Especially last night.

A thud sounded overhead, loud enough to shake dust from the rafters.

"Quick, get into position," Risa urged her.

"Risa, wait."

Risa scurried back to the corner and lay down on the floor. "There's no time. Put the hood back over my head."

"No, wait. I know who Chaos is. It's not Dom."

Footsteps echoed from above, followed by the sound of men's voices.

CHAPTER 47

The stench of mold and mildew choked Luka. His throat was raw, every breath an effort. His head pounded. He opened his eyes—it was almost too much work to bother, returning to unconsciousness was so very tempting. He was lying face down on an ancient braided rug between the coffee table and the sofa. Someone knelt on the small of his back and the pain jolted him to full awareness. His wrists were pulled together as handcuffs ratcheted with a metallic snap.

The man rolled off Luka's body to stand beside him. All Luka could see was a pair of expensive leather work boots and jeans cuffed with mud. The man's foot reached out to nudge Luka's shoulder.

"Didn't go overboard with that chokehold, did I?" he asked in a friendly tone. "Hurts like hell, doesn't it? I could have used the stun gun, but I much prefer a hands-on approach when it's practical."

Luka blinked, trying to focus—not only his blurry vision, but his foggy thoughts. He rolled to one side, his back to the couch, hitting Massimo's legs. They felt unnaturally stiff and cold. He pushed against them, mere obstacles as he fought his way to a seated position. His vision swam red with the strain and he closed his eyes, concentrated on his breathing. Massimo was dead. The fact finally penetrated the haze that filled his brain.

Time. Buy time. He'd told Krichek where he was going—if Luka didn't show up soon, he'd send backup. Or maybe his text had gotten through to McKinley and the ERT was on the way. Luka hoped.

"Okay, there? Not gonna barf, are you?"

Luka took another breath, shook his head—regretting the movement as it released a shockwave of pain roaring through his head—and finally found the strength to look up, focusing on the man. Cherise's killer.

Jack O'Brien.

"You never even had a clue, did you?" Jack's grin widened. "I couldn't believe it when you showed up at Risa's building after I silenced the old lady. Knew you right away, of course I did. You're the reason why I'm in this business, how I found my true calling."

"Wha—" Luka couldn't finish the question, his throat tightening like a noose as his brain finally cleared. He swallowed hard, ignoring the pain. "You? Cherise?"

Jack laughed, hands on his hips, back arched, face to the ceiling. The sound emerged more like a victorious howl of a rabid wolf baying at the moon. "You still don't remember me! We met. Once when you dropped her off at our house. My stepsister, Lynne, she ran Cherise's study group."

Lynne Braughman. She'd been one of Cherise's best friends. Devastated after Cherise's death, she'd been interviewed by the police—all the members of the study group had, but Jack's name was nowhere to be found in the police report. No one had thought to question the younger brother—no one had even mentioned him being home during the study group.

Luka searched his memory, could vaguely recall passing the boy on the lawn once when he'd escorted Cherise to Lynne's house. There'd been an arch covered in climbing roses. He remembered thinking that someday he and Cherise would have a house like this, with its well-groomed lawn and lovingly tended gardens, but most of all with an arch they could walk through each time they returned, leaving the world behind as they crossed into their happily-ever-after.

He'd barely even noticed the teenager kicking the soccer ball against the garage wall. Not until he was leaving and the ball hit him square in the small of the back. The kid had apologized and Luka had chuckled, retrieved it and kicked it back, the ball sailing past the kid, hitting what would have been a goal shot if there'd been a net. He remembered thinking that their kid, who'd hopefully both look like Cherise and be as smart as she was, their kid would have a real net. And two parents out there playing with him—or her.

Luka's recognition must have shown. Jack crouched down to Luka's eye level, peering at Luka as if he were an insect under a magnifying glass. "Now you remember."

"Soccer ball."

"Yeah, that's right. You thought I missed, but I hit exactly what I was aiming at."

"You were—fifteen?"

"Seventeen. Hadn't had my growth spurt yet." He stroked his chin. "That came later, after I left for the army. But Cherise didn't mind. She saw my potential, the person I was destined to be. Said I was smart, clever, that sports weren't everything."

Typical Cherise, always finding the best in people. Was that what got her killed?

"Why?" Luka asked the question that had haunted him for seventeen years.

"You, Luka. She rejected me. Not because I was too young or too short or too skinny. Because she said she could only love you." He stood again, towering over Luka. "Do you have any idea how many people I've killed because she said no? Because of you?" Jack motioned with his gun. "Get up. I expect you want to know everything that happened to Cherise. Well, I'm going to show you."

Given the handcuffs restraining his wrists behind his back, Luka was forced to leverage his weight against the couch—taking care to avoid the dead man's legs—in order to push himself to standing.

"Massimo," Luka said, trying to buy time. "Did he know?"

"Not until two seconds before I killed him," Jack answered jovially, one professional sharing trade secrets with another. "But, goodness me, doesn't he make the perfect fall guy? Had you fooled, all of you."

They moved across the room, leaving Massimo's body behind. "And Trudy? Why did you kill her? It obviously wasn't part of your plan."

Jack jerked Luka's arm angrily. "Damn woman wouldn't stop chattering about seeing me in Smithfield. I couldn't risk her telling Risa and Risa putting two and two together once word got out about the guy I'd killed in Smithfield. After all, I was meant to be a hundred miles away that day."

Finally, it all clicked. "Your job. Environmental compliance—"

"Sends me all over. I go where the job takes me, grab a map, throw the dice and let chance guide me from there. Never the same place twice, never the same type of killing twice. I could've kept going for the rest of my life if it wasn't for Trudy."

They reached the front door. Jack opened it, the hollow echo of the rain drumming on the portico roof forcing Luka to raise his voice. "Except it wasn't all random, was it? Not after you targeted Risa."

"Risa." Jack spoke her name like a sigh whispered in church. "I couldn't hide from her, didn't want to—I wanted to share everything with her. I knew she'd see my genius, would fall in love with Chaos as much as she had plain old Jack. With time." He nudged Luka with the gun. "Time we don't have anymore. Thanks to you." Jack led Luka back out to where the van and the Honda sat. "That's good. Stop there."

Stall, just stall, Luka thought. How much time had passed already?

"Was raining even worse than this, that night with Cherise." Jack continued his commentary. "A bit warmer, too. But that's okay."

"Why make it look like a suicide?" Luka kept his tone calm, casual, concealing any hint of his rage—and his fear. He turned to face Jack. If he was going to die, it would be facing his killer, not from a bullet to the back.

Jack's mouth twisted as he considered the question. "You know, I didn't go out there expecting to hurt anyone. I let the air out of her tire during her little study group. Then I followed her. I thought I'd be her Prince Charming, coming to her rescue when her tire went flat. Thought she'd be so happy to see me. And she was. At first."

Cherise always had a good nose for bullshit. Luka bet she saw right through whatever story teenaged Jack had tried to feed her about his happening along just at the right time that night.

"Then," Jack continued, "she tried to drive off. But I jumped into her car with her, took the keys. I tried to tell her how I felt, but she kept screaming and fighting. Wouldn't give me a chance, and she was just so damned loud, I had to shut her up—"

"You strangled her." The words tasted of ash and sorrow. Luka fought the urge to charge the other man—a suicide mission, but if it silenced the roaring rage filling him, seventeen years' worth of fury and anguish, it might be worth it.

"First time I ever hurt anyone. It felt—" Jack's eyes shone in the overhead light, while the rain continued its drumming against the portico's roof. "It felt... glorious. If you've never done it, killed someone just for the pure pleasure of seeing the life—all their hopes and dreams—drain from their eyes, well, you just can't understand." He shook his head as if pitying Luka. "You'll never understand. And just like sex, the first time—it's always special. You never forget it. My Cherise. She was so much more mine than she ever was yours."

Luka bit back his retort. He was no longer the college kid who'd lost the love of life, lost their future together, no longer the boy dreaming of being a poet, using words to inspire and change the world. No. Jack O'Brien might not realize it, but Luka was in charge here.

All he had to do was hold the fort until backup arrived.

Jack led Luka to the van, opened the passenger door, and pushed him onto the seat. Then Jack took the driver's seat. He turned on the ignition. "It was easier with Cherise. You remember, where she went in? The hill leading down to the bluff overlooking the river. All it took was a bit of a nudge."

He hit the gas, deliberately moving the vehicle forward until the van's bumper touched the rear of the Honda. Then he kept accelerating slowly as the sedan began to roll forward, heading toward the river. It slowed as it hit the muddy grass beyond the gravel, but Jack merely sped up, the larger vehicle propelling the smaller one.

"With Cherise I was so worried about leaving evidence. It's why I almost didn't take her ring. But I couldn't resist—I needed a piece of her, something to remember her by." He glanced at Luka. "Smartest thing I did that night. It sold the story. Broken engagement, distraught lover flinging her ring into the river, betrayed by her man, using his own book of poetry to send a final message. Give people a mystery and they want to solve it. But give them a story and they're satisfied, stop looking for answers. Even heartbroken Luka Jericho. Didn't hurt that everyone blamed you."

The Honda came to a stop mere yards away from the river. Jack tried a gentle nudge from the van, but the other vehicle barely moved. Luka held his breath, hoping the Honda's wheels were caught in the mud or on an unseen tree trunk or any obstacle that would make Jack see the risk was too large, abandon his plan.

"It's how I've been able to keep playing my game all these years—no one suspected me, not ever." Jack threw the car into reverse and backed up.

"Until you decided you needed an audience," Luka said. "Someone who would appreciate your brilliance, even if she had no idea who you were."

"My beautiful, brilliant Risa. She surprised even me, how quickly she became obsessed with Chaos. Have to say, it felt weird, I was actually jealous of my alter ego, she spent so much time and energy on him. But you're wrong. I didn't do it for the attention. I did it to save Risa. I hadn't realized how devastated she'd be after she couldn't travel anymore. So I fixed that for her. Just like I saved her from ever again running into danger simply to chase down a story."

Luka turned to Jack, forcing himself to act surprised. "You're the one making Risa sick?"

"I *am* a chemist. With access to any number of industrial poisons. Things no doctor would ever dream of testing for. If you're smart and careful, you can create any symptom you want in a person."

"But why?" Luka was doing more than stalling. If he got out of this, Leah would need as many details as possible to treat Risa.

"She couldn't focus on me—the real me—if she was galivanting around the world writing her stories, now could she? I needed her home, dependent. On me. But Risa, she's like a thoroughbred, strong, stubborn, so independent. So I had to... break her."

"By dosing her with poisons?"

Jack merely shrugged.

"You were meant to be at the hospital with Risa and Leah—"

"I was."

It was clear Jack wouldn't harm Risa, but... "Where's Leah?"

"Safe. For now." Jack's lips thinned as if daring Luka to ask again, to beg or plead for Leah's life.

Luka didn't give him what he so obviously wanted, instead moving to another subject. "How'd you fake the live streaming video from this morning? Vogel's death?"

"I see what you're doing." Jack chuckled. "Pretending to be interested, stalling. As if that would save you." He gunned the van. It roared forward, rammed the sedan, forcing it to the water's edge. "I don't mind. The video was child's play. I simply changed the clock on the camera, synced it to when I had the text scheduled to be sent, drove back to Risa's and waited."

"What's the story you're telling with all this, Jack?" Luka asked. Get him talking about himself, the one topic he couldn't resist.

"The story of a podunk cop who stumbled across a serial killer and let him get away with murder." Jack reversed the van again.

"Kill us and the police will never stop looking for you."

"Not me. Dominic—thanks to his DNA and prints being all over the crime scene. Believe me, no one will ever find his body. As for poor Jack O'Brien, they'll find plenty of evidence on Dom's computer that he's been stalking Jack for years, was obsessed with Risa—also his motive for killing poor, stupid Cliff. After tonight everyone will believe Jack was one more victim of the Chaos Killer, Dominic Massimo."

He nudged the gas and hit the Honda, ramming its front wheels into the water.

Jack slammed the brakes. With his hands behind his back, Luka was jolted into the dashboard. When he caught his breath and was able to push himself back upright in the seat, Jack had reversed the van a few yards, far enough for the headlights to offer a good view of the sedan, its front bumper lashed by the rushing water.

"Perfect," Jack said with a grin. Then he surprised Luka by jumping out and dancing through the rain to Luka's side of the car. He opened Luka's door, grabbed his arm, and jerked him out of the seat. Luka went sprawling into the mud, Jack standing over him.

"Poor, pitiful Luka. The wannabe poet turned wannabe cop—as if carrying a badge would give you what you really need."

"And what's that?"

"Power. You wrap yourself in guilt, as if you had any control over Cherise's life or death. You mope around all sad about losing the love of your life when there are plenty of women out there, if you'd just stand up and take one."

Luka forced himself to a sitting position, ignoring the rain and mud soaking his slacks, ignoring the gun in Jack's hand. There was a way out of this, he just needed time to think. "Like you're taking Risa?"

"Risa is different. She understands me—but she's not afraid. She sees my power and she wants to know more, not run away. That's what makes her special. Different from all the rest of you. You're all so blind, willing to let fate, destiny, God, whatever, control your lives, like you're rats in a maze. Well, I am Fate, I am Destiny, I am God. And it's your turn to play my game, Luka."

Jack dangled a key ring with a handcuff key above Luka's head. "If you want to save your friend, Dr. Wright…" He nodded to the Honda straddling the river's edge. "Just say the word. Your choice, Luka. Come after me, try to stop me—or play the hero. Which will it be?"

He was bluffing, Luka thought. Because… because Jack lied. Maybe he'd never even taken Leah, maybe she was already dead. But could Luka risk that? "Give me the key."

When Jack didn't move, Luka pushed himself up to his feet and lunged toward Jack. "I said, give me the key."

"Sure, Luka." Jack's grin gleamed in the glare of the headlights. He pocketed the handcuff key. "But first, I need to buy some time. Come with me."

He led Luka to the driver's side door of the Honda, their feet sinking into the mud and gravel of the riverbank. All the windows on the Honda were down, Luka saw.

Jack kept his pistol trained on Luka as he opened the door, shoved Luka into the driver's seat, and threaded Luka's handcuffs through the steering wheel. Then he tossed the handcuff key into the back seat. "As promised, the key is all yours. It's been fun, Luka."

Jack raced through the rain back to the van, gunned the engine, and rammed the sedan one final time, sending it fully into the water.

CHAPTER 48

The footsteps above Leah faded away without anyone coming near to the door. She returned to Risa, pulled the hood off her head, and crouched down beside her. "Risa. It's Jack. It has to be."

"No." Her face creased in confusion. "No, it can't be. He loves me, he's helped me—"

"Think. He's a chemist, easy access to toxins, knows exactly how much to give you to make you sick and dependent on him. He's gotten you to move away from your friends in New York—"

"No. That was my idea."

"He planted it, I'm certain. He's isolated you from everyone, kept you from traveling and doing the work you love, and who else would have easy access to your computer files and all your new assignments?" Risa's eyes were tearing up but with her hands still restrained, Leah had to wipe her tears for her. "I'm sorry. But it's him."

"Jack killed Trudy?" Her voice trembled.

"He has a key to the Falconer, right? And Trudy knew him, wouldn't think twice about seeing him up on your floor or letting him get close. He knew about the childproof locks and how to entice Walt out, frame him for Trudy's murder."

"But—why kill Cliff?"

"I think he was angry about Cliff spying on you. Plus, it helped him to frame Dom. Jack knew he had to get rid of Dom and he had to establish an alibi for himself, but he also knew that nicotine has a short half-life and quick onset. So he knocked you out with the GHB, went to Dom's hotel, grabbed him and Cliff, and set up the camera in the car."

"It couldn't be Jack. No, I don't believe it."

"He's a chemist, Risa. He would know about nicotine poisoning, have access to all sorts of other toxins, even know how to make GHB."

"No!" Risa's voice rose as she grasped for one final lifeline. "No. It's not Jack. You were there with both of us when the video came in."

"Cliff was killed hours before we saw the video. I think maybe Jack had the message with the video scheduled to send at a certain time. Then he made sure I was there to witness its arrival. It wasn't just you, he had us all fooled."

Risa sniffed, and fell against Leah's arms as if finally surrendering to the truth. "I thought I loved him."

"You loved the man he pretended to be, the man he wanted you to see. It's not your fault."

"Yes, it is." She pulled back. "How many people did he kill because of me? How many innocent lives am I responsible for?"

"Zero." Leah kept her tone firm. "This is not your fault."

"What do we do?" Risa asked.

"We play to his weakness, just like we planned. But I need you to be strong, Risa. Can you do that? And face him?" Risa nodded, sniffed, rubbed her cheek against her collar. The sound of a door slamming and footsteps sounded from upstairs. This time Leah heard only one man's steps.

"I can do it. Put the hood back on," Risa said.

"We're going to get out of here, Risa. Tell him the truth. Tell him that you know. Don't try to pretend. Be honest with him, shout his name as soon as he opens the door. Maybe he'll drop his guard, rush right into our trap."

The footsteps grew closer. Leah crossed back to her position beside the stairs, fumbling to find the loose end of the paracord. The door above opened.

"Jack! Jack, let me out right now! I know it's you!" Risa's shouts echoed from the cement walls.

Light spilled in through the open door and Leah spied the paracord. The man at the top hesitated for a moment.

"Jack! I know what you've done!"

The man sprinted down the steps and Leah jerked the cord taut just as his front foot landed and his back foot was raised. The force of his body striking it almost tore it from her hands. Then he was flying, twisted, tumbling, arms flailing to grab hold of the railing. He landed on the floor with a thud.

"Run, Leah," Risa called. "Hurry!"

Leah didn't need to wait to be told. She cautiously skirted Jack's body—he wasn't dead, was moaning and struggling to push himself up. She reached the first step and was pushing off for the next one when a jolt of electricity hit her, surging through every muscle.

The pain stole her breath. Inside her head she was screaming even though she couldn't make a sound. She felt Jack's hand grip her ankle. Then the pain stopped, and her body went limp, falling against the concrete floor. She lay there gasping. Jack stood over her, holding the stun gun in one hand, wrapping his other arm around his ribs.

"There's only one reason why you're alive." He drew a foot back and kicked her in the side. "But there's plenty of ways to punish you without killing you. You might want to keep that in mind, Leah."

"Jack, stop it." Risa shook free of her hood and even in the dim light from the open door her furious glare held the power to make Jack forget about Leah. He stepped toward Risa, a small grunt of pain as he put his weight on his left ankle.

"Haven't you done enough?" Risa demanded. "Untie me and let her go."

"When did you know? How long?" He sounded angry that his deception had been discovered.

"I'm not stupid. Or maybe I am. Maybe I should have figured it out a long time ago."

He pulled a knife from his pocket and flicked the blade open. Leah tried to lunge for him, but couldn't even make it to standing, her muscles were all twisted into painful knots.

He stopped and turned to scowl down at her. "Don't make me dose you again, Leah."

"What did you use? Chloroform?"

"Nothing so crude and imprecise. It was a 6.75 percent concentration of monochloroethane. I had to titrate it precisely as anything over 8 percent is lethal." He adjusted his grip on the knife. "Relax. I'm not going to hurt Risa." He stepped toward Risa, focusing on her. "I'd never hurt you."

"No. You just wanted to cage me like a canary. To sing your praises, something like that?"

He crouched down and cut her bonds, then gently helped her to her feet, one arm wrapped around her waist, keeping the stun gun close to her body. "Maybe. Yes. But only because I wanted to take care of you. I never loved anyone the way that I love you."

"How can I be sure of that, Jack? When everything else was lies? How do I know what's true and what's stage dressing?"

"Me. I'm here, right here. The man you fell in love with."

"I fell in love with Jack. Not Chaos."

"No. You see the truth in people, Risa. That's your gift. So when you fell in love with me, when you saw me, you saw my true self. You fell in love with all of me. I'm more than the man you call Chaos, more than Jack O'Brien."

He raised his hands, not to strike her, but to emphasize his point. "Robert Louis Stevenson called it Mr. Hyde. But this need, this drive, this urge I have, it isn't uncommon. Some men turn it on their families, abuse them. Others pick fights in bars. Many allow it to consume them in the form of addiction or being so competitive at work that they'll ruin lives to climb to the top." He shrugged. "I found another path."

As he spoke, Risa leaned her weight so that in order to face her, Jack turned his back on Leah. Leah struggled to regain her feet but could barely manage to breathe through the pain that consumed her.

"You're saying you're like Dr. Jekyll and Mr. Hyde? A split personality that doesn't know what the other half is doing?"

He shook his head. "No. I'm in complete control at all times. But so was Dr. Jekyll. He *chose* to release Mr. Hyde, to vent all those repressed feelings of violence and rage. He did that so he could be a better Dr. Jekyll."

"You're trying to be a better man by killing strangers?" Her voice was taut with disdain.

"Honey, I know this is a lot to take in. But I'm still the man you fell in love with. After all, I could have run. I risked everything to come back. For you."

"You want me to come with you? As your hostage? As the poor, sick woman who depends on you for everything? Isn't that just another game, another living lie?"

"No. Come with me as my partner. My equal. I've never met anyone as smart or beautiful as you, Risa. You're wasted here, telling other people's stories. Isn't it high time you lived a life worthy of legend? A story people will talk about for generations to come."

Leah barely caught all his words, focusing instead of getting up. Using the railing for support, she clawed her way upright, despite the pain. Silently she crept up one step, and caught Risa's eye. Leah continued trying to blend into the shadows so Jack wouldn't notice the movement behind him.

"My story? Or a bit role in yours?" Risa asked. Then she met his gaze head on, took his face in both of her palms. "What if I want to take control this time, what if I want to take care of you for a change?"

"You mean, keep me safe from danger? Hide me? While you—"

"While I have some fun. I mean, why is it always men who are free to explore their dark side? Why not a woman?"

His breath caught. Leah cheered Risa's ingenuity—it was exactly the right thing to say to gain Jack's complete attention. She used the diversion to make it past the halfway mark.

"I could teach you," Jack said. "So many things I could teach you."

"And I you. See, that's what really upsets me, Jack. That you didn't trust me—"

"I couldn't. Not until I was certain—"

She held a hand up and he stopped. "You lied, you cheated me out of so much, you made me feel like crap, and you didn't trust me. I love you but I won't live like that. Not ever again. Do you understand?"

He nodded, eyes locked on hers, waiting for permission. Leah held her breath as well, taking another step. Only six more…

"Say it," Risa commanded.

"I understand. I'm sorry. I should have never doubted you."

"How will you make it up to me? Will you let Leah go?"

"Yes," he breathed. "If you stay with me." He gripped both her arms and turned his head, looking right at Leah. Her stomach dropped—he'd known what she was doing all along. This was just another one of his damned games. His laughter echoed from the walls. "Go on, Leah. Run. But run fast. As soon as I have Risa situated, you'll have my undivided attention."

Leah was torn. He held Risa tight, so tight that she whimpered in pain. "Please don't hurt her," Leah called down.

"I'd never hurt her. She's just going to take a little nap. And then we'll be leaving. For good." He marched Risa backwards until she was pinned against the wall. Then he reached into his pocket for a syringe.

Risa's eyes widened with terror. "Run, Leah!"

Leah was powerless, unable to help Risa. So she did the only thing she could do to maybe save them both. She ran.

The door opened up into a darkened hallway. There were no lights except one coming from the front of the house, barely reaching the shadows back here. Weapon. Phone. Some way to bring help or stop Jack.

She stumbled toward the light. It led to what appeared to be some kind of reception area. Dom sat on a couch positioned in front of a computer. From his pallor and sagging, expressionless features, it was clear he was dead. An old-fashioned phone was on the wall beside the door. She grabbed the receiver. Dead.

She had to find help. Leaning over the coffee table, she spun the laptop away from the corpse and clicked out of the video site, hoping to be able to message Luka or the police. The screen filled with images from surveillance cameras showing multiple views of an empty road, and a building with a white van parked in front of it—the old pumphouse.

Jack's boots pounded up the steps.

But now that Leah knew where she was, she had options. She ran outside, the wind catching at her open parka, billowing it like a cape. Jack's van was parked at the front door, covered in mud, and wet grass clung to its wheels. She tried the door as she passed it. Locked.

With every breath she expected to hear Jack calling her name, taunting her as he closed in on her. No way in hell would he leave without ensuring Leah's silence. One way or another.

She sprinted across the overgrown lawn, avoiding the muddy dirt drive where she'd leave footprints. *Wait. Think, Leah.* Jack would expect her to try to outrun him, head straight to the road. It would be anyone's first instinct. But he had a car and she didn't.

When she was a kid, she had played in the woods between the pumphouse and the railroad tracks—sometimes even on the tracks, crossing the bridge. It was against Nellie's rules, making it irresistibly tempting to a bored, lonely young girl.

The tracks. There'd be no help there, but with the bridge over the marsh, they took a more direct route to Route 11 than Old River Road did. Plus, if Jack got too close, there was a place where she might be able to trap him. The marsh.

As a kid, she'd watched them with their digging machines laying the foundation for the new railroad bridge. Once they'd finished, she'd seen the water reclaim the area as marshland. Land that no matter how dry it appeared was always shifting, greedily pulling in anything that dared try to cross it. When she was a little girl she used to pretend it was quicksand and throw various sized rocks over the new bridge, see how long it took them to vanish.

The larger and heavier, the faster the marsh devoured them.

A bright beam of light stabbed the ground beyond her feet. Jack had found her.

CHAPTER 49

Through the Honda's open windows horizontal rain pelted Luka as the car swayed and lurched in the current. If he was lucky, it'd be weighed down in the mud and silt of the shallows and his only worries would be wet shoes and finding a phone so his guys could intercept Jack.

He pulled his left knee up as high as it would go and with his foot felt blindly for the manual trunk release. Just as he was rewarded with the pop of the latch opening, the current, roiling and swollen with the weeks-long deluge, caught the front end of the car and swung it away from the bank.

The car spun, water gushing in through the floorboards and open windows. Luka spared a moment to glance in the rearview mirror. The trunk had popped all the way open but there was no sign of anyone escaping. What if Leah was unconscious, unable to swim past the water rushing into the trunk? Had he just doomed her?

The car ground to a stop a short distance downstream, its hood facing toward the bank, the rear sinking in the deeper water. Luka's teeth ground together as he tried to keep them from chattering. Still no sign of Leah.

Jack had searched Luka's pockets and taken everything. But he'd left Luka's badge clipped to his belt. Probably so the entire world would immediately know that the corpse in the Honda was the detective who'd failed to catch the Chaos Killer.

It was a mistake. Because behind Luka's gold shield was a small pocket with his credentials and a keyring with two keys: one the universal key for the department's pool vehicles and the other a spare handcuff key. Luka twisted his body and slid as low in the seat as he could go, arching his hip up until his fingers could reach his belt.

They were already numb and clumsy with the cold, and the water surging all around him wasn't helping, but he was able to hang onto the clip and slide it free of his belt. Now came the hard part—fitting the key into the lock.

He closed his eyes, took a breath, and focused on the tiny key slipping between his fingers. It caught on the keyhole, the angle wrong. Slowly, carefully, he stretched to reposition it and finally it slid in, clicked into place. He twisted it and the cuff opened.

Free of the handcuffs, he pushed himself through the open car window. Wind and rain lashed at his face. He didn't try for any kind of fancy dive—no idea what lay below, snags from downed trees, rocks or other debris. Instead he lowered himself into the water, hanging onto the car, fearful that if he slipped or if the current stole it from his grasp, he might not be able to reach it again in the darkness.

The cold was a shock that made him gasp out loud. At the front of the car, the water was not so deep—he could touch the bottom with his toes. Moving as fast as he could, he worked his way toward the rear of the car.

He'd made it to the rear door when his foot slipped on a slime-covered rock and he plummeted down, the water closing over his head. Despite the unrelenting black and the freezing grasp of the current, Luka remained calm. In a way, he'd been preparing for this moment for seventeen years.

After Cherise's death, when it felt as if the entire world blamed him for pushing her over an emotional cliff, he'd been obsessed with what had happened to her, trying—and failing—to understand what she'd gone through and why she hadn't saved herself. The coroner's report said she'd been alive when she went into the water, she could have fought; he was so furious at her for not fighting—for him, for them.

As a way to deal with the maelstrom of emotions that had overwhelmed him, he'd begun swimming obsessively—not just swimming, but drowning. Or as close to it as he could force himself to come. Every time his instinct for self-preservation forced him back to the surface; he lacked the willpower to surrender his life.

Tonight, as he kicked his way back up, aiming at a churning in the current that he hoped marked the location of the sedan, Luka realized that Jack O'Brien was wrong. Not only was Luka not responsible for all the lives after Cherise that Jack had taken, Luka was also not at fault in Cherise's death—and, most importantly, neither was Cherise. Finally, the burning question that had nearly destroyed Luka's world was answered. There was no why. She'd never chosen to leave Luka or their life. They were both Jack's victims, one living a life he'd never asked for, the other who had her life stolen from her.

Relieved of the burden of seventeen years' worth of guilt and doubt, Luka felt energized. He quickened his stroke, a calm certainty filling him, propelling his actions. His hand hit smooth metal—the Honda's rear panel, angled down. He followed the curve, but the car was fully submerged.

His lungs burning with the effort, Luka pushed through the water, kicking against the current until he made blind contact with the sheet metal of the trunk's lid. Ignoring his lungs screaming for oxygen, he felt his way down to the trunk itself, practically folding his body into the space, searching blindly. Breathe, he needed to breathe, but still he forced himself deeper inside until he hit the back seat. Where was she?

His vision darkened and he could barely feel his feet as he kicked to the surface. Rain pelted him as he broke free, the night almost as black as the water below. A few more kicks and Luka could stand, although the mud-and-algae-covered bottom made for precarious footing. He gulped down air, bracing himself for another dive into the black, when he heard Leah's voice in his mind. *Chaos lies.*

Leah wasn't there. She'd never been there. It was just another of Jack's games.

He fought the current, finally hauling himself onto land, and glanced around. The rain and swirling fog weren't helping. The pumphouse was out of sight behind a bend in the river, but he could make out the reflectors that marked the railroad bridge downriver, over the marsh.

Jack still had Leah and Risa. Luka couldn't stop him, not alone. He needed help. Shoeless, numb and shaking with the cold, he fixed a route that would lead him to the closest phone—the Homans' place, God help him. But odds were there'd still be officers there, processing the scene. A scene he'd never have found without Nate and Emily, the thought instilling him with warmth and giving him the energy to keep fighting. Then he took off running.

Luka sprinted through wind-whipped knee-high grass, his sock-clad feet growing numb as the mud clutched at them with every step. He tried to steer a course that would skirt the treacherous marshlands but get him to the road as quickly as possible. The marsh was tricky to navigate in the best of times, grassy meadow giving way to swampy mire without warning. Tonight, with the river at flood level, water skimmed along the soggy ground, making it impossible to tell safe ground from dangerous.

If not for the occasional flashes of lightning reflecting off the river and giving him a brief glimpse of the landscape surrounding him, he'd be totally lost. He was almost to the train tracks when a sudden beam of light bobbing through the trees startled him. Too bright to be anything but manmade, it came from upriver, the direction where the house was.

Jack. It had to be. But who was he chasing after? Luka hurried, heading in the most direct route to the tracks, which would place him just behind Jack. Once he reached the trees that ran alongside the tracks, he grabbed a stray fallen branch to use as a potential weapon.

From this angle he could barely make out the flashlight since Jack's body and the trees blocked it; but crossing into the clearing the train tracks created would leave him too vulnerable, so he kept to the shadows, skirting the tree line, following Jack downriver toward the bridge.

Luka hated the bridge. It didn't attract suicide attempts like the taller bridges in Cambria City, but instead it was catnip for stupid, drunk teens bored and restless. They'd dare each other to walk the length of the tracks over the bridge wearing a blindfold. The bridge was too short to require anything more than a minimal wooden railing—definitely not enough to prevent a drunk teen from toppling over it into the marsh. As a uniformed officer, Luka had lost count of how many idiots they'd been called out to rescue with the help of the river patrol guys. Not all the kids had made it—if the water level was low, they pancaked against a few inches of mud; if the river was high, like now, they could easily be pulled under by the current and swept out into the main channel.

Jack, of course, hadn't grown up around here, and would know nothing of the terrain. Luka sped up, hoping to use that to his advantage. Maybe he could ambush Jack on the bridge, stop the killer before he caught whoever he was pursuing. It had to be either Risa or Leah. If it was Risa, that meant Leah was probably dead already. But if it was Leah, it meant that Jack had Risa under control.

He sidled through the trees, taking the gamble of traveling along the tracks where he could move faster, thankful now for his numb feet, impervious to the biting gravel.

Ahead of him, the bobbing light suddenly stopped, lasering in on its target: a woman standing on the bridge. Luka pushed himself faster, the wind covering the noise of his footfalls, he hoped. Jack seemed focused on the woman, saying something to her that Luka couldn't hear clearly, but he made out her name: *Leah.*

What the hell was she doing? Leaning against the bridge railing as if she'd given up, that wasn't the Leah he knew. What had Jack done to her?

The wind carried Jack's laughter back to him. Luka sprinted forward, only five or six yards away. If Jack heard him, he was doomed—no cover and in easy range of Jack's semiautomatic.

Jack hesitated at the end of the bridge—any sane man would, given that the train tracks were open to the air below, so you had to cross by stepping along the railroad ties. He called out to Leah, gesturing with his pistol, but Leah sank further against the wooden railing, her body almost sagging through the opening below it. Jack yelled again and finally walked onto the bridge, his gait turning awkward as he lurched from one tie to the next.

Luka sped up, reaching the bridge just as Jack reached Leah. Lightning speared down, illuminating the marsh below with a ghastly green glow. Leah clutched the railing, her wet hair whipping against her face, head hung low, ignoring Jack's threats—and his gun. What was she thinking? She was smart enough to know Jack could just shoot her—which meant she knew something he didn't. If Jack wanted to kill her, he could have just shot her from the end of the bridge, didn't need to go to her, get so close.

Leah had a plan. He should've known. Luka began to cross the slippery railroad ties, his shoeless feet allowing him to grip the wet wood better.

"Please," she was begging Jack. Her arms were wrapped around the railing, hands hidden by her parka.

Jack stepped closer, pushing the pistol's barrel between her eyes. Leah didn't move. Then Jack raised his gun hand, ready to strike her.

The movement put him off balance for a split second. Long enough for Leah to spring up from her crouch, hands pushing his gun hand away from her as she launched her body against him, spinning him over the railing.

It was a good move, would have worked, except Jack's other hand had a firm grip on the railing. He fell against the railing, but quickly recovered, bringing his gun down against Leah's skull. Stunned, she dropped, almost sliding under the railing. That's when Luka saw that she'd lashed herself to the vertical support strut. Smart. She stopped her slide by throwing one hand around a train rail.

Jack straightened, taking aim with his pistol. Luka rushed him, swinging his tree branch like a baseball bat, aiming first for Jack's gun arm, knocking the pistol from his grasp, and then on the back swing, hitting him in the solar plexus.

Jack staggered, off balance, his momentum propelling him toward Leah, who was crouched on the tracks. Using the hand gripping the railing above her for leverage, she launched her other fist into Jack's throat. Jack slumped forward over the railing, all resistance vanished.

Luka grabbed his arms and quickly handcuffed him as Jack sputtered and gasped for breath.

"You okay?" Luka asked. Leah had blood trickling down her forehead into her eyes.

She nodded. Together they each took one of Jack's arms and hauled him off the bridge.

"Put him into recovery position," Leah instructed after Luka had placed Jack on the ground and searched his pockets, finding a cell phone along with Luka's service weapon.

They rolled Jack onto his side. Leah checked Jack's breathing, ignoring the glare Jack lasered at her. Luka stood guard over her, his weapon sighted on Jack as he dialed with his other hand. "Where's Risa?" he asked Leah.

"At the pumphouse. He drugged her." She took in a breath, wiped the blood from her face, and pushed to her feet. "He'll be fine, but I need to get back to her."

"I left my guys just down the road at the Homan farm." The road was on the other side of a thin strip of trees. "I'll have them come pick us up and call for an ambulance. It'll be faster than you walking back."

She nodded, but still seemed a bit stunned, taking a beat longer than normal before answering. "Why were you at the Homans'?"

"It's a long story…"

CHAPTER 50

Two mornings later, Leah found herself hugging a pillow to her chest as she sat on the couch of her trauma counselor's office. "How many times can one little girl be traumatized without it causing lasting damage?"

"But was Emily traumatized?" he asked, using that infuriatingly neutral therapist tone, as if they were discussing the cafeteria's lunch menu and not her daughter's life. "From my understanding, she was never in danger and handled the situation with extreme maturity."

"She's six!" Leah flared. "Her life has been threatened twice—three times if you count what happened at the Homan farm—and she saw her father murdered. Of course she's been traumatized."

"And is already in treatment for what happened around her father's killing. Yes, she's been through more than any six-year-old should, and yes, you're worried about her, but I sense there's something more beneath those feelings…"

Silence was one of his favorite weapons, Leah had learned. She understood why—she'd seen Luka use it as well, manipulating the human urge to fill the void with words. But it wasn't going to work, not on her. Silence was her friend. In silence Ian's voice could come through—or what she imagined he would say, always less harsh than her own judgment of her actions. Ian never made her feel guilty or fearful; it was her own voice that did that.

"We've spent almost this entire session discussing what happened to Emily," he continued when she didn't speak. "But how do you feel about what happened to you? You were kidnapped, drugged, almost killed, ran for your life. Then confronted a killer just as you did after Ian died."

"I'm fine." She tightened her grip on the pillow. Why was he wasting her time with this? Emily's welfare was the priority.

"During all that, did you consider the fact that you might need to take another person's life? How did that make you feel?"

"Feel? I was furious. And that's exactly why I did survive. Why I fought. For Emily. I couldn't leave her alone."

"But your survival wasn't solely in your control. No one's is."

Again a lengthy silence, the only sound the clock's soft ticking behind her. Surely their time was up, Leah thought, anxious to leave this discussion and get back to work.

"Are you at all concerned that your new position, working so closely with the police, might place you in danger again?"

"Of course I am." Was she really paying him to ask such idiotic questions?

"Then why not quit? I'm sure a talented physician such as yourself could find other opportunities."

This time he didn't break the silence that followed his question. Leah had answers—Emily's need for stability, their financial security, etc. But none was the real answer. She knew it and, obviously, so did he.

Finally came the chime announcing the end of their session. Leah bolted upright, throwing the pillow back onto the couch. The therapist stood, reaching the door before her, blocking her path. "Before our next appointment, I'd like for you to think about what attracts you to a life filled with emergencies—whether as a physician treating patients or now as a consultant for the police."

She frowned at him. "Saving lives and helping people isn't good enough for you?"

His banal smile was more infuriating than his silence had been. "I wonder if it's enough for you. I wonder if perhaps there's something more fulfilling or rewarding that your chosen careers provide you? If we can explore that fully, perhaps we can also find ways to mitigate any attendant danger in the future." He opened the door for her. "Just a thought. See you next week."

Leah left, feeling a bit sheepish. Deep down she knew exactly what he meant. Once a colleague had accused her of having a savior's complex, needing to try to save every victim that came into her ER. But she'd brushed him off, never explored the why behind her actions. It had to be more than a need for control, more than being an adrenaline junkie.

She turned to stare at the closed door, wondering if she'd find the courage to return. Decided that, for Emily's sake, she would.

Leah crossed the street from the outpatient clinic building to Good Sam's inpatient tower and began her rounds. First, she saw Mrs. Czury, the elderly victim of a vicious mugging. Mrs. Czury was finally awake, moving from the ICU to the neuro-psych unit where she'd receive intensive therapy for the stroke her head injury had caused. It would be a few days before Leah could do a complete forensic interview for Luka, but Leah was hopeful that the old lady would make a fair recovery.

Next was Walt Orly, Trudy's husband. Dr. Chaudhari had fine-tuned his medication regimen and he was much calmer, able to be transferred to a long-term placement. The home in Smithfield that Trudy had hoped for didn't have an open bed, but a very nice facility in Hershey did. The curious thing was that in Walt's mind, Trudy was still alive and well, living with him at the hospital, just out for a cup of coffee when Leah stopped by. She saw no need to torture the man with the truth. Sometimes denial was the best medicine.

Which left her final patient, Risa Saliba, who was undergoing chelation therapy for heavy metal toxicity. But when Leah got to Risa's room, she'd already been discharged. Leah tried calling her, but it went straight to voicemail.

"Hello, you've reached Risa Saliba's number. I'm out in the field for the near future, because life is too short, and the world is too big to be a prisoner of your own life. Leave a message if you want, but I probably won't be checking. People to meet and places to go. *Ciao*."

Leah listened to the message twice, enjoying the strength and passion that colored Risa's voice. At first, she'd thought Risa might tip into a crevasse of depression and guilt, but the reporter was proving more resilient than Leah imagined. Good for her.

She left Good Sam through the ER, smiling and waving at the nurses and other staff who greeted her. It'd been such a thrill, rushing Risa into the ER two nights ago, feeling like her old self for the first time in a month. It made her aware that her new job wasn't as different as she thought. Which reminded her of her therapist's final question. Maybe she didn't have all the answers, was maybe a coward, afraid to search too hard for them, but she was slowly discovering her own truth.

Surviving without Ian had felt like a betrayal. But now she realized that hiding in shadows of guilt and grief were the last thing he would have wanted. He'd want more for her. Not just to merely survive but to learn how to live again, to embrace her new life, as painful as it was.

Living without him didn't mean living without his love. Far from it. Every time she looked at Emily, it was clear that Ian was never truly lost.

She drove over to her next appointment: volunteers from Ian's church were meeting her at her old house to help her sort through their possessions, pack the ones she wanted to keep, and take the rest to their charity shop.

She arrived early, just as she'd planned. Not only in case she had another panic attack, but also because she wanted time alone with their home, with Ian. This time she strode straight up to the door. Despite the tears blinding her eyes she managed to get the key turned and walk inside without any sense of panic. In fact, she felt the opposite—she felt a bit giddy, like when Ian took her hand and they danced their first dance as husband and wife.

He was with her, a comforting weight supporting her, a warm hand guiding her. And he'd never abandon her—or her him.

EPILOGUE

17 days later...

Luka straightened his tie in his truck's rearview mirror. He couldn't believe the crowd that had gathered along the river to celebrate Cherise's life. He was the only one dressed in a tie and suitcoat— everyone else had followed the instructions on the invitation and came in jeans and work boots. He nodded and smiled to them—old college friends, friends from work, Cherise's family, even McKinley and Ahearn, Leah, Ruby, Emily, Pops, Janine, and Nate, holding Rex's leash in one hand and a shovel in the other.

Luka took his place standing on the rock where he'd left the dead irises. What a difference a few weeks made. The sky was blinding blue, as if competing with the flowers crowding the back of his truck. The river gurgled a happy tune, its angst and roiling rage vanquished. The grass was green, the trees were budding, and a breeze carried the scent of pine down from the mountain.

"Thank you all for coming," he began. "I'll keep it short and then we can get to work. First of all, a huge thanks to someone who couldn't be here today, Risa Saliba. She orchestrated all this, getting the county to turn this land into something to truly honor Cherise's life. Welcome to the Cherise Sumner Community Garden."

The crowd applauded, even Cherise's parents, who were both wiping tears away between clapping.

"As you know, a famous poem by one of our favorite poets was used to mark Cherise's death. So now, I'd like to remedy that miscarriage by reciting a poem I've written in tribute to both Cherise and Langston Hughes."

He pulled the well-creased and sweat-stained slip of paper from his pocket and unfolded it. Like the original Langston Hughes poem, his was only twelve words long, but he didn't want to risk messing it up. Every word had been carefully chosen to mirror Hughes' "Suicide's Note." A study of opposites and contrasts. He hoped.

"Beloved's Letter." He read the title. He cleared his throat and began—he'd never performed any of his poems without Cherise in the audience, but now as he looked out over the crowd of faces, he realized she was here, in each and every one of them.

> *"The vibrant,*
> *Warm touch of your lips*
> *Invites me to live forever."*

He finished and looked up. Silence greeted him and for a moment, he feared he'd made a fool of himself, desecrated Cherise's celebration.

But then, a few anxious heartbeats later, applause broke out, all at once as if the crowd was obeying the commands of an invisible orchestra conductor. Several openly wept—including Harper and McKinley of all people.

"Enough tears," he said. "Let's get planting."

As the crowd broke apart, grabbing tools, soil, and the plants for the garden, Leah approached him. She carried a box wrapped in Christmas paper. "Sorry, it was all I could find at Nellie's."

"What's this?" They sat down on the rock, facing the river. The water was the last thing Cherise saw, Luka thought, another poem beginning to crystallize in his mind.

"Open it."

He didn't need to be asked twice. He tore the paper off and tugged the box flaps apart. Inside were a dozen or more books, slim volumes of various sizes. Books of poetry. Tennyson, Dickinson, Frost, Eliot, Robert Hayden, Chinua Achebe, Rainer Maria Rilke, Rita Dove. And more.

Luka glanced up at Leah. He recognized these books, knew exactly where they came from: they were Ian's. "Leah, are you sure? This is a treasure trove—shouldn't it go to Emily?"

"Emily has plenty to remember Ian by. When he wrote code, he said it felt like writing poetry, so I thought of you."

He placed his palm over his heart. "Thank you, I'm honored."

Nate and Emily raced past, Rex leading them both as he chased a butterfly.

"You're doing a good job with him," Leah said. "Seems like he's starting to open up."

"More like I'm opening up to him." Luka smiled at the children, feeling as warm inside as outside. "You know, a very wise person said something that I'll never forget. She said you can't go your whole life trying not to love. I've decided that she's right."

"Cherise would agree." Leah rubbed her wedding ring, glinting in the sunlight.

"As would Ian," Luka said, knocking his shoulder against hers. He stood and reached a hand down to help her up. "C'mon, let's go plant some memories."

A LETTER FROM CJ

I want to say a huge thank you for choosing to read *The Drowned Woman*. If you did enjoy it, and want to keep up to date with all my latest releases, please sign up at the link below. Your email address will never be shared and you can unsubscribe at any time.

www.bookouture.com/cj-lyons

I'm often asked about the "themes" of my novels. I love this question because it gets to the heart of why I write.

Critics and reviewers have commented on the fact that grief and loss play a recurring role in my books. I don't deny it—anyone who has read my full bio on my website knows that I've been both haunted and inspired by the tragic loss of a friend who was murdered when I was twenty-five.

However, I would argue that my books aren't really about loss, and my theme isn't actually grief. Rather, my books are about courage. The courage to hope. To heal. To find the strength to live and laugh and love despite tragedy.

As Maggie (the wisest young person in Craven County!) says in the first Jericho and Wright thriller, *The Next Widow*, "Grief is the price we pay for love. But love is what saves us from grief."

This journey from tragedy to hope is one many of my characters undertake, just as I myself have faced it, time and again. It's the emotional heart of my thrillers, and hopefully what sets them apart from other mystery and suspense novels, as exploring the